T0161941

A ROYAL ROMANCE

Visit us at www.boldstrokesbooks.com

A ROYAL ROMANCE

by
Jenny Frame

2015

A ROYAL ROMANCE

© 2015 BY JENNY FRAME. ALL RIGHTS RESERVED.

ISBN 13: 978-1-62639-360-8

THIS TRADE PAPERBACK ORIGINAL IS PUBLISHED BY
BOLD STROKES BOOKS, INC.
P.O. BOX 249
VALLEY FALLS, NY 12185

FIRST EDITION: MAY 2015

THIS IS A WORK OF FICTION. NAMES, CHARACTERS, PLACES, AND INCIDENTS ARE THE PRODUCT OF THE AUTHOR'S IMAGINATION OR ARE USED FICTITIOUSLY. ANY RESEMBLANCE TO ACTUAL PERSONS, LIVING OR DEAD, BUSINESS ESTABLISHMENTS, EVENTS, OR LOCALES IS ENTIRELY COINCIDENTAL.

THIS BOOK, OR PARTS THEREOF, MAY NOT BE REPRODUCED IN ANY FORM WITHOUT PERMISSION.

CREDITS

EDITOR: RUTH STERNGLANTZ
PRODUCTION DESIGN: SUSAN RAMUNDO
COVER DESIGN BY SHERI (GRAPHICARTIST2020@HOTMAIL.COM)

Acknowledgments

Firstly, I have to thank Radclyffe for taking a chance on a beginner and allowing me to join the BSB family. Thank you to all the Bold Strokes staff who work tirelessly behind the scenes and fellow authors who have made me feel extremely welcome.

A huge thank you to my editor, Ruth Sternglantz. You have made the editing process a wonderful teaching experience. I truly appreciate your guidance, advice, and good humour.

Lily Hoffman, thank you for always being there to help, and giving me the benefit of your talent and knowledge. This book wouldn't have been possible without your help, encouragement, and belief in me. Your friendship means so much.

Thank you to my friends Amy and Govita who have supported me from the start, believed in my stories and listened to my endless anxieties, self doubt, and craziness. Also to Christine, and Kat Old Chap! Your friendship and support are greatly appreciated. I hope you enjoy the book.

A big shout of thanks also goes out to the online Amazons who have followed my writing since I first got the courage to share my work on the Web.

Thanks to my family for always being there in good times and bad, and supporting whatever I wanted to do.

Lou, I would have no love stories to tell without you. You made me believe in knights in shining armour, fairy tales, and happy ever after. Thank you for putting up with all the days and nights obsessing over one story or another, and for having an unshakable belief in me, even when I didn't. I'm so grateful to you and Barney for giving me more love than I could have ever dreamt of.

Dedication

For Lou
AETERNI VESTRI FIDELITER
Forever yours, faithfully

PROLOGUE

Bethnal Green, London
2044

Beatrice Elliot ran downstairs as quickly as she could. She checked her appearance in the mirror at the bottom. Her long dark-blond hair looked unruly. *I'm going to be so late, and I look a mess.* She quickly gathered her hair up into a ponytail, making herself a bit more presentable.

From the living room, she heard her mum shout, "Bea?"

Beatrice popped her head round the door and said, "Yes, Mum?"

Her mother, Sarah, sat on the couch facing the large TV projection on the wall. "Are you coming to watch with me? It's Princess Georgina's investiture as Princess of Wales."

Beatrice gave her mother a scowl. "Mum, you know I have absolutely no interest in that shower of spongers."

Sarah pointed towards the TV and said, "But Bea, the pageantry, the tradition, and she's going to be the first woman to become Queen ahead of her brother, and the first openly gay monarch. Surely you of all people should understand that."

Bea sighed. She was getting fed up having this argument with people and hearing the name of Princess Georgina. "They take money away from our country's essential services. You and Dad should know why that makes me angry."

Her mother nodded, but not before Bea caught a look of pain on her mother's face, and she felt guilty for causing that. She walked behind the couch and put her arms around her mother's neck. "I'm sorry, Mum, but I have my student union meeting. Remember I told you about it last night? It's our last meeting before the charity fundraiser."

Sarah patted her daughter's hand. "Oh yes, I remember, sweetheart, be careful then."

"I will. Will Dad be in soon?"

"Yes, another half hour or so. He hoped he would be back in time to see the ceremony. Off you go then, and leave me to my pageant."

Bea laughed softly and gave her mother a kiss. "Enjoy it then. See you later, Mum."

After Bea left and Sarah heard the front door close, she picked up her cup of tea and settled down to watch the TV special that the country had been buzzing about.

She watched the cameras span the grounds of Caernarfon Castle in Wales. The castle surrounded a triangular area of grass. In the middle of the grass sat a dais made of Welsh slate, on which the ceremony would take place, and around the three sides were the raised seating areas for spectators.

On the dais sat three thrones, while to the side sat the members of the extended royal family. The royal fanfare began and Sarah said to the TV, "Volume, up five." The fanfare filled the room and she could almost feel like she was sitting there among the spectators.

"Reg is going to be mad he missed this."

The voice-over began…

And we see the King and Queen emerge from the castle and make their way up, past the spectators, towards the dais. They are escorted by heralds, resplendent in their ancient dress, the first minister of Wales, and senior peers of the principality and are guarded by men and women of the Household Cavalry. The Welsh National Choir is providing the choral accompaniment to the occasion, and it sounds magnificent, I think you'll all agree. What an atmosphere. The crowd is applauding King Edward and Queen Sofia as they walk past. There is a joyous feeling amongst the crowd, a feeling of celebration and hope for the future.

Sarah watched the tall, imposing-looking King, dressed in his ceremonial Royal Navy uniform, escort his elegant wife into her seat on the dais, and then take his own seat. To Sarah this was what Britain did best—tradition, ceremony, and pageantry—and she wished her daughter could see that. She understood her hostility. Beatrice believed the monarchy took money away from much-needed organizations such as the National Health Service, schools, and community groups.

The Elliot family knew first-hand what it was to be at the mercy of an underfunded health service.

She had always been a fan of the royals, and especially the very popular King Edward and Queen Sofia. King Edward was a few years older than herself, and so she grew up watching the friendly boy prince become a man and meet his true love, Sofia.

Sarah, along with the nation and two and a half billion people around the world, fell in love with the couple as they watched their fairy tale wedding. Now it was his firstborn daughter and heir's turn to be invested as Princess of Wales and recognized as heir apparent to the throne.

Sarah heard the front door open and close as her husband hurried to join her for the royal broadcast.

"Reg? Hurry up, it's started."

Her husband eased himself down on the couch and gave her a kiss.

Sarah cast a glance down to his hands.

"Reginald Elliot, go and wash those mucky hands. You can't watch a royal broadcast with dirt and muck on your hands."

Reg got up quickly and ran to the kitchen to wash up, mumbling as he went, "As if they can see me anyway."

Reg, who owned his own small landscaping business, usually came home in a less than pristine state. He washed up and hurried back.

"It's getting to the good bit Reg." They both eagerly watched the scene unfolding and listened to the voice-over announcer.

The King stands, as the Earl Marshal, the Duke of Norfolk, approaches the dais. The King instructs him to order the Garter King of Arms to bring the Princess from the castle tower.

Sarah and Reg watched in awe at the almost medieval scene that played before them. The sense of history and tradition was brought alive with the bright colours and the vivid livery of the participants in this ancient ceremony. It was history made alive in their own living room. To Sarah and those royalists like her, the rituals and traditions of Britain, and the monarchy, gave the country a feeling of stability, a connection with the past, but also of continuity. That was what today was all about. The King and the country recognizing not only the heir to the throne, but that Britain's system of government, led by the constitutional monarch, was in safe hands and the succession of the House of Buckingham was secure.

"Look, Reg, the Princess," Sarah exclaimed.

And we have our first view of Princess Georgina, who is led from the Castle by the Garter King of Arms and walks past her family seated on the right. We can see her brother, Prince Theodore, Duke of York, and also her grandmother, Queen Adrianna, the Queen Mother. Beside her sits Georgina's aunt, Princess Grace, along with other members of the family.

The Princess of Wales looks resplendent in her Army uniform of The Blues and Royals, the characteristic black uniform, with gold braid, and a red stripe down the side of the trousers, and spurs on the heels of her boots. She has no officer's cap, as she is to receive the coronet of Wales during the ceremony. The Princess has recently completed her officer training at Sandhurst military academy and is about to be deployed with her regiment on a six-month training mission in Canada. Of course in her regiment, she is simply known as Lieutenant Buckingham. Also notice—diagonally across her tunic she wears a blue sash, to signify she is a member of the Order of the Garter, which is the highest honour of chivalry. Behind the Princess, the regalia of the Princess of Wales are carried on red velvet cushions. A sword, a coronet, a mantle, a gold ring, and a gold rod.

Sarah thought that Georgina cut a dashing figure. In her smart military uniform, and with her tall broad-shouldered physique and blue eyes, the Princess was her father's daughter. But her colouring—her sallow skin and dark collar-length hair—was all her mother, Queen Sofia. Although born and brought up in Britain, she was actually a part of the Spanish royal family, and she had passed on her dark looks to both of her children.

We see Princess Georgina make her way up the steps and onto the dais. She kneels before the King on the hassock placed there for her. A hush comes over the castle grounds as the King steps forward towards his daughter.

As the first minister of Wales read the proclamation in Welsh, King Edward took the sword from one of the Welsh peers, who carried the regalia of the Princess of Wales, and draped the Sword of Justice, which was attached to a leather strap, over her head. The strap ran across her chest, leaving the sword at her side. The coronet was then brought forward, and the King reverently placed it upon his daughter's head as a symbol of her rank. Next the signet ring was placed on her finger; she would keep this on to remind her of her duty as Princess of Wales. The last two items were brought forward—the Golden Rod which symbolized government, and finally the King placed the royal robes around her shoulders.

As the King fastened the robe at her neck, he looked down at his beloved daughter and gave her a smile and a wink.

Now we will see the most formal part of the ceremony. The Golden Rod will be taken from her hands, and the Princess of Wales will now make her pledge to her King, her father, and the nation.

Sarah nudged her husband and said, "Did you see that? The King winked at Georgina. He's a great man."

"I saw it, dear."

Sarah took her husband's hand and said, "They're such a warm family, not like some of the royals we've had in the past. Oh, look, she's taking her oath."

The still-kneeling Princess raised her clasped hands. The King held them between his own and she said, first in English and then in Welsh:

I, Georgina, Princess of Wales, do become your liege woman of life and limb and of earthly worship and faith and truth I will bear unto you to live and die against all manner of folks.

The King then bent over and kissed his daughter on the cheek. The royal fanfare was sounded from the castle walls to signal the end of the ceremony.

The Princess of Wales stood and, taking the hand of her father, was led down the dais, followed by her mother, the Queen. The King led her up onto the castle balcony and presented her to the cheering crowds outside.

"Did you see the pride on the King's face?" Sarah asked her husband. She dabbed a tissue at the corner of her eyes. "Magical, just magical. This is what this country does best."

CHAPTER ONE

Sandringham House
1 December 2053

Princess Georgina stood, hands clasped behind her back, looking out of her bedroom window at Sandringham House, the Christmas residence of the royal family. Normally Georgina would look forward to this time of year, spending Christmas within the warmth of her family, but not this year.

"Diary." The computer on the desk came to life and signalled with a beep that it was ready. "Begin. Today is the first day of December. Normally I cannot wait for the Christmas period, but this year will be different. It's hard to believe that only two days ago, I was serving aboard my ship, *HMS Poseidon*, blissfully unaware of what was unfolding at home. I received word that the captain wished to see me on a private matter, and I knew it must be bad news about Papa. The King's doctor had informed the family of my father's illness a few months ago. He had an aggressive virus that was proving to be drug resistant. I was angry, and I'm ashamed to admit I took my anger out on the doctor. I found it impossible to believe that a virus could put him in so much danger. I called for a second opinion, and then a third, and I was given the same conclusion: he was dying before our eyes.

"I couldn't take it in—I expected to have my father for a very long time, and here he was being taken away from me. I was so hurt at the thought of losing my beloved Papa that I refused to see him for weeks."

Princess Georgina felt the guilt deep in the pit of her stomach. *How could I shut out my father, my hero?*

She moved from the window and took a seat at her desk, and twirled the ring that her father gave her at the ceremony in Wales.

"Of course Mama knocked sense into me. She is the most caring woman I have ever encountered, but when needed to be, she can be as strong as an ox. Between Mama and Granny, it's a wonder my father got a say in anything during his reign." Georgina smiled wistfully, thinking of the family's two formidable matriarchs.

She reached out for a model ship that was sitting on her desk half-finished and, as she always did in times of stress or when she needed to relax, began building as she spoke. Attaching the tiny parts in order brought calm to her mind.

"I apologized to Papa, and the doctor assured us that he would do everything he could for him. I made peace with the fact that he might have a short time left with us, and promised to make the time we had left together as a family count, and to create some very happy memories. To everyone outside the family, my father is the King, a strong and well-respected man. To us he is a much-loved and adoring father, and to my mother the love of her life. Between Papa and me there is a special bond—ever since I can remember, I have followed his exemplary way of life. Not only have we shared a great deal of the same interests, but he has trained me ever since birth to follow in his footsteps. Where my brother Theo could be let off the leash, so to speak, I had to be trained for a life of duty and service. To that end, we spent a great deal of time together, he teaching me the correct way to lead and to behave. I believe he was most proud when I swapped services to the Royal Navy. Papa had spent his youth in the Navy and passed on his love of the sea and sailing to me. I have spent the past five years serving aboard ship on *HMS Poseidon*. I thought I had many happy years of service ahead of me, until Papa's illness. As he worsened, he contracted pneumonia and had been moved here, to Sandringham, in the hopes that the fresh country air would help."

Georgina dropped her model ship and stared blankly ahead, as she thought back to being informed of his grave condition.

"The ship's captain informed me that my father the King was not able to fight off pneumonia due to his weakened condition. I was to leave duty and return to Sandringham immediately. As I packed my kitbag, I knew I would never be returning to my post. As well as losing my beloved Papa, I was losing my life as I had made it up until then. Duty was calling me, as I always knew it would—I just didn't think it would be for a very long time. As Papa has always told me, duty to the country and the people comes first, second, and last."

She heard a knock at the door of her bedroom. "Diary end." The computer saved her words and powered down. "Come."

Georgina's personal aide and dresser, Captain Skye Cameron, or Cammy as she was known, entered, gave a brief nod, and said in her thick Scottish brogue, "Your Royal Highness, the doctor has called for the family to attend the King's bedside."

Georgina's heart sank. She stood and walked towards the drinks cabinet, determined to pour something to calm the sick feeling in her stomach. As she lifted the crystal decanter to pour, her hand started to shake and the glass clinked uncontrollably against the decanter.

In a second Cammy was there, taking the crystal from her hand and placing it back down. She grasped her comrade and friend by the shoulders and said, "George, take a breath, man. You can't go in there like this. Just breathe in and out. One minute more won't do any harm."

Cammy enjoyed a familiarity with the princess, which no one outside the family did. Only her family and Cammy ever called her George, although the captain was not ignorant of protocol. In public or where ears were listening, she was always Your Royal Highness or Ma'am.

With deep breathing the shakes began to lessen, and George knew it was time to assume her dutiful role as the eldest and heir of the family dynasty. She looked down at Cammy, who was a good six inches shorter than her, and said, "I'm ready."

"Do you still want that wee dram for your nerves?" Cammy asked.

George shook her head. "No, it wouldn't be appropriate to have alcohol on my breath. I don't want to disappoint Papa."

"Is there anything else you need from me, Ma'am?"

George looked down at her casual dress of jeans and wool jumper. "I think I will have to do as I am, Cammy."

"Very well. I'll look after your formal dress uniforms." Cammy was the consummate professional. Even in George's sadness, it was her job to think what would come next and anticipate her commanding officer's needs. With the expected death of the sovereign, George would need her formal attire pressed and ready. These little things made George's life so much easier, especially at a time like this.

George clapped her on the back. "Thank you. You always look after me."

"That's my job and my pleasure, George."

She opened the door and felt a deep sorrow in the pit of her stomach. Not only was she losing her beloved father, but she was also losing the small bit of freedom she had enjoyed. George thought of the words said by many historical commentators of the past. As soon as the sovereign took his final breath, the heir entered into a life sentence, with no early release for good behaviour. Outsiders would see the luxury and the riches, but those within the family and staff understood that George would be entering a gilded cage, with her entire life mapped out for her. The relative freedom George enjoyed in the Navy would be no more.

This was the last time George would be the Princess of Wales. When she returned to her rooms, she would be Queen with all the responsibility that brought.

❖

George stopped in front of her parents' bedroom door; she took a breath before walking through. She found the scene that she had dreaded since learning of her father's illness. King Edward was in the grand four-poster bed, his breathing raspy and shallow. George felt her chest tighten as she watched her brother Theo on his knees at the side of the bed, gripping his father's hand. The tears ran down Theo's face; their mother stroked his hair, trying to soothe him. King Edward's doctor approached her side and waited, as protocol demanded, for George to initiate the conversation.

"Doctor, what is the King's condition?"

"The King is nearing the end of his life's journey, Your Royal Highness."

George bit her lip to keep under control. She was now becoming head of the family and was determined to act as such. "How long does he have?"

"It could be minutes or a few hours. It's hard to say Ma'am." George met her mother's tear-filled eyes, and she gave a shake of the head.

She walked towards them, past her Aunt Grace, the Princess Royal, and her grandmother, Queen Adrianna, who both reached out to her as she passed.

As she approached the bedside, she heard her father say in a breathy voice, "Lis…ten to…your sister…my boy. I love you."

It broke George's heart to see the King like this. He had been such a strong, athletic, and vibrant man all her life, and here he was, thin, ashen faced, and struggling for breath.

The Queen leaned over and said to her husband, "Eddie, my darling? George is here." Placing her hands on her tearful son, she encouraged him to stand and let George approach her father.

The princess knelt and took the King's hand. She looked into the blue eyes so much like her own and said, "Papa?"

"George? My girl?"

She kissed his hand. "Don't speak, Papa. Save your strength."

"I must, I'm dying. I must talk." He reached out a shaky hand and touched her cheek. "I'm so proud of you. You will be a fine Queen."

"Don't say that, Papa. Hang on please."

"Too tired. Listen, I have trained you well. The crown is safe."
Every word was a struggle to get out, but the King was determined.
"Look after your Mama, and your brother."

The tears were rolling down George's face now; she knew this
was the end. "I give you my word, Papa."

"Remember duty and service come first..."

George was well aware of this phrase. It had been taught to her
all her life. Duty and service to the country and its people come first,
second, and last.

"You will be the first. Make Uncle George proud."

Georgina was named after her Uncle, Prince George, whom her
father had loved and looked up to a great deal. Her father was in fact
the second child of the late King Alfred II and Queen Adrianna, now
the Queen Mother.

His brother George was the eldest and heir to the throne, and
his younger sister Princess Grace, the Princess Royal, the youngest.
George was a remarkable young man, very much liked by the people.
He was the first openly gay prince and would have been the first openly
gay monarch.

Edward was very proud of him and named his eldest daughter
after him. Edward never expected to sit on the throne himself, although
it was expected that his children would inherit. Stem cell reproduction
had been in its infancy at that time, and Prince George was unlikely to
produce a legitimate heir.

This became academic, however, when Prince George was thrown
from his horse and killed. His parents and siblings and the country were
distraught. From that moment on, Edward knew he would sit on the
throne. George understood how much the family, and especially her
father, adored her namesake and always felt it her duty to live up to her
uncle's memory. This became even more pertinent when she explained
to her parents that she was gay. The family couldn't have been more
supportive. Edward now thought for certain his daughter was destined
to carry on his brother's legacy. Not only would she be the first female
to inherit the throne ahead of her brother, but she would be the first
openly gay monarch, and because of the major advances in reproductive
technology over the preceding years, the line of succession would be
secure.

George could actually feel the heavy weight of expectation
suddenly resting on her shoulders. "I will try to make you proud. I love
you, Papa."

"Love you. Sofia?"

George swapped places with her mother, who held her husband's hand and stroked his head, all the time whispering words of love. This was the example she and her brother had been shown all their life. Their parents were devoted to each other, and hopelessly in love.

George looked up to see Theo, being held in their grandmother's arms, racked with grief.

The tightness in George's chest grew worse as the King's breathing grew shallower and shallower. Another few minutes passed, and nothing could be heard from the King. The Queen convulsed in tears, holding Edward's head to her chest and rocking him.

"My darling Eddie, I love you. I love you my darling."

George looked round the room in shock. Her grandmother cried as she cooed and tried to comfort Theo. Her Aunt Grace sat on the corner of the bed, holding her face in her hands.

The doctor at the other side of the bed said to the Queen, "May I, Ma'am?"

Queen Sofia quickly brought herself under control. Her grieving would be done in privacy. The doctor took the King's pulse, and then looked at the Queen. "The King is dead." He then retreated from the bed.

Sofia dabbed her wet red eyes with her handkerchief, and a look of calm dignity came upon her. She stood and took her daughter's hand, kissed her knuckles with reverence, gave her a bow of the head, and said, "Long live the Queen."

At that moment, the tightness that George had felt in her chest made her heart feel like it was going to explode. She collapsed into her mother's arms. "I can't do it, Mama. I can't…"

Sofia, who now in a matter of minutes had become the Queen Mother, took her daughter's head in her hands and looked deeply into her eyes. "George? Look at me, look at me. Take deep breaths."

George did as she was asked and her sobs began to lessen and breathing to calm.

"That's it. Calm down. I know the pressure you feel, and I know the hurt that is tearing at your heart, but you have been trained for this moment all your life. You can do it my darling. You are your father's daughter, and it's time to make him proud."

George stood up straight, lifted her shoulders, and wiped the tears from her eyes. George brought some control back and remembered her father's words. *Duty and service come first.*

"I understand, Mama."

"Good girl." Queen Sofia kissed her on each cheek and stepped to the side, where her grandmother, aunt, and brother stood, waiting to pay homage in the way her mother had. After Theo bowed and kissed her hand, George enveloped her younger brother in a hug, and his tears started anew.

"He's gone, Georgie."

I have to be strong for my family. "Everything will be fine, Theo. I will take care of everything." George kissed her brother on the head and said to her mother, "Mama, I'm just going to take a moment, and then I'll speak to the palace officials."

George guided her grieving brother to her mother and gave a last look to her father before bolting from the room, her mother's shout echoing in her ears.

❖

"George!" Queen Sofia shouted.

"Leave her to me, my dear." Queen Adrianna told her daughter-in-law and set off as fast as her aged legs would allow.

The trademark clatter of her walking stick reverberated up the hallway of Sandringham House. The King's private secretary, Sir Michael Bradbury, bowed as she approached.

"Is my granddaughter in the late King's office?"

"Yes, Your Majesty. I spoke with Dr. Forsyth and immediately came to see if I could render any assistance. My sincerest condolences to you and your family, Ma'am."

"Thank you, Sir Michael. It is a very sad day."

Queen Adrianna could see the tension in Sir Michael as he gripped his tablet tightly. The death of the King put everything into flux, for the staff as well as the family. She was sure he would be worried for his own position as private secretary to the monarch.

"I understand that this is a very difficult time, Ma'am, but I wanted to get permission from the Queen to announce the King's death to the staff, and we need to start thinking about releasing information to the press. I tried to talk to the Queen, but she wishes to be left alone."

"Let me talk to Her Majesty, and we'll take it from there, Sir Michael."

"Of course, Ma'am."

Adrianna walked into the late King's office to find George staring at her father's desk, unmoving.

"It won't bite, my dear."

George turned to speak to her grandmother. "How can I ever begin to follow Papa, to fill his shoes?"

Queen Adrianna tottered over to George. "You can follow him because you have been trained, and you know you can achieve great things with the proper training, and you won't fill Eddie's shoes because you will make your own path. You will take all the best parts of your father's legacy and add your own. Modernizing and adapting along the way."

"Granny I…"

"George, do sit down, please? My old bones could do with a seat, but I cannot sit before the Queen."

"I'm sorry, Granny, of course." George quickly sat at what was now her desk. Her grandmother walked round the desk and sat at the other side. George suddenly realized where she was sitting. "Granny, you tricked me."

Her grandmother gave her a small smile. "It's not a trick. I'm here to give you a swift kick up the jacksy, my dear."

George clasped her hands in front of her. "I just need some time."

"That is not a luxury you have, my dear. There will be time for private grief. You are the head of the family now, as well as the nation. The family, the staff, and the nation need you to lead them in *their* grief. The people especially need to see you to know that the monarchy is safe and secure. Remember, we need to be seen to be believed."

"I know what my duty is, Granny, but I've just lost my papa."

"George, I have just seen my second son die. It is the worst thing imaginable for a parent to bury their child, but I know I have to be strong for your mama, and especially your brother. He's only a young man, and he doesn't have your strength of character. He needs to know you are taking care of things, and that everything will be all right. That's what leaders do, and you are now our leader."

George blew out a breath. "Am I that strong? I don't know."

Adrianna brought her hand down sharply on the desk. "Of course you are. You are a Queen of the House of Buckingham. Your whole life has been dedicated to duty and doing the right thing, and you have behaved in a very appropriate manner. You've accepted the responsibility that came with your birth without question. Theo, on the other hand, has struggled with the responsibilities and limits placed on his life. I love him more than life, but I and the country thank God that you were destined for the throne."

"I will do my duty and I will look after Theo, Granny. I promised Papa. He is a good boy—he is just more free spirited than I. I promise I won't let the family or the nation down."

Her grandmother quirked an eyebrow in a way so much like the late King. "You never could, my dear. Do you not think your father had these same worries? Remember, he had no idea that he would ever inherit the throne. Your Uncle George was the heir and so Eddie didn't have the same training, but when it became clear that George would not produce any children, Eddie knew he would perhaps have to bear that heavy burden. You, my dear, have a head start. You have always known what your destiny would be. Now just let your training take over and do it, and when at the end of the day you find yourself alone, then do your grieving."

George closed her eyes and tried to regain control. She twisted off the ring she wore as Princess of Wales and placed it on the desk.

When she reopened her eyes, she was calm, in control, and ready to be Queen. "What's first, Granny?"

Adrianna patted her on the hand and said, "Good girl. Sir Michael is waiting outside. He will take you through the protocol. Use his experience."

CHAPTER TWO

Not a chance Danny, I'm not doing this." Beatrice Elliot stomped around her charity director's office angrily.

Danny Simpson reached for his heartburn medication and shot the aerosol into his arm, something he was doing more and more while trying to keep the small hospice charity afloat, in these harder economic times.

"Bea, please. Do you know how lucky we are? Just to be chosen as one of hundreds to receive the patronage of Queen Georgina is lucky enough, but for Timmy's to be chosen as the main charity she wants to publicize in the run up to her coronation is beyond lucky. It's pure gold. The Queen has graciously asked to tour every Timmy's hospice in the country. She wants to understand how we work, and the needs of our patients and staff. You need to be her guide—you are regional manager. You know all the staff and sites inside out."

Bea was fuming. She loved her job, it was more than a job it was a vocation, but the thought of escorting the Queen around their sites for six months was not her cup of tea.

She sat at Danny's desk and laid her feelings on the line. "Danny, you know better than most my private feelings on the royal family. I am a republican. I believe the monarchy is an outdated organization and should be abolished. It's a waste of my time to be babysitting some blue-blooded upper-class scrounger who's never done a hard day of work in her life. I need to be doing real work."

Beatrice graduated from university with top honours in public policy and management. She had offers from many organizations, but she had always raised money for hospices and those who needed them whilst growing up, and so she chose the relatively small charity Timmy's and had made herself indispensable.

"Bea, listen to me," Danny said with a hard edge to his voice. "We are a small organization, and we are struggling to keep our network of hospices open and properly equipped. You've seen the projections—

the Queen's patronage will give us a very high profile nationally, and donations from both big business and people on the street will quadruple."

"Maybe organizations like ours and the health care system wouldn't be struggling if the government didn't spend millions upon millions supporting the monarchy."

"Listen, Bea, I'm only going to say this one more time. You are our regional manager and no one knows all the sites like you do. The Queen has asked to tour every one of our hospices. I'm told the goal of our charity means a lot to her personally. This patronage is like winning the lottery for us, so you will do it, and you will do it with a smile on your face."

"Fine, but I strongly disagree with this." Bea stood and walked angrily towards the office door, the sound of her high heels clattering on the polished floor echoing around the room.

Just as she had her hand on the door, Danny shouted, "Bea, the Queen will be visiting headquarters tomorrow for a briefing about the tour. Check your mail for a list of royal protocols the palace sent."

Bea didn't look back as she stormed out and slammed the door.

❖

Queen Georgina heard the crunching sound of boots on gravel and walked to her bedroom window. She saw Major Jock Macalpine of the Pipes and Drums, 1st Battalion, Scots Guards in position under her apartment, in his traditional Royal Stewart tartan kilt, sporran, and black tunic. At precisely nine o'clock, the whining drone of bagpipes began to play, signalling the official start to the monarch's day, a tradition for two hundred years.

As he marched up and down below her bedroom window, she saw the other daily morning sight of a palace page, in his red and black livery, walking her dogs. The exuberant black Labrador, Shadow, and Baxter, the boxer, were pulling the young man off his feet.

Captain Skye Cameron joined her at the window and looked down on the scene.

"Shadow and Baxter are taking my page for a walk, as usual, it seems," George said, before returning to finish getting dressed by the bed.

"Aye, as usual, Your Majesty."

George pulled on her black wool jumper over a crisp white shirt and dark blue jeans. She was as casual as she could ever be. "Cammy, I can see your disapproving looks from here."

Her personal aide and dresser walked over and started adjusting the collars and cuffs. "Are you sure I can't interest you in one of your suits? You don't look half dressed, man."

George appraised her look in the mirror and ran her hands through her dark collar-length hair. She was more comfortable in a suit or uniform but was trying to look less intimidating.

"This is my dressed-down look. You know I'm going to the charity meeting today. It's an unofficial event, and I want people to be relaxed around me. I'm always either in a suit or uniform, and I think it makes people uptight."

Cammy picked up some of George's discarded clothes and replied, "There's nothing wrong with being smart, George."

"I know, I just want to seem more approachable. I'm still wearing black for Papa's mourning period. Don't worry, I'll be back to normal tomorrow. It's all right for you, Captain, you get to wear your army uniform every day."

Captain Skye Cameron was never out of uniform when working in an official capacity. Her black dress uniform with red peaked cap was always impeccably smart.

"Don't you think I'd rather be in my military uniform?"

Since the King's death, George's life had changed overnight. Two days later had come her ascension day. She stood before her privy council, read her ascension declaration, and signed the declaration documents using her new signature: Georgina Regina. Up and down the country, proclamations were read out at all the royal residences.

Her advisors set the date of the coronation for fourteen months' time, with the Duke of Norfolk in charge of the preparations. As well as seeing to these official matters, George also had her family to attend to.

Her brother, Prince Theo, struggled with their father's death; at twenty he had never been through the death of a close family member, and the day of the state funeral was extremely hard for him and his mother. George didn't have the option of falling apart, although she had wanted to.

Life had started to settle into a daily routine of visits, government documents, and state functions, which were all part of being a British constitutional monarch. The overriding feeling she had in her life was loneliness. Everyone deferred to her as Queen, and she had no one to share the burden with.

Cammy gave her a smack on the arm. "I know you'd rather be aboard ship. How about you tell me what tune the pipes are playing?"

George smiled. This was a game they played every morning as they listened to the official alarm call. It amused George that this tradition was originally meant to awaken the sovereigns of the past, whereas she herself had already gotten up, been to the gym, and had breakfast. Nevertheless George loved tradition.

Cammy came back from putting discarded clothes away. "Well? What's the tune?"

George closed her eyes and listened carefully. She had been around pipe music all her life, and unlike most people her age, found the sound strangely comforting. "Hmm, has to be a tune from the country of your birth. Glasgow Police Pipers?"

"Aye, it is that. A real foot tapper."

George smiled at her friend and comrade; she could always cheer her melancholy mood. Cammy was as close to a real friend as she could possibly get. She kept all of George's secrets and did nothing but support her. When George had ascended the throne, she had given Cammy the option of returning to her post in the military police and continuing her career, but ever loyal, her personal aide had chosen to stay at her side.

Captain Skye Cameron had a more unusual background than the average officer type. Born in Inverness, she was fostered out to a family in Glasgow at age ten. Luckily she was born with a determination to make her life better, and lucky that she placed with the same foster family for all of her high school years. Her foster mother was a teacher and saw in the young Skye Cameron an intelligent and highly motivated young woman.

With encouragement, she was very successful with her studies and had many options open to her. She attended Sandhurst and passed out as an officer; from there she was assigned to the Royal Military Police regiment and undertook further training as a close protection officer. It was during this training that her superiors singled her out as a candidate for assignment to the then Princess of Wales.

"So? Do I look ready to face my day?" George asked.

Cammy raised an eyebrow and said, "You'll do, George."

She gave Cammy a smile and went off to meet with her private secretary and start the business of the day.

❖

Queen Georgina sat at her desk, ready to work through the red boxes containing the government papers that demanded her attention. This morning there were five of them, and there would be more this afternoon. In a world where almost everyone had moved away from paper, by tradition all her government papers from Number Ten were always printed on paper and locked in the famous government red boxes. Only she and her private secretary had a key to the boxes.

Having a few minutes before her private secretary arrived, George thought she would have a look at the newspapers. She had already watched the morning news over breakfast, but she still had the papers to read. Her late father had taught George that it was part of her job to read every mainstream daily newspaper, to keep in touch with ordinary people's concerns and views of the news events of the day. It normally took her all day, grabbing five minutes here and there to read, but she did finish by evening.

She activated the small computer on her desk and said, "Display Racing Post." The image of a small newspaper appeared above the computer and she began to flip through. This was her favourite read, as it was about one of her well-loved country pursuits, horses. George owned three stud farms and stables, and she had enlisted the help of her aunt, the Princess Royal, and her daughter Lady Victoria to help her run them.

There was a knock at the door. "Come."

Sir Michael Bradbury entered carrying his tablet, which ran a great deal of George's life. He had been delighted to stay on and serve her as he had done for her father. The Queen felt it important to have someone as experienced in palace and government matters to help her get used to the job, though George had appointed her own people below Sir Michael, as deputy private secretary and ladies-in-waiting.

"Good morning, Sir Michael." She greeted him and minimized the Racing Post.

"Good morning, Your Majesty. I trust you slept well?"

"Yes, thank you, Sir Michael," she lied. The truth was that she had not slept properly since her father's death. George felt the intense pressure of staying strong for her family and not grieving, not to mention the pressure of being constantly reminded by her advisors and the media, that she was special, she was the first monarch of her kind. George could feel every ounce of expectation lying on her shoulders. Gay groups were championing her, women's groups and the young; all felt Queen Georgina was their figurehead. And this kept her staring into the darkness most nights.

"So what's on the agenda this morning?"

"Well, Ma'am, as well as your usual government papers and your mail, there is a proposal document from the Duke of Norfolk and the government regarding the coronation celebrations. It has been suggested that given the historic nature of your ascension, the royal family would take part in a river pageant, down the Thames, as some of your ancestors have done at significant points in their reign."

George thought about it for a minute and said, "Yes, that sounds like a very nice idea. I will look further into the proposal, but you can indicate to the Duke of Norfolk that I would require community groups and members of the public to have equal share, if not more of the places in the pageant, as the dignitaries. Perhaps each community could nominate some deserving people?"

"I will intimate that to the duke, Ma'am." Sir Michael put his tablet in front of the Queen and asked, "Could I ask that you sign these two letters before you attend to your mail and government business? One is your response to the Archbishop of Canterbury, and the other is to the Muslim Council of Britain."

George scanned over the first letter and second letter and quickly signed her e-signature.

"How many letters today?"

"Your ladies-in-waiting have forwarded one hundred and fifty letters they feel need your immediate attention, Ma'am."

Good God, George thought. "The volume seems to increase every day."

Hundreds and hundreds of e-mails were sent into Buckingham Palace every day. If the Queen's ladies-in-waiting could reply on the Queen's behalf, they would do that, or if the correspondence was about a particular problem, they would refer it on to the Queen's private secretary's office, who would then contact the relevant government or local government body who could help the writer. A selection of all the mail was sent to the Queen herself, to give her a flavour of the issues people were facing or if the ladies-in-waiting thought that a certain mail would interest her.

"Indeed, Ma'am. There seems to be a growing excitement over Your Majesty's reign."

Don't I know it. I feel every bit of everyone's expectation. "So it seems. Is there anything else?"

Sir Michael took back his tablet and checked through the upcoming business. "Oh yes, just to remind you, Ma'am, it's very likely that the general election result will be clear quite early Wednesday morning, so I would expect Your Majesty would be required to invite the winner to the palace just after lunchtime. Everything is arranged for court to decamp to Buckingham Palace tomorrow."

"Very good." Normally the family would stay in residence at Sandringham until early February, but the previous government had called a snap election, and the winner would need to be received at Buckingham Palace on Wednesday.

George had decided the whole family would cut their stay short and travel back to London, instead of travelling herself. She felt the family would benefit from having some distance from where her father passed away.

She sat back in her chair and smiled. "Tell me, Sir Michael. Who is the bookies' favourite to be meeting with me? The charismatic Labour leader, Boadicea Dixon, or the very sensible, but dull, Conservative leader, Andrew Smith?"

Sir Michael smiled at the Queen's betting analogy. "I'm told that, going by the polls, Ms. Bodicea Dixon is the odds-on favourite, Ma'am."

Two women at the top of government. Interesting.

"Well, thank you, Sir Michael, I'll get on with this mountain of work then."

Sir Michael bowed and exited the room. George looked at the pictures of her family sitting on the desk, until her eyes settled on the one of her father wearing Royal Navy dress.

"Papa? I hope you're not too disappointed with me so far." Her eyes went to the large stack of red boxes waiting for her. Real old fashioned paperwork first or mail? George instructed her mail to open. "Open mail folder. Password: Poseidon."

An image of a screen appeared. She scanned down the titles of the messages quickly and stopped when she saw one that her ladies-in-waiting had titled *Child's Picture*.

"Open child's picture." The child's drawing then filled the screen; it depicted a rough drawing of herself and the late King in crowns and robes. At the bottom it said, *To the Queen. I'm sorry about your daddy. Love, Jessica. Age 8.*

George felt the tears coming to her eyes and a lump to her throat. As usual, though, she gulped the feeling down.

"Mail off." The screen disappeared immediately. George used her key on the top red box and pulled out a folder of papers from the Ministry of Defence. *Some dry, boring paperwork will be better to start the day with, I think.*

She began working her way through it carefully, signing and approving items as she went. A persistent beep coming from her computer told her she had an incoming call. "Answer. Hello?"

"George? Have I caught you at a bad moment?" her mother asked.

"It's fine, Mama. I'm going through my boxes, but I always have time for you. I wish you would use face call." George carried on working her way through her papers.

"Good Lord, no. Who knows who might be with you, and I might not be presentable."

George grinned at that thought. She had never known her mother not to be presentable. She was an elegant, beautiful woman and never appeared outside her bedroom without make-up.

"Mama, you know you're always beautiful. So how can I be of service this morning?"

"I wanted to check that you had no engagements this evening. Granny and I thought we should have a private meal together tonight, before we head back to London. Just you, Theo, Granny, and I." Sofia's voice cracked with emotion. "I think your Papa would have liked that."

George sighed. The extended family had all gone home after the funeral, leaving them to their grief. "Of course I will be there, Mama. I only have a charity meeting this afternoon. I'm taking the helicopter, so I won't be long. I know a part of you thinks we are abandoning Papa, but I think we're doing the right thing."

"Of course you made the right decision, my darling. Papa always said, after Uncle George died, that keeping busy and getting on with things was the best medicine for grief. You know I'll always support you and follow your lead. Could you have a word with your brother? He is reluctant to return to art college and public engagements."

"Of course I will, Mama. I'll handle him."

"Thank you, my darling. Have a pleasant afternoon."

"Goodbye, Mama."

George sat back in her chair and looked at her father's picture. Everything was a blur after the late King died. Duty and performing those duties kicked in straight away, without any time for grieving or taking stock. She thought back to her ascension day.

George had met with her privy counsellors and read and signed the declaration, before watching as it was read to the gathering public outside.

Whereas it has pleased Almighty God to call to his mercy our late Sovereign Lord King Edward XI, of blessed and glorious memory, by whose decease the Crown is solely and rightfully come to the high and mighty Princess Georgina Mary Edwina Louise.

We, therefore, the Lords Spiritual and Temporal of the Realm, being assisted with these His late Majesty's Privy Council, with representatives of other members of the Commonwealth, with other principal gentlemen of quality, with the Lord Mayor, Aldermen, and Citizens of London, do now hereby with one voice and consent of tongue and heart publish and proclaim, that the high and mighty Princess Georgina Mary Edwina

Louise is now, by the death of our late Sovereign of happy memory, become Queen Georgina by the grace of God, Queen of the realm, and her other realms and territories, Head of the Commonwealth, Defender of Faiths, to whom her lieges do acknowledge all faith, and constant obedience with hearty and humble affection, beseeching God by whom Kings and Queens do reign, to bless the Royal Princess, Georgina, with long and happy years to reign over us.

God save the Queen.

As the proclamation was read, George could have sworn she heard the gilded cage door shut and locked.

She looked around the empty office, with only the noise of the ticking antique clock, and felt utterly alone.

CHAPTER THREE

Bea checked her appearance in the office mirror before smoothing down her skirt. When she left home this morning, her mother had been beside herself with excitement about her daughter meeting the Queen. Bea refused to see today as anything other than a normal one and was determined not to make any special effort. She had come downstairs this morning for breakfast to find her outfit had been cleaned again, pressed and hung waiting for her, and her mum giving very special attention to her high heels.

Sarah had made her daughter promise she would not say anything inappropriate in the presence of the Queen.

To which she had replied, "Mother, I'm not an idiot and I am a professional. I wouldn't make a scene at my work."

What had bothered her more than anything was that over the past few days, Timmy's had been wasting money, as she thought, upgrading the facilities. The smell of fresh paint was everywhere she turned, and she resented it.

Bea glanced at her computer display where she had the protocol guidelines, sent by the Queen's equerry, on screen. The first three really stood out:

1) Please refrain from touching the Queen. When shaking hands, wait for Her Majesty to extend her hand to you.
2) On first meeting, please address the Queen as Your Majesty, then Ma'am as in *ham*, not Ma'am as in *the farm*.
3) When in the presence of Her Majesty the Queen, please do not turn your back on her.

"Bloody cheek. Computer off." It powered down with a barely audible whine.

"Right, Bea, let's go and meet the toffee-nosed bitch with whom I'll be spending the next six months touring the country."

George sat in the back seat of her armoured unmarked car, on her way from the helipad to the Timmy's charity headquarters. She used the time to read the brief her equerry had prepared for her on the visit and the staff.

As it was an unofficial visit, she only had Cammy and one other police protection officer with her. She gave a small smile as she scanned over the information about Beatrice Elliot, who would be her guide for months to come. Her equerry, Major Archibald Fairfax, had written to the side of Miss Elliot's picture: *Could be trouble. Has voiced republican and anti-monarchist views throughout university. The director insists she is the only one qualified to guide Her Majesty throughout the country.*

George looked at her picture and the image of the beautiful woman did not look like trouble to her. "Cammy, does this young lady look like trouble to you? Major Fairfax thinks so."

Captain Cameron looked over the young woman's picture. "No, Ma'am. She looks like a bonnie wee lassie."

Hmm…intriguing, thought George.

The Queen followed closely as Danny Simpson stood at the top of the conference table, talking through his presentation. Around the table sat other members of the board of trustees and senior staff, including Beatrice Elliot.

Danny pointed to the computer image he had displayed and said, "So as you can see, Ma'am, we have twenty-two sites in all, three of which are only in the building stage. We also have ten fundraising projects. This is our regional director Beatrice Elliot's project. Her idea is to get the community involved in the fundraising and upkeep of their local hospice; this then gives a sense of ownership to the local people, and hopefully encourages them to care about the ongoing funding of the hospice. These projects are attached to schools, community groups, and church groups. It's worked very well, Ma'am, and we're very excited to show you over the coming months. Miss Elliot will start by taking you to…"

George looked over towards her guide. Beatrice was even more beautiful in the flesh. Her delicate features and creamy skin enhanced her elegance and beauty. George had noticed that Beatrice didn't look too happy, and that was very unusual. She was used to people being genuinely pleased to see her, or even if they didn't like her personally, they would fawn over her because of her position. This further intrigued her.

"Ma'am? Did you have any questions?"

George was quickly shaken from her thoughts. "No, Danny. I would just like to say to you all, I am grateful for this opportunity to help Timmy's. Every one of you does such a wonderful job and I admire the dedication you show. I hope we will be able to bring some much needed attention to Timmy's. Thank you all for your time today."

"Thank you, Ma'am. We have some tea set up in the other room, if you would like to follow me."

George leaned over to Danny and said quietly, "Could I have a word with Miss Elliot privately before we go through?"

"Of course, Ma'am. Beatrice?" Danny walked over and spoke to his colleague, and George noticed her face fell further into melancholy.

I wonder what I did to deserve that.

Everyone else filed out of the room, and Beatrice walked over to where George was sitting.

George, always courteous, stood. "Do sit down, Miss Elliot."

"I prefer to stand if you don't mind, Ma'am." Beatrice's tone was highly unimpressed.

"Oh...of course." George remained standing and clasped her hands behind her back. "I just wanted to have a few moments with you, get to know your thinking about what you would like to achieve. We will be spending a lot of time together over the coming months."

"Don't I know it," Bea whispered under her breath.

George let that go and continued. "I noticed during the meeting, and while talking to you, Miss Elliot, that you seem to be less than impressed with your new assignment. Could you tell me what's bothering you? Perhaps it can be fixed."

Beatrice sighed. "Ma'am, due to the protocol demands your equerry made sure we understood, it would be difficult for me to express my private feelings without it reflecting badly on Timmy's."

"Oh, that? It's just a guideline. Please speak freely. We are on our own, no staff to get you into trouble, and I give you my word, nothing you say will affect my patronage of Timmy's. Please, do go on."

George leaned against the windowsill, arms folded, waiting to hear what the intriguing Miss Elliot had to say.

After seconds of silence, Beatrice said, "I begged Danny not to give me this job. I don't want to do it, but apparently there is no one else qualified to do it. I don't want to do it because I'm a Republican—I believe the monarchy is not only an outdated institution, it also is a drain on public funds. The money that is supporting your family could be spent on the National Health Service, and perhaps charities like us would not be needed as much. I don't believe you are any better than I am and I think it's ridiculous that I have to bow and curtsy to you, not to mention the rest of the stupid rules on your protocol document."

George was both stunned and amused at the same time. Never had anyone outside her family spoken to her in such an irreverent manner. She smiled inside at the fire in those green eyes. *They must sparkle when you smile.*

She cleared her throat and said, "I thank you for your extremely frank response. It's most refreshing. I can only tell you this. I have very personal reasons for choosing this charity. As you know, the late King died before Christmas. When he was dying, I realized, even in my sadness, how lucky my family was. We had twenty-four hour care with specialist doctors and nurses. The King was also able to stay at home where he was most comfortable, the equipment and drugs coming to him rather than the other way about. To that end, I decided I wanted to give something back to those who don't have that luxury. I think we both share the same goals, Miss Elliot. I don't have the time to debate the monarchy with you at the moment, but perhaps that's something we could discuss as we travel the country. As for the other matters, if we are alone, I give you permission to call me whatever you want."

It looked as if she had surprised Beatrice with her response.

"So I can call you anything I want?"

"Well, my family and friends call me George."

The angry fire in Beatrice's eyes had changed into a mischievous glint. "George is a bit serious, how about Georgie? Like Georgie Porgie from the nursery rhyme."

George threw her head back and laughed heartily. The young woman's totally irreverent attitude towards her was highly amusing.

"Oh, thank you, Miss Elliot. That's the first time I've laughed in…I don't know how long. My brother has called me Georgie ever since he was a little boy. You reminded me of more carefree and happier times."

She watched Beatrice's gaze wander over her, trying to gauge her response. She had clearly been a surprise to her.

"I'm glad I made you laugh. You can call me Bea. Everyone does."

"Thank you very much. So, have we come to an understanding, Bea?" George started to walk towards her.

In an instant, Beatrice's fire returned. "And what about these stupid protocols I was sent?" she said angrily.

"What is so terrible about the blasted protocol document? What on it disturbs you?"

"Well for one thing it says, *Please refrain from touching the Queen.* That's just ridiculous."

George raised an eyebrow and said with a hint of amusement. "You wish to touch me, Bea?"

Beatrice's cheeks went bright red. "What? No, I don't mean that. It's the fact that we ordinary people are unfit to touch you, as if we might contaminate you. Well, let me tell you something, Georgie, you are not special, you are not chosen by God to lead the British people, as some think, and I am certainly not your subject."

George was unsure as how to handle this. No one had ever tried to debate with her before, and she was starting to feel rather defensive of her role and the monarchy, which her family had worked so hard over the years to protect, and in which she believed wholeheartedly.

"As I say, Bea. I have neither the time nor the inclination to debate my constitutional role with you at the moment, but if I had the opportunity, I would vehemently defend my family's position. I will say this to you though. You are welcome to your views—this is a free country after all. Whether you wish to think of yourself as a subject or not is irrelevant. This country, a democracy, has a constitutional monarchy of which I am the head of state. As such you are my subject, whether you like it or not. To that end, I have given you permission to address me in an informal way in private, but around others you will address me correctly, or we will have to make other arrangements. The dignity of the monarch's position must be upheld. Do we understand each other, Bea?"

Beatrice's face was now one of thunderous rage. "Yes, Your Majesty. I think we understand each other perfectly."

George groaned inside. She knew that the goodwill and friendly feeling they had built up had now evaporated. "I'm glad. Oh, and for your information, the no touching rule is simply to insure I don't get overwhelmed by people as I walk through crowds. So, shall we rejoin the others?"

Beatrice indicated for her to go first. "I wouldn't want to turn my back on you. That's another rule."

George simply sighed and walked out of the room. *I know. My life is guided by rules, Bea.*

❖

Bea walked in the front door of her family's little semi-detached house and immediately relaxed. After a trying day, it was wonderful to come home to a warm, loving home. She could smell her mother's cooking, wafting through down the hall from the kitchen. She hung up her jacket, kicked off her high heels, and made her way to the kitchen. Her mum was standing at the cooker making dinner.

"Is that you, sweetheart?"

Bea walked up behind her mother and kissed her cheek. "Hi, Mum. What's cooking?"

Sarah turned quickly and said, "Never mind what's cooking, tell me about the Queen."

Bea put her hand on her hip. "Mum?"

Sarah pulled her daughter by the arm to the kitchen table. "Bea, please, sit down and indulge me."

She rolled her eyes but sat down waiting for her mother's grilling.

"Well? What was she like? Was she charming? Polite? Oh, she must have been regal. She always holds herself with such dignity, and she's just your type too. Big, strong, and powerful, and those dreamy blue eyes. She plays polo, sails, and climbs mountains and all sorts. A real action woman."

"Mother, I do not have a type, and I think you read celebrity magazines a bit too much."

"Are you having a laugh, sweetheart? Your last two girlfriends were a footballer and a rugby player. Do I need to say any more? A mother knows her girl."

Bea scowled. She knew her mother had a point, but she wasn't going to admit anything. Her short but disastrous history of girlfriends was something she was trying to forget.

The back door opened and in walked her father, covered in soil as usual. Reg kissed both his wife and daughter as he made his way over to the sink to wash off the dirt of the day. "How's my best girl?"

"I'm fine, Dad." Bea gave her father a warm smile.

"Don't distract her, Reg, she's going to tell us about meeting the Queen today."

"Wait for me then." Reg got a bottle of lager from the fridge and took his place at the table. Now both of her parents looked at her with eager smiles.

What do they find so exciting about her? "She was…very nice to all the staff. Listened very carefully to what they all had to say."

"And?" asked Sarah.

"And what?"

"What did she say to you of course." Her mother was becoming exasperated.

"Well, she said I could call her what I liked. I said how about Georgie?"

Sarah looked aghast. "You asked if you could call the Queen of Great Britain *Georgie*?"

She was highly amused by the look of horror on her mum's face. "Don't worry, Mum, it made her laugh. She said I could call her whatever I wanted in private." She recalled how much younger the Queen looked when she laughed. So different from the stoic, serious mask she had worn during the meeting.

One thing she did remember from the meeting, though. While Danny talked figures, she lifted her eyes and caught George looking right at her, appraising what she saw with interest. Bea felt a fluttering in her stomach at the memory, then shook it away.

"That's my girl. On first-name terms with the Queen," Reg said proudly.

Sarah reached out and took her husband's hand. "So, when are they going to announce this to the press? Can I tell your Auntie Martha?"

Bea knew this was what her mother had been waiting for. A chance to show off a bit to her snobbish cousin Martha. Sarah and Martha were not close by any manner of means. They had always been like chalk and cheese. Whereas Sarah had a fun-loving, easy-going personality, her older cousin Martha was stuffy, pompous, and a social climber. Although coming from a working-class background, Martha had been extremely proud of herself when she married a doctor. Since then, her mum had had to listen to her cousin being entirely too pleased with herself and her two children.

"It should be on the news tomorrow, so you can tell her anytime. Can I go and get changed now?" Bea was becoming fed up talking about the royal visit.

"The Queen must have said more to you than that, sweetheart."

With a huge sigh, she replied, "She asked to speak to me privately, to discuss the trip and any concerns I had. I told her that I didn't ask for this role, and I didn't feel comfortable with it, but I had no choice but to do it."

Sarah looked horrified. "Oh, Bea, you didn't. What will she think of you?"

I've had enough of this for one day. If one more person mentions the bloody Queen I'll scream. "Mum, Dad. It's been a long day. I just want to get changed and relax. The precious Queen is an arrogant woman full of her own importance, and she snapped me back into line, okay?"

She stomped out of the kitchen and up the stairs.

❖

"Shadow, Baxter, heel." George walked along the corridor leading to the family's private dining room, followed closely by her ever-faithful dogs. After returning from Timmy's, she had attended to some more paperwork before making sure to change her jeans to black suit trousers, knowing her mother and grandmother would not appreciate the dressed-down look.

As she approached the door, the page stationed outside bowed at the neck. When he opened the door, Shadow and Baxter immediately shot off to see the Queen Mother's and the Dowager Queen's dogs. The royal family loved their dogs.

The dogs barked as they greeted each other, all except her father's Labrador, Rex, who rushed over to George, wagging his tail and twirling around excitedly.

"Rex, sit. Wait," George commanded, and Rex obeyed immediately.

Conscious of her mother and grandmother standing, she went to greet them first. Everyone had to know their place in the royal family, even the dog. She walked over to the dinner table where she gave her grandmother a kiss on each cheek. "Good evening, Granny. Please, do sit down."

"Good evening, my dear. Theo is late as usual."

"Give him a few minutes, Granny. He'll be here." George then greeted her mother with kisses and a hug. "How are you doing, Mama?"

Sofia gave her daughter a brave smile and said, "I'm doing well, my darling."

George knew that her mother was struggling. Often she found her with red eyes, obviously very recently crying, but she was trying not to show it to be strong for her daughter.

"Are you sure, Mama?"

"I will be fine. Please don't worry darling. It's poor Rex that needs help."

George looked over to where the Labrador was still obediently waiting for attention.

She knelt down and said to the dog, "Rexie? Come." She was immediately engulfed with hugs and kisses from the dog. "What's wrong with him, Mama?"

"He won't play with Mabel and Daisy. He just lies in the corner, whimpering and crying for your father. He hardly eats anything either. I'm worried. The only time he is happy is when he sees you. I think he associates you with Eddie."

George ruffled his ears and gave him kisses on the head. "Are you sad, Rexie? I'm sorry, boy. I know you miss him, but we all love you too." Rex gave her lots of licks on the face.

Queen Adrianna then said, "He needs a strong alpha to make him feel secure, my dear. He doesn't know his place any more."

"Is that right, Rexie?" George asked the dog. "We all need to know our place, don't we, boy?" She turned to her mother. "I'll take him if you want, Mama."

Queen Sofia smiled. "Oh, would you, George? I hate to see him so unhappy. He was such a good companion to your father."

"Of course. Would you like that, Rexie?"

The dog wagged its tail vigorously and licked her face. "Shadow, Baxter, come." Her two dogs trotted over to her. "Look after Rexie, go play." Shadow, the leader of her two dogs, gave Rex a lick and a soft bark, as if sensing the dog needed looking after. The three trotted off to play with the others.

George took her seat at the head of the table.

"Well done, my darling. We can always count on you to sort out family problems," Sofia told her daughter.

George clasped her hands in front of her. "That's my job, Mama."

Queen Adrianna added, as Theo hurried through the door, "Now you just have one more to sort out."

"Sorry I'm late, Mama." He hurriedly greeted his mother and grandmother with a kiss.

He quickly took his seat and she gave him a stern look. "Theo, it's not us you have to apologize to. It's the staff that you've inconvenienced."

Theo looked up to the page who was standing by the door and said, "Jones, please convey my apologies to the staff for keeping them waiting."

"Very good, sir." Jones walked to Queen Sofia's side and asked, "May we serve now, Ma'am?"

George had made it clear to the staff that the Queen Mother was still in charge of domestic affairs. George was going to be a different kind of Queen. She had no idea about flower arrangements, banquet menus, or table settings. So until she had a Queen Consort who she hoped would be interested in those things, it was down to her mother.

The first course was served and they began to eat. George looked up at her brother and he was simply playing with his food. His appearance was scruffy, his already unruly dark curly hair was longer than usual, and he was clearly unshaven. He looked like a little boy lost.

Theo had always been different; he was a free artistic spirit, who struggled with the confines of their royal roles and duties. Although he was very different from her and her father, Theo had adored the King, as well as his big sister. Edward had given him leeway, as he was not going to have the responsibilities of the throne. Theo felt safe doing his own thing, going to art college, travelling all over the world, knowing that he had a stable family at home.

He feels adrift, just like us all. I need to have a good chat with him, bring him back to safety.

"Theo, how about a game of cards after dinner? Just you and me?" This was something the two siblings used to do with their father after dinner most evenings. They would talk about everything and anything out of earshot of their mother and grandmother.

Her brother looked up hopefully. "Are you sure you have time, Georgie? You've got so much work to do these days I—"

"I can always make time for my brother."

Theo was suddenly full of smiles. "That would be wonderful, Georgie, thank you."

Queen Sofia gave her daughter's hand a squeeze in thanks.

As the first course was cleared away, Queen Sofia asked her, "How was your visit today?"

George smirked, remembering the feisty blonde who had talked to her like an ordinary human being. No one outside her family had ever done that, and even then, her family still followed rules of protocol. Since returning from Timmy's she had found that her mind had been lingering on Miss Beatrice Elliot.

"It was…intriguing."

"How so?" asked her mother.

"The young lady who is to be my guide is…well, she is something I haven't come across before."

"What? A woman, Georgie?" Theo teased.

"Theodore." Sofia gave her son a look that could kill.

George chuckled at her brother's comment. He always liked to rib her about her lack of experience with women. "No, my dear brother, it was for another reason. Her name is Bea, Beatrice Elliot, and she is a republican."

"Oh my. How interesting," Queen Adrianna exclaimed.

"Yes," George said wistfully. "I've never come across an anti-monarchist personally before. Of course I've seen the small band of republicans that hold placards outside the palace occasionally, but someone has never admitted it to my face."

Queen Sofia looked concerned. "Was she rude, my darling?"

Beatrice had been a little rude, but for some reason she wanted to protect her. "Not rude, Mama. I asked to speak to her privately, and only after I asked her to speak freely would she tell me. She was totally unimpressed with my position, and I found her forthrightness refreshing."

Adrianna said, "Well, my dear George, it is your challenge, over the course of your time together, to impress this young lady and bring her to our way of thinking. The honour of the House of Buckingham rests on your shoulders."

George and her mother grinned, but Theo burst out laughing. "God help us all, Granny, if the honour of the Buckinghams relies on Georgie impressing a woman."

Luckily for Theo, the staff came in with the main course before his grandmother could clip his ear.

After dinner, George and her brother sat at the card table, the three dogs sprawled in front of the fireplace.

Theo threw his cards down. "You win again. You want another drink?"

She gathered the cards up and started shuffling. It hadn't gone unnoticed by her that while she was still on her first drink, Theo was on his third. "I think I've had enough, and I think you have had enough too, Theo."

He looked at the bottle and with a sigh put it down.

"Sit down, Theo."

He sat and kept his gaze on the floor. "I know what you're going to say."

George sat back in the leather chair. "What am I going to say?"

"You're going to say that I have to do my duty, I have to get back to normal, but I'm not like you Georgie, or Mama and Granny. I can't sweep my feelings under the carpet. Our father is dead, gone, and I can't just snap out of it," Theo shouted.

If only you knew, Theo. "Is that what you think we are doing? Sweeping our feelings under the carpet? We are doing what we've been trained to do—our duty—and grieving privately. At Christmas we all sat round this table, all our cousins, aunts, and uncles, and made a commitment to take on a portion of Papa's charities. We made a commitment, and those organizations need us. It's our duty to the people to get back to work."

Theo stood up angrily and shouted, "Bugger the people. I've lost my papa."

Rather than reacting with anger, George stood and took her brother in her arms. "Shh, shh, now, it's all right."

She stroked Theo's head as he sobbed against her shoulder. "I miss him, Georgie. I miss him and I'm so angry that he left us. When Mama said you had decided we should go back to London, I felt like everyone just wanted to forget about him."

She took her brother's head in her hands and said, "Listen to me. We are not forgetting Papa. We are doing what he would have wanted, doing our jobs. Mama, Granny, and I know that it is not only our duty to get on with things, it is good for us to get working and take our minds off our grief. Don't you think I miss him? Don't you think I cry for him when I'm alone? You know how much I loved him."

"Yes, I know you do," he replied quietly.

"Yes, but I don't get the opportunity, or the luxury of time, that even you get. Government business and messages from the public land on my desk twice a day—if I stopped to grieve the way you want to, I would go under. The affairs of the nation would pile up, and I would not only be letting the people down, I'd be letting Papa down. Duty was everything to him, and we honour him by carrying on with ours. And remember, Theo, as a royal family, we have to be seen to be believed."

"I'm sorry for complaining, Georgie. I know your life is a lot harder than mine—I'm afraid of losing you too. Everything has changed now."

"You don't have to be sorry, Theo, just do your duty, so that Mama and Granny won't worry. They have enough on their plates. You will never lose me, Theo. I may be busy, but I will always be there for you, even if it's at the end of a phone sometimes. And please understand that if I make a decision for the family, it is in the best interests of the family. With the election, I have to get back to headquarters at Buckingham Palace."

They both sat down again. "So, what's first up in your diary?"

Theo wiped his eyes and said, "I have to open a new art department at a secondary school. Don't you ever get fed up with the endless rounds of opening schools and hospitals, and unveiling one plaque after another?"

George gave him a smile. "Remember what Granny has always said on the subject?"

Theo chuckled along with her. "Oh yes." He put on a high-pitched voice imitating Queen Adrianna and said, "We are the royal family and we adore unveiling plaques."

"Good boy. Things will get easier, Theo, and you know I will always look after you. We have a busy year ahead."

"I know, and just think, Georgie, all of Europe's aristocracy will be trying to catch your eye, hoping to become your wife and Queen Consort. I have heard that Princess Eleanor of Belgium has suddenly come out of the closet."

George was only too well aware that it was the Queen's duty to find a consort and produce an heir. This she had known from when she was very young. "So I've heard. The thought does not fill me with joy," George said wistfully. Getting married did not worry George; she was in fact a very traditional person. She longed for someone who would love her and support her in the role as Queen, but at the same time see past her position. George craved a relationship like her mother and father's but feared she would not find that person in time and would be obliged to marry someone she did not truly love.

"Georgie, I have faith you will meet someone like Papa did, and probably where you least expect to find her. Now. How about a rematch?"

CHAPTER FOUR

Boadicea Dixon's car pulled in through the high gates of Buckingham Palace. Her assistant, spin doctor, and close friend Felix Brown met her eyes and grinned. "You've done it, Prime Minister. You've made it."

"It's been a long time coming, but we're not done yet. I'm not Prime Minister till I get on my knees and swear fealty to the sovereign."

"How do you feel about that? Kissing hands, as they call it."

"You know better than anyone that I don't go down on bended knee for anyone."

Felix certainly knew this to be true. Felix had met Bo at Oxford University, where they both studied politics.

Bo was a larger-than-life character who was hugely involved with many of the political clubs within the university. She always was determined to become a career politician and get to the very top. Felix, who had a talent for speech writing and a good understanding of how the media worked, made it his mission to help his friend achieve her goals. Bo was a no-nonsense woman who had an extremely tough reputation and was not averse to trampling on others to get where she wanted. Her nickname in the House of Commons was the ball-buster and, while spending two years as the leader of the opposition, had been known to make grown men cry.

She was a woman who believed in her own destiny and would use everything at her disposal to get what she wanted, and she had gotten it—the first female leader of the Labour party, and now moments away from becoming only the second woman prime minister in British history. The media were calling it a new modern age. A gay woman on the throne and a female Labour prime minister.

"How do I feel?" Bo tapped her perfectly manicured fingernails on her handbag on her lap. Felix felt a thrill rush through him at the power she exuded. One thing he didn't know about his friend, that no one knew, was what happened in her personal life. She had never married and no one knew whether she was gay or straight. People speculated, especially since she was quite an attractive woman, but Bo seemed to thrive on the ambiguity of it. It was just another tool at her disposal.

"I *feel* that our new Queen is riding a wave of popularity and it will suit our purposes to be part of that. I think I will make sure we have the goodwill of our sovereign."

❖

Queen Georgina stood alone, apart from her three dogs who lay in the sunlight by the window, in the audience room at Buckingham Palace, awaiting the arrival of the prime minister designate. As it was a formal occasion she'd elected to wear her Royal Naval dress uniform, with her blue sash across her chest, and diamond Order of the Garter badge.

She checked her appearance in the mirror, smoothing her neat collar-length hair. This was her first of what she hoped would be many prime ministers, and her first major government duty. George had to admit to being a little nervous, but as with any royal duty, she hoped her training would kick in.

George and her mother had arrived back at Buckingham Palace yesterday, with the Dowager Queen Adrianna going to her own residence at Clarence House, and Prince Theodore to his apartments at St James's Palace. George had watched the election results with interest. She found the prime minister to be an interesting character and was looking forward to meeting her. Her father had met her on several occasions while she was leader of the opposition, but George had never had the pleasure.

George heard the knock at the audience room door and took her place quickly. The Queen's equerry ushered Ms. Dixon into the audience chamber. They both bowed by the door, then Major Fairfax said, "Ms. Dixon, Your Majesty."

George extended her hand and Bo walked forward to take it and bow once more, as protocol demanded.

"Ms. Dixon, how nice to meet you. Congratulations on your win. Do sit down." *Well, Ms. Dixon, let's see if you live up to your reputation.* "You must have had a very tiring night, although I find adrenaline does keep one going at times like this."

"Indeed it does, Your Majesty, and I'm sure I will start to really feel it over the next couple of days."

"I understand from your election campaign that you mean to do a lot of modernizing, sweep away old ideas and ways of doing things."

George watched the prime minister designate sit back in her chair and cross her legs in quite a seductive manner. Are you testing me, Ms. Dixon? I don't think your charms will work as well on me as on your fawning ministers.

Queen Georgina's gaze remained impassive and focused, never once lingering down Bo Dixon's legs. George thought she was a very attractive woman, but her domineering nature was not to George's tastes.

"Yes, Ma'am. I believe this country has been sleepwalking for the past ten years, under the previous government, and I intend to shake things up a bit. One thing I would like to make clear is my unending support for you and your position as Queen. May I speak freely, Ma'am?"

"Of course, Ms. Dixon."

Bo sat forward and said, "I know some of the people in my party have a reputation for being anti-monarchists. I just want to make clear, I do not share that view, and neither will your cabinet. We are at a turning point in history, Ma'am. Two women at the top of government, leading the nation. We are at the start of a new age, and historians will look back to this day as the point when Britain became a thoroughly modern country, with Your Majesty as head of state and myself leading your government. I hope we will be able to help each other along through our time together."

My, my, you are very full of your own importance, Ms. Dixon. You are forgetting one thing though. Prime ministers come and go, but monarchs are unchanging. "I thank you for being very frank with me, so let me be equally frank. I take my constitutional responsibility very seriously, and as you know it is my duty to advise, guide, and warn. I will enact my duty to you in our weekly meetings, which I hope, as we get to know each other, will be valuable to you."

Bo gave her an unreadable smile. "Of course. I'll look forward to it."

"Excellent. Now shall we get on with the formalities?" Queen Georgina stood, preparing to receive the prime minister's homage by kissing hands.

Bo stood quickly, then knelt before the Queen. As George prepared to say the formal words, she wondered how many times and with how many different prime ministers, she would go through this ritual.

"The duty falls upon me as your sovereign to invite you to become prime minister, and to form a government in my name."

Bo looked up at her with the suggestion of a smile and said, "I will."

She held out her hand and the prime minister brushed her lips across her knuckles.

"Excellent." Queen Georgina walked back to a side table and touched a discreet sensor to signal for her Equerry. "My warmest congratulations again, Ms. Dixon, and I look forward to seeing you at our first weekly meeting."

Major Fairfax opened the doors to escort the prime minister out.

"Thank you, Your Majesty." Bo walked backwards out of the audience room, so as to not turn her back on the Queen.

CHAPTER FIVE

By the time February came along, Bea had visited two hospice buildings with the Queen, and things were going reasonably well. Their own relationship was very polite and cordial. She had to admit that the Queen seemed genuinely interested in learning about the hospice and its staff.

Bea had also been impressed by how hands-on the Queen was with patients. She was not afraid to hold a hand, hug, or lift a child into her arms. Wherever she went, the Queen seemed to leave the patients and staff uplifted and with smiles on their faces. This she couldn't understand; George was an ordinary woman just like everyone else, but she seemed to possess a quality within her, that left those touched by her happier than she had found them.

There was one incident, Bea remembered, that did show the real woman under the stoic mask of monarchy. They were visiting the room of a young boy who didn't have much time left. The Queen extended the visit by an hour, so that she could sit by his bed and chat to the boy and his parents. He loved dogs, and so George had shown him some pictures and videos of her three dogs. She held his hand and simply gave the young man her time. When it came time to leave, Bea saw the emotion on the Queen's face, which was then quickly brought under control. It had touched her that the Queen had genuinely shown and given care to one ordinary boy and his parents.

Later that week, Bea received a call from the hospice to tell her that the boy had passed away peacefully, and that his parents wanted to thank the Queen for her kindness to their son. George had gone back to the hospice privately, taking her dog Rexie to meet him. The boy and his parents had been overwhelmed by the Queen's generosity and Bea realized that even though she didn't agree with her position, the Queen had an extremely kind heart.

Today was Friday and the end of Bea's working week, but they had a busy day ahead. The Queen was about to leave for a four-day visit to Canada and New York, so they were squeezing two Timmy's visits into her schedule before she left. This morning they were visiting a hospice in Cambridge, and in the afternoon they would take the high-speed royal train to a school in Edinburgh, who were raising money for the building of a local hospice.

Bea stood by the hospice door ready to introduce the Queen as she arrived. Further up the path was the Lord Lieutenant of the county, in his black and red uniform, ceremonial sword hanging at his side. She had been surprised to learn that at each official visit the Lord Lieutenant of the county must meet and escort the Queen around his particular area. More useless pageantry.

The road outside the hospice and up to the entrance was lined with local people and schoolchildren, all cheering and waving flags as they watched the Queen's royal limousine pull into the hospice grounds. Surprisingly the limousine stopped well short of the entrance and the assembled dignitaries. She saw the police protection officers get out first, and then Captain Cameron held the door open for the Queen, who made her way over to the waiting schoolchildren. The crowds were delighted to be given the time with the Queen before she went inside for the visit.

The nursing manager standing next to Beatrice said, "Isn't she wonderful?"

Bea simply smiled and turned her attention back to George, who was working her way down the crowd, laughing and joking with them, shaking hands and accepting flowers and pictures from the children.

People just seem to love her. As she watched George, who was today dressed in a tailored black suit, she felt that unfamiliar flutter in her stomach that she had already experienced on a couple of occasions while in her company. *It must be the excitement of the event,* she tried to convince herself. She couldn't deny that the Queen looked, in her very unique way, a combination of both beautiful and devilishly handsome.

Having finished her impromptu walkabout, Major Fairfax introduced her to the Lord Lieutenant, while Captain Cameron handed over to their driver the piles of gifts given by people in the crowd.

Before long the Queen was next to her. "Miss Elliot. Delighted to see you again." George gave her a warm smile and a very quick wink. "Would you like to take us from here?"

Bea was momentarily knocked off balance. *Did she just wink at me?*

"Miss Elliot? If you would?"

"What? Oh yes, of course." She mentally kicked herself. *What is it about her that makes you lose your concentration?* "Your Majesty, may I present the nursing manager, Julia Corrigan."

After her initial stumble, Bea settled down and the visit went well. After meeting the staff, they met the patients and families using the hospice. The Queen listened intently, made the people laugh where she could, but above all made everyone feel as if they had been heard.

Bea directed them to the last room on the corridor. "This is the last room, Ma'am. Julia, could you give the Queen some background before we go in?"

"Of course. Your Majesty, Billy Evans is in his final stages of life. He has no family and has not had any visitors—he's quite alone in the world. Billy's been so excited about your visit, Ma'am, he was in the Royal Marines."

The Queen nodded and followed Julia into the room. Bea was sure she saw a flash of emotion in the Queen's demeanour when she looked at the patient, but almost as soon as she had noticed, it was gone, replaced by a stoic mask.

George looked over at the nurse, who was explaining to Billy that the Queen was here, and propping him up. He held a hand over his eyes, the bright light of the media and TV cameras obviously bothering him.

"Major Fairfax? Can you get everyone out, I'd like this to be a private meeting. Only Miss Elliot and Captain Cameron to stay."

"Yes, Ma'am."

As everyone filed out, George leaned over and said to the nursing manager, "Do you know what rank Mr. Evans held in the Royal Marines?"

"It says on the picture by his bed Sergeant Evans, Ma'am."

Once everyone was gone, the Queen clasped her hands behind her back and turned to Cammy. "I think an old comrade needs to remember happier times. Will you oblige us, Captain Cameron?"

Cammy nodded in understanding.

What are they up to? Bea wondered.

Cammy stood by the bed and said, "Officer on deck. Attention."

Billy pulled himself up as best he could on the bed. "Sergeant Evans at your service, Ma'am," he rasped.

George looked over to Bea and smiled. "Sergeant Evans, what service were you in?"

"Royal Marines, Ma'am. Four-five squadron, based at Arbroath."

George walked closer, looking very much like an officer on parade. "Ah, Scotland? Captain Cameron's old stomping ground. Captain Cameron is Army though, Evans, not Royal Navy like you and me. What do we call the Army, Evans?" George looked over to Cammy with a cheeky smile; Cammy smiled back and shook her head.

"Knuckle-dragging gorillas, Ma'am."

Bea watched as the man who was at death's door brightened and smiled, enjoying the banter between the three. *Maybe Julia was right. Maybe she is wonderful...*

George sat down by the bed and talked to him about all his tours of duty, and the conflicts he took part in, all the while covering his hand with her own. Bea was astonished; talking with his commander in chief seemed to breathe a bit of new life into the man.

"Now, Marine, I'll have to leave shortly, but I'm going to contact the Royal Marines Association, let them know you're here, and I'm certain they'll be out to check up on you. So you keep that in mind while you're here on your own."

"Thank you, Ma'am." Billy was tiring and starting to struggle with his breath again. "I'm very sorry about the King. He...he would have been so proud of you. I wish I had a daughter like you."

In a second Bea watched George's face drain of colour and her breathing become shallow. "Bea—is there somewhere I can catch my breath?"

Seeing the Queen in distress had her over to her and taking her hand in seconds. "Captain Cameron, could you wrap this up?"

Cammy nodded. "Evans? Her Majesty expects you to keep morale up and do exactly what the nurses ask of you. Is that clear?"

"Yes, Captain."

In the meantime Bea had pulled George by the hand through a side door, away from the waiting media, and into an unoccupied room.

Bea heard the gasping breaths and watched as George pressed her hands against the wall in front of her, trying to regain control. She immediately recognized this as a panic attack. She had watched her mother suffer with them over the years, and watched as well as her father helped get her through them.

Bea grasped George by the shoulders and turned her round. "George, Georgie? Look at me. Concentrate on my face."

This seemed to get through to George as she looked very intently into Bea's eyes.

"Good. Now I want you to breathe in through your nose, and out through your mouth for a count of five. Come on, Georgie, breathe with me. In one, two, three. Out one, two, three, four, five. That's it, and again."

Bea held George's hands tenderly as they repeated the process until her breathing started to calm.

"That's it. You feel better?" As Bea looked up into George's emotional blue eyes, she had to stop herself from tucking an unruly lock of dark hair behind George's ear. She pulled back immediately, getting some distance between them.

"Thank you, Bea. I…don't know what to say. I must apologize. I'm sorry you had to see that and I'm sorry I inconvenienced you."

She could see that George was horrified that she had shown herself to her in this state, and given her opinions on the monarchy was no doubt worried that the story would appear all over the news sites the next day. "You didn't inconvenience me, Georgie, I wanted to help, and despite our differences, I give you my promise that no one will hear a word about this from me. Can you trust me?"

George met her eyes for a few seconds, and said, "Yes. I do."

Bea walked towards her. "Then trust me that I will never break your confidence. We might have different views, but I could never hurt anyone like that. Especially anyone who has a kind heart like you."

George's face brightened with a smile. "You think I have a kind heart?"

"Yes. I know all about you going back to visit the little boy with your dog, and what you did in there? That was exactly what that man needed. So yes, you are kind, and it's all right if you let your emotions show once in a while. You can't be butch and stoic twenty-four hours a day."

This brought a laugh from the Queen.

"Have you been having panic attacks often?" Bea asked.

George sat on the bed in the empty room and indicated for Bea to sit also. "Is that what they are? I don't really know. I haven't told anyone about them."

"Do you get tight chest, tight throat? Feeling like you can't breathe?"

George nodded. "Yes, and I break out in a cold sweat, and my vision seems to narrow. It's happened about five times—this was the worst though."

"Yes, that's a panic attack, my mother used to get them when I was younger. That's why I knew how to get you out of it."

"Well, I thank you, Bea, for your kindness."

"I'm sorry, but I had to break the stupid no-touching rule."

George covered Bea's hand with her own. "I think at this stage we can forget that protocol."

Bea felt something when they touched, a connection that made them both pull their hands back quickly.

"So? Why do you think this has been happening, Georgie?"

George let out a long breath. "It's since my father's death. When I was with Mr. Evans there, I was back there by my father's bedside. I don't know why I called to you for help."

"Sounds like you need time to grieve, Georgie."

All of a sudden the Queen completely closed herself off to her. She stood and smoothed her hair, buttoned her jacket up, and said, "Thank you for your help and your concern, Bea, but my duty to my family and to the nation do not allow me the luxury of time. If you'll excuse me, I have to get back to my duty."

George walked out and left Bea sitting, wondering what had just happened. *What is wrong with her? Just when I think I'm talking to a normal human being, she starts that upper-class stiff-upper-lip nonsense.*

CHAPTER SIX

The royal train set off for Edinburgh. The distinctive claret train was nine carriages long, and at the front there were carriages for the Queen's staff and invited guests. Bea knew there was also a full kitchen and chef at the Queen's disposal, and the Queen's private carriage was a home away from home, with comfortable bedrooms for the monarch and her consort, en-suite bathrooms, and sitting room with comfortable couches where the monarch could conduct the business of the day and take meals.

She despaired at the waste of public funds.

Bea had been directed to a normal looking carriage near the front, where she was sitting next to the Queen's administrative and PR staff.

In the seat across from her a rather busy looking woman was working on her computer and talking on her ear phone. "No, the Queen has no plans to meet with Princess Eleanor privately, or at anytime in the near future. The princess may be attending events leading up to the coronation, but so will many other royal figures and members of the aristocracy."

Princess Eleanor? I wonder who that is, and what she has to do with Georgie? I should listen to Mum more often—I'm sure she would know.

Bea took out her tablet and did a quick search. The first hit to pop up said: *Will the Princess of Belgium become our new Queen Consort?*

After the unexpected outing of Princess Eleanor, speculation has been growing that the youngest daughter of the King of the Belgians has her sights set on our very own Queen Georgina.

Sources close to the princess claim that they were close as children and have always maintained a strong friendship. It is thought that Eleanor would make a good consort for our first lesbian monarch.

Wow. Princess Eleanor looked like a fashion model. They would make a beautiful couple, but somehow she just couldn't see Georgie with this woman in the picture.

"Excuse me, Miss Elliot?"

Bea quickly touched the power off symbol on her tablet. She looked up and saw the rather stiff looking Major Fairfax.

"Yes? How can I help?"

The major looked left and right, clearly uncomfortable at delivering his message with so many others around. "Miss Elliot, Her Majesty wonders if you would join her for lunch in her private carriage."

"Me?" She looked around and a couple of the people sitting near looked suspiciously at her.

Major Fairfax leaned closer and whispered, "The Queen hoped you would accept her invitation to lunch. If you would just follow me."

Without giving her a chance to reply, the major marched off down the carriage.

I suppose I don't have much choice then. She gathered her things together quickly and tried to catch up with the major. When they eventually reached the other end of the train and stood outside the private carriage, he stopped and turned to her.

"I will enter and announce you. When you hear your name come into the room, curtsy, walk towards the Queen, wait for the Queen to extend her hand, and then take it."

"Major Fairfax, I've just spent the whole morning with her. Is that really necessary?"

The major gave her an incredulous look. "Yes, it is necessary. Please remember when you are in the presence, at no time turn your back on the Queen."

"The presence?"

"Yes, that's what it's called when you're in Her Majesty's company."

For goodness sake, you would think I was meeting a God. I think the major would have a fit if he knew I called her Georgie.

Major Fairfax announced her. When she entered the Queen's private quarters, she forgot she was on a train. It looked even grander than she had imagined. Directly in front of her, the Queen stood by her comfortable-looking couch. Strewn around the couch and the table in front were papers and files that had presumably come out of the red boxes, which were piled five high by the side of the table.

Bea heard Major Fairfax clear his throat, and she remembered the instructions she was given. Just to be annoying she gave the most exaggerated curtsy possible. When she walked forward, she observed the Queen smirking at her attempts.

"Miss Elliot, I'm delighted you could join me. Please sit down." The Queen indicated the couch opposite her own. "Major Fairfax, could you give us five minutes before you send in the steward?"

"Of course, Ma'am." He bowed and left them alone.

George fidgeted with her collar nervously. She had dispensed with her suit jacket, and her shirt sleeves were rolled up to her elbows. After an uncomfortable silence George said, "I...asked you here because I wanted to apologize for this morning."

Bea sat back and crossed her legs. *I'm going to enjoy making you work for this.* "Oh? What happened this morning, Georgie? Or will it be Your Majesty?"

"It was very discourteous and abrupt, the way I left. You had been so kind to me, and well...I'm sorry."

"Are you worried I'd tell someone?"

"No, of course not. I told you I trusted you and I mean it. May I be absolutely frank with you?"

"Of course, I would rather you were."

"I was embarrassed this morning. I have never broken down like that and shown my emotions with anyone outside my immediate family, and even then, not to that extent. I'm not used to anyone seeing my emotions, but somehow I..."

Bea knew George was struggling with this, and even though she shouldn't care, she felt she had to make things easier for her. "Listen, it's okay. For some reason you feel you have to keep this stoic mask on, and that's up to you, but I accept your apology. You don't have to offer me lunch for that. I'll just go back to my seat."

She stood to leave just as the Queen's steward knocked and entered. "Would you like to order lunch, Ma'am?"

"Could you come back in a couple of minutes, Walters?"

"Of course, Ma'am."

George hurried to the door and reached out for Bea's hand. "Please, Bea. I wasn't trying to ingratiate myself by asking you to lunch. I would love it if you would have lunch with me. I'm on my own a great deal, and it would be wonderful to have some pleasant company. Unless you had other plans?" George suddenly found her shoes very interesting.

For a Queen, she certainly doesn't have much confidence in herself. She gave George a warm smile. "How could I turn down lunch with the Queen? My mum will be so proud."

"Wonderful. Take a seat and I'll ask Walters to bring us something," George gushed.

❖

"Well, this is delicious." Bea was polishing off the simple meal of sandwiches and soup in no time.

George smiled. She was delighted to see Bea enjoy her meal with such gusto. "Really?"

"Uh-huh. Oh yes."

George felt her heart begin to pound at the throaty moans of pleasure coming from her lunch companion.

"It wasn't what I was expecting. I thought it would be something like partridge or foie gras, and on gold plates of course."

George managed to calm her heart rate but decided to play with her dining companion a bit. "No. We don't bring out the gold plates when we're dining with commoners."

Bea froze as she took a gulp of her water. "What, you think I'm—" Bea paused. "You're having me on, aren't you?"

"Of course I am, Bea. I have very simple tastes, and the only time you'll see a gold plate is at official state functions at the Palace."

"Oh, you do have a sense of humour, then, Georgie?"

"I hope so." George found herself so captivated by the eyes and the smile of the young woman opposite her, that she forgot about the rest of her own food.

"Do I have something in my teeth?"

George was shaken from her lingering gaze. "Oh…no, I was… sorry."

"Can I ask you a question?"

George pretended to think very carefully. "Only if I can reserve the right to ask you a question in return."

Bea answered confidently, "Of course."

George opened her arms wide and said, "Then you can ask me anything."

"That's the thing, I see everyone bowing to you and being very formal. Why do you allow me to talk to you this way?"

"When I first met you, Bea, I had never come across someone before who would talk to me like I was an ordinary person. I enjoyed it, and I enjoy talking to you. Even my family has certain formalities in the way we behave towards each other. You are like a breath of fresh air to me, and as long as it's not in public, it's perfectly all right."

"So I'm a token commoner?"

"No—"

"It's okay, Georgie, I understand."

At that moment, Cammy popped her head round the door. "Sorry to interrupt, Ma'am. I just wanted to let you know, I contacted the Royal Marines Association, and they are going to send some people to visit with Mr. Evans."

"Thank you, Cammy."

After Cammy left, Bea said, "You really have surprised me, Queen Georgina."

"May I ask you why?"

She dabbed the corners of her mouth with her napkin. "To be honest, I thought you just went around shaking hands like an automaton and instantly forgot about the people you meet."

George sighed with disappointment. "My, my, you do have a poor impression of the royal family. My Granny, Queen Adrianna, tells me it's my task to persuade you that constitutional monarchy is the right thing for Britain."

"You've told your family about me?" Bea said with surprise.

"Of course. We do talk about our day, you know, like any normal family."

"I just can't imagine that."

The stewards came in to clear away the dishes and bring in the tea tray. Walters approached to serve them. "Tea, Your Majesty?"

"Yes, please. Miss Elliot, would you care for tea?"

She nodded. "Yes, thank you."

When Bea took her first sip her face screwed up. "Oh my goodness, that's strong."

"I'm sorry. They make it strong for my taste. I'll ring for some fresh for you." George reached to ring for the steward.

"Oh no, please. It's fine. I'll just add some sugar."

"If you're sure. I got the taste for strong tea in the forces. They used to say that in the Navy they made the tea so strong, you could stand up in it."

George sipped her tea and tried not to stare too much at Bea. Between her beauty and cheeky personality, she found her captivating.

"We're not aliens, you know," George said out of nowhere.

"Excuse me? Who said you were aliens?"

"You said you couldn't imagine me with my family, talking over our day. Despite the unusual nature of my family, we are very close." It hurt George for Bea to think they were abnormal in some way.

"I'm sorry, really. I seem to keep making assumptions. I didn't mean to offend you."

"You haven't offended me. I'm just very defensive about my family. If you get to know me better, perhaps you will see how important they are to me." George felt an awkwardness come between them, which annoyed her.

Bea gestured towards the red boxes piled high and asked, "Am I keeping you from your work?"

George looked over at the work left undone and knew she would have yet another late night, just in order to catch up. "Oh, don't worry—I have to stop for lunch anyway." The truth was, this *was* keeping her from her work, but she didn't want to bring their time to an end before she had to. She found talking to Bea very soothing. When they were together, she could feel like she was a normal person for that brief moment. "I'll finish later."

"How much paperwork do you have to do every day anyway?"

George began tidying away some of the files and papers into the red boxes. "Well, I get them delivered from Number Ten in the morning and the evening. There can be anywhere between three and six on a busy day."

Bea sat forward and rested her head on her hand. "Even on a day like today, when you have other engagements?"

George gave her a wry smile. "Oh yes, I'm always on duty. Three hundred and sixty-four days a year. They like to give me Christmas Day off," she joked.

"I remember from my studies at university, that as monarch and head of state you have the right to see everything, state secrets, the lot. But does it really matter? I mean, what would happen if you just didn't do your boxes?"

George was heartened by the fact that Bea seemed willing to learn, and that in itself was progress. "As a constitutional monarch, it is my responsibility to advise, guide, and warn the government of the day, and especially the prime minister in our weekly audience. I could hardly do that if I didn't keep up to date with government business, could I? There are also a great deal of papers I have to sign."

George knew how to be a bit mischievous herself. She quirked her eyebrow and said, "Remember, it is my government after all."

"And here I thought I was living in a democracy," Bea said sarcastically.

"Oh, you are, Bea, but this is a British democracy." George was beginning to love these verbal sparring matches.

Bea sat back on the couch and crossed her legs, causing her short skirt to ride farther up her legs. George looked, transfixed, her heart thudding inside her chest.

"So?" Bea seemed to be waiting for a response, but George had been mesmerized by her legs, completely unaware Bea had continued talking.

"So, what?"

Bea sighed, unaware of what had taken George's attention. "I asked you what you thought of the election result. I bet all of your upper-class cronies were extremely unhappy to have a Labour government at last."

George tried to ignore the intense feelings of attraction and not look down Bea's legs, but it was extremely difficult. All she could think was, *she's so beautiful.* "Um…what did *you* think about it?"

"I asked you first."

"As I'm sure you are aware, I am not allowed an opinion on party politics. Are you trying to trip me up, Miss Elliot?"

Bea leaned forward to whisper, but in the process exposed some of her cleavage. "You must have an opinion, Georgie. I know you're not allowed a public opinion, but you must have private ones. You can tell me."

Good God. George jumped up and began to pace so she wouldn't be tempted to ogle Bea. "No, as I've said before, I take my role very seriously, and so I am above politics as a good constitutional monarch should be."

George wanted to know more about Bea. She wondered if there was someone waiting for her at home, or at least someone special in her life. She thought of the care and compassion Bea had bestowed on her this morning and tried to imagine her giving that care and attention to some other man or woman, and her stomach knotted up.

"So, my turn for a question," George said.

"Oh yes, I did promise. On you go then."

George sat back down on the couch. "What does a young woman like yourself do on a Friday evening? Let me live vicariously through you."

Bea looked confused. "Why would you want to? You're a Queen, why would my everyday humdrum life interest someone who does exciting things all the time?"

George laughed out loud. "You think I do exciting things? Bea, my life is governed by rules, regulations, and a schedule. My diary is booked two years in advance. Every minute of every day, all year, is accounted for. Even when I go on holiday, work follows me."

"I think any ordinary person would gladly switch places with you, Georgie. You live a life with riches and splendour."

"Really, Bea? Would they really? I have never been to a bar, a club, a cinema, or out to a restaurant. Security means I could never be free to pop out to see this, do that, or simply take a walk. I live in a cage—it may be gilded, but it's a cage nonetheless. That's the price, you see. As the monarch you have a simple deal. You live a life of great importance and privilege, but the price is that you can't live your life as you like. Duty and service come before everything. So forgive me if I'm interested in the simplicity of your life. Let's forget I asked."

"No, please. Forgive me, you've been so open with me, it's the least I can do. Well, I usually meet my friends on a Friday night. We sometimes go to dinner or the cinema, then get a few drinks at our favourite pub, and have a good chat about our week. We're not really that wild."

George smiled warmly at the thought of an evening spent like that in Bea's company. "Do you have a boyfriend or…girlfriend to take you out?"

Bea had a hollow laugh. "Not for a year or so, no. I'm single and content with that. I seem to go out with women who are commitment phobic. I feel like I want something more now, you know?"

"Like what?" George's heart was thudding again. For some reason the fact that Bea was gay made her very happy.

Their eyes locked together, and the room melted away. "I just want someone to love me. Just love me. That's not too much to ask, is it?"

George looked intently into Bea's eyes.

A knock sounded, and Cammy entered. She cleared her throat loudly. "We're half an hour from Edinburgh, Your Majesty."

"Ah, yes. Thank you, Cammy. Would you excuse me, Miss Elliot? I have to freshen up before the next engagement. Cammy will escort you back to your carriage."

"Of course. Thank you for lunch, Your Majesty." Bea took George's outstretched hand and looked surprised when George pressed a soft kiss to her palm.

"Thank you for your company, Miss Elliot. It's been a pleasure, and to answer your question—no, it's not too much to ask."

CHAPTER SEVEN

As Bea took a taxi to meet her friends in town, she reflected on her day. After her lunch in the royal carriage, it had been quite ordinary. Apart from escorting the Queen around the school in the afternoon, she hadn't had any more private time with her that day. When she had returned to her own seat on the train, she had noticed a few looks coming her way from some of the Queen's staff. She had found herself thinking a great deal about George since this afternoon, and that bothered her. Bea wanted to dislike George so much, but everything about her was making her do the opposite. She also felt sorry for her; she seemed too isolated, and her only friend to speak to on a daily basis was Captain Cameron. When Cammy had escorted her back to her carriage, she had taken Bea into a side room, and the memory of Cammy's words annoyed her.

"Miss Elliot, I wanted to have a word with you. The Queen is in a unique position, and it is very difficult for her to meet and become friendly with people, even more so to trust people. She seems to enjoy talking with you."

"Are you implying something, Captain Cameron?"

Cammy gave her a penetrating look. "Not a thing, Miss Elliot, I just wanted you to realize the importance of whom you were chatting with and that you need to keep anything she says to yourself, since you have no respect for the institution of the monarchy."

"I have respect for the Queen as a fellow human being, not as a monarch, Captain Cameron."

"You will find all of us who serve Her Majesty do respect that institution and are extremely loyal to it. The crown and the human being are indivisible, Miss Elliot. Everything that makes the Queen who she is, is George, and vice versa. You cannot pick and choose which you respect. If you had any idea how hard the Queen works, and how much

good she does, then you couldn't fail but to have the utmost respect and reverence for her."

Bea was getting really angry by this point in the conversation. "She may do, Captain, but she also has plenty of luxury and money to ease her suffering, while ordinary people who work very hard do not have that reward, and in the meantime, schools and hospitals suffer through lack of equipment in order to prop up this outdated institution."

"Well, when you get home tonight, lassie, and kick off your shoes and get ready to relax for the weekend with a few drinks with your friends, remember your Queen is still hard at work, usually till well into the wee hours of the morning."

"Can I go now?" a furious Bea asked.

"All I ask is that you don't take advantage of her," Cammy said, her tone softer now. "She's not only my sovereign, she is my friend."

"You have my word, Captain."

Cammy nodded with acceptance and took Bea to her seat.

"Here you are, miss." The taxi driver shook Bea from her thoughts.

"Oh, thank you."

She paid the driver and smoothed down her short black-and-white print dress, and then made her way into Mickey D's, the girls' favourite gay bar.

The music pumped in the background, and she felt many pairs of eyes following her as she walked across the busy bar to the corner table. She hated the long walk across the bar, feeling extremely self-conscious, but when she saw her friends, she let out a sigh of relief. Normal people at last.

The four of them had met at university and had worked hard to keep their friendship going through leaving university, new jobs, and marriage.

There was Holly, a feisty redhead who liked to call herself the group's token heterosexual and self-confessed man-eater, who worked as a hair and make-up artist and designer.

Greta, the married woman of the bunch, had married her childhood sweetheart Riley straight after graduation and proceeded to have three children in short order.

Then there was Lalima Ramesh, a stunning woman of Indian descent, who was also Bea's best friend. Everyone said that Lalima could have been a model or a Bollywood actress. Her skin was flawless, her bone structure perfect, and her unusual blue-green eyes sparkling. Lalima, like Bea, had always had a strong social conscience, and after university became involved with a homeless charity, where she was now director.

"Here she is. Beatrice Elliot, friend of the royals," Holly shouted.

"Oh, please. I've had royalty up to here." Bea flopped down onto the chair. "I'd like one evening without thinking or hearing about the blessed Queen."

"Here, we got a drink in for you. Take a sip and relax," Lali said.

Greta grasped her hand and gave her a desperate plea. "Oh, you've got to tell us something, Bea. I'm a harassed mother of three, and the only exciting adult conversation I get is when I come out with you girls. We saw you on the news, leading the Queen around. Is she as gorgeous in the flesh as she is on TV?"

"Gret, really?" exclaimed her three friends.

"What? I'm married, am not dead."

Holly turned to her and said, "Does poor old Riley know you lust over the Queen?"

Greta playfully hit her friend. "I do not lust over the Queen. And poor old Riley gets plenty of my attention, believe me. Come on, Bea, give us some titbits. You have to admit, she is quite the dish, and just your type."

Oh, not again. "I do not have a type. My mum said the exact same thing."

The three women laughed at their bemused friend.

"What?"

Lali placed a hand on her best friend's back and began to stroke it in a soothing fashion. "I'm afraid you are guilty as charged, Bea. Every woman you have ever gone out with or liked has been the rugged, sporty, butch type."

Bea thought back to her only two serious girlfriends, and thought of the way the Queen had made her stomach dance with a thousand butterflies, and was forced to concede her friends might be right. "Well, maybe I have a certain type, and maybe Georgie is a rather attractive example of said type, but that doesn't mean I like her, or what she stands for."

"Wait a minute, Georgie? You did not call her that did you?"

"I don't think the whole pub heard you, Holls, could we keep this between ourselves?" Bea pleaded.

Holly gave an exaggerated whisper, "Well, tell us the goss then."

Bea, gave in with a sigh, as she had done with her mother. "I told her my views, and annoyingly, she seemed to find it amusing. She told me I could call her what I liked, so I picked Georgie. I had hoped to pierce that upper-class pomposity, but she just laughed."

Lali grinned and said, "The Queen does have a reputation for being approachable and kind. I think you picked the wrong royal to try and annoy."

She knew this was true. No matter how hard she tried to dislike her monarch, she found it impossible. "She is very kind to the people she meets and seems to genuinely care about their problems, but she shouldn't be in that position. We should have an elected head of state, not waste money on people who are there simply by an accident of birth."

Greta rolled her eyes. "That doesn't alter the fact that she is gorgeous. Imagine marrying her, and becoming the Queen Consort. The first gay couple to rule the country. It would be a fairy tale."

Yes, whoever married Georgie would be a lucky woman.

"They say that the Belgian princess is keen on being the lucky woman," Holly added.

Bea felt her stomach clench uncomfortably. She'd had just about enough of the Queen for one day. "Look, could we change the subject? I'm out here to forget about work and spend time with my friends."

Her friends looked at her with shock. She was not normally prone to bursts of anger, and she immediately felt guilty.

"Listen, I'm sorry. I'm just really tired, and it's been a really stressful week. I'll go and get another round in, okay? Same again?"

Lali gave her hand a squeeze. "Do you want any help?"

She gave her friend a smile. "I'll be fine. Be back in a sec."

❖

Bea leaned on the bar, waiting her turn to be served. At nine o'clock in the evening, the bar was busy but not yet overflowing with the clubbers who would pour in later for drinks, before heading to the club next door.

Bea was warring with herself. She had wanted a break from thinking about the Queen for one night, as her thoughts seemed to be filled with her recently. At first it was annoyance and anger, and now something else, and it was the something else that made her uneasy.

She couldn't get the image of the Queen from this morning out of her head. What she had seen then was not the Queen, but Georgie. Georgie, although still strong and capable like the Queen, was underneath it all emotionally vulnerable and, Bea sensed, very lonely, and she was so drawn to that.

"What can I get you, sweetheart?" the bar woman asked.

She shook herself from her thoughts quickly and gave her order. While she was waiting she glanced up at the large projected screen on the bar wall. The screen was showing lots of different channels at once. Sports, news, music channels, popular reality shows. The news channel caught Bea's eye. It showed long rooms at Buckingham

Palace, and lined down each side were ladies and gentlemen in evening dress. The banner along the bottom of the screen read: *Her Majesty Queen Georgina hosts a diplomatic reception for foreign ambassadors.* Although there was no sound, Bea could still feel the majesty of the event. She watched as the royal trumpeters in their gold livery, with *GR* emblazoned on the front, began playing the royal fanfare, huge doors were opened, and the Queen walked in, leading her extended family behind her in order of precedence. Her brother, Theo, the Queen Mother, and the Dowager Queen behind her. She didn't recognize the other members of the family.

Captain Cameron was right. With all that they'd done today, George was still working tonight. *Do you ever get to do what you want, Georgie?*

Bea's eyes were transfixed on the Queen, who was wearing white tie, with a blue sash and diamond encrusted badge across her chest. Greta was right—she was gorgeous.

The camera panned in on the Queen's face, and she gave a dazzling smile to the ambassador she was introduced to. Bea forced herself to look away when she felt that ever more familiar tingle.

"Here you go, sweetheart." The bar woman plonked down her tray of drinks.

Bea swiped her mobile phone to pay.

"Thanks, luv."

Before heading back to the girls, she took a sip of her drink. As she brought the glass to her lips, she noticed the crown stamped on the glass. *Good God, I can't get away from her.* These symbols had always been there, but she had taken them for granted, only now really seeing just how much the monarch impacted on British life.

Bea was just about to lift the tray when she felt a hand on her arm.

"All right, darlin'?"

She sighed inwardly. She often saw her ex, Ronnie Lassiter, at Mickey D's, usually with women very much younger than herself. She'd been a fresher when she'd met Ronnie at university, and Ronnie in her third year. She had been dazzled by the extremely cool and good-looking woman. Ronnie was meant to be studying law but spent most of her time playing for the university rugby team and drinking too much with them in the bar. Bea, on the other hand, was very serious about her studies.

"Ronnie, stop trying to sound like an eighteen-year-old from the inner city. You're the daughter of a High Court judge who's lived her whole life in Chelsea." Ronnie's need to fit in the younger crowd and pretend she didn't have every advantage growing up infuriated Bea.

Her ex-girlfriend held up her hands in a defensive posture. "Okay, okay. You sound like my mother."

"I hope not." Ronnie's mother had never been impressed with her daughter's choice of girlfriend. Bea's working-class background, lack of good breeding, and lack of private education were not deemed acceptable for the daughter of Sir John and Lady Hillary Lassiter. All through her relationship with Ronnie, Lady Hillary made her disapproval abundantly clear.

"Come on, Bea, I come in peace. I just wondered how you're doing. I haven't seen you here in a while."

Bea turned and faced her ex-lover. Ronnie was older than her, now into her middle thirties. At first she had found her youthful exuberance exciting, but as she left university and started her working life, Ronnie's immaturity started to affect their relationship. After a long week at work, Bea would have liked to have a romantic meal together, whereas Ronnie was more interested in going out with her rugby friends, drinking and clubbing.

"I've been busy with work, and the girls and I are normally going home by the time you're just arriving."

Ronnie moved closer to Bea and stroked her hand. "I saw you on TV showing the Queen around. Mother was impressed."

Well, I wonder why? she thought cynically. Bea pulled her hand back from Ronnie's grasp. "Yes, I have a lot on at Timmy's at the moment. So, how are you Ronnie? Working at all?"

"Eh? No. Father got me a position at a law firm in the city, but I left it a few weeks ago—a couple of my mates have started a band with me, so I'm going to concentrate on my music."

In other words, you got the sack. "And what did your mum and dad think of that?"

Ronnie looked a little sheepish. "Father wasn't too pleased, but Mother's going to fund our recording studio time, so it's all good."

You're a spoiled brat. Ronnie had opportunities other people could only dream about, and she was just wasting her life. George might have been born in even greater privilege, but at least she recognized it and worked hard, trying to give back what she could to the country.

"Well, I'll be off then." She went to pick up the tray but Ronnie stopped her.

"Wait."

She sighed and said, "What?"

Ronnie stroked her fingers down the side of Bea's face. "Listen, why don't you come to the club with us later? We could have a few drinks, and a dance, maybe go back to mine later. I still miss you. We were so good together."

Ronnie had tried to seduce her once or twice since they had split up, but she was certain this attempt was more to do with her newfound royal connections, than wanting her. Everything Ronnie did was driven by ego, and Bea was sure she just wanted to prove she could still have her.

"No, I don't think so." Bea's attention was drawn to three girls, who looked no more than eighteen or nineteen, who were standing on their seats, drinks in hand, and chanting, "Ronnie! Ronnie!"

Bea shook her head and said, "Your fan club is waiting for you, Ronnie."

She lifted the drinks tray and walked away, and Ronnie shouted after her, "Bea, come on. Give me a chance."

She just carried on walking and didn't look back.

❖

Bea walked back to the table with the drinks and noticed they were missing Holly. "Here you go, girls. Where's Holls?"

Greta pointed over to a dark corner of the bar, where Holly was laughing and flirting with a good looking young man. "She managed to find the only straight man in a gay bar as usual."

Bea giggled. "She's unbelievable."

"Was Ronnie bothering you?" Lali asked.

She handed out the drinks. "No, just hoping she would catch me in a weakened moment as usual. I can handle her."

They were interrupted by the ringing of Greta's mobile phone. When she answered, her partner Riley's face appeared on the screen. "Hello?"

"Sweetheart, I can't find Jessica's cuddle bear, and Jamie won't go to bed. He says you let him have a chocolate bar before bed."

Lali and Bea laughed into their hands, and Greta rolled her eyes in frustration. Every Friday, Greta left her partner written instructions for taking care of their children, and every week without fail, Riley would call with some crisis or another. Sometimes the girls would bet each other how long it would take for Riley to call.

"Excuse me, would you, girls? I need to go and shout at Riley."

As Greta walked away to try and find a quieter corner, they heard her say, "One night a week, Riley, one night, that's all I get to be out of the house."

"Poor Riley," Bea said to her friend.

Lali and Bea were alone for the first time all night. "Are you really all right, Bea? You seemed a bit stressed earlier."

Bea let out a long breath. "Yes. I'm just a little off balance."

"Why? Is it your job?"

"I suppose. When Danny told me I would be traveling the country with the Queen, I was furious. I mean, you remember what I was like at uni."

Lali giggled. "Yes, you used to always be doing things with that group, Free Republic. I remember you all went to that protest outside the palace with placards."

Bea took a sip of her drink. "Everything seemed so black and white then. Now I seem to see everything in shades of grey. I can't help but like her—no one can help but like her, it seems to me. She's very charismatic, and she cares, genuinely cares, about everyone she meets. I've seen Georgie go out of her way to help people, when others wouldn't have bothered." *And I've seen the Georgie underneath the mask of Queenship. The one she wants no one to see.* That thought was something that she would never share with anyone, and would gladly protect.

"Is it a bad thing that the Queen makes you realize that maybe she is doing a good job? I mean let's face it, anti-monarchist and republican feeling has never been lower. The country loved her father and now loves his daughter even more, so it's not likely that they are going anywhere. Do you remember our politics lecturer at uni?"

"How could I forget? He didn't like me."

"Is it surprising? You argued your way through the whole topic of the British constitution."

With a small smile Bea said, "Perhaps I did. He was an arrogant old fool, though."

"Maybe, but I always remember he said: *Monarchy is dependent on the people. It's in the people's hands whether or not it endures.* And since every gay woman I know, and some of the straight ones too, are in lust or love with her, and the rest of the country thinks she is a jolly good sort, I don't see us becoming a republic with a president anytime soon. So why don't you give yourself permission to like her. Do you think Abby would have liked her?"

Bea gave a soft smile thinking of her sister. "I know she would have. Abby loved horses. I know a lot of young girls do, but we didn't have access to the country being complete townies. When we were young, Dad used to take us to a city farm, and Abby fell in love with the horses. She collected pictures and horse magazines. Georgie was quite often featured in the magazines, taking part in gymkhanas and country horse events, and I remember she always said what a dream it would be to meet the princess. I think the freedom of the country appealed to her, and the feeling that you could go anywhere in those wide open country spaces. Freedom."

When she realized she wouldn't see the Queen for almost a week, she felt something she wasn't expecting—a longing ache to be near her.

Why do I miss you Georgie?

❖

Princess Eleanor crawled up the body of her panting partner and kissed him thoroughly.

"My dear Princess, you are truly a wicked woman."

Eleanor looked at Julian, Viscount Anglesey, with a self-satisfied smirk. When Princess Eleanor had come to Britain with the sole purpose of hunting down Queen Georgina and becoming Queen Consort, Julian had seen the perfect opportunity to use her for his own ends.

"You do seem to have a talent for inspiring my wickedness." Eleanor rolled off him and reached for her champagne.

Julian sat up and poured some more champagne for himself. "I must say your lesbianism is going very well."

They both laughed. "Oh, don't worry, My Lord Anglesey. For our sovereign Queen Georgina, I will be the perfect lesbian."

Julian reached out for one of his cigars, and lit it; the smoke billowed in clouds from his mouth.

"You know it is illegal to smoke, Julian," Eleanor joked.

"Oh, Princess. You sound like my wife. I can do what I like. I am a Buckingham and the son of the Princess Royal, but we'll keep the smoking between ourselves shall we?"

Viscount Anglesey had met Eleanor on occasion as they grew up, but they hadn't spent a lot of time with each other. Given her reputation, he was very surprised when she had very publicly come out of the closet.

Julian blew out a smoke ring and said, "Now, I will get you invited to the right places and close to my cousin, the rest is up to you. Do you think you can do it?"

Eleanor ran a long fingernail down the center of Julian's chest. "What do you think?"

"I think you will eat her alive, my dear. My cousin is a strong individual of mind and body, but with women she is a novice. If you do what you do best, she will be eating out of your hand."

Eleanor kissed Julian's chest and circled his nipple with her tongue. "Hmm…and I will be the Queen Consort of Great Britain, the Commonwealth, and two billion people worldwide, not to mention one of the wealthiest people on earth."

"Princess, you have done your homework. Some people might think you are only interested in power."

The princess bit Julian's nipple, making him jump. "Who would not want to be the Queen Consort of all that? My older brother the king and my sister think they outshine me at home in Belgium, but once I get my claws into Georgina, everyone in the world will notice me."

Julian stubbed out his cigar and rolled Eleanor underneath him. "Just remember the price you pay, Princess. You use your persuasive powers and I get whatever I want, when I want it."

Eleanor placed a finger on his lips. "You will get anything you wish. I promise."

Julian grabbed hold of Eleanor's hair, a little too hard. "I better, Princess, and just in case you forget who got you into my bitch of a cousin's bed, I have recorded our little discussion." He pointed to the tablet on a desk across the room.

"Very clever, Lord Anglesey. I would hate to have you as an enemy."

He released her hair from its tight hold and changed to gentle stroking. "Just remember that Eleanor, when you are on your back servicing my cousin."

Princess Eleanor laughed. "You really do hate your cousin, don't you?"

Julian's mood grew dark. He had always resented George's position in the family and despised having to defer to her. Not only a woman, but a lesbian was now sovereign and head of his family. When Eleanor had come to Britain and he'd discovered her plan, he saw a way to become the power behind the throne.

"Everyone in my family, especially my mother, brother, and sister, thinks the sun shines out of her arse. I am the only one who sees her for what she is—a pervert who needs to be controlled before she ruins the reputation of my family dynasty—and I am the one to do it."

He'd had to bow down to George and her brother all of his life, but his hatred was complete when, after the late King's death, he had to pay homage to the new Queen.

He remembered how humiliated he felt, kissing George's hand and swearing fealty.

Filled with disgust, Julian began to take his frustrations out on the body beneath him.

CHAPTER EIGHT

The Queen's deputy private secretary, Sebastian Richardson, placed a file onto the desk in front of George. "Finally, Ma'am, if I could just get you to approve the changes to your speech tomorrow."

George scanned the document quickly. "Have the foreign office approved the changes you suggested?"

"Yes, Ma'am. I understand the prime minister was particularly pleased with them," Sebastian said with obvious pride.

George was very pleased with the young man's fresh approach and new ideas. When George had ascended the throne she was very aware of her duty to the late King's existing staff, in particular the King's private secretary, Sir Michael Bradbury, who had been a faithful servant to the Buckinghams. She had made no changes but with an eye to the future had recruited Sebastian, a highly thought of young man from the foreign and commonwealth office. He was being groomed for Sir Michael's role, and George was delighted with his advice and ideas.

"Thank you, Bastian. Could you call Captain Cameron on your way out? I will have to dress shortly."

After he left, George walked over to look out the window of the hotel's large penthouse suite. Due to the amount of staff and security personnel, the Queen's entourage had taken up two floors of the hotel building. She had been on a four day state visit to Canada and had now travelled to New York to give a speech to the UN. Tonight the president was hosting a reception for all the visiting heads of states and dignitaries, and tomorrow she would give her speech.

George looked over the dark city skyline and sighed. The loneliness she had felt since taking the throne seemed to deepen over the time she had been on her overseas trip. *I wonder what you are doing this evening, Bea? Having fun, no doubt.*

Captain Cameron emerged from the bedroom door. "Your Majesty? I have your clothes laid out if you are ready to dress."

"Thank you. Yes, I'm ready."

The Queen entered the bedroom first and Cammy followed behind. George began to slowly undress down to her underwear.

Cammy handed her a dressing gown and said, "The shower is running, Ma'am."

George nodded. "What time are we leaving?"

"Major Fairfax gives us two hours, Ma'am."

With another audible sigh the Queen picked up her towel from the bed.

"May I speak freely, Ma'am?"

"Of course. You know you can always speak freely with me."

Cammy stood with her arms crossed and a questioning look upon her face. "What's wrong with you, man? You've been moping about looking like a wet weekend for days now."

"It's nothing. I'm fine."

"Is it something to do with that wee lassie?"

George's head shot up and she looked at Cammy. "What wee lassie?"

"The charity lassie, Beatrice Elliot."

George felt her cheeks go a shade of red. "Why would it have anything to do with her? I'm fine anyway."

Cammy put her hands on the Queen's shoulders and said, "George, we've been through a lot together, we've fought side by side as comrades. You'll find no criticism or judgement from me."

George's thoughts had been filled with Miss Elliot. It was hard to admit though. She wondered how she could miss seeing someone she had only known for a few weeks. Feeling slightly awkward, George stood and walked over to look out of the bedroom window. With her back to Cammy, she could now admit the truth.

"I will say I have missed her company. I like to talk to her, she speaks to me like no one else, and I had hoped she might become a friend."

"Are you sure of this woman's intentions? It could be dangerous to allow a familiarity to breed between you."

George whipped round to face Cammy, feeling displeased with her friend. "Miss Elliot has already had the power to ruin my reputation. That morning at the hospital, she saw me in a distressed manner but did nothing but help me, and there has been no stories in the press about it. She is a very caring and sensitive woman, Cammy."

"That is true. I worry though about her lack of reverence for your position and family, Ma'am."

"It does us good to keep us on our toes. My grandmother challenged me to convince her that a constitutional monarchy is a good thing, and I intend to do so. I have never had a friend of my own choosing, Cammy, apart from you. All through my childhood, friends were provided for me from other aristocratic families. I understand why—it was for my own protection and security. Miss Elliot is the first person I've socialized with outside my family's sphere of influence, and I like her. To her I am Georgie, someone who she met through work, not the Queen."

"If you're happy, then that's grand. Would you like me to get her contact details so you could give her a phone call?"

George was taken aback. "What, speak to her, you mean?"

"Aye. Have a bit of a chinwag with Miss Elliot. That will cheer you up."

"But…" George stammered, her heart speeding out of control. "But what if she's busy? What would I talk about?"

Cammy walked up to George and patted her on the shoulder. "Anything. Start by talking about your plans with the charity and see where it takes you. Now you get in the shower, Your Majesty, and I'll speak to your protection command. Superintendent Lang will I'm sure have ways to get contact numbers."

Captain Cameron had exited the room before the Queen could reply. *Why did I have to open my big mouth?*

❖

George sat in full white tie dinner suit, staring at the computer screen on her desk. True to her word, Cammy had gotten Bea's contact details and left her to her call, after making sure the line was secured.

George felt her palms grow sweaty with nerves. Why was she even doing this to herself? She stood and began to pace up and down the sitting room area of her suite.

I'll just leave it. Yes, I have no need to speak to her, and she's probably busy anyway.

George sat back down and said, "Display Timmy's website."

The computer screen displayed the home page that she had looked at countless times over her trip. A video of herself and Bea touring around the school project they had visited in Edinburgh was one of the main items posted. It captured the moment that George had been invited to play football with the children. She had noticed a small boy who wasn't getting involved, looking nervous around the older children, so she whisked him onto her shoulders and the pair dribbled their way down the playing area to score a goal. The staff and children were delighted and cheered for her and the little boy, but George's favourite part of the short video was when the camera panned to Bea and captured her in an unguarded moment, laughing warmly and looking on with what she could only describe as pride.

"Go back five seconds and pause action." The projected screen instantly obeyed her commands and paused on the close-up image of Bea. *You are truly beautiful, Beatrice Elliot.* She reached out as if she could touch Bea's face, but her fingers just went straight through the image.

"Take still picture and save to my private folder, password Regina one."

I want to talk to her. Come on, George. You meet kings, queens, emperors, presidents, and prime ministers and never get tongue-tied or nervous.

"Private call. Beatrice Elliot."

Bea had retreated to her bedroom after dinner to go through some work from the office. It had seemed a strange week so far. She had become accustomed to being out and about with the Queen over the last few weeks, and being back stuck in the office had made for a very long week.

As she looked over her plans for the next two royal visits, Bea found her mind wandering to George. She had made a point to watch the news every night with her mum, to see what the Queen was getting up to on her state visit. She saw George visit all sorts of places, give speeches, inspect the troops, and even take part in a sailing event. Through the entire trip, the Queen was full of smiles and warm words, and the media declared the trip a huge success as hundreds of thousands turned out to see her. Bea saw something different: she saw Georgie doing her duty, but very alone. This was encapsulated in the carriage procession to her official welcome. Crowds lined the route, waving hands and flags at Queen Georgina, who cut a lonely figure sitting on her own in the carriage. As Bea had watched, she ached inside.

Georgie you do need a consort. I hope you find someone to share the burden with, and someone to give you the care and support you need.

Bea's thoughts were interrupted by ringing coming from her tablet. Caller withheld. Who could that be? "Answer call." The screen suddenly filled with the image of Queen Georgina, looking extremely dapper in white tie. Bea's mouth hung open in surprise and shock.

"Bea? I hope that this is a convenient time, and you have no objections to my calling you."

"Well...no...yes?"

George quirked an eyebrow, confused at Bea's response. "It isn't a convenient moment or it is?"

There were a few seconds of silence as Bea tried to calm herself. "Yes, it is a convenient time. I'm sorry—you just surprised me, that's all. It's not every day the Queen calls me."

George smiled warmly. "Oh, good. I didn't want to interrupt anything."

"No. I'm just looking over our schedule for next week actually."

There was a knock at the bedroom door and Sarah shouted, "Would you like a cup of tea, love?"

Bea felt her cheeks go bright red. "Would you excuse me one moment, Georgie?"

"Of course."

After explaining to her mother that she was on the phone with the Queen—and following her mother's excited squeal and a lot of shushing—Bea returned. "Sorry, my mother got a little excited there."

"You live at home with your parents?"

"Yes. I like to be around for mum for various reasons, and since I'm not in a relationship, it suits me too. I apologize for the squealing. My mum is very much a monarchist."

"Really?"

"Oh yes. She and Dad are great fans. They've been to tour Buckingham Palace many times, and she has a collection of memorabilia they bought there and at Windsor Castle."

George gave her a big smile. "Well, I'm glad I'm popular with one of the Elliots."

"Mum's not the only one. I told you I respect how you go about the job you've been given. We just differ on how the country should be run—which reminds me, I haven't forgotten you promised me a debate on the monarchy."

George held up her hands in a defensive gesture. "I promise the next time we have some time between visits, you and I will slug it out."

This made Bea laugh. "You are funny. How's the tour? I've been following you on the news."

"It went well, I believe. I'm in New York at the moment, to give a speech to the UN on climate change."

"Oh? What's your opinion on it?" Bea asked.

"As you well know, I leave the policy decisions and opinion to my Government."

Bea chuckled. "I'm sorry Georgie, I just like to keep you on your toes. You look very nice—are you going somewhere?"

"Oh, just a reception for the heads of state and dignitaries in for the UN meeting." *She thinks I look nice.* Her heart did a happy dance.

"You say that as if it's an everyday occurrence. I'm not keeping you back, am I?"

George said, "Well, it is an everyday occurrence to me. It's just part of my job, and no, you're not keeping me back. I have forty minutes before I leave."

"Was there something in particular you called for?"

George searched around in her brain for a reason, apart from the real one, that she had just wanted to hear her friend's voice. "Well, I was thinking about…" Then suddenly she had it. "I was thinking about ways we could raise more money for Timmy's, and make something very special for my coronation build up. How about we organize a concert to take place on the Mall outside Buckingham Palace, and you can use the palace forecourt if need be too."

George seemed to stun Bea into silence again, and she felt she had to fill the silence. "We could call it the Coronation Concert or something similar. The palace has been used like that many times in its past. What do you think?"

"Wow—that would be utterly fantastic. Think of how much money we would make, and how much we would raise the profile of Timmy's. Oh, wait a minute. Don't you have to ask if it's okay?"

George laughed a little. "I am the Queen, remember? I'll get my private staff to seek the necessary clearance from the local council and any other relevant authorities, and liaise with you on it. I'm afraid the planning will have to be up to you—I have no idea about modern bands and singers. That's more my brother's department. I'm rather old-fashioned in my musical tastes."

"I'll do it. Thank you so much, Georgie. This is going to do so much good, you have no idea. Thank you."

Bea beamed with joy.

Goodness. This was all it took to make her happy? George felt such pride in being able to have this effect on Bea. She looked stunningly beautiful, light and full of joy. George decided then and there that she had to have this woman's friendship in her life, one way or another.

"No trouble at all. I'll have my deputy private secretary, Bastian, contact you to begin the preliminaries. I wonder, may I…"

"What is it, Georgie?"

Just ask you fool. She won't bite. George gulped hard. "Well, I think you've probably gathered that I enjoy our discussions. It's the only time someone will speak to me as if I'm an ordinary human being, and when I'm overseas or on visits, I can get isolated. Would it be acceptable to give you a call from time to time? I don't have many friends because of my position."

Bea responded immediately. "You have a friend now, Georgie, and of course you may call me. I'd be delighted to chat with you."

George let out a breath she had been unconsciously holding and felt immensely lighter. "Thank you, Bea. You are very kind. Well, I suppose the UN reception beckons me."

"Do try and have fun, won't you?"

George nervously fiddled with her bow tie. "UN receptions are not fun, I assure you. They are a duty."

"What is fun to you? What makes you happy Georgie?"

Bea's question took George by surprise. No one had ever asked the Queen what made her happy. "Lots of little things, I suppose. Spending time with my family, sailing—I love my boats. I feel such a sense of peace out on a loch somewhere, among the mountains and valleys. I make model ships to relax when I have a moment to myself too. I like working on my estates at Sandringham and Balmoral, whether it's just walking my dogs, helping to dig out the ditches, put up fencing, or tending to my horses at the stables. I love my horses."

"My sister liked horses," Bea said wistfully.

"I didn't know you had a sister."

Bea suddenly looked uncomfortable. "I did have a sister. She died when I was little, but that's another story."

George recognized that Bea had brought the conversation to an end. "I'm very sorry to hear that. If you ever want to talk about her, I can lend a broad shoulder."

Bea replied, "Yes, I've noticed you have two very broad and muscular shoulders."

George saw a blush tinge Bea's cheeks, and she sat a little taller in the chair.

"Oh, I do apologize, Ma'am. Sometimes we talk so easily together that I forget who I am talking to."

Hmm. You've noticed me then, Bea. "Yes, we do seem to talk very easily, and please don't worry yourself. As I said before, I enjoy feeling like a normal human being for once. Now I really must go Bea, or Cammy may have me shot. I'll see you at our first visit next week."

"Yes, and thank you for calling. The concert is a wonderful idea."

"My pleasure. Goodbye."

As the screen disappeared, George felt almost giddy. "Cammy, I want you to arrange something for me."

CHAPTER NINE

Felix Brown knocked on the door of the prime minister's private office.

"Come."

"Bo, can I have a quick word?"

"Shoot."

Felix always found his heart skipped a beat at the sight of Bo, sitting at her substantial oak desk. She had an aura of power without even trying.

"I've had a report from MI5 that you need to be aware of, Prime Minister."

Bo, who had been working away on her computer, shut down the screen immediately. "Talk to me."

"They have been monitoring Internet chatter from various subversive groups. There has been a consistent theme emerging from the surveillance, and it centres on the Queen."

"And?"

Felix took a seat in front of the desk. "It seems that at least three different groups believe that it will be detrimental to this country to have the first openly gay monarch. They have threatened to do something about it."

Bo sat forward in her seat. "Get me the heads of the security services and the head of the Queen's protection unit here this afternoon. I want to know what we're dealing with, and how we can assure the Queen's safety."

Felix watched the prime minister's face take on a hard expression.

"You have seen the polls—my popularity is riding the coat-tails of our new, popular monarch. My legacy is intertwined with our good Queen's, and you know how important my legacy is to me. In a hundred years' time, they will still be talking about Queen Georgina and Boadicea Dixon, leading Britain into a new age of modernity. That would not be the case if her brother was king, or anyone else for that matter. I will make sure that woman is crowned at Westminster Abbey even if I have to mobilize every police officer and every soldier in the land. Make it clear to everyone that the Queen's safety is my top priority."

"Yes, Prime Minister."

❖

Over the next three weeks, February turned to March, and a lot had changed for George. Her friendship with Bea had blossomed, and on days when they were not scheduled for a Timmy's visit, George always tried to call her. They would talk about everything and anything, from the coronation concert plans, to family and friends. George enjoyed hearing about Bea's eclectic university friends and all they had got up to, and Bea seemed to enjoy listening to George's tales about the many varied places she had been and the people she had met.

George hungrily took any time Bea gave her; she felt a happiness and peace around Bea, which she hadn't felt in a long time, and her panic attacks lessened greatly. On the downside, her protection had been beefed up following a briefing with the prime minister. George refused to curtail her public appearances but reluctantly accepted that security had to be increased.

The royal court had now moved to Windsor Castle, where it would stay until after Easter. After an extremely busy schedule, George finally had a day to spend with her family and was out on a ride with Theo around the grounds of Windsor Great Park. The siblings trotted slowly through the leafy park, enjoying the quiet and trying to ignore the protection presence secreted in numbers around them in a perimeter.

"They're not very good at looking discreet are they?" Theo indicated the officers standing by the trees, trying to look inconspicuous.

George sighed. "I know. I hate the increased protection. As if my life wasn't restrictive enough. I protested, but the prime minister insisted."

When the Queen had been informed of the threat, she was sceptical. She didn't believe any one of her subjects would go through with such a threat. The prime minister had pointed out that if she didn't accept the security, she was putting innocent bystanders around her at risk. George was horrified at the thought of anyone being hurt because of her and so reluctantly agreed, but she refused to curtail any of her engagements. The royal protection squad was doubled, and Captain Cameron was armed with a standard issue MI5 weapon.

"I for one am glad, Georgie. Anything that keeps you safe and secure gets my vote."

"I can't imagine you taking it so well, Theo." George pulled the reins, directing her horse to walk closer to her brother's.

"That may be so, my dear sister, but you are far more important to me and the nation. If anything happens to you, Georgie, I will give you one swift boot up the arse myself."

"You sound like Granny." Theo looked aghast at that comment, making George chuckle.

"You're not funny, Georgie. So I hear you have a new friend?"

George gave her brother a surprised look. "Yes, Beatrice Elliot. How do you know?"

"You know courtiers are terrible gossips. She has lunch with you and all sorts, so I'm told."

"Are you? Well, yes. It's nice to have a friend and I enjoy her company."

"She's the anti-monarchist, yes? The one who Granny challenged you to convert?" Theo smirked at his sister.

"The very one."

"So? How goes Granny's challenge? I seem to remember the honour of the House of Buckingham rested on your shoulders."

"Well…"

The promised debate had happened without fanfare the previous week. After spending a few hours at a community project and having lunch with the children, it emerged that a threat had been made regarding the Queen's safety. While the royal protection squad checked over the car and the surrounding area, they kept the Queen secured in the manager's office inside.

"Your Majesty, if you could stay in here, we'll get the area swept as quickly as possible."

"Thank you, Superintendent. I'm anxious not to hold up the staff here any longer than necessary."

"Yes, Ma'am."

George took a seat behind the desk and sighed in frustration.

"Can I get you anything, Ma'am?" Cammy asked.

George's thoughts went immediately to Bea. They had been bidding the staff farewell, when Superintendent Lang and his officers had bundled the Queen back into the building and she and Bea had been separated. "Could you bring Miss Elliot, Cammy? It would be nice to have someone to chat to."

"Certainly, Ma'am."

A few minutes later, a rather annoyed looking Bea entered the office.

"Are you okay, Georgie? No one would tell me anything."

George had stood as soon as she entered. "I am absolutely fine. My protection squad are probably just being over cautious. Do please sit down."

"I can't believe people would threaten you for being gay in this day and age." To George's delight, Bea seemed extremely concerned over her safety.

"There will always be people who do not approve of me in some way or another. There are many people that don't like the head of state being a woman, and a gay woman at that. As monarch I am a symbol of what Britain stands for—equality, freedom, and tolerance. My job is to bring my people together and represent them, whatever their colour, creed, or sexuality, and that does not suit those who seek to cause division. My father took his role seriously, and I intend to do the same. At my coronation I will take a vow, before God, to defend my people's rights and freedoms. Some would prefer I did not have the chance to do that. Being so openly gay doesn't help, I'm sure."

"You really take your coronation vows seriously, don't you?"

George was confused. "Of course. Any vow is serious, and when you take such a vow you are bound by honour to uphold it."

"Does that extend to a marriage vow?" Bea asked quietly.

"Of course, why do you ask?"

"I read on the Net most days about the various women you are connected with. I just wondered…No, I'm sorry. That's a private question. I shouldn't ask you things like that."

George tried to contain a smile and said, "It doesn't usually stop you, Bea."

Bea's cheeks went red. "Well, I—"

"Ask away. What do the gossip columns say?"

"They say you are linked with many members of the European aristocracy, but that the main contender is Princess Eleanor of Belgium. Apparently you played together as children, and she is your childhood sweetheart."

George could not help but laugh out loud at what Bea had said. "Dear God, wait till my brother hears this. I assure you I have no childhood sweetheart, and I think I may have met Princess Eleanor all of twice at royal functions as I was growing up, and she is known in our circles to be a bit of a man-eater."

"A man-eater? But she came out only a few months ago."

George sat back in her chair and crossed her legs. "Let's just say that my family and I are quite astonished at the number of European princesses and members of the aristocracy who are suddenly coming out since I inherited the throne."

"You mean…?"

"I mean that I think Princess Eleanor is more in love with the idea of being Queen Consort, than the thought of loving me."

"Then she is a fool," Bea said indignantly.

An awkward silence fell upon the room, as George wondered what to make of what Bea had said.

Finally, George said, "I will have to marry eventually though. It is my duty."

Bea looked up at George with searching eyes. "Your duty? Why?"

"Well, for one I must produce an heir, for the succession."

Bea laughed. "Are you some sort of a prize bull? Or will you be a breeding heifer?"

George leaned forward on the desk and said in a low voice, "Oh, I think it's quite clear I'm the prize bull." She was sure she could see Bea give a little shiver. "My brother often reminds me he would like to be bumped from first in line to the throne as quickly as possible. He can't think of anything worse than taking over as king if anything happened to me."

"You know, I wouldn't have believed that someone wouldn't want your job until I met you. I can now understand why you wouldn't want that burden."

"Yes, indeed." George sighed, then continued, "The other main reason is that the monarch was never meant to do this job alone. I need the support of a Queen Consort to help me in my duties. There is an office waiting back at the palace for my consort. She has just as important a role as I do."

Bea tapped her manicured nails on the desk. "What if you don't meet someone you love?"

A wave of sadness rushed George all of a sudden. "I can only pray I will find someone I truly love to make my Queen Consort, the way my father loved my mother. If not, I can only hope we will be friends and a support to one another."

"You would marry someone you didn't love, for duty?" Bea's anger was evident in her voice.

With a certainty that came from a life of training, George said, "Of course. Duty comes before self for the royal family, and especially for the monarch."

"I don't know how you could even think that. You do realize that it's not the Middle Ages, don't you?"

George became defensive in her reply. "It is the reality of my position, Bea. I must have a wife and produce an heir. I don't expect you to understand, but I have been trained since birth to put the country, its people, and duty before my own private wishes, and that is exactly what I will do."

The room was again in an awkward silence, until George felt she should break the ice. "I apologize for this delay. I will stay as long as you need me to at the next venue, or we can come back at a later date."

"Let's see how long it takes first. Do you have any engagements tonight?"

"Yes, I have a reception for one of my charities, Wounded Heroes. It raises money for injured servicemen. I've invited some business people and some representatives of the armed forces, to try and raise funds."

Bea gave George a smile that melted her heart. "I sometimes forget you have other charities apart from Timmy's. You really do give us a lot of your time."

"I try to do as much as I can for all of my charities—I'm the patron of over eight hundred—but I wanted to choose one to be the main focus of my coronation year, and I'm so glad I chose Timmy's. Not only do you do fantastic work around the country, but I wouldn't have met you, Bea, and I value your friendship greatly."

"I appreciate it hugely as well, Georgie."

George met Bea's eyes and felt Bea could see deep inside her, past the stoic mask, to a place where there was no Queen, just Georgie and Bea.

Cammy cleared her throat, and George jumped up, realizing they had been caught. "Cammy? Yes, what news?"

"Superintendent Lang estimates we will be held up for another half an hour, Ma'am. If you could just stay put here for a while longer."

"Thank you. Please let us know when we can set off." Cammy bowed her head and left.

George saw the edges of Bea's mouth rise into a smile. "It seems I have you as a captive audience, Your Majesty."

George was relieved to have her emotions back on an even ground and chuckled at Bea's words. "I appear to be at your mercy indeed. What would you do with me?"

Bea sat back into the chair, looking confident. "I think it might be time for that debate on the merits of monarchy you keep putting off."

"I do not put it off. I am simply busy, but if you think you can hold up your end of it, then let's have at it."

George shifted in her saddle, remembering the passionate look that Bea had had at the thought of a good debate, and wanted to see that look again.

"Well, Georgie?" Theo asked.

George's horse snickered and whinnied, bringing her back from her thoughts. "I made progress, I believe."

"Progress? What did you say to her?"

"I gave her the facts. Most presidencies cost more to run than a monarchy. The monarchy represents stability, continuity, and ethics, and I pointed out that we are above politics and so more able to represent Britain abroad without the grubbiness of political debate upon us."

Theo thought for a moment and said, "I do hope you explained that the monarchy brings billions in revenue into the country each year, and we only cost the taxpayers a few pounds each."

"Of course I did. She seemed to take some things on board but needs further convincing. It's hard to see the real value of our work unless you come face to face with it. I hope I can make her see it."

"You haven't told me the most important thing. Is Miss Beatrice Elliot beautiful?"

George grinned. "Bea is absolutely beautiful. Stunning even."

"Well, well. I don't think I've ever heard you describe a woman so enthusiastically, Georgie. I can't wait to see for myself, since I am the expert on the female of the species."

George gave her brother a serious look. "Just remember she is off limits to you, Theo. She's a lesbian, so you'd be wasting your time."

"I know, don't worry. How about I race you back and see if we can lose these protection officers?"

George grinned at the challenge. "Last one back mucks out the stables."

The siblings shot off at a canter, leaving the running police officers lagging behind.

CHAPTER TEN

B ea was working when Danny stopped by her office.
"Have you got a minute, Bea?"

"Of course. Computer off." He sat down at her desk, barely able to keep the smile from his face. "Danny? You look like the cat that got the cream. What is it?"

"I've had the first donation figures since the Queen gave us her patronage."

"Well?" Bea asked expectantly.

"In just two months of patronage, donations and fundraising are up by seventy percent. The number crunchers predict that we will hit one hundred percent by summer."

Bea jumped up and shrieked, "Oh my God. Really? You're not kidding, are you?"

"Never. We can afford to finish building and equipping our new units, and start work on the overseas respite centre."

She ran round the desk and hugged her friend and boss. "I can't believe it. All because we have a royal walking about, shaking hands and waving."

"Yes, indeed, but I have even more news." Danny let go of her and stood back.

What now? Was it a good news/bad news scenario?

"Don't look so worried. Listen, remember when the Queen was in America?"

Bea did indeed remember that time fondly. It was when Georgie had first called her and they'd cemented their friendship. "At the UN conference, yes?"

"Yes. Well, apparently at one of the glitzy affairs, she spoke to some business people. One of them, an expat Brit, was very impressed with our Queen and asked which charities she was involved with. Queen Georgina told her all about us and our work."

"Tell me. Please."

"The businesswoman's secretary just called me to say we would be receiving a donation from her company of twenty million dollars."

❖

Bea walked around in a daze the rest of that day. A smile was permanently attached to her face, and all she could think of as she tried to work and as she made her way home was George's warm smile and deep blue eyes.

She walked through her front door and shouted, "Mum, Dad, I'm home."

"We're in the kitchen, dear. Come and see. It's so wonderful."

What on earth has made Mum so excited? She hurried through to the small kitchen, to find her mum and dad sitting at the kitchen table with a large picnic basket.

"Look, sweetheart. This was delivered an hour ago."

Bea dropped her handbag and began to look through the basket. There were jams, marmalades, biscuits, fruits, meats, and even fresh juice. They all bore the label: *Produce of the Sandringham Estate, Norfolk.*

Bea looked at her parents quizzically. "How did this get here?"

"I'd just pulled up outside the house, and this big Land Rover pulled in behind me. These huge blokes got out, and I thought I was in trouble, I tell you."

"What kind of blokes, Dad?"

Reg shrugged his shoulders. "Looked like plain-clothes policemen or something. They asked if I was Mr. Elliot, I said yes, and he says he's got a delivery for me and my wife, and that the card would explain everything."

Sarah handed it over to her and said, "It's handwritten and everything."

Bea read the note out loud.

Dear Mr. and Mrs. Elliot,

Please accept this small token of my esteem, from my estate at Sandringham. Everything in the basket has been either grown or made there, and I hope you will enjoy them. Your wonderful daughter has told me of your long and unstinting support for my family, and for that I am very grateful.

Yours faithfully,
Georgina R

"I can't believe she would do this," Bea said in shock.

Her mother pulled her into a hug. "A personal gift from the Queen. It's astonishing, and that's not all. This was inside." Sarah handed over a larger envelope, which had a large handwritten card inside. It read: *The Lord Chamberlain is commanded by Her Majesty to invite Mr. and Mrs. Elliot to a royal tea party to be held at Buckingham Palace, October 5th.*

"A royal tea party. It's wonderful, isn't it, sweetheart? Did you tell the Queen about us?"

"Yes. I told her that you love the royal family, and about your collections and things. I'm astonished that she took in all that and did this."

"Reg, I'll need to buy a new hat and dress. Oh, I can't wait," Sarah said excitedly.

Oh, Georgie. You've been so kind. You really listen to me don't you? "Mum, I'm just going to get changed, okay? I'll be down in a while."

Bea ran up the stairs to her bedroom and activated the computer on her desk. She had no idea how she could contact the Queen. Georgie always called her on a secure line when they spoke. Then she realized— Cammy, of course. She had Captain Cameron's details in case any problems with the visits came up.

Bea kicked off her high heels and said, "Call Captain Cameron." After a few seconds the image of Cammy appeared.

"Hello? Ah, Miss Elliot. How are you?"

Bea moved to her desk. "Hello, Captain, I'm sorry to bother you."

"Not at all, Miss Elliot, and please call me Cammy. How can I help?"

Bea sensed that the captain had warmed up to her over the past few weeks, and she was glad. "Thank you, Cammy, please call me Bea." She went on to explain about the news she'd heard from Danny at work, and then coming home to find the kind gift the Queen had sent. "And so you see, I just wanted to thank her for her kindness. I really am overwhelmed at what she has done for Timmy's and my family."

Cammy smiled. "Of course I will let her know you called, Bea. She is with the Queen Mother at the moment, but I will speak with Her Majesty at the first opportunity."

"Thank you. Well, I'll let you get on—"

"Before you go, Bea, I just wanted to apologize for the way I spoke to you on the train. I was concerned because Her Majesty has never opened up like that to an outsider. She doesn't have friends— well, she has her cousins and myself, but no one outside the royal family or palace walls. She is very guarded, usually, but when I saw her behaving so freely with you, I'll be quite frank, I was worried."

Bea was buoyed by the knowledge that the Queen trusted her enough to be open, and she realized then what a special friendship they were developing. "You needn't worry yourself, Cammy. I understand why you are protective. I haven't known the Queen as long as you, and I already feel that urge to protect her." *And care for her.*

"I was worried, but not now. You've seen her at her lowest and you didn't go running to the press. You've proved your loyalty, lassie."

She smiled at Cammy's pleasant sounding Scottish brogue. "Thank you. Anything the Queen tells me will be kept between us, I promise."

Cammy rubbed her chin in a nervous fashion before saying, "I may be speaking out of turn here, but it appears to me that the Queen really cares about you and your friendship, so be careful with her, please?"

"Of course, Cammy. You have my word."

"Good enough. Cheerio then, Bea."

"Goodbye, Cammy." As the screen went blank, Bea thought, *Georgie cares about me?* Somehow deep inside she'd known that already, by the way the Queen looked at her, but she wasn't prepared to think about what that meant.

I know how I can thank you, Georgie. She quickly called up an Internet shopping site and looked through all the items.

I have no idea which one to choose. I bet Dad would know.

Bea opened her bedroom door and shouted downstairs, "Dad? Can you come and help me?"

"This looks fine, Mama. Whatever you think is appropriate. You've been doing this a long time."

The Queen and Queen Mother were discussing the upcoming banquet to be held at Windsor Castle. These events, known as dine-and-sleeps, were held several times a year, and various dignitaries were invited, depending on the occasion. This particular event was a thank you from the whole royal family to politicians on all sides, religious leaders, and community leaders, for their support since the King's death. The event would also mark the end of his mourning period. The King, ever aware of putting duty before self, left instructions that he was to have a short mourning period. He wished the public and political parties' focus to be on his daughter, the new Queen, and not on the King that came before.

"It is my pleasure to ease your burden, George, but you would do well to find a wife to help you in the long term. Your reign will be one of fresh ideas, modern ways of doing things, and in that you will need a younger woman helping you, not your old mother."

George took a sip of her coffee and regarded her elegant looking mother with a smile. "You are not old, Mama, and as for the wife part… well, I know my duty."

Queen Sofia sat closer to her daughter on the small armchair and took her hand. "Remember, there should be more than duty my dear. There should be love. Our family history is filled with couples who married for duty, and it brought great unhappiness to both parties and in some cases damaged the monarchy itself."

"I know, Mama. I will try, but there is no one of our acquaintance that I feel that way about." As George said those words to her mother, Beatrice Elliot's face floated across her mind, and her heart sped up just a little.

"I have faith that the right consort for you will pop up, my dear, and you will give me some beautiful grandchildren. You are too guarded, perhaps, with the ladies, too careful. Let them see the warm, wonderful person inside. Your brother, on the other hand, shows too much of himself to the ladies. I fear he will never settle down."

"Don't worry so much about him, Mama. He has grown up a great deal since Father died. I will look after him."

"I know you will, my dear. The family all look to you for strength and guidance. Just as they did with your father before you. That is why a consort to share your burden is so important."

George was feeling uncomfortable. The one person who had seen her at her worst and soothed her soul was Bea, and she was very unsure what to do with those thoughts. She reached down and patted the dogs lying at her feet. After playing with her mother's dachshund for a while, the pups settled down to sleep, cuddled up together.

"So, the whole family is going to be on parade?"

"Yes, all have confirmed. Your aunt Grace has been helping organize the family. It will be nice to have everyone together again."

George sighed and rubbed her forehead. "I must make some time to talk to Aunt Grace and Cousin Vicki about the stables, with the polo and riding season coming up. I must see how the horses are doing, but I've just been so busy I—"

Her mother stroked her cheek tenderly. "I understand how hard you've been working. Those red boxes never end, do they? Your father kept many late nights trying to get through it all."

"Papa never complained and neither will I. Duty before self."

"Indeed. It must be done. Oh, before I forget, your cousin Julian has asked that Princess Eleanor be asked to the dine-and-sleep."

George raised an eyebrow. "Why? We are thanking people who have supported the family since Papa's death. What has Eleanor to do with it?"

"Apparently he and his wife Marta have met her at various social events, and she has expressed a hope to be received by you. I know that you think her presence here is somewhat…underhanded, but courtesy dictates that you receive a visiting royal. At least at a function like this, you will have plenty of reasons to circulate and not have your time monopolized."

With a huge sigh, the Queen acquiesced. "Very well. I wonder why Julian cares so much."

"I have no idea, but he did ask Granny to put in a good word for her also."

"Hmm. Suspicious if you ask me. I wonder if he will manage not to sneer at me for the terrible crime of inheriting the throne, just for this one night."

Queen Sofia chuckled. "He always was an envious little boy and far too proud, in the worst possible way. So unlike his brother and sister."

Lady Victoria and Lord Maximilian Buckingham, known as Max, were very close to George and Theodore. They grew up together, spending holidays together having fun, and they all shared a love of horses. Julian, on the other hand, always kept himself somewhat separate from them all.

George had a thought pop into her head. "Mama, is it too late to add one more invitation?"

"No, we always keep space for a few more in case of cancellations. Who would you like to invite, my dear?"

George suddenly found the cup and saucer in front of her very interesting. "I would like to ask Miss Beatrice Elliot to come."

"Miss Elliot? Is she something to do with the charity you've been touring with? The republican?"

George stood and walked, hands behind her back, to the large window in her mother's sitting room. Rex, who was now extremely attached to George, got up and followed after her. "Yes, Mama. She is the regional director of Timmy's, the hospice charity. We have become friends and she has been a great support to me. And I would like to thank her." George stroked Rexie's head as he stood at her side.

Queen Sofia smiled and said, "Of course, George. If that is your wish, I shall send the invitation out as soon as possible. I'm sure Granny would be delighted to meet her—I don't think she has ever met a republican face to face."

George walked back over to her mother, feeling much more relaxed. "I have been working on putting our views across, as Granny challenged. I hope Miss Elliot's views may be softening."

"Excellent. I have every faith in your powers of persuasion."

CHAPTER ELEVEN

After meeting with her mother, George returned to her office, followed by her dogs, to continue with her paperwork. Just as she sat down, Sir Michael came in with another six red boxes to be done. George's heart sank, but she made no outward sign to her private secretary.

Two hours later, George was struggling with a headache and blurry vision, one sentence seeming to merge into another, so when Cammy interrupted her work, it was most welcome.

"Good God, man, you look awful."

George had to smile. "Thank you very much, Captain. That's a lovely way to talk to your Queen."

"Well, who else is going to tell you? You need to take a break, and I have the excuse. Miss Elliot called me earlier."

George immediately brightened. "What for?"

"It seems that her parents received your note and your gift. She wanted to thank you personally, but she didn't know how to contact you."

George tried not to appear too interested in this new information. "Oh? Did she seem pleased?"

"She seemed over the moon."

George looked at the time. "Ten o'clock. Do you think it's too late to call back?"

"No, Your Majesty, I'd go for it."

"I will. Thank you."

Cammy opened the door to leave, then turned and said, "Oh, and George? She is a lovely wee lassie. I had my reservations at the start, but she's been a loyal friend to you."

George couldn't help the huge smile which now adorned her face. "Thank you, Cammy. I appreciate that."

"Ring for me when you're ready to turn in, Ma'am."

"I will do. Could you organize something for my head? It's a little sore."

"Of course, Ma'am." Cammy gave a quick head bow and left.

❖

Bea lay on her bed cuddling her teddy bear, the TV playing absently in the background. She had found it difficult to concentrate on anything, as thoughts and feelings buzzed around her head; all that she believed in seemed to be turning upside down.

The tablet by her bedside came to life and announced, "Caller withheld." Her heart started to pound. There was only one such person who called her regularly. She jumped up and ran her fingers through her hair, trying to tidy it up a bit, and then looked down at her nightie with the bunny cartoon character on. "Oh God. Why didn't I wear my silk nightie?" With no choice, Bea answered the call.

George appeared on screen and immediately beamed with a smile. "Good evening, Bea. I hope you aren't annoyed that I've called so late. I only just got the message that you called, and I didn't want you to think I was ignoring you."

"No, I'm delighted you did, Georgie. I was anxious to speak to you—I want to thank you for your kind gift to my parents. They were so excited."

"I'm delighted they liked it. It's just a small token, I hoped you wouldn't mind."

"Of course not, and the invitation to the tea party? My mum is overjoyed. I know there are hundreds of people there and only very few meet you, but just to be asked…"

"They will meet me—I'll ask for them to be introduced. My staff go through the crowd to pick out interesting people for me to meet, and I'll make sure your mother and father are first on the list."

She is too good to be true. Bea gave a coy smile and said, "Are you trying to butter me up, Queen Georgina?"

"Why would I do that?" George looked stricken. "I'm your friend, I thought—"

"I'm only kidding, Georgie, it was very kind." Bea was constantly amazed at how unsure of herself George was. She watched her on public engagements, and a more confident woman you could not see, but with her, in private, she seemed to react differently.

"Well, it was my pleasure."

She saw George's eyes rove over her, and again she wished she had chosen something nicer to wear to bed. "I'm sorry. I'm a bit underdressed."

George smiled at her. "On the contrary, I'm the one that called you at this late hour, and I think you look very cute."

Bea felt her cheeks flush. "It's not very appropriate when talking with the Queen though, is it?"

George's look became serious. "When I talk to you in private, I don't want to be the Queen—I just want to be George, just George."

There was a hint of longing in her friend's voice that touched her somewhere deep inside; she wanted to soothe that part of George, if only through friendship. "Okay, Georgie. You'd better meet my bedmate then."

George looked very uncomfortable all of a sudden. "Ah, I don't think this—"

Bea held a traditional teddy bear. "This is my bedmate every night, Rupert."

George let out an audible sigh and began to chuckle. "Oh, that's your bedmate? A teddy bear?"

"You didn't think…?" Bea started to ask in surprise.

"It doesn't matter, please do ignore me."

Bea looked her friend in the eye and explained so there would be no misunderstandings. "Georgie, there is nobody that shares my bed, apart from Rupert here, and even if there were, I would never expose your privacy by letting anyone else hear our conversations." Bea looked at Rupert and stroked his fur. "I value our friendship too much."

"I appreciate you saying that."

Bea felt something change between them in those few words, and even though physically they were miles apart, she felt somehow connected to this extraordinary woman. "Danny told me about the American donor."

George thought for a second and then replied, "Ah. Yes, she spoke to me at the UN reception. She was very keen to donate to one of my charities—and publicize the fact, most likely. I immediately thought of Timmy's."

"Do you know how much that money means to us? Not to mention the fact that our UK donations have gone through the roof."

"That's my job, Bea. I'm the head of Britain PLC, and it's my job to promote British interests around the world. Do you see why I take my job so seriously? You might think the traditions silly, and the institution outdated, and maybe if we were starting the country from scratch tomorrow, we wouldn't have a monarchy, but we're not. The monarchy is part of the British brand, and I will fight tooth and nail for this country and its people wherever I am, every business, every charity. I hope you can appreciate that."

Bea was finding herself swayed more and more by the sheer belief George had in what she stood for. "I appreciate what you do, Georgie, and you've opened my eyes to that. You work so hard and you really care, but every monarch is not like you, and the people have no control over who comes after you."

As the conversation continued, George felt she was really getting somewhere with Bea, and it came to her mind that Bea was exactly the sort of person the monarchy needed. Someone to challenge the old ways of doing things, come up with fresh ideas, and question and counsel, when the monarchy needed it. Above all else, Bea was dedicated to the service of others.

A perfect Queen Consort.

George mentally slapped herself for even thinking that and hoped Bea didn't notice the crimson she felt creep up her face. "So, tell me about Rupert," George blurted out.

"Rupert was my sister Abigail's bear."

George felt stupid for asking. Bea had always clammed up when the subject of her sister arose. "Please, forgive me. I shouldn't have asked."

"No, please. I'd like to talk about her. I can't really talk to Mum and Dad about her a lot. They still get very upset."

"I would be glad to listen—I know it's helped me a great deal talking to you about Papa."

Bea absent-mindedly played with the bear's slightly worn ear as she relayed the story about her sister. "I was too young to realize that Abby was going to die. I just thought she'd always keep getting ill and going into hospital. Abby had a rare form of leukaemia—she fought it for three years. Then when she was eight, the doctors told Mum and Dad she wasn't going to get better. I hated when she went into hospital—it was a sterile, scary place to me as a child—but when she started to go into the hospice instead, it was different, better in some ways. I didn't know that meant there was no hope anymore. I just saw a bright, friendly place where my sister could be comfortable. The walls were painted with children's characters and there were toys…things didn't seem so bad."

Tears started to fall from Bea's eyes, and George felt frustration that they were so far apart and she couldn't offer her friend comfort. "How long did she live after that?"

"Two months. Mum said even though it was at the end of her life, hospice was a time when Abby and the family were most at peace, because of the drugs and therapies available there."

Bea held Rupert to her chest tightly, as if trying to get closer to her sister. "There was a shortage of beds, though, and she was in and out of the hospice all through that time. As I grew up I knew I wanted to make things better for kids like my sister, and that's why I get so angry about the budget given to the health service. I've raised money all through school and university for hospice and cancer charities, and when I graduated, I knew what I wanted to do."

She wiped away the tears and said, "I miss my sister every day, and I always wonder what kind of woman she would've become, but I feel close to her when I have Rupert here. Abby died holding him."

George felt her arms physically ache with the want to hold Bea, but all she could do was offer her words of support. "I'm sure she would have been a fine young woman, and wherever she is, I'm certain she's proud of all you have achieved, Bea."

"Do you think there is a wherever else? A heaven or afterlife?"

George answered immediately with conviction. "Of course. I am the defender of faiths, remember? At my coronation next year, I will take my vows before God, and you know I don't take vows lightly. I know my papa is looking down on me, guiding me as best he can, as Abigail does you. That's my belief anyway."

Bea smiled at her. "Do you visit the King's grave often?"

"Oh yes. He is buried here at Windsor, in St. George's Chapel, along with his brother. When I'm in residence, I go down to the chapel to think, to pray and talk to Papa and Uncle George. It gives me great comfort. Was Abigail buried?"

"Yes, but I don't get there very often. Mum won't go, she can't face the pain, even to this day. I know Dad goes and tends to the flowers he has planted around the grave, but he and Mum don't really talk about it, and I don't like going on my own."

On a whim George said, "Could I escort you there?"

Bea looked up in shock. "You? But you can't just go to somewhere like that in private, cameras will follow you, and think of the security—"

George held her hand up. "Listen. I have ways of getting to certain places as privately as possible, if you allowed me to organize it. I would like to—you've supported me through a difficult period in my life, and I would like to do this for you. As long as you don't mind sharing this private time with me."

"I would like that, Georgie. I would like that very much."

❖

The arrangements were made, and two days later an all-terrain vehicle arrived to pick Bea up. As it turned out, the unremarkable vehicle was a state-of-the-art bullet- and bomb-proof car. In front sat Cammy in plain clothes, and in the driver's seat was a police protection officer. The car was self-drive, but the officer would need to take control in case of any security scare.

Following at a discreet distance was another car of police protection officers, all fully armed.

Bea entered the vehicle and looked surprised to find George decked out in a washed-out scruffy army camouflage jacket, jeans, and baseball cap. George explained, "Do excuse my somewhat shabby appearance, but it helps me to go unnoticed."

Bea held a bag containing flowers, a ceramic teddy bear, and her little gift for George. "I think you look great."

"Don't tell Cammy that—she hates when we have to dress down." Cammy sighed from the front seat and they shared a laugh together.

"Thank you for doing this. It's very kind, Your Majesty."

George appreciated that Bea always made sure she was respectful of the Queen's position when outside ears were listening. Her instinct was to reach out and touch Bea, but she pulled her hand back in time before Bea noticed.

"Don't mention it. I'm happy to be your friend and offer any support to you that I can, just as you have done with me. I hope you don't mind, but I took the liberty of bringing some flowers to lay at Abigail's grave." George picked up a tasteful bunch of white lilies.

"Of course not, Ma'am. That was very thoughtful."

"Did you tell your parents where you were going?"

"I just said I was going with a friend, otherwise Mum would have made such a big fuss of you that the whole street would have been likely to hear."

George smiled and joked, "If only I had that effect on all the Elliot women."

It was a dry but dull day at the Sunny Hill graveyard. Inspector Lang of the Queen's protection unit had chosen the time—midmorning on a workday—to limit the number of people who would be there. He had come a few days before to work out the best positions for his team, so they would have a good view of the Queen, but not draw too much attention to her. George and Bea stood at the graveside, and Cammy strategically sat on a bench, a few graves up from them.

Bea set her flowers down and placed the small bear statue on the gravestone. "I hope you like him Abby. I'm taking good care of Rupert for you."

When she stood back, George laid down the flowers she had brought and bowed her head before coming back to stand next to Bea.

Bea's gaze was glued to the moving image of her sister that was on the stone.

The sisters looked very similar, although Abigail's hair seemed to be a lighter shade of blond.

"She was a beautiful girl," George said.

Bea wiped away tears. "She was, and so talented. She loved to ride horses and was quite good for her age. We never got to go into the country, only ever rode the horses at the city farm, but she dreamed of going to one of those horse gymkhanas in the country. I tried it a few times, but didn't have the confidence to enjoy it."

"I must introduce you to my horses. They are my pride and joy, and you wouldn't be nervous of them. I have some that are very good with beginners."

Bea smiled, but kept staring forward to Abigail's picture. "Abby would have liked you. I remember when I was about ten, Mum and Dad took us to Buckingham Palace—it was a special birthday, I think, for your grandmother. The people had lined the streets for a parade and then swarmed up to the palace gates on the Mall, waiting for a balcony appearance. It was a big deal at the time, I remember, there were going to be gun salutes and a fly-past by the Royal Air Force."

"I remember, I think it was Granny's sixtieth birthday," George said.

"It was a magical day, surrounded by all those people. You felt part of something, part of history, something greater than yourself. Then the noise, when your family came out onto the balcony to wave, was louder than anything I've ever heard. Were you scared, looking down at everyone screaming and shouting?"

"No, it was normal to me because I was brought up with it. I do remember always feeling happy and proud that the people liked my family enough to come and cheer for us. Every time we would stand there, looking down upon the crowds, Papa would say to me, *George it is your duty to always put these people first. We are here only by the will of every man, woman, and child here, never forget that, and never let them down.* I never did forget."

Bea smiled and said, "My dad said to us, *Never forget this moment, we are witnessing history.* We each took turns at sitting on his shoulders. Abigail liked it most when she saw you because she'd read all about you in her horse and pony magazines. She would have loved to have met you." Fresh tears came to her eyes.

George couldn't stop herself from touching Bea any longer and reached out to hold her hand. Neither said anything, but George knew Bea was grateful for the offered support by the squeeze she got in return. "I've met her now, Bea. I know she is looking down on us and, I hope, happy that you and I are friends."

"Oh, she would be. I'm certain. Could we sit down?" She gestured to the bench behind them.

"Of course." George didn't let go of her hand.

After a few minutes Bea said, "Sometimes I feel so guilty that I survived, that I get to experience everything in life that she didn't get the chance to."

"On the contrary, I'm sure she is so proud of her sister and everything she has achieved." George was silent for a minute. "I understand the feeling though. Do you know about my Uncle George?"

Bea gripped her hand tighter. "Of course, he was to be the first openly gay monarch. The country was very excited until…"

"He died." George finished the sentence for her. "I wasn't born yet and didn't know him, but I know my father adored him and made sure I knew everything about him."

George looked away from Bea and stared off into the distance. "I was named after him so his name would inherit the throne as he should have done, and when I told my parents I was gay, well, Papa was even more convinced that I was destined to be everything that Uncle George would have been. My father didn't mean it to exert pressure, but I've always felt a heavy weight of destiny placed upon me to be what he would have been, and I know I'll never achieve that."

Bea looked confused. "Why would you not?"

George turned to Bea. "You must have seen footage of him—he was brilliant in anything he tried. He was an excellent horseman and sportsman, and so charismatic. The people loved him for good reason. He lit up any room he walked into and made people laugh with ease. I'm not like that. I've had to work hard to learn the art of talking in public, and I'm sure he never had a panic attack in his life."

"Is that how you really see yourself, because it's not what the world sees."

"What do you mean?"

"Georgie, people adore you. You know how sceptical I was at the start, but even I couldn't fail to miss the way the public reacts to you. You work your way through a crowd as if it was the most natural thing in the world, and each person you meet feels that you have really listened and appreciated the time you've spent with them. All the kids you've met have loved you too—remember the football match at the school? And you put the little kid on your shoulders? He'll remember that forever."

George knew she was blushing. "Well, that's just my job, and I like playing with children, that's not hard."

"It's not only children. Every person we've met touring the hospice sites so far has been brighter and happier for meeting you. Although you live a privileged and sheltered life, you manage to find common ground with everyone you meet, whether it's a young boy or an old soldier."

George laughed softly out of embarrassment. "You do wonders for your sovereign's ego."

"I think even Queens need encouragement from time to time. Oh! I nearly forgot." Bea rummaged around in her bag and took out a gift-wrapped box. "I got you a gift. I wanted to thank you for what you've done for Timmy's and for sending my mum and dad the hamper from your estate."

George took the gift. As Queen, she received gifts from every country she visited, and from every visiting head of state and politician. But they weren't personal gifts like this, and she usually saw them for all of five minutes before they were whisked off to sit in government vaults or become part of the royal collection.

"You didn't have to do that, Bea. I didn't expect anything in return."

"I know you didn't, and that's exactly why I wanted to get you something. This is for Georgie, not the Queen."

The fact that Bea knew the difference between those two things made her even more perfect in her eyes.

George began to rip the paper off carefully.

"I hope you don't already have this one. My dad helped me pick it out."

When she saw what the gift was, she was both shocked and over-whelmed at Bea's kindness.

"I wasn't sure what to get, I mean, what do you buy for a Queen who has everyth—"

George threw her arms around Bea and gave her a hug. "Thank you, Bea. I have never been given a nicer gift." She felt Bea's arms circle her back and held on tight.

"It's just a silly little thing really," Bea replied.

George pulled back slightly so she could make eye contact, but didn't let go. "It's not silly. No one but you would have thought of this. You listened to the things I said and knew what I liked. You see *me*, Beatrice Elliot, and not the crown."

At that moment George was overwhelmed with the urge to kiss Bea. The shock of her rising passion forced her to let go and make some space between them. She hoped Bea hadn't noticed the passion in her eyes.

"You don't have that boat already, do you?" It was a model of the *HMS King George*. "Dad helped me choose it. I thought since it was named George, it would be a good choice."

"No, I don't. It's an extremely thoughtful gift. Thank you, I shall take great pleasure in building it."

"I'm so glad. I hoped it was one of the boats you didn't have."

George started to laugh. "It's a ship, Bea, not a boat. I really need to teach you the difference."

Bea gave her a miffed look and said, "Oh, I suppose you've got five boats and six ships that cost the tax payer millions in upkeep."

George decided to play along. "More like twenty boats and one royal yacht, and technically all the ships and frigates in the Royal Navy are mine. They are called Her Majesty's ships after all."

"You're having me on, aren't you?"

"Well, just a bit. I do have quite a few boats—I sail a lot up at Balmoral, our Scottish summer residence, and I do have a royal yacht we take holidays on—but I pay for that out of my own private money. So you don't need to get your republican knickers in a twist," George teased.

Bea gave her a seductive look and said, "Oh, Georgie, it takes a good deal more than that to get my knickers in a twist."

Bea's tone and comment hit right to George's core. She shifted uncomfortably in her seat and refused to meet Bea's eyes.

"So? Do I get to see this boat...*ship* thing when it's finished?"

Grateful for the change of subject, George smiled warmly and said, "Of course. I was going to ask..." George hesitated, unsure of the response she would get.

"What? Tell me."

"The dine-and-sleep that's coming up at Windsor?"

"Yes, I was really surprised to be asked, Georgie. Are you sure it's right for me to be there? I mean, if government officials and politicians are going, maybe I shouldn't be there. I'm just a charity worker."

George almost lost her temper. "You are not just a charity worker, Beatrice Elliot. This banquet is to thank all who have supported my family since the King died, and none of the others deserves to be thanked more than you."

"I've been a pain in the bum, more like," Bea retorted.

"Not at all. You have opened up a new world to me. I was terribly isolated and lonely, but these past few months with you have brought light to my darkness, and I can't wait to see what the rest of the year brings." George reached out to touch her cheek, but stopped a few inches away, realizing she had maybe said too much.

George turned away quickly, suddenly feeling exposed. "What was it you wanted to ask me?" Bea asked after a few seconds.

"What? Oh yes. Well, every guest leaves first thing the next morning. I wondered if you would stay for the day and spend some time with me. I could show you the stables and some of the sights."

"I would be delighted."

George simply nodded, and for the next few minutes they listened to the sounds of the graveyard, the birds chirping, the wind blowing gently through the leaves. And George tried to come to terms with the feelings churning inside her.

"Thank you for coming with me today, Georgie. It means a lot. It would have meant a lot to Abby too."

"It's an honour to share this with you Bea. Thank you."

Chapter Twelve

L ali Ramesh sighed dramatically at her best friend. "Bea, would you stop looking in that box. It's perfect."

The two friends had spent the day searching some designer shops in London for a dress. Bea had wanted something special for the banquet at Windsor Castle. After hours of searching, Lali had persuaded her to buy a long midnight-blue dress that had showed off her petite figure wonderfully. They had stopped at a smart cafe for a well-earned bite of lunch.

"I don't think it suits me, Lali. It's very…grand. I'll be paying my credit card off for a year."

"It's supposed to be grand, Bea—you're going to a banquet at a castle."

Bea closed up the box and fidgeted nervously. "I really don't think I can carry it off."

Lali shook her head. "You can carry off any style. You've been a nervous wreck about this event ever since you got the invite, and I don't know why. Bea, you're a regional director of a charity and a very accomplished woman. You've been to lots of big charity events."

Bea took a sip of her coffee and said, "This is a very different thing. The prime minister and some big name politicians will be there, not to mention the Queen's family. I mean, I got a protocol book and timetable for the whole day."

"I'm sure that's just to make things easier for you."

"Oh, it is, but it makes me feel really nervous. I don't want to let Georgie down."

Lali reached for her friend's hand and gave it a squeeze. "I know you never could. From what you've told me, she's a very kind and considerate person. She'll be delighted to have you there."

Bea sat silently.

"There's something else bothering you, isn't there?" Lali asked.

There was one thing she had been unable to stop thinking about, ever since she saw it in the press. Princess Eleanor was going to be there. It had even been suggested that they would soon be an official couple. Despite George's protestations to the contrary, Bea was very aware that George would have to marry someday. The princess was a renowned beauty, and if she was determined to pursue the Queen, she might get her wish. After all, the princess was royal and an ideal candidate. The thought of Eleanor with George made Bea's stomach ill.

"You like her, don't you?"

Bea looked up sharply. "Of course I like her. After our rocky start, you know she's become my friend."

"No, I mean you *really* like her. I think you care about her."

"I do care about her. She needs a friend. She has a heavy burden to carry and I want to be there for her," Bea said defiantly.

"Is this my friend the anti-monarchist talking?" Lali smiled quizzically at her.

"Do you know how hard she works, Lali? I've been exhausted trying to keep up with our engagements around the country, but I get to go home and relax every evening. Georgie doesn't get that luxury, and she's quite isolated. I want to support her all I can, because no matter what I think about the monarchy in general, she has a heart of gold and always thinks of others first."

"You're falling for her, aren't you?"

Bea opened her mouth, but no sound came out. "I…don't be ridiculous. Queens don't have serious relationships with working-class women, unless they take a mistress, and you know I would never be anyone's mistress. So can we just drop it?"

George relaxed as the ancient turrets of Windsor Castle came into view, and she saw the Union Flag that always flew when the monarch wasn't in residence begin to descend. As soon as her car arrived inside the castle walls, the royal standard would be raised. The family liked to spend most weekends here. If Buckingham Palace was headquarters of the Buckingham dynasty, then Windsor was their home.

Her morning engagement had gone very smoothly, and now she was looking forward to seeing Bea tonight. Cammy had not accompanied George for this engagement as she had to go ahead and arrange the Queen's personal belongings and take the dogs down to Windsor. George didn't like to be away from her pets for long. Instead of Captain Cameron, George had taken her old school friend and senior lady-in-waiting, Olivia Henley, Duchess of Monkford, Mistress of the Robes.

"It's good to be home." George sighed.

"Indeed, Your Majesty. I wish all your engagements were as straightforward as this morning," Olivia replied.

George leaned back against the headrest. "It's going to be an extremely busy year. What am I talking about? It's going to be a busy life. After the coronation, I'm going on a six-month world tour."

She and Olivia had been friends since they attended the same boarding school in the Scottish Highlands. The tough outdoors-oriented school had been tough on the very feminine and beautiful Olivia, who panicked if she broke a nail. George had looked out for her and helped her navigate the perils of a school whose ethos of hard and often manual tasks, such as sailing, rock climbing or orienteering, were extremely demanding. After school they remained friends. George even introduced Olivia to her husband, the Duke of Monkford.

"If you'll forgive me for saying, Ma'am, you need a wife."

After another big sigh, George said, "You sound like my mother and granny."

"I don't mean you need to find a wife for duty—you need the support and care of a partner who loves you."

George turned and looked at her. "Please don't tell me you're lobbying on behalf of Princess Eleanor."

"Good gracious, no. Everyone knows she's the biggest man-eater around. Her sudden lesbianism is somewhat see-through. Why? Who is lobbying for her?"

"Cousin Julian. He's been to see Granny and Mama. He pushed for her to be invited tonight. I feel he seeks to have some influence to prosper his position within the family, but I'm not that stupid, I hope."

"Of course you're not. Viscount Anglesey has always, shall we say, struggled with his position within the royal family."

George chuckled softly as they pulled up to the private entrance of the castle. "That is a very polite way of putting it, Lady Olivia."

"Thank you, Ma'am."

The car came to a stop and George turned to her lady-in-waiting. "I have a new friend coming to the banquet tonight. She's not used to this type of royal occasion, and I know she has been very nervous. Would you watch out for her? Perhaps introduce her to some of the other guests. As you know, I will have to circulate."

"I'm intrigued. Of course, Your Majesty. I'll look out for her."

"Thank you. I'll see you tonight."

❖

The banquet hall of Windsor Castle looked resplendent. After weeks and weeks of hard work by the staff, everything was ready for the Queen's inspection. The hall could easily seat two hundred, but tonight it was set for a more intimate number of eighty. The Queen Mother led the way, followed by the Queen and the Master of the Household, Air Marshal Sir Hugh Blair.

The senior page, the yeoman of the cellars, and the royal florist were waiting. The staff all bowed, and Queen Sofia immediately went to the task of checking the table arrangements.

"Simpson? Any problems?" Sofia asked the senior page.

"None, Ma'am. Everything has gone very smoothly so far."

No matter how often George had seen the banquet hall laid out for guests, either at Windsor or Buckingham Palace, she was always impressed by the display. The light from the large gold candelabras situated at regular intervals along the long table dazzled off the crystal glasses and gold plates. Fresh plump fruits groaned from the bowls at easy reach of the guests' plates. A red and gold carpet ran the length of the banquet table, giving the room a feeling of opulence. Huge bouquets of flowers were placed at regular intervals up the table, and on wrought-iron stands in the corners of the room. The side walls were punctuated by a series of arches, allowing the staff access to serve and clear. The arches were guarded by mounted suits of armour and heraldic shields from the royal collection. The ceiling was equally impressive, made up of oak beams running the length of the room, and there was a small balcony where the band of the Welsh Guards would play the music for the evening.

The Queen Mother checked the table settings with a keen eye; George knew the staff were always nervous at this point as her mother was a stickler for details.

"This looks wonderful. Well done, Simpson."

"Thank you, Ma'am."

The Queen checked where she would be sitting at the head of the table. "So, I'm here, next to the prime minister?"

Sir Hugh stepped forward. "Yes, Ma'am, and since the prime minister doesn't have a partner or guest accompanying her, we placed the next ranking guest, Her Royal Highness, Princess Eleanor, with the Queen Mother on her right."

"I don't think that's appropriate, Sir Hugh. This is a dinner to thank those who supported my family after my father's death. She does not merit such a high-ranking place."

Sir Hugh looked panicked at displeasing the sovereign and turned to the Queen Mother for guidance.

"Perhaps the next highest ranking politician instead, Sir Hugh? The Chancellor of the Exchequer would be an idea, and place Princess Eleanor in his vacated spot."

The Master of the Household was grateful for the Queen Mother's diplomatic suggestion. "Very good, Ma'am."

The Queen was beginning to feel the princess pushed upon her at every turn, and she didn't like it. "Was my guest Miss Elliot placed next to Prince Theodore, as I asked?"

"Yes, Ma'am." Sir Hugh replied.

Thoughts of Bea being close went some way to assuaging the annoyance she was feeling.

"Your Majesty? Aren't they beautiful?" Sofia nudged her daughter.

"What? Oh…yes, beautiful. Thank you, ladies." These housekeeping tasks were the most boring of George's duties, and she was delighted to delegate them to her mother, but being Queen, she had to do this final inspection, until she had a consort of her own.

"Where are we sending the flowers this time?" George asked Sir Hugh. It was tradition that after these types of big events, the floral arrangements were broken into smaller bouquets and distributed to local hospitals, retirement homes, and other community institutions.

"We thought, Ma'am, that we could send them to the royal military retirement home. The late King was patron there and his first equerry lives there now."

George nodded. "Yes, excellent choice, Sir Hugh. I'm sure he would have been pleased with that. Do you agree, Queen Sofia?"

The Queen Mother smiled softly and looped her arm through George's. "Indeed he would. Why don't you speak with the yeoman of the cellars while I check the menu?"

George gave her mother a kiss on the hand and walked off. "Of course, Mama."

❖

Bea had been at the castle for two hours. The Queen had arranged for a car to pick her up and bring her to the castle. Her luggage had been collected earlier in the morning. George had explained that would make it easier for the staff. Bea had been a bag of nerves when she had said goodbye to her parents, and her anxiety was made worse by her mother, whose excitement had been near fever pitch for the past few days.

When she had arrived at the private entrance, she was conducted up to her room by the senior page. The bedroom was beautiful and grand, white-panelled walls edged with gold, but it was the view from the window that really took her breath away. Bea had been in the public part of Windsor Great Park with her family many times, but to see it all laid out in front of her was something special.

She had changed into her gown, a long midnight-blue chiffon with a split to the side, and was now applying her make-up at the antique dressing table. Bea had been surprised to find, when she was shown to her room, that everything she had packed in her luggage had been put away, her dress and other clothes hung up, her make-up unpacked and arranged tidily on the dressing table. Even her bear Rupert had been placed on her bed.

She looked in the mirror. *What are you doing here? You don't fit in with these people.* "I'm here for Georgie. If she wants me here, then that's where I'll be."

I'm falling in love with her. The thought came out of her subconscious and was impossible to ignore.

❖

"George, would you keep still. You're fidgeting like some poor lad on his wedding day." Cammy was doing her best to fix George's collar and white bow tie. George had been jumpy all through the dressing process.

"I'm sorry, I feel a bit on edge."

"A bit on edge? You've been a bag of nerves, man." Cammy finished with the tie and walked over to the drink decanters. "How about a wee dram before the off?"

George continued to fiddle with her collar and cuffs. "I think that would be wise. Did you ask Prince Theo to drop in before he goes downstairs?"

Cammy brought over the glass of whiskey and said, "Of course. He'll be here any minute, I'm sure."

"Good. Pour yourself one, Cammy."

Cammy smiled broadly. "Thank you, Ma'am, I wouldnae mind a wee dram." She poured out the drink and rejoined her. "So? Is it this wee lassie that's making you so jumpy?"

George nearly choked on her drink and started coughing. "What? Why would you say that?"

"Who knows? Probably the fact that you spend all the time you can speaking to her or talking about her, and because you're never nervous about these functions."

George sat down in resignation. "Do I?" Then with a big sigh she said, "Maybe I do. I've never met anyone like her, Cammy. She sees me, just me, not the Queen. When I'm with her, I feel lighter. Like all the responsibility and stress I feel is halved."

"What does she feel, Ma'am?"

George swirled the drink around in her glass. "I have no idea. Women are not my specialist subject, as you know."

"Aye, most Naval officers are supposed to have a woman in every port, but not you, George. You could have had any woman, but you didn't."

"Unlike you, Captain Cameron," George joked.

Cammy smiled and raised her glass to her friend. "Too true."

"All I know is that she is my friend. Anything more than that, then I'm at a loss. What would you suggest I do?"

"If you were an ordinary person, Ma'am, I'd advise you to ask her out."

George snorted in disgust. "I'm not a normal person though, am I? I can't take her to see a film, out to dinner, go to a bar for a drink, nothing." She downed the rest of her drink and slammed the glass down.

"Your Majesty, you may not be able to go out and do those things, but you can easily achieve them just by doing them on your own patch. You have so many advantages—use them. You've already started by asking her to spend the day with you tomorrow. Make it special."

"I'll try. I thought I'd take her out riding, maybe have a picnic?"

"That sounds a cracking idea, Ma'am. You do…ah, no." Cammy hesitated.

George stood and walked over to her. "What? Tell me."

Cammy stood to attention, her hands behind her back. "It's not my place to say, Ma'am."

George patted her on the shoulder and said, "Cammy, we've been through a lot together. You know all my secrets and are my most trusted member of staff. Tell me."

"Well, you do realize what the reaction will be to Miss Elliot as a possible partner for Your Majesty. A woman from a working class family and an anti-monarchist. If you want this woman, you'll have to fight for her."

"I know that. What I don't know is if she even likes me in that way, and even if she does, to be with me would be a life sentence. Who would voluntarily want to be a part of this lunacy?" George sat down and held her face in her hands.

"A certain Belgian princess, I hear."

George turned to Cammy with a look of steel. "That's exactly why she will never get the chance, Captain. I would never allow someone like that to rule beside me."

Cammy got the Queen's black dinner jacket from the hanger and brought it over, holding it out for George to slip her arms in. "Then I suggest, Ma'am, that you simply enjoy your time with Miss Elliot and see where it takes you. I know what pressure rests on your shoulders, George, and if someone is willing to share in the burden, for the right reason, then you have found your Queen Consort and wife." Cammy got a clothes brush and began to brush off any specks of lint from her jacket.

"So you're saying, play it by ear?"

"Indeed, Ma'am."

There was a knock at her door. Cammy opened it and let Prince Theo in.

"You wanted to see me, Georgie?" George thought Theo was looking better than he had for a long time. His unruly curly hair had been cut smartly, and his face was bright and full of smiles.

"Yes. Could you give us a minute, Captain?"

Once Cammy had left, George poured a small drink for them both. "A small snifter before the off?"

Theo laughed at his sister. "You are starting to sound like Papa."

"Perhaps. I wondered if you would keep an eye out for Miss Elliot. She's not coming with a partner, and you know that my time will be spread amongst the guests."

Theo took his drink and sat down. "Of course. Young ladies are always safe in my hands."

George was suddenly enraged. "Theo, that is not—"

"Calm down! I would never chase a girl you liked, you should know that."

She was taken aback that her brother had noticed. Cammy had certainly noticed, and she wondered if anyone else had noticed. *Has Bea?* "Why would you say that, Theo? She is my friend."

Theo finished his drink and stood. "Your face lights up like a giddy teenager's whenever you mention her name, and you are allowing her to stage a huge concert in the Mall, just to make her happy."

"It's for charity."

Her brother gave her his best dazzling smile. "Of course, Georgie. Now I promise I will be a perfect gentleman, and don't worry, I've read my notes for a change and know everything that is expected of me. I won't disappoint you."

For events such as these, every member of the royal family received an information pack on the guests, who they would be sitting with and where.

"Good man." She walked forward and pulled her brother into a hug. "You're doing well, Theo, and you could never disappoint me."

Theo looked delighted he had pleased his sister. "Well, we better get off or Granny will have my guts for garters."

"Quite," George said with a smirk. "Oh—I asked Lady Olivia to keep an eye out for her too. Between the two of you, I'm sure she can navigate this evening."

When Prince Theo was halfway out the door, he turned and said, "Can I have your permission to offer my assistance to Miss Elliot for the concert? I know a lot of musicians, bands, and artists that could help."

"Of course. That would be very kind of you."

He's going to be fine, Papa. I know it, she thought proudly.

CHAPTER THIRTEEN

Bea followed one of the pages down the grand staircase to be shown to the receiving line. This was the part that had been terrifying her. The thought of making conversation with all these eminent and important people was a daunting task.

She looked around her and tried to take in everything about the castle. She was under orders from her mum to give a detailed description on her return. The walls had red covering and gold cornicing, which along with the many magnificent and historic paintings covering the walls gave a feeling of opulence and majesty. The republican part of her wanted to be angry; all these riches could help to pay for so many of the country's services. But then she thought of George, holding a dying child's hand, feeling his pain but bringing some smiles and laughter back to the child. These conflicting notions were constantly at war inside her head.

At the bottom of the stairs and lining the route were men dressed in the Tudor style, with scarlet ceremonial dress with *GR* emblazoned on the front. On their heads they wore black Tudor hats, and they each carried a long spear.

"Excuse me, sir. Are those beefeaters?" Bea asked the page.

"Oh no, miss. Their uniform is similar, but they are the Yeoman of the Queen's bodyguard. They take part in ceremonial events, and are all senior ex-servicemen."

Bea had to admit that the sight was spectacular. It felt like she had stepped back to medieval times. She remembered something George had said to her when they were debating the subject: *Monarchy is magical, Bea. All the pageantry and strange rituals that are lost in the mists of time are important for one reason. It honours the dignity of our constitution. Monarchy represents what we were, where we are, and what we aspire to be.*

The page stopped at the back of a line of people. "Miss Elliot, if you would wait here to be called. You will be announced to Her

Majesty, then walk forward, give a bow or curtsy, and wait for the Queen to extend her hand. Then please move swiftly on to Her Majesty, the Queen Mother, and repeat the same process. From there you move on to the drawing room in front of you, where you will be greeted by members of the royal family and other members of the household."

"Thank you."

She was sixth in the line to be greeted by the Queen, and everyone in front of her was in a couple. Bea suddenly felt very alone. As the line moved up, she got her first glance of George. She looked stunning in her white tie dress suit, with a blue sash set diagonally across her chest.

Bea felt her traitorous heart began to thud wildly, and a nervous tremble began in her hands. *I can't do this. I don't belong here.* Bea took a deep breath to calm herself.

I have to do this. I have to do this for Georgie.

❖

George had been introduced to around half the guests so far and was anxiously waiting for her first sight of Bea.

"Miss Veronica Chase and Mr. Steven Crawford," the senior page announced.

The couple moved along and bowed before the Queen, looking rather nervous. George was well-practised at this ritual of receiving guests and always managed to put people at their ease.

"Good evening, Miss Chase, Mr. Crawford. I'm delighted to have you here. May I introduce the Queen Mother?" Since George didn't have a consort, Queen Sofia took the place of cohost. As the Queen lifted her head to meet the next guest, she caught her first glimpse of Bea. The whole room dropped away, and she stopped breathing as her gaze filled with the vision that was Beatrice Elliot.

George had never seen a woman look as beautiful as Bea did. Her normally straight golden hair had a soft wave, which gently cascaded down her bare shoulders and back. Her dress was a midnight blue with a bodice that accentuated her already ample bosom.

She was mesmerized. George had never seen or imagined anyone as beautiful as Bea. She was her perfect dream of what a woman should be, shining with goodness and blessed with the kindest heart she had ever encountered. Not that she had as much experience as her ladies' man of a brother, but plenty had tried to catch her eye through university, and her mother had tried to introduce her to many eligible young ladies. But seeing Bea in this moment made George realize exactly what she'd been waiting for.

Sofia nudged her daughter. "Your Majesty? George."

The Queen was knocked from her private vision. "What?"

Queen Sofia pointed quickly to the next approaching guest.

"Oh, sorry, Mama. I was lost in my thoughts," George whispered.

"Yes, and I can tell exactly what thoughts you were lost in, my dear." Queen Sofia smiled knowingly.

George extended her hand to the guest and said, "Good evening. It's wonderful that you could join us."

After a few more had passed, it was finally time for Bea to be announced. George felt her mouth dry up. *Get a grip on yourself.*

Moments later the page announced, "Miss Beatrice Elliot."

Bea gave the Queen a deep curtsy, and when George took her hand, she was sure she could feel electricity pass between them. "Good evening, Miss Elliot. I am so glad you could join us. Have the staff been looking after you?"

"Oh yes, Your Majesty. Thank you."

George beamed with happiness. "Jolly good. Let me introduce Queen Sofia, the Queen Mother."

"Hello, Miss Elliot. I've heard a great deal about you from the Queen. I look forward to talking to you later."

"Thank you, Your Majesty." When Bea looked unsure of what to do next, George stepped in and said, "If you go through to the reception room, my brother will meet you there."

As she watched Bea walk off, she ached to be with her, to escort her. *She should be with me.*

Bea felt like she had met hundreds of people, despite the fact there were only eighty guests. As soon as she entered the reception room, she was approached by a smiling Prince Theodore. Bea liked him very much; he was a great deal more laid back than George, but she supposed they had different demands placed upon them.

At the moment she was meeting the siblings' cousins, Lady Victoria and Lord Max Buckingham. Like George, they were both tall and well built, although unlike George and Theo had fair hair.

"Delighted to meet you, Beatrice. Do call me Vicki, and this one here is Max. We've never thought he was serious enough to be a Lord."

Max laughed and gave his sister a playful swat. "Don't listen to her, Miss Elliot. We are very happy to meet you though. Our elder brother Julian is schmoozing with Princess Eleanor, so you'll need to meet him later. George has told us a great deal about you."

"She has?" She needn't have been nervous about meeting George's family. They were warm and welcoming, not like she'd imagined at all. On the other hand, she had a sick feeling at the thought of Princess Eleanor. She hadn't been introduced and had only seen her from afar, but the long-legged brunette looked like a model.

"Oh yes. You're the anti-monarchist."

Bea almost died of embarrassment, but the three royals didn't show any discomfort or anger; instead they looked amused. "Well, yes. Queen Georgina and I have a lively debate on the matter, but she has shown me that there is another side to the story."

"Good old Georgie," Theo exclaimed. "Granny challenged her to persuade Bea here of the merits of monarchy."

She watched them laugh together. They seemed a close family. Coming from a small family, she envied George her brother and cousins.

"I understand you're staying on tomorrow, Miss Elliot?" Vicki said.

"Yes. The Queen wanted to show me around."

Vicki took her hand and said, "Do get George to bring you to the stables. Our mama and I run them for the Queen."

An older gentlemen walked over with a bright smiling face. "Will you introduce me, Vicki?"

"Of course, Papa. Miss Beatrice Elliot, this is our father, the Duke of Bransford."

"Pleased to meet you, sir." Bea said nervously.

"A pleasure, Miss Elliot. Her Majesty has told us a great deal about you. My wife, Princess Grace, is eager to meet you as well, but she's off talking horses with some person or another. I'll find you after dinner to introduce you, if I may?"

"Of course, sir." The duke smiled and left her with Theo.

Theo pointed over to the doors to the banqueting hall where the royal fanfare was struck up by the ceremonial guard. "We better look lively. It looks like we're under starter's orders." Theo offered Bea his arm and guided her to the doors and said, "If you follow the line through the doors, a page will conduct you to your seat. We have to enter with the Queen and Queen Mother, but I'll see you very soon."

Bea smiled at the Prince. "Thank you, Your Royal Highness. You are very kind."

"Not at all. My sister wishes you to be very comfortable here, so I am at your service."

Bea found her seat, but everyone remained standing while the royal family, led by the Queen, entered the banqueting hall in procession, to the tune of the national anthem.

The dinner was spectacular, and although they had not spent any time together as yet, she could feel the Queen's gaze upon her often. She would smile in return before the Queen would go back to chatting with the prime minister.

After the meal was finished a strange droning sound could be heard. Before she could ask, Theo said, "Oh God. Here come the bloody pipers."

The massed band of the Pipes and Drums of the Black Watch entered the room and marched round the table. The glasses and cutlery shook at the loud noise. George had a smile on her face. Theo rolled his eyes. "My sister insists on keeping up this tradition even though everyone under the age of forty hates it. She loves this infernal music just like Papa did."

After the music had finished the Queen stood and the room went silent. "I want to thank you all for being here this evening. My father, the King, would have been delighted by the support everyone has given to us since his death. One of the last things my father said to me before he died was…"

Bea saw the same look of terror on George's face as she had the morning at the hospital. Her breathing became short, and she couldn't force her words out. This was a panic attack and all Bea wanted to do was get up and help bring George back, but that was impossible. Some of the guests started to shift uncomfortably as they watched the Queen struggle.

George looked to Bea in desperation, and the young woman mouthed, *Close your eyes and breathe.*

Never taking her eyes off Bea, George began visibly to calm, and she spoke the rest of the speech as if directed to Bea.

Afterwards the guests were directed through to the library where a display of the royal collection had been set up as an after-dinner entertainment for the guests, while they enjoyed coffee. The curator gave the guests a short talk on the collection, and then the royal family mingled with the guests as they looked round the artefacts.

After several attempts, George finally was able to make her way over to Bea, who was standing with Theo and Lady Olivia.

"Miss Elliot, could I show you around." George offered her arm, and Bea gladly took it. "Excuse us, Lady Olivia, Prince Theo."

When they were out of earshot, George said, "I'm sorry it's taken so long to have some time with you, Bea."

"Not at all, Georgie. You have a lot of guests to attend to, and I'm not as important as these dignitaries around us."

George stopped and looked Bea in the eye. "You're wrong. You are very important to me."

Bea seemed quite taken aback and unsure how to respond, so George took the initiative. "I would like to show you a few pieces of the collection that might interest you, but first, I wonder, could I introduce you to my granny, the Dowager Queen? Besides my mother, she is the other great influence in my life."

"I would be delighted," Bea managed to croak out, clearly nervous about meeting the family matriarch.

George led them to the side of the room, where Queen Adrianna sat with her childhood friend and companion Lady Celia, Countess of Warwick, and the Queen Mother.

The three women stood as George approached.

"Oh, please do sit, ladies."

The Dowager Queen gripped a walking stick with a silver handle in the shape of a horse's head and seemed to really rely on it as she lowered herself back down to the chair.

"Granny, Lady Celia, may I present my friend, Miss Beatrice Elliot. She works with the hospice charity I've become involved with."

"Ah. The republican. Tell me, young lady, would you have us all beheaded in Trafalgar Square?"

Bea was struck dumb for a few seconds, while the three aristocrats around her laughed. Then, to George's surprise, she retorted, "After the beautiful dinner I've just enjoyed, you are all safe for the moment, Your Majesty."

Queen Adrianna snorted with laughter. "Oh, I like this one, George. She's as sharp as a tack."

After that Bea relaxed as they all chatted together, and George was delighted. When George led her off to look around, Queen Sofia said, "I think my daughter is besotted with that young woman."

"Hmm. I rather got that impression, my dear," Adrianna replied.

Lady Celia added, "She seems very nice, but she has a few things going against her. An anti-monarchist and from a working-class background. Has it ever been done? Surely only middle and upper classes have married into the family?"

"Remember the famous saying, Celia," the Dowager Queen retorted. "There is no king who has not had a slave among his ancestors, and no slave who has not had a king among his. There's nothing wrong with a bit of fresh blood. Do you agree, Sofia?"

"Indeed. I just want George to be happy like her papa and me. She's toed the line her whole life, and behaved impeccably. I don't want her to choose someone out of duty."

Adrianna reached over and took her daughter-in-law's hand. "Then I suggest we monitor the situation, and if they appear as close by the summer holidays in August, you invite her to Balmoral."

Balmoral was the traditional testing ground for potential additions to the royal family. It encompassed everything that the royal family enjoyed—outdoor pursuits and community events, all done in the harshest of Scottish weather. The family believed if someone didn't pass the Balmoral test, they didn't have the character to join the family.

Queen Sofia nodded. "I think that would be wise."

"Who is that common little tart draped over the Queen, Julian?" Eleanor asked angrily.

As soon as Julian had spotted the mystery blonde George was giving all her attention to, he had dispatched his wife Marta to find out more. "Just some woman from the charity my cousin has been working with. No threat to our plans."

He looked up and saw his wife walking over. "Well?"

"They are the best of friends, apparently. They talk on the phone most nights, and she has privileged access to the Queen. Don't worry though, Eleanor, I'm sure the Queen just finds her working-class ways amusing. At worst she would be nothing more than a mistress. George knows she must marry someone with breeding."

Julian was worried though, because unlike him, George had no taste for mistresses. The Queen was just like the King before her; she believed in all the guff about setting an example to the nation.

If George did start seeing this woman, she would have only one intention. "Marta, I think it's time we were introduced to this woman, and let Eleanor talk to the Queen. Follow me."

Chapter Fourteen

George took great pleasure in describing the stories and history behind all the treasures on display, and from what she could tell, Bea was enjoying it.

"Of course, there would be a lot more in the collection if it wasn't for Oliver Cromwell and the English revolution."

"Why?" Bea asked.

George pointed up at a painting of her ancestor Charles I. "After Oliver Cromwell and the Puritans ousted and beheaded Charles, Cromwell sold off hundreds of pieces of the collection to pay for his army and government. When the monarchy was reinstated, his son Charles II tried to buy back as much as he could, but some pieces were lost."

George leaned into Bea and said, "I suppose that's what you would have in mind for me, Miss Elliot?"

"What, behead you? No, you're far too good-looking and handsome to lose your head." Bea closed her eyes tightly, as if trying to hide. "I'm sorry. That wasn't appropriate, Ma'am."

George grinned back at her with glee. "I like it when you are inappropriate with me. No one else ever is. Please don't change." *She thinks I'm good-looking and handsome.* The thought filled her with joy.

"Excuse me, Your Majesty?"

George looked up to find her cousin Julian and his wife.

"Would you introduce us to your new friend?" Julian smiled, but it looked forced.

George groaned internally. Just when she thought she had Bea all to herself, her least-favourite cousin and his wife had to appear.

"Of course. This is Miss Beatrice Elliot, and Beatrice, this is my cousin, Lord Julian, Viscount Anglesey, and his wife, Lady Marta."

"I'm pleased to meet you both." Bea gave a very quick curtsy to them both.

Lady Marta looked at Bea like she was something on the bottom of her shoe, and it made George fume.

"It must be a dream for you to visit Windsor."

"It is, Lady Marta."

"Let us introduce you to the prime minister. It wouldn't do to monopolize so much of the Queen's time, now would it?"

"Now look here—" Before the Queen had a chance to do anything, Julian and Marta had whisked Bea off.

Bloody idiots. George didn't want to make a scene in the room full of people, but she would have a chat with Julian about his disrespectful interruption.

"Hello, Your Majesty. We haven't had the chance to talk yet."

George knew by the accent who was talking. "Princess Eleanor. I hope you've had a pleasant evening."

The princess gave a deep over-exaggerated curtsy, which gave the Queen an eyeful of her assets. It did nothing for George, who was annoyed that she had been so obviously manoeuvred into this situation.

"I'm glad to be here to spend some time with Your Majesty."

George scowled and lifted a drink from the tray of one of the passing servers. "This evening was not about spending time with me. It was about remembering the King and thanking all those who have supported my family."

"Of course. Would you show me some of these lovely things?"

George knew she had no choice but to be polite and go along with it.

❖

Across the room Bea was talking with Bo Dixon. Viscount Anglesey and his wife had ditched her as soon as she was introduced to the prime minister. Under normal circumstances Bea would have been riveted, but she couldn't help but be distracted by Princess Eleanor, giggling and laughing at whatever the Queen was telling her.

"She's marvellous, isn't she?"

Bea realized she had been caught staring. "Sorry?"

Bo took a sip of her drink and smiled. "Her Majesty."

"Oh yes. Yes, she is."

"I understand your position, Beatrice."

"What position are you referring to, Miss Dixon?" Bea worried that the prime minister had noticed the adoring way she looked at the Queen.

"I've read about your background. Socialist, anti-monarchist, I believe you were at more than one demo through your university years, and I know about the tragedy that drives you."

Bea was shocked at the information that Bo Dixon had. "How do you know all that? I've never met you before."

Bo put a comforting hand on Bea's shoulder. "I always make it my business to have as much information as possible. Don't be alarmed, but when you are working so closely with the sovereign, a sovereign whose life has been threatened, it is my duty to know everything about you."

"I suppose that's true," Bea said.

"I was like you. I have been a socialist all my life, Beatrice. Joined the Labour Party at university, took part in debates and rallies. I always thought it repugnant that the aristocracy still had a place in modern Britain. People who had titles and money because of an accident of birth. I campaigned for reform of the political system, to curtail the rights of the monarchy and the House of Lords. Britain is a democracy and power rests with Parliament."

"Are you saying your opinion has changed, Prime Minister?"

Bo smiled while slowly choosing her words. "I would say *softened my opinion* is more apt. When I became an MP and started to take part in those ceremonies I thought silly and outdated, I saw them in a different light. You felt like you were taking part in history, something that has remained unchanged for centuries. It gives the people a feeling of continuity. Politicians may come and go, but British democracy will always remain unchanging, linked to a stable monarchy."

Bea looked back over to where George was standing, explaining some work of art to the princess while she edged ever closer.

"My head and my heart are at war, Prime Minister. I have these ideals, these things I've always believed in, and then I've gotten to know the Queen and see what good things she does. She cares deeply about her people, and really works hard."

Bo nodded. "We are blessed that the last few generations of the family have been decent people. No scandals like they've had in the past. When I became leader of the opposition I began to spend more time around the royal family at functions and state occasions. I found the King to be very knowledgeable on a wide variety of subjects, and very approachable. I haven't known the Queen for long, but she seems to be very much her father's daughter. Her popularity in the opinion polls is sky high, so I don't see the people clamouring for a republic in our lifetime."

What Bo said made sense, and it had really helped clear up her messy thoughts. "So you're saying I should just go with the status quo?"

The prime minister laughed softly. "Oh, I wouldn't say that, Beatrice. There are always ways it can be adapted—the success of our constitution is the fact that it constantly evolves and modernizes. We are at the dawn of a new age, Miss Elliot, and I'd rather be on Queen Georgina's side than against her."

Bea lifted her glass in toast to Bo and said, "Thank you, Prime Minister. You make a lot of sense."

"I always do, Beatrice."

❖

Bea awoke the next morning feeling happier. After her chat with the prime minister the previous evening, she had decided to relax and enjoy her friendship with George, without worrying constantly and arguing with herself. The Queen had escorted Bea to her room and promised to call for her at ten o'clock the next morning. George had arranged for breakfast to be brought to her room, to give her some privacy from the rest of the guests.

Bea looked at herself in the mirror and wondered if she looked all right. George had said to dress casually, as they would be walking around the grounds, but she always wanted to look her best. She had her hair back in a ponytail and wore a pair of figure-hugging jeans and a cream cashmere cowl-necked jumper.

"Will I do, Abby? I hope so."

There was a knock at the door at precisely ten o'clock, and immediately the butterflies started to flutter around her stomach.

She walked to the door and grasped the handle. *Okay. Deep breath, Bea.*

When she opened the door, she found a smiling George standing waiting for her. "Good morning, Bea. Are you ready for our sightseeing walk?"

She gave a quick curtsy. "Oh yes, Your Majesty." George looked wonderful in a wool cricket jumper and jeans. Bea imagined herself placing her head on George's chest and snuggling into the cosy jumper.

"If you don't mind, there are some people I'd like you to meet. Can we come in?"

Bea was slightly puzzled. "Of course."

They went into the room and George said, "All dogs, come."

In trotted her faithful companions, tails wagging. "Sit." The three dogs sat in a line awaiting their next command.

Bea reached out and grasped the Queen's arm. "Aww, you brought your dogs? They're so sweet."

George was full of smiles. "They go everywhere with me, so I hoped you wouldn't mind them coming with us."

"Mind? They're adorable." Bea got down on her knees so she was eye level with the first dog, a big black Labrador. "And who's this big boy?"

"That's Shadow, he's the leader—well, below me obviously. Shadow, shake."

The black dog lifted his paw for Bea to take. She shook his paw and clapped his big head. Shadow rewarded her with licks to the face, making Bea giggle.

The dog next to Shadow barked with impatience.

"Baxter, wait," George commanded.

"It's okay, Georgie." Bea patted her lap. "Come on then. So this is Baxter the boxer?"

"Yes. He's the silly one of the bunch. He's not the brightest, but he's very loving and he loves to play."

Baxter was just about sitting on her lap and gave his new friend lots of kisses. "Oh, you are a handsome boy, Baxter." Bea scratched his ears and kissed his head.

George put a hand on her shoulder. "They'll make a mess of your clothes. You look beautiful, by the way."

She looked up at George and smiled. "Thank you, and don't worry, I love dogs."

Rex had been sitting apart from the other two dogs looking over shyly. Bea noticed he wasn't joining the others and got up and went over to him. "Are you a shy boy?"

George knelt beside them and clapped the dog's head. "This was my father's dog, Rex. He's struggled since he died. I took him because he seemed to be happier around me. Haven't you, Rexie? He's been very nervous around other people."

Bea held her hand out for him to sniff, without feeling pressured. The Labrador sniffed and then tentatively licked her hand. "Good boy, Rex. I won't hurt you."

Rex looked into her eyes as if he was thinking hard. He then got up and walked over to her and began peppering her face with kisses.

"Oh, you are a good boy, Rexie." Bea put her arms round the dog and hugged him.

"How did you do that, Bea? He's distant with everyone, even my mama."

Bea looked into George's eyes and smiled. "I know what it's like to grieve. He just needs love and understanding. When you lose someone that close to you, you need someone who understands your pain."

"Thank you. You don't know how much I appreciate your friendship, and now I think Rexie will be your friend for life."

"I'll be here as long as he wants me to be."

The double meaning in Bea's statement was deliberate. When she had watched George with Princess Eleanor the night before, she'd realized she was on borrowed time. It might not be Eleanor, but somebody like her would come along eventually. A suitable aristocrat or middle- to upper-class woman would someday take George away from her, and she knew it would break her heart.

Princess Eleanor was furious. She had thought she could persuade George to spend some time with her today, but she had been informed by the Queen's private secretary that she was entirely unavailable. When she returned to her room, she found her cases sitting packed and ready to depart. She stormed into Viscount Anglesey's room. He and his wife had long ago given up sharing a bedroom. "Who is this woman, Julian? I couldn't get George's attention from her last night, and now she's spending the day with her."

This turn of events had taken Julian and his plans by surprise. He had seen the way George looked at this woman, and it worried him.

"I'll admit, this situation has taken me by surprise. My cousin has never had a female friend like this before, but I won't let it affect our plans. I'll get someone to look into her background—I'm sure there's something that will discredit her. Besides, my family does not accept working-class brides, Eleanor."

"They better not, Julian, because all this should be mine."

He stood up quickly and grabbed her by the hair. "Remember who's running the show here." He loosened his grip and kissed her lips. "I'll work out a way to get rid of this woman. Your next opportunity to be with her will be at the races at Royal Ascot. Don't waste the opportunity."

George led the way through the ornate corridors and rooms, followed by Bea and the dogs. Rex was glued to Bea's side and looking a great deal happier.

As they walked through the castle, they passed a few members of the housekeeping staff, who would stop what they were doing and bow. George always acknowledged them and apologized for disturbing them.

"If you spot anything you would like to know about, Bea, just shout out and we'll stop. I didn't want to overwhelm you on your first visit, so I thought we'd start with interesting places in the grounds and then have a picnic for lunch. I'm so glad it turned out warmish and dry today."

"That sounds lovely, Ma'am."

"My granny used to take us on these sorts of tours when we were younger. She wanted us to understand everything about our dynasty and where we fit into that. There's one room I want to show you inside."

She opened up two huge wooden doors, and they entered into the most spectacular wood-panelled room. The floor was covered with a huge red and gold woven rug and a banquet table, much like the one they sat at last night, only smaller, sat in the middle of the room.

George spotted that they had disturbed two members of staff both working at the fireplace halfway down the room. The two men got up quickly and bowed. George said, "I'm sorry for the intrusion. Please just ignore that we're here." Bea found it sweet that George apologized to the staff—after all, it was her house. But that was George. Considerate and kind.

"The man tending the fire is the royal fender. His team is in charge of maintaining all the fires and fireplaces in the castle."

"That's someone's job?" Bea said, somewhat surprised.

"Yes, we like to keep all of the old skills alive. Besides, in a place this big you need the heat from the fires as well as modern heating. The other chap is the royal clockmaker—he takes care of all the clocks on the estate."

"My goodness. This really is like stepping into the past."

George stood with her hands in her pockets and rocked on her heels nervously. She truly hoped these opulent surroundings didn't make Bea angry. Shadow and Baxter trotted over to the sumptuous carpet and lay down, but Rex stayed sitting beside Bea. She reached down and clapped her new friend.

It struck George that Bea was showing the same care to Rex as she had done with her. She saw the hurt inside them both and wanted to ease the pain she found there. Never before in the Queen's life had she wanted to say the words *I love you*. But she did now, and it was agony to keep these words inside.

"Tell me about the room then. You were so good at explaining the history of the things on display last night," Bea asked.

"I enjoyed talking to you about them. You're so easy to talk to." George looked at her feet shyly.

"Did you enjoy telling Princess Eleanor?" Bea asked coyly.

George looked her right in the eye and said, "No. She wasn't interested in what I had to say."

Bea teased, "Was she more interested in your prize bull qualities?"

George burst out laughing. She could always rely on Bea to release any tension she was feeling. She put her fingers above her head, making the horns of a bull, and scratched the floor with her foot as if it was a hoof. "Moo, moo."

"I think I'll call you Bully." Bea giggled.

"Well, since you're interested in more than my prize bull qualities, I'll tell you about the room."

"Please do, Your Majesty." Bea bent down in an exaggerated curtsy.

George shook her head with a smile. "Well, Miss Elliot, this is the Waterloo chamber. It was built to commemorate the final battle at Waterloo in 1815, when Napoleon was finally defeated. If you look up to the roof, you can see the beams were made to look like the bow of a ship."

Bea peered up at the ceiling. "Oh yes. That's clever."

"The wooden panels on the walls are in fact a lot older than the room. They were carved for the then royal chapel in the 1620s. When it was demolished, they were salvaged and put up here. The paintings around the room are all politicians, royals, and important people from around the time of the war with France."

George watched Bea gaze around the room in silence. She couldn't tell if she was impressed or appalled at the treasures on show. "I know what you're thinking."

Bea crossed her arms and looked at her friend quizzically. "Oh? Do tell, Georgie."

"That all these treasures and valuable things could pay for a great deal in this country, but I don't actually own these things, I'm just the trustee for my lifetime. They belong to the nation, and even if I wasn't here, they could never be sold. They would still have to be kept just as they are."

"I wasn't thinking that, actually, Georgie. I was thinking of how beautiful it all was, but since you brought it up, how do the people get to enjoy all these beautiful things?"

George took her hand and led her over to a rather large painting of a man in what looked like religious garb. "This painting is Pope Pius VII by Sir Thomas Lawrence. It only arrived back two weeks ago—it's been at the Royal Portrait Gallery for the past six months. Museums and galleries up and down the country submit requests to borrow the paintings and other items. They all go out on a rotation. And Windsor is open to the public all year, apart from Easter court and during Ascot."

Bea smiled. "You've convinced me, Georgie."

George never let go of her hand and then quite naturally pulled her in closer.

Bea pulled back from her abruptly when Sir Michael entered the room and cleared his throat to get her attention.

"Can I help you, Sir Michael? I did say I was having some private time until this afternoon."

Sir Michael walked a few more steps into the room and bowed. "I'm sorry, Your Majesty, but I thought you might want to see the guest list for Your Majesty's birthday celebrations. Number Ten want the invites to go out this week."

George sighed and spoke softly to Bea. "Excuse me for one minute." After a quick word, Sir Michael hurried away. "Are you ready to continue our tour?"

Bea nodded and followed George from the chamber, closely followed by the dogs. Bea asked, "I'm keeping you from your work, aren't I?"

"No, of course not. I got started on my boxes early this morning, and I'll finish up the rest this evening. Sir Michael knew I asked for some personal time, he just didn't realize how important it was to me. I simply let him know my time with you is sacrosanct. Come on."

As George and Bea approached the steps to the medieval-looking St George's Chapel, George turned and addressed the dogs following them, "All dogs, stay. You know you can't come in." Shadow and Baxter went off to play on the grass, but Rex sat and began to whine. Bea crouched down and hugged the dog. "It's all right, Rexie. We won't be long." After a final kiss on the head, Rex trotted off after the other two dogs.

"You're amazing with him, you know," George said.

Bea stood and walked up the ancient stone steps with her friend. "Thanks. What about them?" She pointed to Inspector Lang and his men, who had joined them discreetly as the Queen left the safety of the castle.

"Don't worry about them. They'll take up position outside until I come out."

George opened the huge oak door and waved her inside. Bea gasped at the beauty of the ancient church. The black-and-white stone tiles that ran the length and breadth of the church, gave it the look of a giant chessboard. The wooden pews ran down both sides of the building culminating in the worship area at the top.

"It's simply astounding, Georgie. It's like a smaller version of Westminster Abbey. The stained glass alone is beautiful."

George pointed up to the glass windows and said. "That's always been my favourite one. St. George slaying the dragon. When I would sit here during services, I would imagine I was my namesake, riding my horse into battle. Come on, I'll show the sovereign's stall."

Bea followed her up to the front, where a large oak booth, set apart and covered in tapestries, sat. "What's this?"

George climbed up the three stairs to the side and sat down. "This is the sovereign's booth, my seat for attending services here. You see, no one can sit higher than the sovereign, so my chair has to set higher than the rest of the pews."

Bea put her hand on her hip. "Oh, really?"

"I thought that might annoy you." George winked down to her.

Bea raised an eyebrow, knowing she was being played with. "Does anyone else get their own seat? Or do the commoners just have to take what's left?"

George walked down the steps to rejoin her guest. "The Knights of the Garter each get their own seat for life." She pointed up to the coats of arms on display above the wooden pews.

"I've heard about the Garter knights, but I don't really know what it means. Is it another hereditary thing?"

"Oh no. The sovereign appoints knights based on what they have done to help the nation. Unlike most of the other honours, this one is not in the Government's hands—it's entirely within my gift. It was started by Edward III, the man who founded this chapel. He wanted to create a Camelot-style round table of knights. There are only ever twenty-four knights, plus the royal knights. My father made me a knight following my installation as Princess of Wales. There is a service every June, where all the knights gather for a service here, and then we walk in procession down to the castle and have a meal together in the Waterloo chamber."

Bea thought for a moment and said, "Is that the thing where you all wear the big blue cloaks and a hat with a long feather? I think I've seen it on the news."

George smiled at Bea's description. "They're called Garter Robes, and there's no higher honour in the United Kingdom. It's a very solemn ceremony."

Bea closed her eyes and took a breath. "You can almost feel the history in the atmosphere of this place. It feels ancient, think how many people have sat in this church. Ordinary people and kings and queens."

"A lot of them are under your feet."

Bea looked down at her feet and jumped. "What do you mean, Georgie?"

George walked up to her and whispered, "There's a royal vault beneath your feet"—she pointed down—"all the way back to Edward IV in 1483. There's Henry V, Henry VIII, all beneath your feet."

Bea reached out and held on to her arm. "Don't tell me that, Georgie. That's creepy."

As if it was the most natural thing in the world, George put her arm round Bea's shoulder, and guided her down the left wing of the chapel. "Don't worry, I won't let the ghosties get you."

She immediately relaxed in the crook of the Queen's arm. "Where are we going?"

"To a special part of the church called King Edward XI memorial chapel. I want you to meet my papa."

Chapter Fifteen

Viscount Anglesey and his wife Marta were on their way back to their London home.

"Should I expect you home this evening, Julian?"

"No, and don't pretend that news upsets you." Julian and his wife had not married for love and had always led separate private lives. Marta wanted the Viscount's position as a member of the royal family and Julian rather liked the large fortune Marta's father had left her.

"I would never pretend to miss you, Julian." After a long silence Marta said, "I heard an interesting rumour from one of the pages at Windsor. Would you like to hear it?"

Julian looked at her with a sneer. "And how did you obtain this information? Try and keep your assignations away from the staff, my dear wife."

"Do you want to know?"

"Tell me then," Julian said with growing frustration.

"The Queen Mother and Queen Adrianna were overheard to say—"

"What?"

"To say that if George continued in her attentions to that common little bitch, then they should invite her to Balmoral, and you know what that means."

"Have they gone mad? They would let some common little charity worker pollute our bloodline?" Julian shouted.

"Don't shoot the messenger, darling. I thought you would like the chance to do something about it," Marta said defensively.

Julian activated the car's on-board computer and called his private secretary.

"How may I assist you, sir?"

"I want every bit of information you can find on a Miss Beatrice Elliot. I want to know about all the skeletons in her cupboard. Contact any of the Queen's staff who you think would talk and find out what exactly is going on with this woman."

"I will do my best, sir."

❖

The chapel was a lot bigger than Bea initially thought, with many parts of it leading off the main part of the church.

They approached a stone sarcophagus set atop a large stone platform. The King's still body was carved into the top of the sarcophagus, like the ones Bea had seen on a trip to Westminster Abbey.

"Do sit down, Bea." George pointed to the pews in front of the tomb. "I come here to think. I miss his good advice. He always knew the right thing to say or do." She sat next to Bea.

"How have the panic attacks been?"

George smiled. "A great deal better, since I met you. It's been a real comfort to me, having someone who understands these stupid things."

Bea took George's hand and gave it a squeeze. "They aren't stupid—it's just your body reacting to stress."

George sighed. "It makes me feel weak. I hate feeling out of control, and I think I've been worrying about this upcoming week."

Bea turned round to fully face George and absent-mindedly stroked the back of her hand. "What happens this week?"

"There's a memorial service at Westminster Abbey. It's to mark the official end of the late King's mourning period, and the start of my coronation celebration year. Dignitaries are flying in from all over the world, and it's being shown live on TV. I have to make a speech about my father and his legacy. Every time I think about it, I just imagine the walls of the cathedral closing in on me, and I get that tight feeling in my chest. I wish you could be there. I know I would feel much calmer," George hinted.

Bea wanted nothing more than to be there for her friend but knew it was impossible, just as impossible as loving her. "I wish I could too but…"

George's face lit up. "Would you come if I got you an invitation?"

"It wouldn't be appropriate for me to be there, Georgie. It's not my place."

The Queen's face turned from smiles to anger in a second. "Is it any more appropriate for the dozen European aristocrats being there, who are more interested in my crown than paying respect to my papa? Or the countless politicians who I have never met in my life, when all I need is you?"

She stood and stormed off angrily towards her father's tomb.

Bea was left astonished at what she had heard. *I'm not imagining it, she feels something too. What are we going to do?* She got up and walked over to George, who was resting her palms against the cold marble tomb. She placed a hand on George's and just waited for her to speak.

"I'm very sorry for my outburst Bea. I'm just feeling under a great deal of pressure. I understand your point and I won't ask again."

All George could think of was having Bea at her side always, as her consort, and then it would always be appropriate. *Papa, I've found my Queen Consort, and I can't have her. Tell me what I should do?* she silently prayed.

"Georgie? Will you look at me?"

George turned, but she feared Bea could see the overwhelming emotions barely being held back, behind her eyes.

"You don't have to apologize. I know you're feeling under strain. I would like to be there for you, you know I would, but I have my work. The days I'm not out of the office with you visiting the sites, I spend trying to catch up with my work."

George got hold of herself and let her controlled persona fall into place.

"Oh no, don't go all stoic on me again, Your Majesty." Bea opened her arms.

George leapt on the invitation and engulfed Bea in her arms, trying to soak up everything about her, the woman who brought calm to her soul. Bea burrowed her head into George's chest, and after a minute of soaking up everything they could give to each other, George said, "How about we put this behind us and enjoy the rest of our day?"

"Sounds good." Bea pulled back from the hug and smiled.

"Come on then, I promised my Aunt Grace and Vicki that I would take you down to the stables."

❖

Bea had enjoyed her visit to the stables or, as the Queen had corrected her, the Royal Mews. Princess Grace was very warm and open to her, just like Lady Vicki, Lord Max, and their father. So unlike Viscount Anglesey, who'd looked at her with utter contempt the previous evening.

As well as showing Bea around, George caught up with her aunt and cousin, discussing the progress of various horses. Bea had become a little lost in their conversation, but she did work out that one of the

Queen's horses, Time for Tea, was one of the favourites for Royal Ascot this year.

They were now walking, with the three dogs, to the picnic spot George had picked out.

"I hope all the horse talk didn't bore you, Bea. I just haven't had the time to check on the progress of my horses very much, and it's getting awfully close to Ascot."

"Of course not. It was really interesting, actually. When you said stables, I thought it would just be ten or so stalls, but that place is like a whole other estate."

George whistled for the dogs to catch up. "All the horses that serve the royal family are housed there. From the little Shetland ponies for the younger members of the family, right up to the race horses, polo horses, and ceremonial horses. It's a big operation—that's why I'm so glad I have my aunt and Vicki to run it in my absence. I hope I can get you to ride the next time."

Bea laughed; despite everyone's insistence she had avoided taking a ride. "Maybe another time. Where exactly are we walking to?"

George pointed ahead of her. "Just over by that old oak tree. Do you see it? It's one of my favourite spots."

Bea saw a young page standing under the tree up ahead. When they got closer, she found a large blanket had been placed on the ground, and an old-style picnic basket placed on it. "This is wonderful, George. It's like a real old-fashioned picnic."

The page bowed and the Queen said, "Thank you, Jamie. Do you have the box I asked for as well?"

"Yes, Your Majesty." He handed over a medium-sized box. "Would you like me to serve, Ma'am?"

"No, thank you. We'll be fine." The young man bowed and walked away. "Dogs, go play."

Shadow and Baxter ran off, full of barks and yelps, but Rex lay down on the grass next to Bea. "Don't come on the blanket, Rexie."

Bea looked around and marvelled at the view of the estate. "This is just magnificent, Georgie."

"I think so, it's a home to me. We try to come here most weekends. It might be an ancient castle, but it's a living, breathing home and community, not just a relic."

"Mum and Dad brought us here quite a few times over the years, but I've never seen it from this angle. Is this part private?"

George indicated for them both to sit. "Yes. The majority of the grounds are open to the public. It's very popular with dog walkers, families, and of course we have polo club and Windsor cricket club."

"It really is a little community," Bea said.

"Before we eat, I want to show you something." George opened up the box the page had given her, and took out the model battleship Bea had given her. It had been fully built and painted.

"Is that the model I gave you?"

George handed it over to Bea to examine. "Yes. I enjoyed it a great deal. I wanted to show you before I got it mounted in a case."

Bea handed it back carefully and smiled. "It's beautiful. I'm glad some silly little gift gave you some joy."

George lifted Bea's hand and kissed her knuckles. "It was the most thoughtful gift I've ever gotten, thank you. Now, shall we eat? I'm not sure what's in here—I got my mother to pick the food. I have no idea about these things."

She opened up the large basket to find several containers of food, a bottle of champagne, bottles of water, as well as a flask of tea. The plates, cutlery, and glasses were strapped to the lid of the basket.

"This looks amazing, Georgie. Would you let me serve you?"

"That would be wonderful. I'll get the champagne though. A lady should never open a bottle of champagne, only be served it."

Bea looked up from her task of filling the plates with food. "My, that was smooth, Your Majesty."

The cork gave a gentle pop, and George poured the liquid into the two glasses. "I wasn't trying to be smooth. It's something that Granny has always said, and I always do what Granny tells me. It's easier in the long run."

"I'm not posh enough to be a lady," Bea said with a touch of sadness in her voice.

George reached over and placed her fingers softly under her chin, lifting Bea's head gently. "It takes more than an accident of birth to make a lady."

"Well, if I'm a lady, what are you?"

"The prize bull of course," George said with a wink.

Bea giggled. "Of course you are, Bully." She handed over a full plate of food and received her glass of champagne. "I feel quite decadent. I've never had champagne at lunch, and this food is beautiful." She began to dish out her own plate.

"All my family loves a good picnic. Especially up at Balmoral—in the summer, we have a barbecue by the river. It's beautiful."

"I thought you would have some poor servants carrying tables, chairs, and all the cutlery and glasses, so you could dine in style. That's what you see the royals doing in all the films."

"Don't forget the gold plates," George teased. "Only joking. We only do that if we have Granny with us. Would you have the Dowager Queen sitting on the ground?"

When Bea thought of the formidable older woman sitting on the grass, it just didn't compute. "Fair point, Your Majesty."

There were a few minutes of silence while the pair began to eat, and then George said, "You won't tell Theo you call me Bully, will you?"

"I won't call you it if you don't like it." Bea was fascinated by the way the Queen could turn from confident monarch to extremely shy woman in a matter of moments with her. When she saw George like this, trying not to meet her eyes and all bashful, she just wanted to kiss her so badly.

"No. I like it—it's just that Theo would give me a fearful ribbing about it."

Bea put down her plate and helped herself to a bottle of water from the basket. "I like your brother very much, he's great fun. He asked to help with the coronation concert."

"Yes, he asked my permission to ask you. I'm glad you like Theo. He's a good boy."

Bea stopped midchew. "Your permission?"

George looked confused. "Yes, why?"

"Why does he need your permission?"

George refilled both their champagne glasses. "I am the Queen and head of the family. They look to me for leadership and everyone knows their place."

Bea shook her head in amazement. "You really are the bull of the herd aren't you? Sometimes I don't know whether you're being completely serious or not."

"I assure you, Bea, I never joke about matters like that. It's just the way my family works. We do things in a very traditional way."

Bea thought she had touched a nerve, so she decided to leave the subject alone. "I'll be delighted with the help. He knows a lot of the artists and bands we hope to attract. Theo's very different from you, isn't he?"

George looked as if she was choosing her words very carefully. "He has had fewer restrictions placed on him."

"He is very open and funny too, not the playboy that the media like to portray."

George smiled ruefully. "He does like the ladies, but he's just a young man with no responsibilities."

"And what about you, Georgie? I'm sure you've had the ladies falling at your feet. Not only a princess, but a dashing naval officer. A girl's dream."

George put down her plate and gulped down the last of her champagne. "Sadly, not."

Bea began to stroke a sleeping Rex, who had managed to edge his way onto the picnic blanket. "Come on, you must have had a girlfriend or two. Do you just not want to talk about it?"

"Oh no, it's not that. I trust you completely, Bea."

"What is it then?"

George rubbed her face nervously. "You have to understand, Bea, because of who I am, I have to live in a certain way, different even from Theo. The media follow every move I make—they have done since I was born. I am the first woman with a younger brother to succeed to the throne, and now I'm the first openly gay monarch. If I wanted to start seeing a girl, the press would have us down the aisle and have her my consort by the end of our first evening out together. I don't think that would be fair to either the girl or me. My father brought me up to respect my position and any girl I was interested in. Because, as monarch, my duty is to marry and produce an heir and a spare."

"So what exactly are you saying? You haven't had a girlfriend or..."

"I haven't been with a girl in any way."

Bea was gobsmacked. "No one?"

George shook her head, her cheeks reddening by the second.

There are so many things you haven't experienced, Georgie. "Surely if you had been discreet? It didn't stop many of your ancestors."

"That's the point. So many of my ancestors brought shame and scandal to the family in the past, and it threatened the very institution of monarchy, but there hasn't been a divorce in the family since my great-grandfather's time. The family stopped arranging marriages with the most suitable partners and allowed everyone to find their own partners." She then took Bea's hand and looked into her eyes. "I don't want to be discreet and run about with lots of girls, Bea. All I've ever wanted is to meet the right girl, get married, and have children. I'm a very ordinary sort of person, despite everything."

Bea's gaze locked with George's.

"Bea, I—"

From the nervous look on her face, Bea knew George was about to say something from which they couldn't return to friendship, so she interrupted her quickly. "Well, I'd better get these plates cleared up, Your Majesty."

With that the conversation was brought to an end.

❖

After returning home, Julian retired to his office away from his wife and children. After last night he was enraged. His perfect plan was faltering, and he needed to regroup. Once he had information on Miss Elliot, he would find a way to discredit her. He was appalled at the Queen Mother's and Dowager Queen's reactions to this woman and felt it had shown just how far his family had gotten from the old ways.

"Sir? May I come in?" the Viscount's private secretary asked.

"Yes, come."

"Sir, I have everything I could find on Miss Elliot." He handed him an old-fashioned paper folder.

Julian flipped through the information and then smashed his fist down on the desk. "This woman cannot be allowed anywhere near my family. Common little tart."

"That's not all, sir. I contacted the Queen's private secretary, Sir Michael Bradbury. He has concerns that this woman has an unnatural control over the Queen, and with some work, I believe I could get him to help us."

"Very good. Leave me now, I have some private calls to make." His secretary bowed and left.

Julian thought for a minute, before an idea slowly formed in his head. "Victor? It's Julian. I have a nice little job for you. What? Oh yes, I think you'll enjoy this one."

Bea grew extremely tired after lunch, not being used to drinking champagne at that time of day. Since it was a bright sunny day, George suggested they lie back and close their eyes for a bit. George never fell asleep but simply enjoyed being allowed to lie next to the woman she loved and watch her sleep. On the other side of Bea, her new best friend Rex lay snuggled up to her side.

George leaned on one elbow, looking down at Bea adoringly, smiling. She memorized every inch of her love's beautiful face, the way her nose wrinkled and the corners of her mouth lifted as she dreamed of something pleasant.

The muscles in Bea's face began to twitch and move as she awakened. Her eyes fluttered open and George couldn't stop herself trailing her fingers across her cheek. "You are so beautiful." She couldn't take her eyes off Bea's lips. They tantalized her, and when Bea opened them slightly, George took it as an invitation and lowered her own to meet them. Her heart thudded wildly, and all her fears and insecurities disappeared with the first touch of their lips. The kiss was tender, passionate, and made George feel more than she could have ever imagined possible. She explored Bea's mouth, memorizing everything about her—her taste, the softness of her lips—and she felt her heart was lost to this woman.

George finally pulled away, needing some air, and Bea looked at her with a mixture of emotion and uncertainty. The barriers between them seemed to be gone; the kiss had exposed all of the secrets they kept but still left unsaid.

She took a breath and started to say the words that lay deep inside her heart. "I lo—"

Bea quickly placed a finger against the Queen's lips and said, "No. Please don't say it. Don't say it out loud."

George pulled back, dazed and confused. "Why?"

Bea cupped George's cheek with her hand. "Because one day, Your Majesty, a well-bred and suitable woman is going to come along and take you away from me, and that will break my heart."

"But I would never—"

Bea sat up quickly. "You might not want to, but you will." She was angry and defensive. "Queens don't settle down with working-class girls from East London, and I would never be your mistress. If we leave everything unsaid, we can perhaps salvage our friendship, because that's all we can ever have."

George tried to grab her arm and stop her from standing up, but Bea pulled away. "Please, Georgie, please just leave it. I have to protect myself. Don't mention it again."

She stormed off and stopped by the ancient tree, bracing herself against the trunk, trying to catch her breath. Rex looked at his master and whimpered.

Bloody hell, I've ruined everything, George thought. She got up and walked over to Bea. "Bea? Please forgive me for my behaviour. It wasn't right to put you in that position, but I would never, ever have you as my mistress and hide you away. You are too important to me. I would be proud to have you at my side."

Bea spun round. "Please, Georgie, don't make this any harder. If we say nothing more, we can go back to being friends."

George was aware there would be some obstacles in them being together, but she didn't see them as insurmountable. Bea either couldn't or didn't want to fight for that, so she would take whatever Bea could offer her.

"I won't bring it up again, Bea, but please don't walk away from our friendship."

"I never could." She threw herself into George's arms and hugged her like she was going to disappear. "Georgie, if you get me an invitation, I'll come and sit at the back of Westminster Abbey. I'll take a day's leave from work."

George let out a long breath. "Thank you. I appreciate it more than you know." She stood holding Bea as long as she was allowed, as she didn't know if she would ever get this close to her again.

You are the only one who will ever own my heart. You are my Queen Consort.

Chapter Sixteen

The following few days were quiet for Bea. With no scheduled Timmy's visits till the end of the week, and the Queen's schedule extremely busy, they didn't speak as much as they normally would. Bea wanted some space to think, and to try and get her feelings under control.

The morning of the memorial service came, and Bea was even more nervous than she'd been for the banquet at Windsor. At least there she'd known she would speak to George at some point. Today was a highly formal occasion, and she would enter alone and leave alone.

"What do you think, Mum?" Sarah had been helping with hair and make-up, and she looked at her with pride.

"You look elegant and beautiful. I can't wait to see you on TV. My little girl at Westminster Abbey."

"Mum, I don't think for one minute I'll be shown. I'm sitting at the back, nearly out the door." Bea ran her hands down her new dress, smoothing it out. "Being friends with royalty is certainly making a dent in my bank account."

"Watch your time, sweetheart." Sarah pointed to the clock on the dressing table. "Are you sure you don't want Dad to drive you?"

"He wouldn't get near the Abbey. It's best if I take a taxi. It says on the invitation they have a special drop-off area near the Abbey."

Her mum gave her a cuddle and said, "I'm so excited, and I've made sure your cousin Martha will be watching."

"Hopefully I can slip in at the back unnoticed."

❖

Bea did not get her wish. She was met at the Abbey door by Captain Cameron and directed to the row near the front of the Abbey amongst the politicians and foreign dignitaries. In front of her were the empty pews waiting for the royal family. As she walked down the intimidating aisle of Westminster Abbey, feeling as if a million eyes were pinned on her, she thought, *I'm going to kill you, Georgie.*

As she sat contemplating her discomfort at being alone amongst all these people, she recalled her conversation the previous evening with the Queen.

She hadn't heard from George for a few days, and thought perhaps she was angry with her, but then as she sat at the desk in her room, a call came through on her computer. "Good evening, Your Majesty," Bea said rather formally, not knowing how George would act with her.

"Hello—I hope it's okay to call."

Bea gave a tentative smile. "Of course it is. I wasn't sure if you still wanted to be friends...after the weekend."

"Of course I do, Bea. I was just trying to give you some space. If I wasn't friends with you, there would be no one to call me Georgie or Bully, and I'd just be the bloody Queen all the time," George joked, as if to ease the tension.

"I'm so glad. I missed talking to you," Bea admitted.

"Rexie has missed you."

"I missed him. He's a handsome boy."

George hesitated before saying, "I missed you. I wanted to make sure you were coming tomorrow. If you've changed your mind..."

Bea saw the tension etched across the Queen's face and knew that no matter how much it hurt, she would be there for George, until the inevitable day when the task would fall to a more suitable woman.

"Of course I'll be there, Georgie. I'll be there for as long as you need me." She heard George let out a long breath.

"You don't know how relieved I am. I've been doing these sort of engagements all my life, but I'm dreading this. I have to be strong for my family—Mama and Theo need to lean on me. I feel all the pressure building up inside me, and I'm so worried I'll make a fool of myself."

"Remember what I told you: When you feel the panic starting to overtake you, shut your eyes for a few seconds and breathe deeply. I'll be right there breathing along with you, and if you need to, just look towards the back of the Abbey and know I'm there with you. I know you won't be able to see me so far back but..."

George smiled and said, "Oh, don't worry, Bea, I'll see you."

Bea realized that George wanted her close enough to be able to see her, and her annoyance at the seating arrangement left her.

The archbishop walked into position at the front, and they all stood. A loud fanfare suddenly filled the Abbey with noise, signalling the arrival of the royal family. The Queen led the family down the aisle, dressed in her Royal Navy uniform, the national anthem playing in the background. As the family passed each pew, the person on the end would bow or curtsy. When George passed the row where Bea sat, she saw the solid, stoic mask George put on for these occasions, but Bea knew inside she would be struggling.

The family took their seats and the service began. There were hymns, then readings by the prime minister and from the chairman of the King's favourite charity. Bea found it very moving, even more so knowing how George would feel listening.

The Archbishop of Canterbury took to his pulpit to introduce the Queen. The silver-haired man had a kindly face and spoke of the King and his family with genuine warmth.

"I had the pleasure of knowing and ministering to the late King Edward for many years. Through our many conversations I learned that he thought his greatest achievements and blessings were his wife, Queen Sofia, and their two children, Queen Georgina and Prince Theodore. In the last months of his life, he confided to me, that his greatest dream had always been to hold his grandchildren in his arms, and know the House of Buckingham would go on for generations. Since he came to accept that he wouldn't be able to accomplish that, he realized that he didn't need to see them to know that the House of Buckingham would remain strong, because his two wonderful children had grown up in love, and they in turn would create loving, happy families for themselves. That to me is the King's greatest legacy. He has departed this world but left us with a new Queen to take us forward into a new world. I ask you all to stand with me and listen to the words of our new sovereign, Queen Georgina."

The entire Abbey stood as George walked to the lectern. She looked out over the sea of faces before her and felt her vision narrow, a cold sweat started to form as her chest began to tighten. George desperately searched the faces until she fixed her eyes on a small blond woman, five rows from the front. She remembered what Bea had said the night before. *When you feel the panic starting to overtake you, shut your eyes for a few seconds and breathe deeply. I'll be right there breathing along with you…*

George closed her eyes, took a breath, and when she opened them saw no one but Bea, who gave a soft smile and mouthed the word *breathe*.

She felt herself relax immediately and began to speak. "In May next year, I will be here at Westminster Abbey to make my coronation vows before God and the people. I would never have been able to fulfil that task without the expert tutelage and example of one of the finest kings this country has ever had. If I could be only half the monarch he was, then I will do exceptionally well. My father, the King, had a saying. *Duty and service to the country and its people comes first, second, and last.* That is how I will remember him, and I hope the nation will do too, as a man that would do anything for his people and his country."

CHAPTER SEVENTEEN

As April turned to May, Bea and George returned to the close friendship they had before they had kissed.

This morning Bea and Prince Theo were attending the final planning meeting for the coronation concert committee before publicity material would be released to the press. The committee was enjoying drinks as they wandered round the exhibition of concert posters and promotional material. Bea and Prince Theo stood in front of a huge computer screen that projected from floor to ceiling. It depicted the image of the band that was headlining the concert.

"I can't believe you talked them into it, Your Royal Highness. They haven't spoken in fifteen years, the biggest band of their generation— one call from you, and they're desperate to reform."

Theo gave her a playful wink. "What can I say? It's just my charm. No, seriously, I've been friendly with them as individuals for a while, and I can tell you it wasn't exaggerated how much they dislike each other. They really do, but when they heard it was Her Majesty's concert, they couldn't reform quickly enough. Everyone wants to be part of the lead-up to her coronation. They know it will be remembered for generations."

Bea had noticed this everywhere she went with the Queen. There was a tangible excitement and buzz about the country. Not only on her visits, but on TV and in the press, everyone was monarchy obsessed at the moment. "The royal family does have an enormous pull with people, doesn't it? They're fascinated by you all."

Theo ran his hand through his curly hair, much as George did when she was nervous. "Yes, we do. My papa taught us to use that fascination to bring good causes to the public attention, and to sell Britain abroad. I'm not as good as Georgie and the others, but I am trying very hard to change and be more useful. Georgie needs me to be."

George and Theo were so different in character and personality, but Bea could see how much Theo idolized his sister. "You're very close to the Queen, aren't you?"

"Of course. My sister is a wonderful person, and I love her. She's always been there for me, helping me whenever I've needed her. She is a rock the whole family lean on, and we are so glad she's the head of the family."

Who does Georgie lean on though? Bea asked herself. She felt the answer come from her heart unconsciously. *You.*

She shook off her thoughts quickly, feeling uncomfortable with the answer. "So, the concert is set for the twenty-eighth of July?"

Prince Theo took a sip of his drink and nodded. "Yes, that was the only available date left in the summer months. From Easter onward, my sister's duties really hot up, so that's the last date before the family go up to Balmoral for the summer holidays."

"I can't thank you enough for your help, sir. Timmy's is going to be set up for a few years to come because of the Queen's involvement and this concert."

"I'm delighted to hear it, but less of the *sir*, call me Theo, remember?"

Bea looked around at the small groups chatting around them and said, "Not when there are others around. I'm always as careful with your sister's title too."

Theo laughed softly. "That won't do your republican image much good, Miss Elliot."

"My anti-monarchist image seems to be going down the tubes very rapidly. My republican university group would be horrified. If only you and your sister weren't so nice and charming."

"The Buckinghams are naturally charming. We can't help being likeable." Bea chuckled, along with Theo, but then a serious look came across his face. "My sister really treasures your friendship, you know. I don't think I've ever seen her as happy or content as when she speaks of your time together."

Bea felt the blush coming to her cheeks. "I enjoy spending time with her." They wandered around some of the other exhibits. "I can't wait until the big night. I've never been part of something this big. They say we could charge ten times the price for the tickets and still sell them all," Bea said enthusiastically.

"It will be spectacular. I've called on all the younger members of the Firm to attend. Vicki and Max are particularly excited."

Bea giggled. "Makes you sound like an accountancy business."

"Yes, well, being royal is our business. I hope you'll join us in the royal box, Bea?"

"Oh, I don't know if that would be the right place—"

The exuberant Prince interrupted her. "Of course it would be. You are the organizer, and the Queen will most certainly invite you."

Bea felt like she was getting deeper and deeper into a new world, a world where she could get lost in George's love, only to be left broken-hearted. "We'll see."

"And you're off on a short trip with my sister, I understand."

"Yes. We're going to visit the construction of a new respite facility being built for Timmy's in the south of France. The cameras are going to follow us and get some footage for the concert programme."

"Excellent. Tell Georgie to have some fun while you're away. She works too much."

"I'll probably hardly see her."

"Oh, I think you will," Theo said.

Sarah and Reg beamed with pride as they watched their daughter on the news the next day.

"Look at our little girl," Sarah said to her husband.

Reg lifted her hand and placed a tender kiss on her knuckles. "She's a beautiful girl. We've done well, sweetheart." They listened intently as the newscaster spoke.

After touching down in France last night, the Queen is touring the site of the first overseas respite centre for her hospice charity, Timmy's.

Hundreds of well-wishers lined the streets of the quiet seaside town of Porto Pollo in Corsica, to welcome the new Queen to France. The charity hopes to send young children and their families here to enjoy the sunshine and the warm weather, in between bouts of treatment.

This charity came into the public's eye after the Queen chose them from a whole host of organizations hoping for her patronage, in this her coronation year. She was shown around the partially built site by the architects of the project and by Timmy's regional director Miss Beatrice Elliot, who has been escorting the Queen around the charity's British sites. She is also on the planning committee for Queen Georgina's coronation concert along with Prince Theodore.

After touring the site, the Queen went on a walkabout among the crowds who had shown up to welcome her. The enthusiastic crowd welcomed her like a movie star, shouting and screaming her name. The

Queen will fly back to Britain tomorrow evening after meeting with the British ambassador in the afternoon. In other news…

"Did you hear that? They spoke about Bea," Sarah said excitedly.

Reg squeezed her wife's hand tightly. "I have a feeling that our little girl will have to get used to this type of thing."

Sarah had started to realize her daughter had feelings for the Queen by the way her eyes sparkled when she spoke about her, but she worried she would be hurt, when in the long run the Queen would be compelled to settle with someone more suitable. The way the Queen involved Bea in every aspect of the event made it look as if she was escorting a consort rather than a charity worker.

Sarah could only pray that the Queen felt the same way, and that her daughter's heart would not be broken.

George looked at the readout on her tablet for around the twentieth time in the last few minutes.

"George, would you calm down, man." Cammy was putting the finishing touches to a table laid out for an informal dinner, while George paced up and down the hotel suite.

"She did say she was coming, didn't she? You didn't misunderstand?"

Cammy left her task and walked over to the Queen. "George, Miss Elliot is coming. When I went down to her room to invite her, she seemed delighted and said she would be here as soon as she'd called her parents. She's only five minutes late—give the lassie a chance."

George let out a lungful of air she'd been holding in. "I'm sorry. I know I'm impossible. Did you inform Major Fairfax and Inspector Lang she'd be coming?"

For security reasons, the royal party had taken the whole top floor in the hotel. This gave her protection officers control of the stairs and lifts and access to the floor.

"Yes, they'll call when she is on her way. Why are you so nervous, Your Majesty? I thought you had decided just to take your friendship one step at a time?"

George wandered over to the coffee table and lifted the model ship Bea had given her. She found the gift a great comfort and insisted on bringing it with her. After a minute or so of silence, George admitted, "I kissed her."

Cammy looked surprised.

George felt the heat rising in her cheeks at the memory. The memory that had kept her awake till the small hours since. "When we spent the day together at Windsor, we were so close…it just happened."

"At the risk of sounding prurient, what was it like?"

The speed of George's heart increased as she remembered the utter bliss of kissing her love. "It felt like finding something I've been missing my whole life. I felt complete, and I would give anything to feel that again." George sat down in the armchair despondently.

"How did she react? It couldn't have been that bad, surely?"

"It was. Oh, she responded to the kiss as much as I, but when I went to tell how I felt, she silenced me. She said one day I would push her away for someone more suitable and break her heart." George buried her face in her hands.

"And would you?"

George looked up sharply. "Would I what?"

"Push her away?" Cammy asked gently.

George stood and said, "Never. How could you ask me that, Cammy? You've known me since I graduated from Sandhurst. Have you ever seen me behave in such a manner?"

"I'm sorry, Ma'am. I had to ask. You've always behaved impeccably with anyone who's ever met you. I just wanted to know how serious you were about this lassie."

George slumped back down on the chair. "You have seen her while we've travelled the country, Cammy. She's perfect for the role of Queen Consort. Even today at the building project, while meeting the staff, she took time to listen to everyone, any concerns they had, and left them smiling. Can you imagine having that wonderful woman to support me in this role of mine?"

"She is, Ma'am. I had my concerns, especially about her views on the monarchy, but she has really shown her warm and gentle heart over the time we have known her. The lassie would be an outstanding consort." Cammy came over and sat in front of her friend. "If you love her, George, and I mean love her enough to go against any opposition there might be, then you have to show her, through thought and deed, that she is the only lassie and consort you will have in your life."

"I love her more than enough for that, but she won't let me raise the subject of our feelings. How do I show her?"

"Don't raise it. Do as you are doing—invite her to dinner, and invite her to some of the events you have in the coming months. Wear the lassie down. If she loves you like you love her, she'll give in."

"How did you get knowledgeable about women, Captain Cameron?" George said with a smile.

Cammy stood and smoothed down her uniform. "I might never have been in love, Your Majesty, but I've chased a lot of lassies." She gave George a quick wink.

"So that's what you were doing on shore leave when I stayed aboard ship?"

Cammy smiled enigmatically and said, "So, will there be anything further, Ma'am?"

"And what do you advise I do about the political obstacles in my path?"

"If I were you, Ma'am, I'd take the best advice from the very top, not from some of your more aged advisors, as they have their minds rooted in the past."

"You are right, Captain. I will speak to the prime minister at our weekly meeting. If I know any obstacles can be overcome, then perhaps I can persuade Bea."

Cammy's mobile rang, and she answered. "Cameron…Yes, send her along straight away, Inspector Lang."

George smoothed her hair back nervously. "We're on parade?"

"Indeed, Ma'am. Good luck."

❖

Bea had been surprised to find the dining table in the Queen's suite to be very formally set. When George had invited her for something to eat, and a film afterwards, she thought it would be an informal occasion. She looked at George, dressed in a smart dark navy suit, and regretted just pulling on her jeans and a cream blouse.

As George approached her, she gave her a small curtsy. "Your Majesty, if I had known you were going to so much trouble, I would have dressed more appropriately."

"Not at all. You look beautiful as always, Bea." George took her hand and kissed it.

The touch of her lips made Bea's heart beat faster. She was led over to the table and helped into the dining chair.

The candles glowing softly gave the room a romantic setting. *Oh, Georgie, you're making it so difficult for me just to be friends with you.*

Once George took her seat, Captain Cameron appeared and poured the wine. "Shall I return in five minutes, Ma'am?" Cammy asked.

"Yes, thank you."

Captain Cameron bowed and left them alone.

"I would have loved to take you to one of the town's best restaurants, but unfortunately that is impossible for me. I thought this would be the next best thing. The hotel does serve very fine food, I understand."

"Of course. This will be perfect, Georgie." Bea was again reminded of the limits placed on the Queen's life. "I can't imagine not being able to go somewhere and do what I want. I don't know how you cope."

George took a sip of her wine before answering. "I live a life of great privilege and importance, and the price for that is I can't do what I like. That's the deal, and I'm used to it. This has always been my life."

George never ceased to amaze Bea; her understanding of her position in life was admirable. "That's a very honest and pragmatic way to look at it, Georgie."

George shrugged her shoulders. "It's the way we're brought up in my family. We're all aware of how lucky we are, and our duties and responsibilities that come with those privileges. Well...perhaps not cousin Julian."

Bea giggled softly. "I did get that impression."

George topped up both their wine glasses and said, "I do sometimes wonder what it would feel like to go somewhere and just be another face in the crowd."

"A lot of ordinary people crave the feeling of standing out in the crowd, of being a celebrity," Bea said.

"I'm not a celebrity. Celebrities court the camera and aspire to be known—I do not. I have never chosen this, but I have been recognizable around the world since the moment I was born, before I was even conscious of it. Mama and Papa were a fairy-tale couple. Their wedding was watched by two-and-a-half billion people around the world, so you can imagine the interest when their firstborn came along."

The thought of being under that much scrutiny was terrifying. "Two-and-a-half billion?"

"Granny told me that there were press teams from all over the world camped out in front of the hospital before I was born. The first pictures of me were taken the day after I was born as my parents left the hospital. So you see, it's all I've ever known."

Bea felt such a sense of sadness for her. She did live an extraordinary life, but she most certainly paid for it. All she wanted to do was wrap her arms around George and soothe her. She thought about the birthday idea she'd come up with and decided to bring it up after dinner.

"Well, Your Majesty, I see it as my task as your friend to show you a bit of normal life."

"Oh, you do, Bea," George said with a smile.

"While you, Your Majesty, can show me the finer side of life, starting with this delicious meal."

George handed her the menu. "I would be glad to."

Cammy phoned the order to the kitchen, and their meal was delivered in no time at all.

"This is delicious," Bea said.

George sat with her hands clasped in front of her chin, simply watching Bea enjoy her food. She ate and enjoyed the new tastes with such a passion, and George wondered if she was equally as passionate in other areas of life.

"This is divine, Georgie." Bea popped another piece of lobster into her mouth. "What's it called, again?"

"Homard de Cornouailles à la nage, sauce vierge." The French slipped off George's tongue with a low burr.

"You speak French?" Bea asked with a husky tone to her voice.

"I speak several European languages. I have to be able to communicate with people as I travel around the world." George had noticed that the atmosphere in the room had changed. She felt a palpable electricity in the air. Bea had a hungry look in her eye, and she was sure it was because of her.

"Say something in Italian for me, and I'll let you have a piece of lobster." Bea lifted a bit of lobster and held it up for inspection.

George, feeling brave, grabbed hold of Bea's wrist and pulled her fingers inches from her lips. *"Ti amo, la mia Regina Bea."* *I love you, my Queen Bea.*

Bea moaned at the words.

"Do I get my prize?" George asked.

Bea nodded, and her lips parted slightly as George closed her eyes and took Bea's fingers into her mouth. She took the piece of lobster from Bea's fingertips. The taste of the lobster was soon replaced by the sensuous feel of her warm tongue, licking and sucking the remaining juices from the tips of Bea's fingers, and she was lost.

It felt like she was making love to Bea's fingers and could only imagine what it would feel like to have Bea naked beneath her, as she kissed her body and coaxed throaty moans from her. The sensation became overpowering, and she knew she had to stop this before it went any further.

She released her fingers, only to hear Bea moan, "Georgie."

Her eyes slowly opened and she found that Bea looked as dazed as she felt.

"Sorry, the lobster was delicious."

Bea looked down at her hands bashfully and appeared to think it best to ignore what had just passed between them. "You spoke Italian beautifully. What did it mean?"

George gave her a wink. "That's a secret."

"Oh, come on, Georgie That's not fair. Please tell me?" Bea pleaded.

It had felt wonderful to George to tell Bea that she loved her, even if her love didn't understand the words. She prayed one day she could say it again, in English this time. "No, not today. Maybe one day. Now, would you like dessert here, or shall we retire to the comfortable couch?"

"I think the couch, and since you refuse to tell me what I want to know, Your Majesty, I'm going to order the biggest and most decadent dessert, and not give you a taste," Bea said with a teasing smile.

George could only laugh at her love's girlish enthusiasm. "As you wish, Miss Elliot."

Bea had indeed shared her dessert, feeding George a spoonful after every one she had, and George loved the intimate act.

"I can't believe this is the type of film you like." Bea set the dessert bowl on the table and moved closer to her on the couch.

George, who had dispensed with her suit jacket and rolled up her shirt sleeves to her elbows, eased her arm along the back of the couch, like a teenage boy at the cinema. Assured that her little move had gone unnoticed, she replied, "What? Why? *Roman Holiday* with Audrey Hepburn is a classic of the silver screen."

"Oh, I agree. I just didn't think a big, tough—sailor? soldier?— whatever you are would like an old romantic, mushy film."

George chuckled and said, "Well, may I remind you that I am very old-fashioned, to the point of being stuffy, Theo says, and I'm not scared to admit I love old-fashioned romance. I don't think it detracts from my prize bull qualities, do you?"

Bea smiled as she watched George arch an eyebrow. "No, it doesn't. I think it's sweet."

George felt her cheeks redden and they both turned back to the screen in front of them. "It was Mama to blame, really. She's a hopeless romantic and watched these sorts of films when I was growing up. You know, *Breakfast at Tiffany's, Casablanca, Brief Encounter.* I like them all, but *Roman Holiday* was my favourite because it was about a princess who got to escape the gilded cage and experience things she would never have had the opportunity to do."

"Pause film."

The image of Audrey Hepburn and Gregory Peck froze instantly, and George looked at Bea, a bit confused.

"Can I talk to you about an idea I've had, Georgie?"

"Of course, Bea, you can talk to me about anything."

Bea sat round and faced her. "When we were at Windsor, I heard your private secretary talking about your birthday arrangements."

"Oh yes, of course. We're having a dinner for my official birthday in June." George reached out and took Bea's hand. "Your name was on the top of the list. I hope you'll come."

"Yes, I'll come if you would like me to, Georgie, but I was thinking about what I could get you, and I wanted to float an idea with you."

Still holding hands with her, George tried to reassure her. "You don't need to get me anything, Bea. The pleasure of your company will be enough. It's not my actual birthday, you know—my real birthday was in November, when I was still at sea. The monarch has an official birthday in June, hoping that the weather will be better for the Trooping the Colour birthday parade."

Bea looked undeterred. "I know, Mum explained that, but since I didn't know you on your real birthday, I thought I would celebrate this one with you. Is that okay?"

"Of course it is. What would you like to do?"

Bea took a deep breath. "I know this will sound crazy, especially with the security problems you have at the moment, but I thought, what is the one thing that Georgie doesn't have? What would she prize above all other things?"

George was certainly intrigued and wondered what she'd come up with. "And what conclusion did you come to?"

Bea looked deep into her eyes and said one word. "Freedom. Freedom for one night to be a normal, unremarkable person lost in the crowd."

George felt her heart both constrict and feel like exploding at the same time. This woman had, in one word, encapsulated and understood the longings of her very soul. Without asking, she pulled Bea onto her lap and into her arms. She held her tight and whispered, "You understand. How can you understand me so well?"

"I don't know, Georgie. It just comes naturally to me. When I look at you, I can see what you keep locked up tight, laid bare." Bea hung onto George just as tightly.

George pulled back a little and said, "But how can I have this freedom for one night?"

Bea gave her a big smile and said, "That's the clever bit. First of all, I'll tell you what I had planned for the night, and maybe you can speak to Cammy and your protection squad and see if it's at all possible."

"I can do that. What did you have in mind?"

❖

George paced up and down in front of Bea, recapping the plan. "So we base ourselves at a London hotel, and your friend Holly, who is a cosmetic artist, will do her stuff and disguise me, make me look like a man?"

"I don't think it'll take much to make you look masculine—you are wonderfully butch—but she will make you look unrecognizable."

"Before we talk some more about your plan, could I ask you something?"

Bea patted the cushion beside her. "Always. Come and sit."

"Do I displease you? I mean, the way I present myself, butch as you call it. I've never given the way I am a name. I've just always been more masculine. It's just me."

Bea couldn't stop herself immediately reaching out and cupping George's cheek. "You could never displease me, Georgie. You are good looking, handsome, beautiful, all of the above. It's what makes you unique, and you will be a very unique monarch."

She could see George's eyes soften as she absorbed the touch of her hand. It was clear to Bea that they both felt the same, they were both in love, but a love that they couldn't allow to blossom. She pulled her hand back, feeling awkward. "So we'll change your appearance and dress you up, and you can experience a night out at Mickey D's with my friends. I want this night to be my gift to you before…" Inside she knew it would be as much a gift for herself as for George. One night to be two ordinary friends, before their friendship came to an inevitable end. "Before your coronation, and your life becomes even more demanding," she lied.

George remained silent as she looked deeply into her eyes.

"Georgie? What is it? Are you worried about my friends? I give you my word, you can trust them. I promise you won't find anything leaked to the press from them. I've known these girls from the first day of uni—they're good people."

"I trust your judgment, Bea, it isn't that. I just can't believe you would think of this for me. I…"

She could see how emotional George was, and as always, Bea was afraid George would say something that could not be taken back. "It's okay, Georgie. I understand. Do you think it's something that could be done? With security and everything?"

"I don't see why not. After all, I'll be fairly hard to recognize. I'm sure Inspector Lang won't be over the moon with the idea, but it's a one-off situation and I'm sure I can convince him."

"Great," Bea said excitedly. "I can't wait for you to meet my friends."

"It will be wonderful. Thank you for the kind idea. It'll be the best present I've ever had."

Bea gave her a soft punch on the biceps and said, "Okay, I think we've kept Miss Hepburn waiting long enough."

CHAPTER EIGHTEEN

S ir Michael Bradbury sat at his desk in the hotel suite below the Queen's. He was nursing his second large whisky of the night. "Bloody woman."

Since Bea Elliot came on the scene, he'd been isolated from the Queen. Before, he'd enjoyed unrestrained access, but ever so gradually, he felt he was being set adrift from her. It seemed like every time he wished to see the Queen, *she* was there. Everyone around the Queen had fallen for her charms, even the Queen's bumptious equerry, Major Fairfax. Added to this, Queen Georgina had been using his subordinate, Sebastian, more and more for tasks normally given to him.

Taking a long swig of his drink, Sir Michael said to himself, "I seem to be the only one to see her for what she is. A scheming, common little piece."

His relationship with the Queen had started to deteriorate since the meeting they had before the late King's memorial service.

Sir Michael handed Queen Georgina his tablet for one final piece of business. "If I could just have your signature on this last letter, Ma'am?"

"What's this one for?" George tried to quickly scan the contents.

"It's a letter of condolence to the French ambassador, who lost his wife this week."

George nodded and quickly signed. "Ah yes. Poor man. I remember meeting his wife and they appeared to be a very loving couple."

"Yes, so I understand, Ma'am. Is there anything I can do for you before I leave, Ma'am?"

George handed back the signed pad. "Yes, I want you to organize an extra invitation for the late King's memorial service. Oh, and make sure you add in all the necessary security passes."

Sir Michael made the note on his computer. "Yes, Ma'am. Where in the Abbey would you like this guest to be situated? The seats are quite full already."

The Queen lifted her next folder of paperwork from the red box and said, "In line with the pulpit and preferably in the first ten rows."

Sir Michael looked up from his pad sharply. "To whom am I to send this invitation, Ma'am?"

"Miss Beatrice Elliot."

Sir Michael hoped the Queen was too focused on her papers to catch the look of annoyance he knew passed over his face. "Do you really think that's appropriate, Ma'am? The first rows are set aside for some very important people. The late King would not have approved and I don't think—"

George stopped dead and looked up with a look of fury. "Sir, you forget yourself. I will not be told what is appropriate by my private secretary. It's your job to follow my commands."

As soon as he'd said it, he knew he'd gone beyond the limits of his post, but he couldn't help but try and advise the Queen against this. "I'm so sorry, Ma'am. I just wanted to counsel you against—"

"I don't care what you intended, Sir Michael. Just follow my instructions," George said sternly.

"Yes, Ma'am." Sir Michael bowed and began to retreat hastily from the room.

"Oh, and Sir Michael?"

He stopped and looked back at the Queen's penetrating gaze.

"Don't ever presume to tell me what my father the King would have done or approved of."

He bowed again and hastily exited her office.

Since then he'd noticed the Queen giving her more personal tasks to Sebastian. It was clear he was being pushed aside. "She has a blind spot where that woman is concerned. Beatrice Elliot will make a bloody fool of her."

His computer came alive and began to ring. "Answer."

The image of Viscount Anglesey filled the screen, and Sir Michael sat up in his seat and pushed his whisky glass out of view. "Your Highness. How can I help you, sir?"

Julian gave the private secretary a warm smile. "Sir Michael, I wondered if I could have a word with you. In the strictest confidence, of course."

"Please do, Your Highness. You can be assured anything you say will go no further."

Sir Michael could see the Viscount was speaking from his private office and wondered what he wanted to talk about.

Viscount Anglesey clasped his hands in front of him and looked extremely serious. "I represent a good few members of the royal family who have...concerns, about the Queen's recent behaviour."

Sir Michael was surprised. He'd thought the Queen was universally loved and supported within the family. "May I ask what concerns your family has, sir?"

"We are concerned about a new influence who has entered the Queen's life and seems to have unrestricted access to her."

Sir Michael knew straight away what Julian was referring to. "I understand what you're talking about completely, sir. I have had similar concerns, but I didn't think anyone else shared them."

Julian leaned forward towards the screen. "Believe me, we have. The Queen Mother and the Dowager Queen Adrianna have raised the issue with the Queen but to no avail, so they turned to me."

"I see, and how can I help you, sir?"

George started to awaken and immediately felt something was different. She slowly opened her eyes to find Bea wrapped tightly in her arms, snuggled into the crook of her neck, and the TV playing on in the background. She remembered Bea resting her head on her shoulder as the evening wore on, and they must have fallen asleep. It felt wonderful to have Bea in her arms, and she couldn't help but give in to temptation. She pressed her lips to Bea's beautiful hair and inhaled the sweet scent of her.

"Bea, Bea, wake up," George whispered, while soothingly stroking her back.

"Hmm...too early...sleep," Bea mumbled, and then surprisingly reached up with her lips and kissed George on the chin.

George couldn't keep the smile from her face, as Bea's eyes flickered open sleepily. "Good morning, darling."

From the daze of sleep, Bea's eyes popped open when she found her lips locked to George's face. She leaped off George like she was on fire and started apologizing rapidly. "I'm so, so sorry, Your Majesty. I had no idea I had fallen asleep like that and—"

George stood quickly and tried to soothe her. "Bea, please, it's fine. There's nothing to be sorry about. We obviously fell asleep watching the film and made ourselves comfortable."

Bea hugged herself and said, "Still, you must have been really uncomfortable with me sprawled on top of you like that. I'm sorry."

George stepped forward and took Bea's hand. "Not in the least. In fact it was the best sleep I've had since before my father died." She looked her love directly in the eye and said, "I'm so at peace with you, Bea. You must feel it?"

Bea opened her mouth to answer but was interrupted by a knock from the bedroom door of the suite. "Your Majesty, Inspector Lang has called to ask if it's a convenient moment for his people to do the morning security sweep."

"Hang on a minute, Cammy." She pulled Bea closer to her and said with a hint of desperation, "What were you going to say?"

Bea gulped and shook her head. "We have a lot on today, Your Majesty. I'd better get back to my room and get ready for our day. Thank you for the lovely evening last night."

She pulled her hands gently from George's and slipped out of the room quietly. George looked up at the image of herself on the TV screen. When the film had ended, it had switched to the rolling news channel, and her visit to France was the main topic for the day. She could feel the bars of her cage closing in around her, inch by inch, until she felt like screaming. George grabbed the bowl they had used for popcorn and threw it at her picture on the screen, but of course the bowl sailed right through the projected screen and smashed on the wall behind.

Bea was furious with herself. After running from the Queen's suite, she jumped into the shower and tried to wash away her overwhelming feelings, but it didn't work. She vigorously brushed her hair back into a ponytail. "What am I even doing here? I'm in love with Queen Georgina of Great Britain, and I can't have her. This is insanity."

There was a knock at the door to interrupt Bea's thoughts. She made her way over and opened the door to find Captain Cameron waiting there.

"Good morning, Miss Elliot. Could I have a wee word?"

"Yes, of course. Come in."

Bea was surprised to see the captain out of uniform, wearing a highly pressed shirt and jeans. "No uniform today, Captain? I don't think I've ever seen you out of that smart red tunic."

Cammy chuckled. "Her Majesty ordered me to wear civvies today. She said I would terrify the weans."

Bea looked confused. "Weans? You've lost me, Cammy."

"Oh, sorry. I forget not everyone understands the Scots language. The Queen is used to it. Weans means kiddies—you know, children?"

"Oh, I see." After looking around the new facility yesterday, today the royal party was going to take part in some of the activities that the children using the facility would use when getting respite here.

"You're looking very nice yourself, lassie."

"So, how can I help you, Cammy?" Bea asked.

"Oh yes, the Queen wondered if you would travel in her royal transport, rather than go separately."

Bea sighed. "I don't think that's a good idea. It's not my place, Cammy."

"Listen, I know you feel awkward after this morning but—"

"She told you?" Bea said furiously.

Cammy held up her hands in a defensive posture. "Hold on there, lassie. The Queen would never tell tales. I popped in early this morning to attend Her Majesty and saw you both on the couch. I left you both in private."

"I'm sorry, I just feel a little exposed at the moment."

"Listen, I may be speaking out of turn here, but the Queen is back there in her suite feeling the same as you, I believe. She feels terrible that you felt so uncomfortable this morning, and that you keep running away from her. She cares deeply about you, Bea. You make her happy. If you don't want the same, then at least give her the chance to make things better between you."

Bea nodded gloomily. "There are always things we want in life, Captain, but we can't always get what we want. Tell the Queen I will be happy to travel with her. Just let me know when to be ready."

"Thank you. We have a bit of time yet. The Queen is going through her most urgent boxes at the moment." Cammy made her way to the door and hesitated before leaving. "When I saw you both this morning, you couldn't have looked more perfect for each other. You held each other with an ease born of many years together. Maybe we can't always get what we want, Miss Elliot, but sometimes you have to be brave enough to take what is offered freely to you."

CHAPTER NINETEEN

When they returned home from France, it was back to the daily grind of appointments and royal visits. There would be no more excuses to spend time with Bea, as they had no Timmy's business scheduled for the next few weeks, due to the Queen's diary.

Today she was having her weekly meeting with the prime minister.

"So, Your Majesty, because of the deepening crisis in the Middle East, we will be deploying ten per cent more military personnel over the next few months. The Americans will also be sending fifteen percent more fighting personnel."

The Queen listened intently. She had, of course, studied the papers in her boxes explaining the situation, but it was always better to get more detailed information from the prime minister herself.

"I understand my former vessel, the *Poseidon*, will be patrolling the nearby waters?" George felt a deep sadness that she wouldn't be on board her ship. This situation was what she had trained for, and now she had to sit back and watch her men deployed without her.

"Indeed, Ma'am. The *Poseidon* was the ideal candidate for the task, according to the defence department. As you well know, Ma'am, it's one of the best equipped vessels in the fleet."

George fiddled the gold cuff on her naval uniform. "Yes. It's an excellent ship, with a lot of fine sailors on board. Prime Minister, with the deepening crisis and increase in troops deployed to the area, shouldn't we organize a royal visit? For morale and to show my support?"

"Your dedication to your duty is commendable, Ma'am. We did discuss the possibility at this week's cabinet meeting. The secretary of defence feels it would be too dangerous to send Your Majesty, given the current threats to your person."

George scowled and said, "Prime Minister, there has been absolutely nothing new since the threats started. I have been going about my normal routine. I don't think we should take this seriously. I feel I should be with my troops."

Bo Dixon sat forward in her seat and said very seriously, "Ma'am, I understand you feel the need to show your support on the ground, but if Your Majesty was injured, or God forbid kidnapped, I don't need to tell you what a position that would put not only this country in, but also our allies. I must advise that you stay but send another member of your family."

The Queen did indeed understand the danger. To capture or injure the monarch would put Britain in an unimaginable position. "I understand, Prime Minister. Who would you advise I send?"

"We would advise two visits spread over the next three months, Ma'am. The first by Her Royal Highness, the Princess Royal, in her capacity as Commander-in-Chief of the Welsh Guards, who are stationed over there at the moment. The second by the His Royal Highness, Prince Theodore, in his new role of Commander-in-Chief of the Coldstream Guards."

"I agree, Prime Minister. You may move forward with those plans."

"Thank you, Your Majesty. I must also inform you that Lord Buckingham is very insistent about being deployed with his regiment, the Irish Guards, to the Middle East. My advice is that with the utmost secrecy and a bodyguard, we could allow him active service at this time."

George was very proud of Max. Since she'd ascended the throne, he was the last royal in active service. She knew how it felt as a royal officer to watch your men go off to serve without you, and if at all possible, she wanted to give him the chance to go with his regiment.

"Prime Minister, as long as it can be done without endangering those men and women around him, I fully support Lord Buckingham's decision to be deployed."

"Very good, Ma'am. That was everything I needed to inform you of, Ma'am. Was there anything you wanted to raise personally?"

George felt very nervous all of a sudden. "I did have something I wanted to seek your advice on. A constitutional matter, you understand."

"Of course. Anything I can do to help you, I will. I am ever at your service."

George couldn't sit any longer. She stood, and when Bo Dixon also stood, George said, "Oh, do please sit. I am more comfortable on my feet." George walked a few paces with her hands clasped behind her back, then turned again to face Bo. "I want to ask for both your advice on the constitutional position regarding a possible relationship and future marriage, and what your and my government's position would be on it."

"I'm sure both the country and your government would be delighted with any marriage you might make, Your Majesty. I know that the people and the government are always happier when a new monarch is married and the succession is secured."

"Perhaps not as much in my case."

When George hesitated, Bo said, "Your Majesty, as you know all our weekly meetings are in the strictest of confidence, but let me reassure you that you can confide in me, and I will do what I can to help you."

George nodded. She did like the new prime minister but knew that she was a very shrewd operator and always played on the side that suited her best. "Prime Minister, let me be frank. I have met and fallen deeply in love with someone I would like to make my Queen Consort."

Bo smiled warmly. "Congratulations, Your Majesty."

George sighed and then sat back down across from Bo. "If only it was that simple, Prime Minister. The lady in question is someone you've met. Miss Beatrice Elliot."

"I see, and you believe there may be problems because of her views?"

"Yes, I fear so. Her views, I'm happy to say, have changed somewhat, but I wondered what you would think the reaction to Beatrice as Queen Consort would be?"

The prime minister lifted her briefcase and brought it to her lap. "May I show you something, Ma'am?"

George was certainly confused about what Bo Dixon was up to now. "Of course."

"I have been expecting that this issue might come up, and I took the liberty of making some enquiries for you."

"Prime Minister, how could you possibly know that this might be an issue? My own mother doesn't even know," George said rather sternly.

Bo clicked open her briefcase and pulled out an old-fashioned paper folder. "If you will permit me for being so bold, Your Majesty, I think you would be surprised. Those who see the way you look at Miss Elliot can see the affection you hold for her. More importantly than that, Your Majesty, I am your prime minister, and it's my job to support you as my monarch."

The Queen raised an eyebrow. "So what are you telling me here, Miss Dixon?"

"Ma'am, I am a politician and it's in my DNA to know which way the wind is blowing. I know that a royal wedding between Your Majesty and someone from Miss Elliot's working-class background, and with her somewhat sceptical attitude towards authority, would be extremely popular with young and modern thinking people. It would be the ultimate fairy tale, and I want to help you with that, Ma'am."

"Prime Minister, this is my life and happiness, and it sounds like you are directing a public relations exercise."

"I am a politician, Ma'am."

She opened the folder and began to look through documents silently. There were copies of online articles and some police documents reporting on incidents involving the anti-monarchist group Free Republic.

"As you can see, Ma'am, Free Republic is an organization involved in demonstrations against not only the monarchy but also government institutions. There have been arrests at these demonstrations, and Miss Elliot was herself arrested once. If you look at the picture at the back of the folder you'll see a picture of the incident at which Miss Elliot was arrested."

George's heart sank as she looked at the image of a young Bea being held by two policewomen, while her compatriots fought with another officer and a Union Flag lay burning on the ground.

"This doesn't look good, Prime Minister. I just can't imagine Miss Elliot going that far. She is one of the kindest and most empathetic people in my acquaintance. I realize young people tend to be more militant, but—"

"Your Majesty, by giving you that folder of information, I am showing you what will be available to the press when they eventually take an interest in Miss Elliot. I think you'll agree they could make her character look pretty unpalatable."

George nodded solemnly. "And you still wish to support me in this relationship, Prime Minister?"

Bo went back into her briefcase and brought out another folder. "I wanted you to see the worst of what was out there, Ma'am, but there is another side to the story."

George took the second folder and prayed it held better news.

"If you look at the police report and witness statements, you'll find that Miss Elliot was released without charge. She was indeed taking part in the demonstration, but according to her witness statement she was becoming increasingly concerned about the militant nature of Free Republic, and when the leader of the movement started to burn the flag, she tried to stop him and was assaulted by him. It's all backed up by the other witness statements."

George was so relieved that her judgement of Bea's character was not wrong. "And she left Free Republic after that?"

"Yes, Ma'am. She was never involved with them again, and you can tell from the various press reports in there that since then, she's only ever been in the newspapers because of her charity work. She's raised a great deal of money for various charities and has received awards and commendations for her good works."

"So do you think the British people could accept her?"

Bo gave her a broad smile. "I believe that with the proper press management we could make Miss Elliot extremely popular. That's why I had to show you both the best and the worst information, Your Majesty. Left alone, the press could paint a very bleak picture of her, but it wouldn't be a true reflection of the facts. It must be managed."

George handed her back the folder and asked, "How can we achieve that?"

"Your deputy secretary, Sebastian Richardson? He's a very able young man—have him work with my right-hand man, Felix, and between the two of them, if and when your relationship hits the press, they will be able to manage it and change any negative public opinion."

"I will." The Queen stood and extended her hand to Bo. "I can't thank you enough for this, Prime Minister."

"If you do persue this relationship, Your Majesty, there will be some opposition from some of the more...traditional sections of the House of Commons, particularly the Conservative party, but I believe you will get cross-party and public support once the full facts are presented."

Now I just need to show you, my love, that you are the one for me.

When Bea and George resumed their Timmy's visits, Bea started to lose the awkwardness she'd felt since their trip to France. The emotions that had been so close to the surface there were kept more firmly under control when travelling around the counrty. Today she and George were attending a lunch in Birmingham, to meet and thank faith and community groups, who had come together to raise funds for their local hospice. A local Indian celebrity chef was making the food, and George had told her how much she was looking forward to an authentic curry for lunch at the community hall.

After meeting and greeting everyone, the Queen sat at the top table, alongside the mayor and Bea. While the mayor's attention was on the local faith leader who sat beside her, she and George got the opportunity to chat. "You look as if you're looking forward to this."

"Curry? Yes, I love it. Do you?"

Bea smiled. "Yes, as long as it's not too hot. So is everything still on for your birthday night out?" With their six months together soon coming to an end, Bea thought it the perfect present to give to George, before they inevitably parted ways.

"Oh yes, Cammy helped me persuade Lang, and they're going to do a couple of dry runs to the pub, just to get an idea of the layout and any potential problems. I can't wait."

Bea smiled excitedly. "Me too. It'll be such fun to introduce you to my friends."

"I have one condition, though," George told her.

"What kind of condition?"

"Since this night out is a celebration for my official birthday, then it seems only right that you come to the ceremonial element of it. Will you and your mother and father be my guests at Trooping the Colour?"

"Trooping the Colour? Is that the marching-up-and-down thing they show on TV every year?"

George smiled and shook her head. "Marching-up-and-down thing? Really, Miss Elliot, you ought to listen to your mother when she talks about the pageants on TV."

Unseen by the other guests, Bea poked George in the ribs under the table. "You tell me what it means, then, Your Majesty."

"That hurts."

Bea giggled and stuck her tongue out.

"You'll be in trouble if a photographer caught you doing that."

"I'm sure. So tell me."

"It dates back to a time when soldiers used their regiment's colour, or flag, as a rallying point on the battlefield, so each regiment would march past to assemble at their colour. Then in the seventeenth century, the ceremony began to be used at the monarch's birthday. I ride down the Mall to Horse Guards Parade, inspect the troops, then take my place at the saluting base, and the whole of the Household Cavalry march past me in salute. It's basically a chance to show the professionalism of the British Army. Very difficult manoeuvres are performed to music, and it's quite a spectacle, I think."

It suddenly dawned on Bea that she'd watched it before. "Oh yes, the soldiers wear the big black hats?"

George laughed softly. "Bearskins, yes. They are a challenge to wear, I can tell you."

Bea smiled coyly. "You'll be wearing one?"

"Indeed. So you'll come?"

"I don't think Mum would let me refuse." The waiters came round and placed a plate and various bowls of curry around the diners.

George rubbed her hands together in glee. "I'm going to enjoy this."

❖

It was a bright and sunny June morning for Queen Georgina's first Trooping the Colour ceremony as monarch. George stood in front of a large long mirror as Captain Cameron inspected every inch of George's Scots Guards uniform. She walked round the Queen looking for any stray bits of lint on the bright red tunic. The three dogs had been banned from the Queen's presence this morning so that none of their hair would find its way onto her uniform.

George had been so nervous last night she hadn't slept a wink, and she wasn't much better today. "Was this collar always so tight?" George pulled at the tight-feeling gold collar with the gold embroidered thistle.

"Your Majesty, would you stop fiddling, man. I've just got everything the way I want it." Cammy batted the Queen's hands away and fixed the collar back to her standards.

"Well, as long as it meets your standards, Captain Cameron... Sometimes I feel like a dressmaker's dummy," George grumbled.

Cammy adjusted the Queen's blue sash upon which her service medals from both the Army and Royal Navy sat proudly. "As long as I am judged by the way you're turned out, Your Majesty, then I'll make sure every part of your uniform is in its proper place."

George placed a hand on Cammy's shoulder. "I'm sorry for grumbling, Cammy. I'm just very nervous, but my uniform looks perfect. I can see my face in these gold buttons and shoes."

Cammy straightened one last button and said, "I should bloody well hope so. I spent all day yesterday polishing and cleaning everything, every last button and buckle."

"It certainly shows, Captain." George adjusted the gold sash and ribbon round her waist and turned to check the back.

"So why are you so nervous, Ma'am? You've done plenty of Colours ceremonies before."

George walked over to the window and looked out at the crowds assembling down the Royal Mall. The guardsmen lined the route, ready to protect the royal party.

"But I wasn't the monarch. I was always riding behind Papa, and he was the focus of attention. I'm worried I'll do something wrong and disappoint Mama and the family."

"George, get a grip on yourself."

George turned round, surprised at Cammy's outburst.

"You've never put a foot wrong, no matter what you do. You've done countless rehearsals, so you know exactly what you have to do. What's really bothering you?"

"Bea's going to be watching, and I want her to be proud of me. I'm frightened of looking like an arse in front of her and her parents."

"You never could. I've seen the way she looks at you, like you could do no wrong. She adores you."

George walked over to examine the bearskin hat sitting in a large box on the table. "I wish that were true. It's days like today I realize how much I love her, Cammy. She'll be there watching, so close to me, but I won't get to see her at all. She should be by my side. It would make me the happiest person in the world to know that she was waiting for me back at the palace with my family."

"You need to tell this wee lassie how you really feel. The two of you are dancing around each other and getting nowhere."

"She doesn't let me. Every time I try to tell her, she changes the subject."

"Hmm. Maybe this night out you're having with her will be a good thing. I know I haven't been too enamoured with the idea because of security, but just the two of you spending time with each other in an ordinary pub, like an ordinary evening out, will be a good idea."

"Perhaps. One thing she did say is that she likes me in uniforms and is looking forward to seeing me in this one."

Cammy lifted the impressive bearskin hat from its box. "Well, let's make sure you look like a perfectly turned out and very proud royal colonel-in-chief."

The Queen had dispatched Archie Fairfax to look after her guests for the day. She'd sent the major and a car to pick up the Elliots and transport them to the stands for invited guests on Horse Guards Parade. When Bea saw they were sitting in amongst the VIPs, she was very glad that they would have the major at their side. There were high-ranking members of all the armed forces and all the recognized churches, politicians from the Queen's government and Her Majesty's opposition, and then the Elliots, a working-class family from Bethnal Green. It was surreal.

"These are our seats here, miss, and if you look over to the side of the parade ground, you can see the projected screen, so we will be able to follow Her Majesty from Buckingham Palace." Major Fairfax sat between Bea and her parents so that he could talk them all through what was happening.

As they took their seats Bea felt a murmur go through the VIP section. She looked around and found lots of looks coming her way, and it made her uneasy.

"Look Reg, there's the prime minister," Sarah said gleefully. Ever since the Queen had invited them, her mother had been the most excited Bea had ever seen her. She was glad that she could share this unusual friendship she had with the Queen with her parents. When Bea looked over, the PM smiled and nodded to her.

"I see her, Sarah. There's the opposition leader, Andrew Smith, too," Reg told her.

Bea had never met Mr. Smith, but as she looked up at him, he gave her an unimpressed look and whispered something to his wife. She'd noticed a lot of people whispering whilst looking at her. *Surely they can't be gossiping about me. Nobody knows about my friendship with George.*

❖

Upon arriving at the palace, Julian had headed straight for the reception room and poured a whisky from the decanter there. He desperately wanted the alcohol to dull the panic and nerves he'd been feeling all week. The little warning he'd arranged for his cousin had started to feel like a bad idea. He'd been shouting at his wife, his children, his staff, and all the time the words he had said to his underworld contact had echoed through his mind.

I want a warning shot to remind the country that this Queen of theirs is a an unnatural freak, and a disgrace to the House of Buckingham.

He walked over to the window and saw the crowds that had gathered to see today's spectacle. They waved their flags and held up their placards, all excitedly waiting on George.

"What do they think is wonderful about her? Peasants."

It wasn't just the people. When he arrived, he'd had to witness the extended family fawn all over her, particularly his parents and siblings. *It should have been me.*

He glugged back the rest of his whisky. "She has to be stopped. At any cost."

❖

"If you look to the screen now, Mr. and Mrs. Elliot and Miss Elliot, the parade is about to start." Major Fairfax pointed over to the large projected screen, which showed the front of Buckingham Palace.

The bands of the Household Cavalry started playing and the carriages emerged from the archway in front of the palace.

"Is that the Queen Mother in the first carriage, Major?" Reg asked.

"Yes, Mr. Elliot, along with the Dowager Queen Adrianna and the Duke of Bransford to accompany them."

"Such elegant ladies, aren't they, Bea?" her mum said.

Bea was so happy to be sharing this with her parents, her mum especially, having endured so much unhappiness in her life. It was wonderful to see her face light up like this. "They are, Mum, and very nice people too."

"The Queen Mother must be sad though—her first Trooping the Colour without the King. They were a very loving couple, weren't they, Major Fairfax?"

"Indeed, Mrs. Elliot. I'm sure I'm not speaking out of turn to tell you that the King's death has been a huge loss to the whole family, but Queen Georgina has been a rock of strength for them all."

Bea listened and thought that not even her family, or any of the close family staff, knew what an emotional toll her father's death had taken on the Queen—the panic attacks, not sleeping well. *She is their rock, and in turn, she comes to me for comfort.* She wouldn't let herself think about what would happen when they no longer saw each other.

They watched the rest of the family follow out of the gates past the Life Guards regiment, looking resplendent on their magnificent horses and wearing their distinctive gold helmets with white plumes.

The last carriage went past, followed by the colonels-in-chief, both royal and non. They took their place in front of the Life Guards, and the bands stopped.

"Here comes the Queen now, Miss Elliot," the major told her.

The lone figure of a guard's officer on a magnificent white horse came through the palace arch. If it hadn't been for the blue sash across her red guard's tunic, marking the officer as royal, and the major explaining what was happening, she would never have known it was George. The tall bearskin covered most of her face, but then the screen changed to a close up and she would have recognized those eyes anywhere.

Bea gasped, and Major Fairfax thought she'd asked a question. "Sorry, Miss Elliot?"

She looked at him and stuttered, "I just wondered what uniform Queen Georgina had on. It's very striking."

"Ah yes, of course. Well, she is entitled to wear many uniforms, as she is commander-in-chief of the military as a whole, but she also inherited the role of colonel-in-chief of many regiments. Today Her Majesty has chosen to wear her Scots Guards uniform."

They heard the parade commander shout, "Royal salute! Present arms!" All the Guardsmen lining the route and the cavalry waiting to escort the Queen came to attention.

Queen Georgina and her horse strode through the gates and stopped, while the national anthem was played.

Major Fairfax whispered, "Once the anthem is played, she will make her way down the Mall."

Bea thought it was wonderful watching the Queen ride through the crowds. They cheered, shouted, and waved flags, delighted to be part of the pageantry. Her people loved her, and so did Bea.

Bea had to admit, the whole occasion was magnificent. The marching and manoeuvres the soldiers performed on Horse Guards Parade, with only a few shouted commands, were remarkable. And as she watched the woman she loved taking the salute of all the regiments, it brought home to her just how important her role as monarch was. She couldn't help but feel a tremendous pride in the country, the military, and the ceremony, and that was something she'd never expected.

The ceremony was now in its final stages as the procession moved from the parade ground back up the Mall towards the palace.

❖

George smiled and nodded to the crowds as she trotted back down the Mall. She breathed a sigh of relief as she neared the end of her first birthday parade. *It couldn't have gone better, Papa.*

Then she felt a small thud against her chest. She looked down and her tunic was splattered with what looked like black dye. The horse bucked and neighed at the noise of the shot, and George struggled to get it back under control.

There were screams from the crowd and the Horse Guards behind her rushed up to surround the Queen and drew their swords. The remaining mounted and foot guards surrounded the other members of the royal family. Above the chaotic scene, a message was projected on the screens that lined the route:

TODAY WAS A WARNING. THE NEXT TIME YOU WILL DIE. YOU WILL NEVER BE ALLOWED TO REMAIN ON THE THRONE. LEAVE, OR FACE THE CONSEQUENCES.

❖

The Queen insisted on finishing the parade, much to the parade commander's chagrin. A lone extremist would not be allowed to ruin the day.

After the family made the customary balcony appearance, the Queen met with Inspector Lang, Colonel Fitzpatrick the parade commander, and representatives of the security services involved in the day's security.

"Ma'am, an investigation will be launched into today's events, but there was nothing from the main groups we've been monitoring that would have suggested this. I think we have a lone operative here," the MI5 commander said.

George nodded in agreement. "Seemed like a lot of parlour tricks to me. Lang?"

"I'm not sure, Ma'am. I recommend we have a cross-agency meeting. When the necessary Internet chatter has been monitored, someone may claim responsibility."

"Yes. That sounds like a fair plan. I'll be talking with the prime minister shortly and I'm sure she will make some recommendations. Thank you, gentlemen."

As they made their way out, Cammy came in to see her. "I have the Elliots, Ma'am."

George stood, smoothed back her hair, and pulled down her red tunic. She'd asked Cammy to contact Major Fairfax and have him bring them to meet her at the palace, as she knew Bea would be very worried. "Show them in, Captain."

Bea came rushing in and, forgetting royal protocol, threw herself into George's arms. "Georgie, I was so worried."

George held her tight, breathing in the scent of her golden hair. "I'm absolutely fine. It was all a lot of stuff and nonsense."

Bea pulled back, looked into George's eyes, and said, "I've never been that scared." Bea looked uncomfortable and took a step back. "Your Majesty, this is my mum, Sarah, and my dad, Reginald." They bowed and curtsied.

"It's a pleasure to meet you. I've heard such a lot about you both. You'll have to excuse the state of my tunic, but as you saw, we had a bit of excitement earlier."

"Your Majesty, we're so pleased to meet you," Sarah said.

"I hope this didn't spoil your enjoyment of the day."

"Not at all, Ma'am. It was a day to remember for my wife and me," Reg told George.

She indicated to the comfortable couch she had in her office. "Will you all take a seat? I've called for some tea."

When they all sat, Bea said sadly, "We'll have to cancel your birthday night out now, I suppose."

George shook her head. "Oh no, Miss Elliot. You're not getting out of it that easily."

Chapter Twenty

Bea paced up and down the hotel room, waiting for the Queen to arrive. Holly had all her equipment laid out, ready to transform Georgina into Rex. "Maybe she's not coming. Maybe Inspector Lang has convinced her it's a bad idea."

Holly sighed, having heard variations of this for the last half an hour. "She told you she was coming. Her people have checked out Mickey D's and are going to have officers in plain clothes throughout the pub, and they've booked out this floor of the hotel. They've put in extra security since the Trooping the Colour incident. I don't think she'd go to all that trouble and not turn up."

Bea looked at herself in the mirror and smoothed down her little black dress nervously. "I suppose."

"You're in love with her, aren't you?"

She snapped her head round at her friend, but before she could reply, there was a knock at the door. She hesitated before opening it. "It doesn't matter what I am, Holls, we live in different worlds."

Bea opened the door and curtsied, before allowing the Queen and Cammy to enter.

"Good evening, Bea, you look absolutely stunning." She felt George's eyes rove over her body.

George handed her a beautiful bunch of flowers, making it feel ever more like a romantic occasion.

"Thank you." Bea heard Holly clear her throat behind her. "Oh yes, Ma'am, Cammy, let me introduce my good friend, Holly."

Holly walked forward and bobbed a curtsy.

"Delighted to meet you, Holly. I understand you're going to make me unrecognizable."

"Yes—I'm going to try my very best, Your Majesty."

"Excellent, now please just treat me as normal from now on, Holly, or I may be discovered."

Bea had already warned her friends Lali and Greta not to curtsy when they all met at the bar.

"Of course, Ma'am."

George indicated to Captain Cameron. "This is my aide, Cammy." Holly and Cammy shook hands. "I do hope these clothes will suffice. It was hard to get the captain here to agree to anything as informal as this. I took advice from Theo as to what was acceptable to wear to a pub, since I only ever wear suits, a uniform, or jeans and a dress shirt. I'm not what you would call fashionable, and well, I hope it's okay." George had on designer jeans with black boots, a white T-shirt, and a green army-style jacket, and sticking out of her pocket was a matching baseball cap.

Oh God, she looks gorgeous. "You look wonderful," Bea said. She felt her cheeks start to burn but saw George had a broad smile on her face. "Why don't we let Holly start, then, Your Majesty?"

"Of course." George clapped her hands together. "Where do we start?"

Holly stepped forward with an inconspicuous-looking box and handed it to Cammy. "Perhaps the captain could help you with this part, and then I'll work on your facial features. You'll find instructions inside."

Cammy peeked inside the box and said, "Yes, I think that would be wise. Ma'am, if you could follow me to the bathroom?"

George looked intrigued and followed her aide. Once the bathroom door was shut and locked, Bea asked, "What did you give her, Holls?"

Holly smirked. "Everything she needs to change her body's appearance to Rex."

Bea's eyes went wide. "You mean…"

"Yes, I do mean, and I know you've always liked *that*." Holly left the word hanging in midair. There were no secrets between Holly, Lali, Greta, and herself. They talked about everything, and now Bea wished they didn't.

Bea felt panic gnaw at her stomach. "Holls, please tell me you just gave her something for show—tell me you didn't give her Intelliflesh?"

Intelliflesh was a technology that had revolutionized the medical world and Holly's own world of cosmetic art. It could be fashioned into any shape, and when attached to the body could provide a full sensory experience. It was used both medically, for prostheses, reconstructive surgery, and gender reassignment, and in the movie industry to change the appearance of actors. And it was also very popular for more intimate use as well.

Holly shrugged her shoulders and smiled coyly. "Of course I did, it's what I work with every day, and I'm going to be using it to change her appearance."

"You know what I'm talking about, Holls, the downstairs department? And don't tell me you work with them every day because I know you prefer the real thing," Bea said, getting more worked up by the second.

"I thought the Queen would like the full experience."

Bea threw her hands in the air in frustration. "The full experience? This isn't just some new friend, Holls, It's the Queen of Great Britain and the Commonwealth. She shouldn't even be going on a night out like this. She's doing it for me because I stupidly thought it would be a great birthday present. She's going to be so embarrassed now."

Holly looked in surprise at her friend. "What are you so worried about? That she'll react to you and you'll have no choice but to see and feel how attractive she finds you?"

Bea couldn't answer; the thoughts whizzing around her head were so confusing. "I'm going for a walk. I need some air."

❖

George hung her jacket on the back of the door of the large bathroom. "So, what's in there? Something to bind my chest, I suppose, such as it is." She was small-breasted, which suited her well, as she'd always felt more drawn towards masculinity than femininity.

"Yes, it's an Intelliflesh binding."

"Intelliflesh? Ah, I suppose Holly uses that a lot in her business. It will be interesting to see what it feels like. Let's get on with it then." George pulled off her T-shirt and compression shirt, ready for Cammy to put the flesh-coloured binding on. It looked like a rectangular piece of thin rubber. "How does this thing work?"

"According to the instructions, I pull it tightly around your torso, Ma'am, and it will shrink and merge more naturally with your skin."

After it was pulled tightly, George felt herself pulled in and held very firmly. "Bloody hell." She imagined this was what a corset must feel like.

Cammy walked around the front to examine the effect. "Is it too tight, Ma'am?"

"No, I can live with it, Captain. How does it look?"

"It looks excellent, it fits in perfectly. No one will see anything, even with your tight T-shirt on. See for yourself." Cammy pointed to the mirror on the bathroom door.

George was amazed to see herself with a flat, muscular chest to match her muscular shoulders and arms.

"Do you have sensation? You can usually feel something after a few minutes."

George stroked her fingers across her chest and gasped. The feeling gave her goosebumps all down her arms and thighs. "It's so strange, the feeling…" Suddenly she realized what Cammy had said and turned around sharply. "Wait, you've used this before?"

"No, Ma'am, I used another version of the product."

George saw Cammy trying her best to hide a smile but let it go. She pulled her T-shirt back on and admired her shape. "So is that it then? Am I manly enough?"

Cammy directed her gaze down to the Queen's fly and smirked.

"Oh, I see. Something to give me a bulge down there?"

"Yes Ma'am."

George smiled and rubbed her hands together. "So, Captain, what do you have for me?"

Cammy opened the box and pulled out the Intelliflesh strap-on. "Holly has provided us with exactly what you'll need."

George quirked an eyebrow to her friend. "Impressive size. Holly flatters me. Still, I am a Queen."

"It goes by your height and build, Ma'am," Cammy told her with a smile.

"Wait—is this the same as the chest binder?" George panicked.

Cammy nodded. "Yes, it's functional—in a limited way, obviously. Is that a problem? If you're uncomfortable with it, Ma'am, I'll come up with something else for you."

George thought for a moment. She was nervous about using it, but had always wanted to explore that side of her sexuality. "No, I'd like to try it, I think. Is this the other version of the product that you've used, Captain Cameron?"

Cammy laughed and said, "An officer never tells tales about her liaisons with the lassies in her life."

"Oh, please, Captain Cameron. Going by the ladies who've lined up to wave you off at whatever port we were leaving, I would say you kept them happy. You've used one?"

"Yes, Ma'am, and enjoyed the experience very much."

"I'll give it a try. It's just for show of course."

Cammy handed the strap-on to her. "Of course. Now I'll leave you to it. Attaching it is a personal thing."

❖

Bea had taken a walk to clear her head, but nothing seemed to calm her nerves, so she made her way back up to the floor the Queen had taken over. George's protection officers waved her past the security checkpoint at the lift area. As she approached the hotel room and saw Inspector Lang standing guard at the door, she realized how surreal her life had become.

In that hotel room, Queen Georgina of Great Britain was being fitted with a strap-on and chest binder, to accompany her out to Mickey D's disguised as a man. *Insane!*

"Thank you Inspector. I suppose you think this is ridiculously odd."

She hadn't ever seen the large, gruff-looking policeman smile, but he did then. "Miss, when you work for the royal family, you see and do many strange things, but it's a privilege to protect them. I had my concerns about this evening, but I think it was a very kind idea, Miss Elliot. She deserves one night of normality."

Bea had noticed that all the Queen's staff were fiercely loyal to her, not just because they were doing their jobs, but because they genuinely liked her and had huge respect for her role as sovereign.

"Thank you Inspector, I'm going to try and make sure Her Majesty enjoys her evening."

When she entered the room, she found George sitting at the dressing table being worked on by Holly. She couldn't see her face yet, as George had her back to Bea.

"How's it going, Holls?"

Holly added one last brush of make-up and stood back to admire her handiwork. "I'm done. What do you think, Ma'am? I haven't added too much, just enough to give you the effect of some very light stubble and sideburns."

"It's looks top notch, Holly, thank you." George stood and faced Bea. "What do you think, Bea? Will I do?"

Bea looked, transfixed, at George. Holly was right—she hadn't had to do much to give George a more male appearance. Her face looked a little fuller, and with the completely flat chest and bulge in the correct place, she doubted many would suspect Rex of being Queen Georgina.

When Bea didn't answer, George asked Cammy and Holly if they could give them some privacy.

"We'll be outside, Ma'am, just tell us when you're ready to go," Cammy said before holding the door for Holly and ushering her out.

When they were gone, George walked up to her and said, "Do I look that bad?"

Bea shook herself. "No, you look handsome and beautiful, but you always do, Georgie, with or without any cosmetic help. I'm just surprised because I thought you would look really different, and it would be like going out with a stranger, but it won't."

George took her hands and said, "I suppose I don't need much help to look male. It's probably a lot easier than making me look feminine."

Bea laughed gently. "It's your prize bull qualities shining through."

George took another step closer to her. "Do you like my prize bull qualities?"

The air around them seemed to be charged with an energy that was pulling Bea to George. This was more than lust, or even love. Bea had thought she'd loved Ronnie, but nothing could have prepared her for the deep need she had for George. She felt powerless against it. Bea reached up and cupped a newly stubbled cheek. "I love your bully qualities, but no matter what Holly had done to you, I realize now I would know you anywhere from those eyes of yours. I know them."

"I know. You always know me." George's arms went around her waist and pulled her close.

Bea didn't stop her. She was tired of fighting her heart, sick of constantly worrying about the pain that she felt was inevitable. "Remember, Georgie, tonight you are Rex. You have no responsibilities to anyone, no throne, no family, no press to worry about. You are just a man called Rex enjoying an ordinary night out at the pub with his friends. It's your night, so enjoy it."

"As long as I'm with you, I will." George lowered her lips towards her and Bea wasn't going to stop her. At this second there was nothing that mattered more than George's lips on hers. They were inches apart when they heard a clap at the door.

"Ma'am? Lang has the cars at the front of the hotel when you're ready."

The spell was broken and Bea stepped back quickly. "We'd better get going, Rex, come on."

Cammy drove them to the pub in an ordinary looking but fully armoured all-terrain vehicle, to make it look as if they were simply four friends on a night out. Inspector Lang and one of his officers followed behind discreetly, and he had both male and female officers spread throughout the pub, to react to any threat to the Queen immediately.

They pulled up at the front of the club, where an officer was waiting to take the car and wait to pick up the party of friends later. Cammy and Holly got out first, leaving George and Bea alone for a minute.

"Are you ready for this, Georgie?"

"I can't wait to see what a normal evening out is like. Before we go in, I just wanted to tell you how much I appreciate you doing this for me. No one else but you would have realized how valuable being someone else for the evening would be."

"I just hope it lives up to your expectations. Just remember—this is your chance to do what you want. You are Rex, and Rex has no restrictions on his life."

George nodded in understanding. "Just one more thing, before we get out and I become Rex. Your *Georgie* wants to tell you that you look absolutely beautiful, and I will be so proud to be out with you tonight."

Bea smiled and she kissed George on the cheek. She wanted so much more. "You are such a sweetheart. Let's go get Rex a drink. I hope Rexie doesn't mind you stealing his name for the evening," she joked.

"Never—he was delighted that I was going to spend the evening with you."

"Told you that, did he?" Bea looked sceptical.

"Of course, would I lie to you?"

Bea laughed and said, "Come on then, Rex."

George was normally a very confident person in public, or could at least appear confident, but walking into a pub for an ordinary evening out was a different thing altogether. She prayed that no one would recognize her, or her one chance to spend an evening like this with Bea would be over.

When they walked through the door, George was delighted by the absence of the looks that would normally follow her; but as they followed Holly and Cammy across the bar, she became aware that a lot of the women at the bar and the tables turned and hungrily appraised Bea. George felt a hot surge of anger go right through her. It was a foreign feeling, but her body seemed to react on instinct, and without thinking in a rational fashion, her hand shot out and took hold of Bea's in a proprietary manner.

Before George got a chance to admonish herself, Bea smiled up at her and squeezed her hand in response. George was delighted and felt immense pride that she was the one Bea wanted to be close to, wanted to hold on to. When she looked back around the bar, those who looked at Bea with hunger had turned back to their drinks and friends in defeat. George felt smug, and she didn't care if that was bad or not. It was the truth. *I want you to be mine, my darling Bea.*

Holly stopped at a large booth in the corner of the room and took her seat beside two women, who looked nervous.

Bea smiled proudly to her friends. "Lali? Greta? I would like you to meet my new friend, Rex."

Lali and Greta looked up at George with astonishment. "Good evening, ladies. I'm delighted to meet you. Bea has told me so much about you both."

Lali was the first to take George's outstretched hand and unconsciously bowed her head.

Bea whispered, "Lali, no bowing."

"Oh, sorry…I'm pleased to meet Your Maj—*Rex.*"

George smiled and turned to Greta. "You must be Greta." Greta managed to shake hands without a bow but still stumbled over her greeting to the Queen. "May I introduce my friend Cammy?"

Cammy shook hands with Greta first. "Pleased to meet you."

When she turned to Lali, her eyes seemed to sparkle, and she lifted Lali's hand and kissed it politely. "And I'm very pleased to meet you, lassie. Miss Elliot certainly has some bonnie friends."

George rolled her eyes and Bea softly giggled. Cammy always put on her best Scottish brogue when she met someone she found attractive.

Lali laughed, clearly knowing she was being chatted up. "Thank you, but you're a flatterer, I think, Cammy."

When George sat down, she took Bea's hand again, and neither of them made comment on it. After some initially stiff conversation, George managed to put Bea's friends at ease, and Cammy was trying to be as charming as possible.

George and Bea were left alone when Cammy went to the bar to buy some more drinks for the group, and Lali and Greta visited the ladies'.

"How are you enjoying being anonymous, Rex?" Bea asked.

George took the opportunity to sit closer to her and put her arm along the back of the couch seat. "It's truly wonderful. Nobody cares that I'm here. I'm just one of the crowd. I can't tell you how much I'm enjoying spending it with you."

George tenderly stroked her thumb across the back of Bea's hand, and she felt full of emotions for her love. She didn't know for certain, but she was sure Bea could feel it too. It felt like they were the only two people in the whole pub. George didn't even notice where her protection officers were, and usually she was only too well aware of their presence.

"I care that you're here. You could never be one of the crowd to me, Georgie."

They got closer, and George thought this time she would get to kiss her, this time she would feel the lips that were so close to hers, but they were interrupted by the voices and laughter of their friends returning. George sighed and Bea moved away from her.

Cammy held a tray of drinks and began to hand them out. She left Lali's to the the end and handed over her drink with a wink. "Here you go, lassie."

"I do have a name, you know," Lali said in an annoyed tone of voice.

Cammy turned around and said, "Aye, bonnie lassie."

George shook her head and chuckled at her friend's attempt to charm Lali. Cammy's manner didn't seem to be working as well as it usually did.

The group become ever louder, joking and laughing. George was starting to feel much more relaxed. She became braver with her touches, and Bea was reciprocating.

After a while, the girls headed off to the ladies' room, leaving Cammy and George alone together.

"How are we enjoying our night, Rex?"

"We love our night, Captain. Bea is being so open with me—she let me hold her hand." Cammy laughed out loud at her. "Why are you laughing?"

"Be bolder. Take the bull by the horns. You're both relaxed—enjoy each other. I don't think she would mind."

"You seem to be making slow progress with Lali. Losing your touch, Captain?" George teased.

"Never, she's just making me work harder, and I can work hard, believe me. She is the bonniest lassie I think I've ever seen."

George sipped from her water glass. She enjoyed the warm glow of feeling a little drunk, but she wanted to be entirely present for the rest of the evening, wherever it took her. When she heard Bea's voice next to her, she looked up at and felt like a bolt hit her. There was never going to be any going back for her. For her heart and her body, there would be Bea and no other.

Be bold. She pulled Bea down onto her lap.

Bea squealed in surprise and put her arms around George's neck. "What are you up to, Rex?"

"I just thought you needed somewhere to sit, and I'm always happy to oblige a lady," George said with a cheeky smile.

Bea licked her lips seductively and wiggled her bottom around in George's lap. "I keep trying to tell you, I'm not a lady," she whispered.

George groaned, and then her eyes went wide in surprise. The usual throbbing she would feel around Bea when she was aroused had an altogether different effect when wearing the strap-on. She saw the recognition in Bea's eyes. *Oh God, what is she going to think?* "Bea, please forgive me, I'm—"

Bea put her finger over George's lips. "It's okay. Don't be embarrassed. I was teasing you." She slipped back into the seat beside her, giving George the chance to calm down.

George took some deep breaths and thought, *This is torture, I need you, Bea.*

❖

Bea had to admit, she couldn't remember ever having so much fun before. George was attentive and caring, and made her feel like she was the centre of her attention. At the moment Bea was giggling and laughing like a schoolgirl. Cammy was trying to charm Lali up onto the floor to dance, but she wasn't having any of it. She'd already been up to dance with Holly and Greta.

Bea tried to encourage her friend for poor Cammy's sake. "Lali, go on, you know you like to dance, and the captain here is willing."

"Very willing and able, Ma'am." Cammy saluted Lali and the whole table laughed.

Lali tried and failed to keep her smile hidden. "Well, I don't see you up dancing, Beatrice Elliot."

Bea smiled at her friend and grabbed George by the hand. "Come on, Rex, let's show them how it's done."

George looked panicked all of a sudden. "Ah…I don't dance."

"You must do. Surely you learned dancing at that fancy school of yours."

"Yes. Ballroom and Scottish country dancing. That's all a Queen needs to know. This type though…"

Bea pulled George up and towards the dance floor. "We'll muddle through. I want to dance with you, Georgie."

George seemed delighted with that, and so scooped her into her arms. Bea giggled as George tried to waltz to the fast pop song that was playing.

"I'm glad I can keep you amused, Miss Elliot." George smiled down at her.

"You are funny. Everyone thinks of you as being this thoroughly modern person because you're a woman, and openly gay, but they don't know *you*. You really are the most traditional person I know. You like bagpipe and band music, making model ships is your idea of a fun night in, and you like mushy old romantic films. I think you were born in the wrong era."

George reached out and cupped her cheek. "Nobody knows that because they don't see me the way you do. You know me, Bea."

Just as they stood still, looking deeply into each other's eyes, the music changed to a slow love song, and they began to sway together. Bea simply couldn't hold back her overwhelming feelings for George anymore. It didn't feel like they were in the bar. It felt like they were dancing on air, somewhere private, somewhere only they knew. Her resistance was gone. She didn't try to stop the Queen's lips as they descended on hers, and she softly and lovingly kissed her.

CHAPTER TWENTY-ONE

The evening wound to a close, and George and Bea were driven back to the hotel by the Queen's protection officers. Cammy had escorted Lali and the girls home. Since leaving the pub, an uneasy awkwardness had set in between them. In the pub with the drink flowing and a jubilant atmosphere, it was easy for George to get lost in her feelings for Bea, but when they walked out the door into the cold of the night, everything didn't seem so simple as it had outside.

They rode the lift in silence, despite the fact that George had a million different things to say buzzing around in her head. They walked in silence towards their rooms, and finally George broke the awkwardness by saying, "Would you come in and help me take off this…?" George pointed to the Intelliflesh pieces on her face.

"Of course I will," Bea said.

George was so happy the evening wouldn't be over yet. She was dreading the dark loneliness of going to bed alone.

All the protection officers took their positions outside the lift and along the corridor, with Lang and a younger officer outside the Queen's door. She nodded to them as she walked past, and neither officer raised an eyebrow at the sight of Bea entering her room with her at this time of night.

"Okay, Georgie, if you'd sit at the dressing table, I'll get this off for you. Holls left some things to help."

George nodded and sat. Bea methodically took off the little pieces of prosthetic that had given the Queen's face a rougher, squarer appearance. She could sense that Bea was trying to build some distance between them, after the closeness of their kiss.

"There we go, I just need to clean the make-up off and you'll be all done." Bea held George's face in her hands while she tenderly wiped the make-up off, and George had to force herself not to pull her love down for a kiss and assuage the ache in her heart.

She searched her brain for something to break the silence. "Your friends are very nice."

Bea smiled. "Thank you, they've been great friends to me. They were so excited to meet you. They were never part of my republican group at university."

"I think Cammy took a shine to Lali," George said.

"Yes, she always has been the most beautiful one of the group. But Lali isn't easily impressed—she's only had one girlfriend the whole time I've known her. She has great respect for herself."

George felt she had to do something to bridge the gap that had opened up between them tonight, or the moment might never come again. She looked up and met Bea's eyes. "Not the most beautiful one of the group, in my opinion. "

Bea looked at her with a mixture of longing and fear, and George prayed that the love she was sure they shared would overcome the fear that Bea clearly felt.

"I think that you're done—Rex is all gone. I'm sure you can deal with the other parts yourself." Bea turned and walked towards the door.

George's stomach dropped like a stone. *She's running away.* She caught up quickly and put her hand on the door so Bea couldn't open it. "Please, stay."

Bea let out a sigh and said, "Let me go, Georgie."

George turned her round and held her by the shoulders. "No, not until I tell you what's in my heart."

"Please, don't," Bea begged.

"You told me this was my night to be, and do, what I wanted, without any thoughts of my throne or my crown. You kissed me tonight and I knew I couldn't hold it in any longer." George put her fist on her chest and said desperately, "The unspoken truth between us is that I love you, I love you so much it's tearing me apart inside. You're all I think about, when I'm lying in bed at night, when I wake in the morning, and when I'm going about my duties. Sometimes when I'm meeting people or doing some event, I turn to smile at you, or to ask you if you liked a particular thing, expecting you to be at my side, and I'm surprised when you're not. I do that because that's where you should be. You work hard for those who are in pain, those less fortunate, and above all, you care deeply about people and their suffering. You were made to be my Queen Consort."

"This is not a fairy tale, Georgie! The handsome prince does not marry the poor village girl, who protested outside the castle walls, and live happily ever after. This is real life, and the handsome prince marries a suitable princess who has the correct breeding and will toe the line," Bea said furiously.

George was desperate and was willing to beg if that's what it took. She held Bea's face and said, "I can make the fairy tale come true, if you'll just let me."

Tears streamed down Bea's face. "You can't give me that."

"Look at me and tell me what's in your heart. Tell me you love me, I know you do."

Bea rested her forehead against hers, and George could feel the desperate pain she was feeling. "Let me go, please. Please, Georgie."

George felt the anger inside threaten to engulf her. She growled and forced herself to move to the side. Bea grabbed for the door handle and ran out, crying.

Bea had lain on her bed crying since returning from the Queen's room. She was angry, angry at herself, angry at George, angry at fate, for choosing as her one true love someone who was utterly unattainable. "Why, Georgie? Why did it have to be you?" Bea asked the empty room.

Her heart answered the question simply. *It could be no other...*

She got up and went to the bathroom to wash the tears from her face. As she looked in the mirror at her red, puffy eyes, she thought about how much George must be hurting, and with nobody to talk to about it.

I told her this was her night to be true to herself, and I couldn't even give her the truth. What will I do, Abby?

"I owe her the truth at the very least."

Having tidied up, Bea walked back along the corridor towards the Queen's room. She couldn't meet Inspector Lang's eye as she said, "Could you ask if I could speak to Her Majesty, Inspector?"

"If you wait here, I'll find out, Miss Elliot. Captain Cameron hasn't long left, so she should still be awake."

When he went in to speak to the Queen, Bea imagined all the officers lining the corridor looking at her, judging her, she knew how loyal all those who served George were to her.

After a few minutes Lang opened the door and said, "Come in, Miss Elliot. Her Majesty will be with you shortly."

She waited in the large living room area of the suite until the bedroom doors opened and George walked out, still wearing the jeans she had on earlier, but now wearing a white sleeveless T-shirt on top. Bea inhaled sharply. Her physique was truly breathtaking.

But her face was stony and unemotional, and it hurt Bea to know she was the cause of that. "Georgie...I want to explain—"

"You've made your position very clear, Miss Elliot. You can be sure there will be no repeat of what happened earlier, and you need not worry."

Bea's heart sank at the formal use of her name. She closed her eyes in despair, knowing that she'd destroyed what they had together.

When she opened her eyes again and saw the same stoic mask on the Queen's face, she nodded her head in acceptance, and the tears tumbled down her cheeks.

George's jaw visibly tightened. She was obviously trying hard to hold her emotions together.

Bea hugged herself tightly, hoping to gain the strength to say what she needed to say. "I understand, Your Majesty, I just didn't want to leave without telling you the truth. You were right earlier when you said I promised you a night to be true to yourself. I just want you to know that no matter how impossible it is, and no matter where our lives take us, I want you to be sure that I loved you, that I do love you more than I've ever loved anyone in my life. I thought being your friend would be enough, but I just fell deeper and deeper."

She held her hand to her mouth in an effort to calm her wracking sobs. George reached out towards her, but Bea continued as she knew she had to get the truth out.

"It scares me so much to know that I'll never be able to be with you, that I'll see you everywhere I turn for the rest of my life with someone who will never love you half as much as I do. I'm sorry I hurt you, Georgie. I just wanted you to know that." There was silence between them for a few seconds, and then Bea turned and walked to the door.

"Bea?" George shouted.

She stopped and turned to look back at her and found George standing beside her, a look of pain in her eyes.

George cradled Bea's face and said huskily, "I need you. I need you like the air that I breathe." George acted on instinct. She pulled Bea to her forcfully, and their lips crashed together in a hungry fashion. She lifted Bea off her feet and Bea wrapped her legs around George's waist.

The feeling of having Bea in her arms was overwhelming to George. She'd never felt a need and desire as strongly as she felt the need to be with this woman. After the initial burst of hungry passion, George rested her forehead on Bea's as they both gasped for air. She took Bea's hand and placed it against her own chest. "Feel what you do to my heart. Please stay with me."

She started to worry when Bea didn't reply, and said, "Forget everything and let us just be Georgie and Bea. Just us. Please."

Bea reached up and tenderly cupped George's cheek. "Make love to me, Georgie."

George grasped her hand and kissed it reverently and with a sense of such relief that her love wasn't leaving her.

Barely seconds later a realization dawned upon her: she was about to make love to the most treasured woman in her life, and she had absolutely no experience.

Perhaps recognizing her fear, Bea took her hand and led her towards the bedroom. Bea shut the door and pulled George to her, so their lips were almost touching. "Don't think about anything—just kiss me, touch me, love me."

George kissed her with renewed passion and felt herself throb. She was suddenly embarrassed, as she hadn't removed her strap-on. "I'm sorry, I didn't have time to—"

Bea placed a finger over George's lips and said, "Shh. Don't be sorry. I like it." She smiled and stroked her hand over the bulge in the Queen's jeans.

"Oh God..." George groaned.

Bea smiled seductively and pulled off George's T-shirt. She ran her hands up and down George's chest, feeling the strong musculature of her chest and stomach. "I need you," she whispered into George's neck, giving kisses and licks as she went.

George's eyes closed as she revelled in her lover's touch, and she didn't move a muscle as Bea stroked her fingertips along her broad shoulders and arms, and down over her compact breasts. Bea kissed her way down her stomach until she was on her knees and nuzzling George's hardness through her jeans.

George groaned with barely restrained lust. "Bea..."

Bea made her way back up slowly. George pulled her back into a deep kiss and then said breathlessly, "Darling, I feel like I'm going to die if I don't have you soon." She ran her fingers through the golden silk of Bea's hair and trailed her fingers down her elegant neck, and over the gentle curve of her shoulders. Her hands shook with emotion as she pulled the zip on Bea's dress and let it pool at her feet. She inhaled sharply when she saw her lover standing only in her black lingerie before her. She watched Bea start to slowly strip her lacy knickers and unclasp her bra, allowing her breasts to tumble free.

"You're simply beautiful, Beatrice Elliot," George said in awe.

"You make me feel beautiful." Bea lifted George's hand and placed it on her chest. "Do you feel what you do to my heart, just by looking at me? Touch me. Make me feel more, Georgie."

She pulled Bea to her and grasped a perfect breast. They both moaned, and George soon realized that her partner's breasts were a very erogenous zone for her, as Bea laid her hand on top of her own and encouraged George to squeeze harder.

The response fuelled her confidence, so she scooped Bea up and placed her on the massive four-poster bed. "I want you so much, my darling."

Bea let her fingers trail over her own hard nipples and said huskily, "Take them off, I want to feel you on top of me."

George stripped off her jeans, leaving her in her tight boxers, with the obvious sign of her arousal. She hesitated to take them off, but then she heard Bea say, "Everything off, Georgie, I want to see all of you, just as you are tonight."

She quickly took off her boxers and was pulled down on the bed, and on top of her lover. Bea's legs naturally parted, and George groaned in pleasure as she eased herself between her thighs, sinking into the first feel of their naked bodies coming together. George's heart hammered and her hand shook as she tentatively caressed her Bea's face, trying to memorize every moment.

She looked into Bea's passionate eyes and said, "I love you. I…"

Appearing to sense George's hesitation, Bea took hold of her hand. "Just touch me, Georgie. Touch me and kiss me everywhere."

George felt a hot rush of passion, and her lips descended onto Bea's neck, kissing and nibbling all the way down towards her breasts. She squeezed one breast while she licked and kissed the other tenderly. Her tongue swirled around Bea's hard nipple, and she was given more confidence by the sounds she was drawing from her lover.

The softness of Bea's ample breasts was something that George would never forget and would gladly spend a lifetime giving attention to. She sucked in as much of Bea's breast as she could and felt Bea's hands on the back of her head, encouraging her attentions, and all George could think of was wanting to thrust inside her.

"Georgie, it feels so good. I want to feel you everywhere." Bea moaned.

"I'll do anything for you, my darling." George could feel her lover's wetness spreading across her thigh and moaned into the breast she was gently sucking. She went back to kissing her lover's lips deeply, sucking her tongue into her mouth. The throbbing in her groin was so intense that she hoped she could control the feeling, and hang on.

"You are everything to me, darling. Please let me touch you, Bea," she pleaded.

"Yes, I need you to kiss me lower."

"Anything." She kissed her way down Bea's body, taking time to kiss and nibble her hips and thighs.

George felt her head being pushed further, encouraging her to kiss where Bea needed her. She parted her folds and moaned at the wetness that awaited her. She took one long lick and hummed in pleasure. The taste of her lover made her own arousal grow so much stronger. Her hips thrust gently against the bed beneath her, seeking some relief. Bea grabbed George's head and pulled at her hair in passion.

She pulled Bea's hips towards her and lifted her legs over her shoulders, giving better access to her sex. George swirled her tongue around the protruding clit, and then teased her wet opening.

Bea held on to her lover's hair and moaned deeply. "Yes, just like that, Georgie. Don't stop."

"Hmm, God, you taste good." George was so pleased that she seemed to be giving Bea pleasure. She was acting on pure instinct and hoped she could satisfy her more experienced lover.

Bea's hips bucked faster and faster until she went still and her manicured fingernails scratched at George's shoulders as she released her passion with a cry.

George gave a kiss to each thigh and crawled up and kissed Bea deeply. "I love you, darling. I think I've loved you since I first saw you."

Bea stroked George's face tenderly. "I love you. I've never met anyone who's touched me or my heart the way you do."

"I was made for you. That's why." George kissed her nose and cheeks.

"You think it's that simple?"

"Don't think about anything else outside of this bedroom. Here, it's just two people that love each other, and that's all that matters."

Bea stroked her fingers down the length of her strong back and squeezed her muscular buttocks. "I want you deep inside me. I want us to come together."

George nodded in understanding and repositioned herself so she could slip inside her lover. They both groaned as she guided the strap-on inside. Bea gasped in her ear and opened up some more.

George stilled and took a moment to fully appreciate the sensation of being inside her lover. It was so overwhelming, she was frightened of losing control and taking things too fast and rough. "Feels so good." She was pulled in deeper when Bea wrapped her legs around her waist. George could wait no longer and started a slow, gentle thrust. "Oh God. Never felt anything like this."

She looked down into's Bea's eyes and at that moment knew she'd been right to wait and share this with the woman she loved. It felt like her heart would explode as well as her body.

As her orgasm built, George thrust faster and harder, making them both moan in pleasure. It further excited George to have her lover holding her by her shoulders, stroking her, and as the pleasure built, digging her nails in and scratching.

"Harder, Georgie, I need it harder."

George obliged by pounding her sex as hard as she could. "Bea, darling, I can't—"

"Yes, come for me, Georgie." She thrust a few more times, and Bea said, "Look at me, Georgie. Look at me."

George forced her eyes to stay open as she tumbled into an intense orgasm and gave a strangled cry, with Bea following seconds later. Looking into her lover's eyes as she came, she felt like she could reach out and touch their love, as if a special energy existed between them that they could only see at that precise moment.

They collapsed into a sweaty, tangled heap, utterly raw and exposed. "I love you, I love you, you are my life," George repeated before kissing Bea thoroughly.

Bea rolled them over and looked down at the strong yet vulnerable woman who she loved beyond good reason. "I love you too. No matter what, I love you." Bea had no idea what would come next. It scared her how much she loved, and how much she felt, but all that mattered was giving George the perfect night she deserved.

Bea kissed George's nose and lips and began to kiss her way down her body.

"Darling, you're making me want you again," George said.

"That's the idea," she replied with a grin. "Just lie back and feel how much I love you."

She swirled and sucked at George's nipples, and then slid down to her flat muscular stomach, which drew more moans.

George's eyes went wide when she grasped her strap-on and squeezed it a few times. "What are you doing, darling?"

Bea gave her a naughty smile. "I would like to suck this all up for you, but first I'd like to taste you without it. Is that okay?"

George leaned up on her elbows and nodded, as she watched Bea remove the strap-on with ease.

She opened George and blew on the overheated flesh.

"I don't know if I could come again, darling."

Bea used the tip of her tongue to gently tease George's clit back to life. It stood up in seconds, eager for more. "Do you want me to stop?"

"God, no."

She took George's clit between her lips. They exhausted each other, learning all about one another's bodies, before finally succumbing to sleep in the small hours of the morning.

George awoke slowly, her body feeling languid and relaxed. She was taking up most of the bed, lying like a starfish across it with the crisp white sheets wrapped around her. She stretched her tired, pleasantly achy muscles, and smiled as she remembered how they got that way.

"Darling? Are you awake?" She turned around and Bea wasn't there, but the bedroom doors were ajar and she could hear the sounds of the television. *Must have gotten up early.*

George jumped up and found her discarded T-shirt and boxers on the floor, next to her strap-on. She put the dildo away in the drawer in case any of her staff came in, and she was so eager and excited to see her new lover, she nearly tripped, trying to pull her boxers on quickly.

"Darling?" She found the living room area empty, no sign of her lover's clothes. *Maybe she's gone back to her room to get changed.* George had to admit, she was a little disappointed that they didn't wake up together.

It was then that the news report on the TV penetrated her consciousness. There was footage of Bea and her touring the country, while the banner at the bottom said, *Royal love affair exposed.*

Her heart thudded loudly. "TV, up ten."

If you've just joined us, it emerged this morning that Her Majesty Queen Georgina has become involved in an affair with charity worker Beatrice Elliot. It had been thought that Queen Georgina was romantically involved with Princess Eleanor of Belgium, but it seems that Miss Elliot, who has been travelling the country with the Queen, promoting the work of hospice charity Timmy's, has caught the eye of the world's most eligible royal. There has been concern over Miss Elliot's apparent republican views from certain sections of the media and from the Conservative Party.

This morning, the media were encamped outside Miss Elliot's humble East London home, hoping for a glimpse of her, but she apparently hadn't been home the previous evening and had to fight her way through the press pack first thing this morning. We later had it confirmed from a source inside the Queen's staff that Miss Elliot stayed the night with Her Majesty.

George held her hand to her mouth in shock at the pictures of Bea being pushed and manhandled as she tried to get in through the door. "Dear God." She watched as Reg came out to rescue his daughter and get her in the house.

There was a knock at the door and Cammy came rushing in. "Have you seen…oh, you have."

George sat in the chair in front of the TV, and the news report continued.

We're joined by Conservative peer Lord Faversham. Good morning, Lord Faversham. We've heard this morning that many in your party are calling this a constitutional crisis, but surely whoever Her Majesty has a relationship with is her own business? What has it to do with the government, My Lord?

The large silver-haired peer filled the screen.

It is the business of Her Majesty's government when she embarks on an illicit relationship with someone who has such anti-monarchist and anti-establishment views and has in fact been arrested for protesting against the monarchy. It is our duty to protect our system of government and our constitutional monarchy, even if that means advising the Queen herself that she may be damaging the institution.

The presenter continued.

Lord Faversham, surely it's a bit early to call it a crisis? We don't know if these facts are true, and Number Ten says it will be releasing a statement to call into question the accusations that the media and your Conservative colleagues have made.

Lord Faversham shook his head vigorously.

You only have to look at the images of Miss Elliot, burning the British flag, to know this is a serious matter, but I have it on good authority from Viscount Anglesey that the royal family are very concerned about the Queen's actions.

George leaped up and shouted with fury, "Julian, fucking Julian. Cammy, get Sebastian and Sir Michael to meet me back at Buck House for a crisis meeting. Inform Number Ten that I need a police presence at Beatrice's house. I can't have her family put through this. Ask Sebastian to call Julian, and tell him to get his fucking arse over to the palace this afternoon, and he can also tell him, I'm going to use a dull knife to hack his fucking bollocks off!"

"Yes, Ma'am. Ah, this letter was on the table at the door as I came in," Cammy said seriously.

George took it from Cammy. The letter simply said *To Georgie* on the front. She opened it up and her hands shook as she read. *I'm sorry, Georgie. You can't give me the fairy tale, and I won't come between you and your throne.*

George fell down onto the armchair and held her head in her hands. "How did it end up like this, Cammy? Last night was the happiest of my life, and now…"

Cammy sat next to her friend. "I take it she came back after I left you last night?"

George nodded. "She came back to tell me she loved me, and the thought of being without me hurt her. We made love, and I thought that we could face anything as long as it was together. I woke this morning and this was playing"—she indicated the TV, now muted—"and she was gone. I need to speak to her, face to face."

"You can't go there, Ma'am. Let's get you back to the palace, and we can try and contact her."

"I can't live without her, Cammy. I need her."

Chapter Twenty-two

Princess Eleanor lifted and impaled herself on Julian as he kept his eyes on the news scrolling across the bedroom wall.

"My, my, Princess, you are feisty this morning. Are you imagining my cousin fucking you like this?" Julian grabbed hold of Eleanor's hips and thrust himself harder into her.

Eleanor moaned and groaned as her orgasm built higher and higher. "No, my dear Viscount. I am imagining being crowned as Queen Consort in Westminster Abbey, alongside Her Majesty, and that long after I am gone, my children shall sit on the throne of one of the oldest monarchies in Europe. My name will never be forgotten."

Julian smacked her on the buttocks and shouted, "Faster."

Eleanor picked up the pace and undulated her hips.

"Good girl. George will be forced to drop this girl like a stone, and then you soothe her grief with what you do best."

"Yes."

Eleanor started to come, and Julian thought as he watched her, *Stupid bitch, I'm going to get a lot more than that if my plans work out. King Julian.*

As he thought about being crowned and his whole family bowing down before him, he followed Eleanor over the edge, jerking inside her.

Bea lay on her bed, clutching her bear Rupert tightly. This morning had been a nightmare. When she'd woken up in George's arms, her lover sleeping so soundly, she'd never been happier. Then she'd checked the news on her mobile phone, but she couldn't quite believe it till she switched on the TV.

She wiped away the tears and cried anew. "Abby, what have I done?"

From outside her bedroom door, she heard the sound of her parents coming upstairs.

"Bea? Bea, talk to us sweetheart?" Sarah said.

"Come on, sweetheart, Mum's got tea."

Bea couldn't ignore her parents any longer. She got up and unlocked the door and fell into her mother's arms.

"Come here, sweetheart. Tell me what happened."

Reg put the tea tray down on her desk and looked up at the news channel Bea had running.

Early polls suggest public opinion is split over the Queen's relationship with Miss Elliot. We have sent our cameras onto the streets of London today to ask what the people think.

An older lady came on screen and said, *A woman with views like these, and coming from that sort of background, should never be allowed near the royal family, and I think the Queen is foolhardy for entering into this relationship.*

A young man and woman gave their opinion next. *We think it's great, don't we?* The young man's girlfriend nodded and said, *Yeah, for someone from this girl's background to make it to be a Queen? That's like a fairy tale—she would just be like us and understand how ordinary people have to live. If she makes the Queen happy, then she should go with it, and not listen to all these old fogies.*

"Bea?" Sarah pointed up to the screen. "Isn't that the man from your group that got you arrested?"

Bea wiped her eyes and looked up to see the leader of Free Republic, Simon West. He was being interviewed on the news broadcast about her involvement in the group.

And you say it was Miss Elliot, who organized the demonstration that day and planned the burning of the Union Flag?

Yes, he answered. *Bea hated everything about the monarchy and the way this country was run and wanted to step up our protests to a less peaceful kind.*

"You lying bastard," Bea shouted at the TV. "Can you believe what he's saying, Mum?"

"I know, I always knew that boy was no good from the first time I met him," Sarah told her.

And what do you think of Miss Elliot now being in a relationship with the Queen? the interviewer asked.

I think she's a traitor to everything we stood for.

The reporter turned back to the camera and said, *When we asked for a statement from Buckingham Palace, an aide told us that there would be no statements from them as Her Majesty does not comment on private matters.*

"What?" Bea exclaimed. "Her Majesty doesn't comment on private matters? Mum, she's just making it worse. We're not in a relationship, and that makes it look like everything the media is saying is true."

Sarah squeezed her daughter's hand and said, "It's just the way the royals do things, Bea. I'm sure when you talk to her, you'll work out what to do."

Reg looked out the window. "Something's going on. Two cars full of police officers have just pulled up. Looks like we've got some police protection at the front anyway. They're moving the press back from the house and putting up some barriers. I'll go and talk to them."

Bea rested her head in her hands. How could things have turned out like this?

❖

Queen Georgina stood at her office window, looking out over the Mall. The crowds that normally gathered at the gates, to watch the changing of the guard, seemed to have swelled this morning, even taking into account that it was the tourist season.

This morning, Cammy had smuggled the Queen out the back door of the hotel, while one of the female protection officers made a decoy run at the front to outfox the waiting media.

I wonder what you're thinking, my darling. She was desperate to talk to Bea but wanted to get as much information as possible from Sebastian and Sir Michael first.

George was furious that this had come out the way it had, before she and Bea had a chance to cement their relationship. She could only pray that Bea would still be willing to give their love a chance.

God knows what Granny and Mama are making of this. She knew she would have to call them as soon as she had a moment. Theo, Granny, and she always spent the weekend together at Windsor, engagements permitting, but with this crisis to be dealt with, George felt she had to be back at headquarters.

She turned when she heard a knock at the door, and called, "Come."

The door opened and Sir Michael led in Sebastian and one of the pages carrying the Queen's red boxes. The three stood at the door, bowed, and walked over to the Queen's desk, then bowed again.

"How many boxes today, Sir Michael?" George asked as she walked over to the desk.

"Seven, Your Majesty. It seems today's events have added to the papers," he said awkwardly.

"Quite." She said simply and sat at her desk. When the page left them, George sat forward in her chair and clasped her hands in front of her. "Before we get into today's events and their repercussions, I want to address how some of this information got out into the media."

Sir Michael fidgeted nervously, while Sebastian stood quite comfortably.

"The information regarding Miss Elliot's past is a different issue, I was expecting that, not as soon as this, but I did know it was out there, and I have a very good idea who tipped off the media about that. I am talking about last night. The media reported that one of my personal staff confirmed that I spent the night with Miss Elliot. Only certain members of my staff knew about the arrangements for my night out. It was top secret, so I want to know who talked. I will find out, gentlemen, because I need to be certain that those who serve the royal family can be trusted to keep our confidences."

Both men said nothing, but George could see beads of sweat forming on Sir Michael's receding hairline.

"Please don't take offence because I will be asking all my personal staff about this. Sir Michael? Could I speak to you first? Bastian, could you wait outside, please?"

"Of course, Ma'am." A quick bow and Sebastian walked backwards out of the room, and the Queen was left with her private secretary.

George looked Sir Michael in the eye and said, "You have served my family with distinction for a great many years, Sir Michael."

"I have always tried to serve your best interests, Ma'am," he said in a noncommittal manner.

George raised a questioning eyebrow. "Indeed. Well, before I ask you about this, I want to remind you that you are addressing your sovereign."

He gave a quick nod and tried, unsuccessfully, to hide his shaking hands.

"Very well. Sir Michael, did you give, or are you aware that any of your staff gave, information to the media, regarding myself and Miss Elliot? I ask you on your word of honour, and as gentlemen."

"Your Majesty…I…" Sir Michael stuttered.

Her gaze bored into him fiercely. "On your word of honour, sir."

❖

George heard a knock at the door. "Yes, come in, Bastian." A quick bow and he was standing back in front of her.

"Bastian, Sir Michael has admitted supplying my cousin, Viscount Anglesey, and sections of the media information about my private life and private engagements. He has therefore been relieved of his post."

Sebastian was shocked. "Ma'am, I don't know what to say. Sir Michael was always so devoted to your service."

"He was," George agreed. "But he listened to the wrong people, presumed to know what was in my best interests, and sought to force Miss Elliot out of my life by turning my people against her."

"I'm sorry to hear that, Ma'am."

"Hmm." George got up and walked, hands clasped behind her back, over to the window.

"Sir Michael will leave his post straight away, and before I offer the post to you, Bastian, I want to be quite clear on my feelings in relation to this issue." George turned to look at Sebastian very seriously. "Miss Elliot and I are in love. I intend to make her my Queen Consort, if I can persuade her that my people will accept her. If you have any problems with that, then now is the time to tell me."

Sebastian had no hesitation in replying, "I have no problem whatsoever, Ma'am. I like Miss Elliot very much, and I wish only for Your Majesty to be happy."

George nodded and walked back over to Sebastian and offered her hand. "Then congratulations, Bastian. You are my new private secretary."

"I am truly honoured, Ma'am."

Although George felt hurt by Sir Michael's actions, she was pleased that this talented young man would now be in charge of her affairs.

"I look forward to working with you. Now to business." George took her place back at her desk. "How goes your work on Operation Elliot? Have you made progress with your opposite number at the prime minister's office?"

"Yes, Ma'am. Everything is ready to go, and with your permission, Felix Brown at Number Ten and I would like to hit the media today and start to clear up these nonsense news stories, Ma'am."

"Of course, get to it, Bastian."

Now I only have to make sure I have a relationship to save.

Chapter Twenty-three

Prince Theodore and Queen Sofia had joined the Dowager Queen Adrianna in her sitting room at Windsor, to watch the TV news.

Queen Sofia asked, "Theo? Did we misjudge this young woman? She appeared to be a very kind and caring person. I know she had some interesting views about the monarchy, but burning the flag and assaulting a policeman?"

"No, you didn't misjudge her, Mama. I've spent a lot of time with Bea, organizing the concert, and I can assure you that she is everything we thought. I don't believe these reports for one second, and even if they were true, well, we all do things we regret at university."

"Quite so, my dear Theo." Queen Adrianna gave her grandson an indulgent look. "I'm more concerned about Julian's part in all this. It sounds as if he has been playing up this idea of constitutional crisis with the Conservatives."

Sofia looked shocked. "You don't think Julian is—"

"Trying to usurp George's throne? I think he may be banking on Theo's well-known relief that he would not have to take the throne."

Theo jumped up in anger. "You mean, if he can cause such a scandal with the public that George feels she has to abdicate, and I don't take it, Princess Grace would become queen, making him heir?"

Sofia clasped her hand to her mouth in shock. "I know he has always been an envious and resentful boy—even Grace, his own mother, can't abide him—but surely he wouldn't do this to his own family."

Queen Adrianna tapped her walking stick on the floor and said, "He has been pushing for Princess Eleanor as a potential candidate to be George's wife. Why would he do that if he didn't have something to gain from it? Julian does nothing without gain. I think he sees what he has always coveted, the crown, and would do anything to get it."

"If that's the case, he's got a surprise coming," Theo said. "If you'll excuse me, Mama, Granny, I'm going to pay Julian a little visit."

When he left, Queen Adrianna said, "That boy is growing up and taking his responsibilities seriously."

Sofia smiled. "He's following the lead set by George. She is such a dutiful Queen. Heaven knows what Eddie would have made of Julian."

"Eddie would have had his guts for garters. Ungrateful boy has never been content with his place in this family. The next time I see my grandson, I will make it very clear what his place is, even if I have to tan his backside." Adrianna emphasized her point by swiping her walking stick through the air.

"I pray George can find a way out of this, because it would pain me to watch her go through life alone, or with someone she doesn't love."

"I don't think she will, my dear. Queen Georgina's reign will be one of the most remarkable in the history of this dynasty, not just because she is the first woman to come before a male in the line of succession, and the first openly gay monarch, but because she will bridge the final gap between the top and bottom of society. I feel it in my old bones, that this young woman will help George do extraordinary things."

"Intuition?" Sofia asked.

Adrianna smiled. "Perhaps I see the hand of destiny on her shoulder."

❖

Bo Dixon walked purposefully into the PR office at Number Ten. The room was alive with sounds of media staff working on computers, contacting the press and every media outlet they could get ahold of.

"Felix? Talk to me, what's happening with the Queen/Elliot story. I don't like these negative headlines I'm seeing." Felix was heading a team working on what, unbeknownst to the Queen, was termed Operation Fairy Tale.

"The palace is going haywire this morning. The Queen has gotten rid of the haughty Sir Michael for leaking to the press and put Bastian in his place, so it might look bad now, but give us both time and we'll get our message across."

"Felix, Prime Minster, look." One of the younger members of the press office pointed to the large screen on the wall.

"It's Andrew Smith. What in heaven's name is he making a statement for?" Felix asked.

"TV, up ten. Everyone quiet," Bo shouted.

The leader of the opposition was speaking outside Conservative campaign headquarters in Millbank, London.

Mr. Smith, what do you think about the Queen's new girlfriend? Would you support an anti-monarchist as consort for Queen Georgina? one of the press pack asked.

I wouldn't normally answer any question regarding a member of the royal family's personal life, but I've had a great many of my constituents and members of the public contact me today regarding this matter. They have great concerns over this situation and what it means for our constitution. You also have to consider the security implications of letting an individual who holds these kinds of views into the highest reaches of government. Remember, the Queen is privy to every government secret, and her position must be protected. I feel it's my duty, as leader of Her Majesty's opposition, to pass on these concerns to the prime minister, so she may better counsel Her Majesty in the right direction.

Another reporter shouted, *What do you think of Viscount Anglesey breaking ranks from the family and voicing his concerns?*

Smith replied, *If he feels something is not right within the family, then we should listen to his concerns with an open mind. That's all for just now Gentlemen.*

The Conservative leader was shielded from the journalists and the cameras buzzing around, as he got into his car and sped off.

"That man is a bigger fool than I thought," Bo said, throwing her hands in the air.

"What are the polls saying, Mai?" Felix asked his team's trend analyst.

"Numbers concerned about Miss Elliot's relationship with the Queen, fifty per cent. Those undecided, twenty per cent. Unconcerned, thirty per cent"

"Those are numbers I can work with. Once I get our people out into the media, we can turn that around."

Bo nodded. "Felix, you and Bastian get going on Operation Fairy Tale. I'm going to call Sir Walter Greengood at MI5. There's something nagging at my brain. Something doesn't sit right about Viscount Anglesey. He's a vicious little tosser."

She closed the distance between them and whispered in Felix's ear, "Now go get me, the country, and the world our fairy tale. I want to be sitting in Westminster Abbey, the camera trained on me as I watch the poor village girl net her handsome prince. Don't disappoint me, Felix."

Bea had asked her mum and dad for some time on her own to think. She was lying on her bed in the dark, as she'd had to close the curtains after a reporter had sent up a camera to take pictures through her bedroom window.

George had called her a few times in the last hour, and she'd let it ring out. She just couldn't handle the thought of talking to George, as she was so confused.

She heard the beep of a message coming through on her tablet on the bedside table. "Open."

The screen popped up and the message appeared. *My darling. I know you're upset and confused, and probably a bit frightened, but please talk to me. I know with our love for each other we can face anything. Just talk to me.*

Bea hugged her teddy Rupert tighter to her, trying to find some comfort in her childhood friend. The tablet began to ring again, and this time Bea knew she would have to answer, or the Queen would just keep calling. She sat up and tried to make herself look less of a mess. "Answer."

George appeared on screen and she looked stressed and drawn. "Hello, thank you for answering."

"We had to talk at some time."

"First of all, I'm extremely sorry for this adverse publicity. I found out who the leak was and he has been dismissed, and I will be dealing with my cousin's part in this later today."

"Do you know how terrifying it was? Coming back to my house this morning and being besieged by the press? They've even had those stupid cameras up at all the windows, trying to get footage of me."

"I am sorry, but I sent over the police officers to you. Is that helping?"

Bea nodded and then there was a long silence.

"Say something, my darling, please."

Suddenly all Bea's bottled up frustrations and hurts came flooding out. "What do you want me to say, Georgie? How about we start with, why on earth haven't you put an end to this story and denied this relationship? You've made things so much worse by saying nothing."

George wore her reliable stoic facade. "For one, the royal family never comments on personal matters, and two, last night we declared our love for each other and made love. Forgive me for assuming that meant we had some sort of relationship, or does sharing your body with me mean nothing to you?"

"Of course it meant something to me, but this is all too impossible. Have you seen the news? Have you seen what they're reporting about me? Do you not want to ask me if I did those things? Are you not shocked about the flag burning?"

"No. I already knew about it, and I know you didn't do anything that they're reporting," George said very matter-of-factly.

Bea was puzzled. "How could you know about it?"

"When we returned from our trip to France, it was clear to me that I couldn't live without you, and I hoped you might share my feelings, so I asked the prime minister for her opinion on any constitutional problems with taking you as my wife and consort. She had a file on you, and all the obstacles to our relationship, and explained what that man from Free Republic did to you."

"What?" Bea exclaimed loudly. "You asked the prime minister about taking me as your wife? You didn't even know if I loved you, and you're scheming and planning to make me your wife? Was I to get a say in marrying you, or was I just going to be commanded?"

"Don't be ridiculous, but as I've explained to you before, my position is unique. I can't just casually date someone and see what happens. As Queen, anyone I'm romantically involved with will immediately be scrutinized as potential wife and consort material, so I have to be sure we have a clear path and there's nothing the press can use against us."

Bea gave a hollow laugh. "I don't think I've heard anything more unromantic in my life. Do you think we're living in medieval times? Why don't you just give me a medical, to make sure I can produce viable offspring for you and your bloody succession, while you're at it?"

"You're just being silly now."

Bea felt her face flame at George's remark. "I'm silly?"

"Look, calm down, please? Because I had that information from the prime minister, we were able to work on a plan to counteract today's press attention. Bastian and Number Ten have been working on a plan to change any negative public opinion on our relationship. They're hitting the press with it from this afternoon. Things will get easier for us."

Bea shook her head in disbelief. "I take it back. I think *that* is the most unromantic thing I've ever heard."

George's calm finally broke. "Well, I'm so sorry I was doing something proactive to try and be with the woman that I love, unlike you who are determined to deny the love you feel for me. I had never made love with anyone in my life before you. Do you really understand what last night meant? We gave ourselves to each other. I love you, and I know you love me, so just forget anything else."

The explosive anger Bea had felt reverted to pain, and her tears started anew. "Sometimes love isn't enough," she said simply.

"What are you saying?"

It was tearing Bea apart to even think this, let alone say it. "I'm saying I don't think…I don't think we should see each other any more. Our charity commitments are nearly finished anyway, and I can have one of my colleagues finish up the last few appointments with you till the end of July."

George looked panicked. "No, don't do that. Just meet with me. If we talk together face to face, I can show you this won't be as bad as you think. Please, let me see you. Let me fight for us."

"I can't, Georgie. If I'm with you, I won't have the strength. We need to end this before it's begun. We live in two different worlds, and I just can't do this."

George said dispassionately, "The police will stay with you until they are no longer needed. If you require anything further, contact Cammy, and I will have someone deal with it."

"Georgie—"

"I'm going now, Bea. No matter what, please remember, you will be the only woman I will ever love. Goodbye."

Bea was left staring at a blank screen. "Goodbye, Georgie."

CHAPTER TWENTY-FOUR

After Princess Eleanor left him that morning, Julian quite happily watched the news with a cigar and a glass of fine malt whisky, in his London flat. This was his bolthole, away from royal life, his family, and wife, and children. He only kept one member of staff here, his discreet butler Palmer.

Julian sat with his feet up on the coffee table, his eyes firmly on the TV projection. He'd been disconcerted to see that some individuals had begun to defend Miss Elliot's behaviour, and on top of that, a very angry phone call from his mother, Princess Grace.

His viewing was disturbed by some raised voices from out in the entrance hall, and before he knew it, a very angry looking Prince Theodore burst through the drawing room door, Palmer trailing behind him. "I'm so sorry, My Lord, I wasn't able to stop His Royal Highness in time to announce him."

Julian put down his cigar and drink and stood to face his furious cousin. "It's all right, Palmer. You may go."

Julian met his cousin's furious stare, daring himself not to bow and show him respect, but he blinked first and gave the smallest bow he could. "Your Royal Highness, won't you sit down? Can I get you a drink?"

"No, thank you. This won't take long. I know what your scheming, traitorous little brain is up to, Julian."

"Oh? What am I scheming?" Ignoring protocol, Julian sat down in the presence of the prince.

"Feeding tittle-tattle to the press, whipping up a storm with those old fools in the Tory party, and turning your back on your sovereign and your family, all because of petty jealousy."

"It has nothing to do with jealousy. I'm trying to protect the dignity of our family line—I'm trying to protect it from a Queen who would invite a common little tart into her bed, and threatens to humiliate us by making her Queen Consort. Surely you see that? How could you or I ever bow and pay homage to a working-class woman from the East End, who has no respect for our position in this country?"

Theo walked closer to Julian and towered over him. "I would have no problem bowing to Miss Elliot because I have never met a more caring, gentle soul in my life, and I would trust Her Majesty's judgement about who she wants to share her throne with. I know what you think of me—I know your traitorous mind thinks I have not the will or the ability for the throne, and I would let the line of succession fall to Princess Grace and, in the end, to you."

Theo pulled Julian up on his feet by his lapels.

"Get off me."

Theo tightened his hold. "Not until I look you in the eye and make my position clear. I'm warning you, Anglesey, if your little plots force my sister off the throne, as much as I would despise the job, I will take her place willingly, out of loyalty to my sovereign, my sister, and the House of Buckingham. You will never get your pathetic, traitorous mitts on my sister's throne or crown. Have I made myself clear?"

"Abundantly," Julian spat.

Prince Theodore let his cousin go, smoothed down his suit, and adjusted his tie. "Just remember my words, Cousin Julian."

Julian watched his cousin walk out of the drawing room, and his anger boiled over. He lifted and threw his glass of whisky against the wall. "I hate you, George. I will bring you down. I swear it."

❖

Later that evening, after Viscount Anglesey had soaked his jealousy, and anger in a large quantity of whisky, he thought back to his afternoon meeting with the Queen.

He was met by a stone-faced Captain Cameron and Major Fairfax and escorted through the corridors of Buckingham Palace to the Queen's office. Every member of staff, from the cleaners to the senior pages, looked at him with disdain. He felt like a traitor being marched towards the firing squad, and he'd wondered why George could engender such loyalty in those who served her. He just couldn't understand it.

When he was shown into the office, the Queen was sitting at her desk, completing some work from her red boxes. Without looking up, she said, "Sit."

Apart from the ticking clock and the dogs gently snoring in the corner, there was silence as George finished up with her last paper.

Finally, she finished writing and very precisely gathered the papers together and closed them up in the last red box.

George looked up at him with a fierce, penetrating stare. It was clear this wasn't to be a cordial meeting. "Viscount Anglesey, your behaviour towards your sovereign and our family causes us great disappointment. You have shamed us. Do you have anything to say for yourself?"

"Only what I did, I did for my family's good name. You talk of shame, and you want to make a common tart your Queen Consort—someone who is so far beneath us, it disgusts me. You will pollute our bloodline."

George squeezed the pen she held so hard that it broke in her hand. "That woman has more decency, breeding, and caring than you could ever hope to have. I am an ordinary person, just like Miss Elliot, just like the man in the street, and just like you, Julian. We are born with great privilege and an important duty to perform for the people, but you seem to think yourself superior to those people. You are not special, Julian—you're not even extraordinary."

Julian jumped up and moved around the desk to lean threateningly over George. "It should have been me, not some disgusting deviant. I should be king. It is my destiny!"

George stood slowly, her height forcing Julian to look up to her. "It is your destiny to be a well-behaved minor royal who supports his monarch. If you ever talk outside of the family again, Julian, or conspire against me, you will be exiled from us. You won't be asked to family functions or royal events, and your income from the civil list will cease. Do you understand me?"

"You can't do that. You can't cut me off from my birthright."

"I can do exactly as I wish. I am head of state and head of this family, Julian, and don't you ever forget it. Everyone has their place in the House of Buckingham. You have just never learned yours."

Julian took a swing for his cousin, but George easily caught his fist in her hand and pushed his arm up his back. "Don't you ever lay a hand on me, you pathetic arse."

His humiliation was complete when the Queen called on Captain Cameron and Major Fairfax, who dragged him out.

❖

A few weeks later, the Elliot's kitchen was alive with the smells of cooking and the noise of music playing in the background. It was Sunday, and a day of familiar family routine. Bea and her mother prepared the Sunday roast dinner—Sarah was mixing the batter for the Yorkshire puddings while Bea peeled and chopped up the vegetables—while Reg watched his football game on TV.

The music they had on in the background changed to an old and emotional love song. As it played, Bea's barely contained sadness washed over her like a wave, and the tears started to roll down her face.

"Oh, sweetheart, come here." Sarah moved to take her daughter in her arms. "You can't live like this. Bea, you love her, she loves you, talk to her and tell her you want to try again."

Bea wiped her tears away quickly. "I can't, Mum. You've seen what it's been like, the TV, the news stories, I can't even go down to the corner shop without being followed, and we're not together. Imagine what it would be like if we were. It's not just George who has to want me. The country has to approve too."

"But, sweetheart, you've seen how things are changing. On TV people are starting to talk about you and the Queen as some sort of magical love story, and Princess Eleanor as some sort of Wicked Witch of the West. Opinions have definitely changed, Bea. You could have the fairy tale if you want it."

Bea slumped down at the kitchen table, holding her head in her hands, "It's not that simple, Mum. George has told me herself what royal life can be like. She describes it as a gilded cage, and do I want to voluntarily walk into that?"

Sarah sat beside her daughter and took her hand. "True, you can stay outside with your freedom and independence, but without the one you love. Are you prepared for that?"

Bea shook her head and sighed. "How could someone like me be a Queen Consort? Me? Beatrice Anne Elliot from Bethnal Green?"

"Not how could someone like you be Queen Consort, but someone like you should be Queen Consort, sweetheart. All you've done the whole of your life is work for others, to try and make their lives better. That's what a consort does. She works hard for charity and the people, listening to their concerns, and trying to do something about them. That's in the job description, and you fit it perfectly."

As Bea considered those words, her dad came into the kitchen, looking shaken. He closed the door and whispered, "There's someone to see you, princess."

Bea and her Mum looked at each other in confusion. "What is it, Reg? You look white as a sheet," Sarah asked.

"It's Prince Theodore."

Sarah jumped up in shock and whispered back, "You're pulling my leg, aren't you, Reggie?"

"No, Prince Theodore is sitting on our couch, in our front room. Large as life."

Bea walked into the living room to find Theo sitting on the couch, taking a keen interest in the football playing on the TV.

"Your Royal Highness, this is a surprise." Bea curtsied when Theo stood to greet her.

"Bea, I do apologize for interrupting your Sunday. I expect you're having Sunday lunch soon?"

"You're not interrupting, sir. We're just preparing it at the moment."

Theo walked forward and greeted her with a kiss on each cheek. "Theo, please, sir makes me feel like I'm ancient."

Bea smiled. "Theo, then. Please sit down. Can I get you tea or…?"

"Oh, I won't if you don't mind. I'm expected at Windsor for Sunday lunch in an hour. I wanted to call on you for a chat about the concert."

"Everything's all right, isn't it? At the last meeting everything seemed to be ready to go."

"Oh, it is. Tip-top and ready to go, it is indeed." Theo fidgeted with his tight collar and tie. "It's about another matter. My private secretary says that you haven't replied to the invitation, for yourself and your friend Lali, to the royal box. Are you intending to come?"

Bea wrung her hands together nervously. "I don't know what to do, Theo. It doesn't seem appropriate, after—"

"Of course it's appropriate. You were the driving force behind this, you planned it. No one has more right than you."

"But seeing Her Majesty again…it will just make things harder."

Theo took Bea's hand gently. "Listen to me, Bea. Georgie is distraught without you. She takes no joy in anything anymore. She goes out, puts a fake smile on her face, and does her duty, but inside she's…it's hard to explain. When you two were friends, it was like she blossomed, came alive with happiness and joy. Now that you're apart, she's like half a person, joyless, incomplete."

The tears returned to Bea's eyes, and she wiped them away furiously. "I'm sorry, Theo. It seems like all I do these days is cry."

"Doesn't that tell you something? Please, come to the concert at least. Georgie will be happy just to see you, even if that's all you can give her."

Bea stayed quiet, looking at the floor.

"I also hear there's a certain Captain Cameron who will be a bit upset if your friend Lali isn't coming too," Theo said with a rakish grin.

Bea laughed, thinking of the smooth captain, who had been so far unsuccessfully wooing her beautiful friend.

"Please come, Bea. Pretty please?"

Bea knew she couldn't say no. Just the thought of seeing George again made her happier than she'd been in weeks. "We'll be there."

Chapter Twenty-Five

One week later, the Mall outside Buckingham Palace had been transformed into a concert venue. The lucky people who had won the chance to buy tickets in the ballot were lined right down the Mall, and the atmosphere was electric with excitement.

Bea and Lali were security checked and taken to sit in the royal box. All of the younger members of the royal family were in attendance, and Bea was happy to see Vicki and Max and was delighted when they told her Viscount Anglesey had been asked to stay away.

The stage went dark, and a spotlight lit up a lone royal trumpeter, announcing the monarch. The lights in the royal box went up, allowing the crowd to see the entrance of the Queen and her brother the prince. All the attendees in the royal box were given a signal to stand in preparation for the arrival of the sovereign. A roar went up when the Queen and Theo appeared and made their way to their seats.

Bea had a quick intake of breath at the sight of George in full Queen mode. Confident, charismatic, and open to her people.

"She looks wonderful, doesn't she?" Lali said, smiling.

Bea simply nodded, her heart thudding at seeing her love again. They were only four seats away from the royal party, but to Bea it felt like miles. All she could think was that she ached to be next to George, holding her hand and loving her.

The music struck up and the whole crowd joined in singing "God Save the Queen." As Bea sang, she took a sneaky look and found George looking back with a small smile. She felt the blush come to her cheeks and looked away quickly.

"You two look like a couple of shy kids at school," Lali teased.

"We do not. It's just awkward. The whole world knows about us, and now we're sitting close to each other, with the cameras trained on us for the world to watch our every step. It's weird, Lali."

A cheer went up from the crowd as the big screen showed the two most talked about people in the world. Lali pointed out some signs in the crowd:

Marry her, Your Majesty!
We want Queen Bea!
Give us our fairy tale!

"I can't believe they would…I'm lost for words," Bea said to her friend.

"You shouldn't be. Everyone wants you two to live happily ever after, because if you two can make it true, then they can hope for the same in their lives. Everyone wants to dream, and they can live vicariously through both of you."

Can that really be true? Bea wondered.

The concert was a resounding success. The crowd, and the audience watching on TV at home, were treated to a wonderful performance by all the acts and the bands. At one point, one of the boy bands announced, "Prince Theodore asked us to sing this song for two people who shared their first dance to it, and I know it means a lot to them. I hope you enjoy it."

Even though they weren't mentioned by name, everyone knew who the couple was when Prince Theodore was named.

Bea looked along to see George whispering into Theo's ear, and he was smiling ear to ear. The song was the one they had danced and kissed to at Mickey D's.

She watched the crowd sing along with the ballad, and the energy of the concert changed. She was pulled into the romantic mood of the evening. At one point in the song, her eyes met George's, and just like when they kissed, everything melted away to leave just two people who simply loved and adored each other. She felt every eye in the stadium on her and noticed the producer of the event was showing them on the big screen at that moment.

The crowd cheered, and for a moment she allowed herself to think that maybe they could have what they wanted, maybe their fairy tale could come true.

The concert wound down to a big finale with fireworks, stunning 3D projections in the sky, and a classical singer leading the crowd in a rendition of the national anthem from the roof of Buckingham Palace.

"Wow," Lali exclaimed. "That was truly stunning. You did such a good job. Abby would be so proud, Bea."

The two friends hugged. "Thank you, I'm really grateful you were here to share it with me, Lali."

"Me too. So what now?"

The royal party left the box, and Captain Cameron strode up to them. "Watch out, Lali," Bea teased. "Your dashing captain is coming for you."

Lali giggled and said, "Shush. You know I don't like those smooth, cocky types."

"Oh, come on, you like her, you're just trying hard not to, and I know you like the uniform."

The captain was dressed in her smart MP dress uniform, with her medals proudly displayed, and Bea saw her eyes go wide when she caught sight of Lali in her golden bejewelled sari. Lali always looked elegant and regal, but tonight she looked especially stunning, and Cammy clearly appreciated it.

"Ladies," Captain Cameron said, "Her Majesty and Prince Theodore wish me to escort you backstage to the after-party. Shall we?"

"Thank you for taking part. You put on a marvellous show." George was working the room, along with her brother and cousins, making sure to thank everyone involved in the concert. She moved around the room, talking to famous singers and celebrities, who all seemed excited to meet her.

George became aware of an excited murmur spreading throughout the room. She looked up and stopped breathing as she watched Cammy escort Lali and Bea into the party. The whole room recognized the aura surrounding Bea. Not only did she look beautiful in her silver evening gown, but she radiated a special natural something that made everyone turn to look and smile.

They locked eyes and seemed pulled together by an invisible thread, and before George knew it, they were standing face to face. Lali and Bea curtsied; Cammy and Lali both seemed to sense they were no longer needed and walked off together, giving George and Bea some privacy.

"Good evening, Your Majesty," Bea said, her eyes never leaving the Queen's.

"Bea, I must congratulate you on a super concert."

"I couldn't have done it without Theo, I mean *Prince* Theo. Sorry, I forget sometimes that he's a prince."

George chuckled. "No need to apologize—he forgets he's a prince sometimes too."

This made Bea laugh and broke the ice a little. "How are Baxter, Shadow, and my special friend, Rexie?"

George was always so touched that Bea remembered her dogs; no one else did that. To everyone else they were just dogs, but to George they were so much more.

"They're fine, thank you, mischievous as ever. Rexie really misses you though. One night you came on the news, and he was whimpering at the screen and trying to give you his paw."

"Really? Aww, he's so sweet. I thought he'd have forgotten me by now."

"Never," George said, very seriously. "You are impossible to forget."

Bea looked down at the floor, as if unsure how to respond.

"Bea? I have to talk to some more of the guests, but can I talk to you later in private? Please?"

"Of course. If you wish, Ma'am."

George nodded. "Thank you. I'll have Cammy come and get you. In the meantime, I hope you and your friend have a good night."

❖

An hour later, Cammy escorted Bea to a curtained-off area backstage, where the Queen was waiting. "If you'll excuse me, Ma'am, Miss Elliot, I have a bonnie lassie to charm," Cammy said with a wink, and suddenly the couple was left alone.

"Thank you for meeting me. I wasn't sure if you would be alone with me."

When George was nervous or unsure, she had this little-lost-boy quality to her voice that made Bea want to hug her and tell her everything would be all right.

"It wasn't that I didn't want to before, Georgie. I just thought it would be much harder for us if we did."

"Well, thank you. You look beautiful, by the way. I didn't get a chance to tell you before."

Bea felt a hot blush come to her cheeks. "Thank you, Georgie. You look very handsome too."

George looked down at her usual suit and crisp white shirt. "Hardly, it's just a suit."

"It's not just a suit, it's the way you fill it," Bea blurted out without thinking. She chastised herself as soon as she'd said the words. Her mind flashed back to the feel of George's mouth on her breasts, their sex-sheened bodies gliding together naturally, as if they were meant for each other. She was trying to remain calm and controlled, but her natural attraction to George just overrode everything.

"I'm sorry, Georgie. I shouldn't have said that, it was inappropriate." Bea looked to the side as a group of rowdy partygoers passed by the small curtained-off area.

George took her hand and pulled her further into the corner, making sure they had some privacy. "I don't want it to be inappropriate, Bea. I want you to be able to say anything to me, I want there to be no barriers between us."

"Georgie I don't—"

"No, I have to say this, because I can't go on living in limbo any longer, hoping that you might come round or change your mind, so please just let me talk and it'll be the last time I ever bring this up, okay?"

Bea nodded. As confused as she was, she knew that this situation had to be resolved as they were both in so much pain.

George took a deep breath as if preparing to bare her soul. "I knew you were special the moment I met you. The irreverent way you treated me knocked me off balance, and I loved having one person in my life who treated me the same as anyone else. Even my mother treats me as a Queen and sovereign, and to you I'm Georgie, just Georgie—well, sometimes Bully, and that's good too."

Bea smiled at the loving familiarity they did indeed share.

"Over the months I found myself falling utterly head over heels for you, and bit by bit everything that my mother told me about finding someone to share the burden made sense. The isolation and loneliness I felt were banished by the care and love you gave me, and I felt a peace I'd never felt before. I knew you were perfect for me and for my consort."

Bea couldn't stop herself from reaching up and cupping the Queen's cheek, and George leaned in, appearing to savour her touch.

"I love you, Georgie, more than I thought it was possible to love someone, but we've got so much going against us."

George took hold of Bea's hand and kissed it tenderly. "I told you public opinion would change and it has. Did you see the signs the crowd were holding up?"

"But—"

George placed a finger over her lips and said, "No buts, my darling. The only thing holding us back is you. I have been in agony without you since we spent the night together. You are my love, my soul mate, and my true consort. There will never be anyone else for me, and I cannot go on without knowing whether you will be mine. Tomorrow I'm going up to Scotland for our family holiday at Balmoral. I always head up early, as I have a few duties to perform first in Edinburgh, and then the rest of the family will come up in a few weeks. Will you come with me?"

"I can't, I…" Bea was so confused. She knew there would be no going back after joining her on holiday.

George nodded her head sadly. "I thought you might say that. I'll be up in Scotland for two months, and you have an open invitation to join me. If you want to come, then just contact Cammy, and she will arrange it. If you don't come, well, I'll know you've made your decision about us, and I won't bother you again."

George kissed her thoroughly and passionately, and when she pulled away and rested her head against Bea's, Bea knew this might be the last time George touched her.

"Remember I love you, I need you, and I would give you the world if you let me. Goodbye."

With one final kiss that made Bea give a deep and throaty moan, George strode off, leaving Bea with her eyes closed, mouth still parted from the kiss, and wondering what on earth had just happened.

"Have you decided what to do yet, princess?" Reg asked his daughter.

"No," Bea said with a sad sigh. She sat at the kitchen table, staring into her cup of tea. "I want to go, but my fear is stopping me. If I go, then that's it, my life is mapped out."

Reg sat down beside her and said, "Do you love her?"

"With all my heart."

Reg covered her hand with his own. "Then go, princess. Don't live the rest of your life thinking about what might have been."

They were interrupted by Sarah coming into the kitchen brandishing a letter. Bea was puzzled. It had been a decade since regular postal service had been disbanded. No one sent letters anymore.

"Sweetheart—a messenger from Kensington Palace brought this."

"Kensington Palace?" Bea asked.

"It's where the Dowager Queen Adrianna lives. Here, open it." Her mother handed over the fine white envelope and sat next to her. "Well? What does it say, sweetheart?"

Bea read and reread the letter before answering. "It's an invitation to tea with the Dowager and the Queen Mother, this afternoon."

"Oh, my goodness. What will you wear? What time do you have to go?"

"Wait, Mum. Let me think. Why do they want to talk to me?"

"Could be they want to encourage you to go up to Scotland?" Reg asked.

"Or warn me off?"

Sarah shook her head. "No. I don't think so."

"Why?" Bea asked.

"I remember reading an article in my royal magazine that Balmoral was a testing ground for any potential new members of the family, because it encapsulates everything it means to be a royal. Being outdoors in all kinds of weather, enjoying country pursuits, and attending events like the Highland Games. Put it this way—I doubt Princess Eleanor would pass."

"But would I?"

CHAPTER TWENTY-SIX

A car picked Bea up in midafternoon and took her to Kensington Palace. She was shown to a very smart drawing room where the two Queens were waiting. To be summoned was nerve-racking enough, but to walk into a room and be faced with the royal family's two matriarchs was terrifying.

Queen Sofia stood and offered her hand after Bea had curtsied to them both. "Miss Elliot, I'm delighted to see you again. I hope you are well?"

Bea's voice shook a little as she answered, "Quite well, thank you, Your Majesty." She felt Queen Adrianna's eyes scanning her and hoped that her dress was suitable.

"Do sit down, my dear," Queen Adrianna said.

"Thank you, Ma'am."

Sofia looked to a page who was standing by the door and said, "We'll have tea now, John."

Turning to Bea, the Queen Mother asked, "I hope your parents are well, Miss Elliot?"

"Oh yes, Ma'am. Very well, and please call me Beatrice or Bea, Ma'am." She found both the Queen Mother and Queen Adrianna intimidating, but especially the Dowager Queen sitting with her silver-claw-topped walking stick.

Once the tea was served, Adrianna said, "Do you know why we asked to see you?"

"I thought it might have something to do with Her Majesty inviting me to Balmoral."

Adrianna smiled and said to the Queen Mother. "No beating about the bush with this one, Sofia."

"No. It seems not. Let us be frank, Beatrice. My daughter is very much in love with you and has been miserable since you stopped seeing her. I want you to tell me the absolute truth, not what you think I want to hear. Do you love my daughter?"

This was surreal. She was sitting in the Dowager Queen's drawing room in Kensington Palace, being asked if she loved Queen Georgina.

"Ma'am, I love your daughter with all of my heart, and the Queen knows that has never been in question. I just don't think I'm right for her—my views on the monarchy and coming from a working-class background…it just wouldn't be right, would it?"

Queen Adrianna snorted. "Beatrice, my dear, you have a strange point of view for someone who purports to have republican sympathies."

"How so, Ma'am?"

"Surely a republican thinks class should be meaningless, and yet you are the only one to mention class, and it's stopping you from being with my granddaughter."

Bea found that hard to argue with. "So you both have no problem with my background?"

Adrianna looked at Sofia and smiled.

Sofia said, "Where you come from and what your parents do? Not at all. Your views might have been a difficulty, but George tells us that they have softened a great deal. Is that true?"

"Yes, I have a greater appreciation for what the monarchy does, and as the prime minister said to me, it's what the people want. They don't wish to have a republic. When you can't beat them, join them, as they say."

"Yes, indeed," Adrianna said. "There haven't been any dissenting voices against the monarchy since the twentieth century."

The page brought in the tea and poured them each a cup. "Thank you, John," Sofia said, and he left the room.

Adrianna began, "Let me tell you a story, Beatrice. I was a young girl who didn't come from a royal or even an aristocratic family. I came from an ordinary middle-class home. I did go to private school, but my parents were ordinary people. My father was a doctor and my mother ran her own business. We weren't poor, but we certainly weren't upper class. I was the first, middle class person to marry into the royal family, when I married George's grandfather, King Alfred II."

Bea looked shocked. "You were? But I assumed…?"

"You assumed I was of aristocratic blood myself? No. Queen Sofia is from the Spanish royal family, but I was simply middle class, and I can tell you, at the time, it was a very big change for the royals to marry outside the aristocracy. Alfred's father and his siblings nearly tore the royal family apart with divorce and scandal. It was a time when people genuinely thought the monarchy could fall, but Freddie was a very independent-minded man, and a loyal man, much like Eddie and George, and refused to marry someone the family deemed suitable. He wanted to learn from the mistakes of the past and marry for love, and he did."

Bea was more than surprised. "Where did you meet? If you don't mind me asking."

The Queen Mother and Adrianna giggled. "You may be aware that I am a keen horsewoman."

Bea nodded. Everyone knew of Queen Adrianna's love of horses and racing. "Yes, Ma'am."

"Well, there was a park that all the local villages had used for a hundred years. It was used for walking, a children's play park, dog walking, nature trails, and there was an equestrian centre where people could come to ride, or ride round the nature trails in the forest. I learned to ride there, and as I grew, I worked part-time, teaching children and looking after the horses. The council, who were short of money at the time, had sold it to a supermarket chain, who were going to demolish the whole thing and build a ghastly twenty-four-hour supermarket. Some of the villagers and staff from the horse stables formed a protest group, and I was the most opinionated member. I bet you can't believe that, Beatrice," she joked.

Queen Sofia snorted and topped-up the teacups. "What do you think, Beatrice?"

Bea smiled back and said, "I couldn't imagine you being so opinionated, Ma'am."

Adrianna knocked her stick on the floor, calling for attention. "I think we've established that I am not shy with my opinions, so our protest went on for weeks, and the bulldozers came in to knock the stable buildings down, and a portion of the forest. We staged a sit in, and the bulldozers couldn't work. Prince Freddie, as he was known in those days, happened to be visiting the area on that day, and ever the modern prince, wanted to come down to the park and see if he could help bring both sides together. Freddie insisted he fell in love at first sight, but I certainly didn't. I thought he was an interfering toff and told him so. He laughed and told me I was a very feisty filly just like one of his favourite horses. I swear if I hadn't been arrested, I would have hit the smug prince."

"What happened?" Bea was intrigued. The Dowager Queen's story seemed so similar to her own.

"He set up a meeting for both sides, and even though he couldn't change the council's mind about selling, he used his influence with the supermarket company to get them to build a children's play park on the site, and for them to buy a patch of land to build stables for the locals."

"Wow. That was kind. Did you begin to like him then?"

Adrianna gave a crooked smile. "Like is probably too strong a word. I would say…I was intrigued by him, more than liked. He clearly wanted to impress me though. He set up a charity horse and pony show, to take place every year in aid of the stables for the local children. It still runs to this day, and I became patron after dear Freddie died. When I saw how much he cared for people, that's when I fell in love. Are you surprised by that?"

Bea put down her teacup and tried to come to terms with what all this meant. "I had no idea. I thought Georgie's…the Queen's family all came from similar backgrounds. I thought you all wouldn't approve of Her Majesty's choice. I know Viscount Anglesey—"

"Oh, please ignore that jealous boy," Queen Sofia said. "He feels himself more important than he is. All that matters to us, Beatrice, is that George is loved the way she deserves. We're not here to persuade you one way or another. I just don't want you both to be in pain if you truly love each other. George has been a dutiful member of the royal family, and she deserves some happiness. As for some of your sceptical views, well, you can help George by bringing a different perspective to the family. You have all the correct skills to be a consort, but it's up to you whether this life is the one you're prepared to live."

Queen Adrianna sat forward in her seat, and pointed her stick towards Bea. "I will warn you though, Miss Elliot, think carefully before you join this family. To be one of us, you have to dedicate your life to the people of this country. It's not all glamourous banquets— you have to commit yourself to a life of service, and that isn't always easy, but you should also think carefully about turning your back on George's offer of love, because you would never find a more loving or more loyal person to spend your life with."

CHAPTER TWENTY-SEVEN

George smashed her axe down ferociously on the log in front of her, splitting it in two the first attempt. She'd been doing this most days, as her need for solitude grew, and it gave her an output for her frustrations and anger. It was three long weeks since she'd arrived in Scotland and last seen Bea. Her hope that their love would conquer all the obstacles in their path was now gone.

As always, however, her isolation was an illusion. The Queen went nowhere, especially at the moment, without her protection officers, who were strategically placed around her. One stood quietly outside the cottage, a few others hidden throughout the trees.

George often liked to come down to Rose Cottage, when she wanted to be alone. It was often used for guests visiting Balmoral, but at the moment stood empty, and George had been grateful to have somewhere to escape to and take her frustrations out on the large pile of logs that sat outside the house.

She'd been going for about an hour, and although it wasn't an exceptionally hot day, the activity made her hot enough to dispense with her jumper and strip down to her black sleeveless T-shirt.

Another ten minutes went by when she heard Cammy behind her. "Your Majesty?"

Not turning round, George shouted back, "What is it, Cammy? Can you not see I'm busy?"

Her three dogs suddenly jumped up, wagged their tails, and started barking excitedly.

"I have something for you, Ma'am."

George sighed and sank her axe into the tree stump she'd been chopping on. "What is it?" She turned slowly and found Cammy standing with Bea. "Bea?"

She curtsied and said, "Your Majesty."

George couldn't believe it and simply stood looking into the eyes of the woman she adored. Cammy took that as her cue to slowly slip away.

"You came. Does that mean…?" George was almost too scared to ask.

Bea smiled and nodded. "I want you to give me my fairy tale, Georgie."

George ran forward and lifted Bea in the air, covering her face with kisses. "I will give you everything, my darling. I love you so much."

Bea held on tight and brought her lips close to her lover's. "I love you, Georgie. I'm so sorry it took me so long to come to you."

Their lips came together with a strong passion, and the relief George felt took over. She kissed Bea ferociously. When they broke apart, George said, "Oh God, I thought…well, I thought you'd never come."

Bea stroked George's hair tenderly. "I couldn't not come, Georgie. There's no one in the world for me but you."

George put her down slowly. "I was so miserable without you."

"You won't be lonely again, I promise. I'll always be by your side and I'm ready for whatever comes next."

George's dogs, who had been waiting their turn patiently, barked at their master. "Oh, looks like there are three furry chaps just as happy to see you."

"And I'm just as happy to see them." Bea dropped to her knees and beckoned them to her. "Come on. Hello, Baxter and Shadow. Kisses?" Each gave her a slobbery kiss on the face. "Where's my big boy, Rexie?" The Labrador nearly knocked Bea over, he was so happy to see her.

"Rex, careful," George warned.

"He's fine. I missed him too."

Georgie's heart swelled as it always did when she saw Bea with her dogs. "You were made for me, my darling." George beamed at her.

"I think so. How about you, me, and these three big boys go up to the castle and snuggle for the afternoon? Get reacquainted."

"Snuggle?" George asked with a raised eyebrow.

"You mean you've never snuggled? Well, I'd better teach you quickly. Come on."

They walked hand in hand back up to the house.

❖

They lay in George's bed, simply holding each other, talking, and sharing kisses, while three happy dogs lay at the foot of the bed.

George's larger frame was spooned to Bea's back, while she enjoyed the soft strokes and caresses that she was getting. "I just can't believe you're here with me, and I don't have to hide what I feel for you," George said.

Bea pulled George's hand from her hip and held it between her breasts. "This is perfect."

George rose up on her elbow and looked down at the expanse of bare neck and shoulder before her and said, "Yes. I love snuggling, my darling." She blew on the exposed skin and felt Bea shiver. Encouraged, she brought her lips into play and brushed them from Bea's hairline down to her shoulder. When she heard Bea moan, she became bolder, kissing and nibbling her way down her neck. It felt like heaven to touch Bea again, and her own heavy beat of arousal was growing with every touch. "You taste so good."

"Hmm…your lips feel so good, Your Majesty."

Then the emotion of the situation came out of nowhere and hit her in the gut. Bea was here with her, loving her, but all her fears were still bubbling under the surface. Would Bea leave her again? Once she realized what a restrictive, difficult life she was choosing, she might leave, and George knew that would destroy her.

Her sudden stillness alerted Bea that something wasn't right. She looked over her shoulder. "What's wrong, Georgie?"

"I…" George tried to form her words carefully, but she just couldn't say what she was thinking. *I'm scared.*

Bea took George's hand from between her breasts and kissed it reverently. "I'm not going anywhere unless you want me to go. You're stuck with me, I promise. I swear to you, I'm ready for everything being in your life means. That's why it took me so long to come here to you. I had to be sure."

George was taken aback. Bea seemed able to read her so easily, it was scary. She pulled Bea into her body even more tightly and rested her head in the crook of her neck. "I never want you to leave. I don't know how you understand me like you do, but you do, and I can't live without everything you bring to my life."

"Then we're both happy, because I can't live without you. I realized that when you left for Scotland."

George kissed her neck softly. "I missed you so much since we've been apart. I thought about you all the time. All through the day, whatever I was doing, you were never off my mind, and at night when I was alone…"

Bea's breathing hitched, and she reached her hand back to grasp at George's hair. "Tell me what you thought about at night, when you were alone."

That one sentence changed the emotional atmosphere to one charged with a desperate need to reconnect. "I thought about how soft your skin feels," George whispered breathily into Bea's ear.

Bea lifted George's hand and placed it on her stomach, and George groaned when she realized what her lover wanted. She began to gently stroke Bea's stomach just under the hem of her T-shirt. "It feels soft and warm, and it responds to my touch."

"Tell me what else," Bea said huskily.

George let her fingers wander up towards Bea's chest. "I lay in bed thinking about how your breasts felt in my hands." That was one of the things she loved most about Bea, how soft she was everywhere. Her own hands were rough and callused in places because of constant handling of riding tack and ropes when sailing, but not Bea. Her lover was everything she was not.

George grew in confidence and clasped a lace-covered breast. "How your nipples hardened in my hand when I gently squeezed."

This time they both moaned, and George felt Bea push her perfectly rounded backside into her groin.

"Uh-huh, feels good," Bea moaned.

George felt the overwhelming urge to thrust into her, but fought hard to keep control and give Bea what she wanted. She lightly trailed her fingers down to the waist of Bea's jeans and hovered over the button. "I tried to remember touching you lower."

Bea's breathing got heavier, and she pushed George's fingers onto the button. "I need you to touch me. I've missed you so much."

George immediately popped the button, pushed her hand down into Bea's underwear, and cupped her sex. "I thought about how wet you were for me."

She slipped one finger into the wetness she knew she would find and softly stroked around her clit.

Bea put her hand behind her and onto George's hip, encouraging her to thrust, and she did. They were gradually losing themselves to each other and to their passion.

"Please, Georgie…I need…What then?"

She teased Bea's opening with her finger, pushing in a little and pulling back out. "I thought about how it feels to be inside you. It feels like nothing matters but being inside you." This time George pushed two fingers deep inside and groaned at the velvety warmth that she found there, while her thumb started to stroke Bea's clit.

Bea reached out in desperation and clutched at George's sleeveless T-shirt, pulling her closer. "Yes…harder."

George gave her what she wanted. "And all I wanted to do was thrust inside you, fuck you till we came." Bea's moans were getting louder to match the pace of her hips, and George could feel her orgasm was close. "But as much as I wanted that, I used every inch of my self control to slow down and make it last as long as I could." To match her words, she slowed her thrusting to a stop and slipped her fingers nearly all the way out.

Bea cried out in frustration, "I was so close, please?"

George smiled against the back of her lover's neck. Knowing that she could have this effect on Bea was giving her much-needed confidence. She hoped that she could always be enough for her. "I only want to savour the feeling, my darling, and make sure you know how much I love you."

Bea turned and looked up at her then, her eyes full of want and need and the beginning of tears about to fall. "I know you love me, because no one has ever looked at me the way you do, touched me the way you have. You are what I've been waiting for all my life."

There were no more words. George slipped back inside her and built up her thrusts slowly, until Bea arched her back and shouted out her release.

When George saw the raw emotion in Bea's tears tumbling down her cheeks, her fear dissipated and she trusted that her lover was here to stay.

She slowly pulled out and gathered Bea in her arms. "Shh, don't cry, darling. I love you."

Bea wiped away her tears quickly and snuggled into George's chest. "I'm sorry, I've never done that before. Cried, I mean."

She reached up to George and cupped her face. "Every time I think I couldn't feel more, I do."

Their lips came together, not with the passionate hunger of their earlier kisses, but as an act of sealing their trust and love in each other. George knew she wasn't alone anymore. She had someone who would argue, talk back to her, and not constantly defer to her, but most of all, Bea would love her. Of that she was certain.

Bea pulled back from their soft kiss and reached for the buttons of George's jeans and said with a cheeky smile on her face, "Now, Georgie, I'm going to show you what you've been missing all those lonely nights apart."

George groaned as Bea started to kiss her stomach while she tried to pull the jeans from her body. She reached down and stroked Bea's blond head. "God, I've missed you."

Just as Bea was about to pull down her Jockey shorts, there was a knock at her door. "Georgie? Leave that young lady alone."

"Go away, Theo," George shouted with frustration.

"No such luck. Granny sent me to interrupt you and tell you she's had the staff make up a room for Beatrice."

George growled and slammed her head back against the pillow, while Bea giggled against her stomach.

"Trust Granny." George fastened her jeans back up, realizing relief for her was a long way off. "I thought you could stay here with me."

Bea crawled up her body and lay by her side. "I suppose it wouldn't look right. The staff and everything."

"Hmm, I'm supposed to be the bloody Queen and I can't even have some private time with my girlfriend," George grumbled.

"Aww, poor baby." Bea gave her a quick peck on the nose.

"Granny also told me to remind you it's time to dress for dinner," said Theo's voice through the door.

"Fine, you've done your duty, Theo, you can go now," George shouted.

"Not a chance. I'm under orders to escort Miss Elliot to her room."

Bea got up and tried to quickly make herself presentable.

George, now thoroughly annoyed, got up and pulled Bea back into her arms. "I could send him to the Tower."

"Don't worry. We'll take up where we left off soon, and you'll have my undivided attention."

"Promise?"

Bea gave her one last long kiss. "Promise. After what you just made me feel, you deserve plenty of one-on-one attention. I love you."

"I love you too."

They walked to the door hand in hand and opened the door. Theo was standing waiting, looking highly amused. He held his arm out for Bea.

"I'll get you back, Theodore," George warned.

Theo snorted. "Let me escort you from my sister's den of iniquity, My Lady."

Bea laughed and took his arm. "Thank you for rescuing me, Your Royal Highness."

George watched them go off together, whispering and laughing, with a huge smile on her face. She couldn't have hoped to find a more perfect partner to add to the royal family.

Now I need to work out how we go forward from here.

Chapter Twenty-eight

George stood outside Bea's door and adjusted the collar and cuffs of her highly starched shirt, making sure she looked as smart as possible. As much as this was a private family dinner, and not a formal occasion, a certain manner of dress was still expected for all the family members, and with it being Bea's first dinner with the family, George wanted to make a special effort.

She knocked, and Bea opened the door.

"Good evening, Your Majesty," she said with a curtsy.

"Good evening, my darling Bea. You look absolutely beautiful as always." George lifted her hand and kissed it gently.

Bea looked down at her short-sleeved silver dress and said, "I hope this is all right. I know you said it was informal, but I wanted to look nice to have dinner with your family."

"Of course it's all right, more than all right. You are effortlessly stunning, my darling." George leaned over and kissed her softly on the lips, then offered her arm.

As they walked off, Bea said, "Who is going to be here, Georgie?"

"Mama, Granny, Theo, Aunt Grace and Uncle Bran, and Vicki and Max. Nothing to worry about."

"What about Julian? Is he here?"

"Oh no. Granny, Aunt Grace, and Uncle Bran have made it clear he's not welcome this year. I doubt he will be again. The only other family you'll see later on are my second cousins, Dicky the Duke of Clarence, and Harry, Duke of Gloucester. They come up a week before the end of the holiday, so they can attend the Ghillies Ball. My ladies-in-waiting come up for that as well, but you've met my Mistress of the Robes, Lady Olivia."

"Oh yes, she was nice. What's the Ghillies Ball?" Bea asked.

"It's not some stuffy formal ball—we do Scottish country dancing. We invite all the staff, and local townsfolk, as a thank you for having us and looking after us. It's great fun, and it'll be even better that you'll be there." George stopped still and turned to face her Bea. "I never thought—will you be able to stay into September? Or do you need to go back to work?"

Bea smiled. "Yes, I can stay as long as you like. I took a leave of absence from Timmy's. Going to work was impossible with the media following me, and Timmy's are delighted with all the publicity, believe me. I will need to pop back and see Mum and Dad though. I've never been away that long from them."

George waited until a footman bowed and passed them, allowing them privacy. "We should invite your parents up for a short break, and then you wouldn't have to leave. We'll have to address certain future family matters while you're here, so it would make sense if they came up. Don't you think?" George said hopefully.

Bea leaned up and gave her a kiss, then said with a smile. "I hope so, Your Majesty."

❖

When they got to the dining room, two pages stationed there bowed and opened the doors for them. Bea saw all the family sitting at the table chatting amongst themselves, and then George's Uncle Bran spotted them and shouted, "Her Majesty the Queen."

The whole family rose as one, either curtsied or bowed, and stood behind their dining chairs.

Oh my goodness, this is an informal family dinner? But then Bea saw the smiles they had on their faces because George was proudly escorting her new girlfriend. It clearly showed they were a loving family, even if they acted a little differently.

George led her to a seat between Theo and Queen Adrianna. She was a bit confused about whether she should curtsy or not, so she gave a quick bob as she approached.

"Do sit down, everyone," George told her family, as she pulled out the chair for Bea. Bea looked up in confusion towards George, unsure of what to do, and without causing any fuss, George told her, "Please sit down, Bea."

With some relief, she sat and realized if she was going to be with the Queen, she was going to need to have some lessons in royal etiquette.

She watched George go around and kiss her mother, who sat at the one end of the table as hostess, her grandmother, and Aunt Grace, before taking her own seat at the head of the table.

The pages came round and filled the champagne flutes. The Queen lifted her glass and stood up. Again, all the family went to stand but she waved them back down.

"Please sit, I only wish to say a few words to you all, before we enjoy this meal together. This year has been a difficult one for our family. Losing King Edward was a huge shock to us all, but we got through it by supporting each other as a family. I know he would be very proud of us all, for carrying on in our duty to the people, and even though we miss him every day, his legacy carries on. I'm so glad that you are all here. Times when we all can get together as a family are rare, so it makes me ever more grateful when they do happen."

George turned and looked at Bea. "I'd also like us to extend a welcome to Beatrice. I can't tell you how much it means to me, that you came to spend the summer holidays with me, and I hope you will be spending a great deal more time with us in the future." Bea's cheeks felt hot as all the family smiled at her. "So I ask you to raise a glass to new beginnings."

When everyone stood to toast, George winked and smiled at her.

I love her so much, Bea thought.

When everyone was re-seated, Queen Adrianna said, "Can we expect some sort of announcement in the near future?"

George's eyes never left Bea's when she said, "Perhaps, Granny, perhaps."

After spending a wonderful dinner and entertaining family evening together, the Queen escorted Bea to her room. "Have you enjoyed your evening, my darling?" George asked as they approached Bea's room.

"Enjoyed it? I can't remember the last time I laughed so much. You have a very surprising family, Georgie."

They came to a stop outside the room. George quirked an eyebrow as she said, "We do? How so?"

Bea took George's hand in her own and caressed it as they talked. "Well, you're all very formal and particular about how you act and behave to each other, yet you couldn't be a more loving family. I mean, I never thought we'd be playing cards and parlour games after dinner. Theo, Vicki, Max, and you together are so funny, always cheating and trying to beat each other. I saw Queen Sofia and Queen Adrianna beam with happiness at you all getting on so well."

"We always have got on well, especially because we are not the type of family who like to sit around watching TV. We see each other less often than a normal family, so when we do get together, we like to be doing things as a family and have a giggle."

"It certainly was great fun," Bea said.

There was a silence between them, and George was unsure of what to do next. She wondered if Bea would want her to stay tonight, or whether she should take it slowly. *Just ask her, George. You know you want to stay with her.*

She looked down at an expectant-looking Bea and took a breath. "Well, goodnight, darling." She mentally chastised herself. *What did I say that for?*

Bea looked disappointed and said, "Oh. Goodnight then, Georgie. I love you. Give the dogs a kiss from me."

George felt like an absolute idiot for wasting this opportunity. "I will. I love you too. Sleep well." She leaned forward and kissed her on the lips. She savoured the taste and again was furious with herself that she wouldn't get another chance till tomorrow.

Bea opened her door and went in. George stood unmoving, cursing her cowardice, when the door opened up again.

Bea grabbed her by the shirt and pulled her into the room. "Get in here." She shut the door and made sure it was locked. "If you want to spend the night together, just say so. I thought we were a couple now."

"We are, but I didn't want to assume—" She was silenced by her girlfriend's lips claiming her.

"Hmm. You are sweet, Georgie, but now I want you to be the Bully that you are and make love to me."

George mimed horns on her head.

Bea giggled and laughed at her antics, but then let out a squeal when George lifted her over her shoulder and carried her towards the bed. Bea smacked her on her behind. "Giddy-up!"

She stopped by the bed and eased Bea down slowly. When they stood looking at each other in the quiet of the room, George felt a nervousness creep into her body. When they'd made love before, they were both caught up in the high emotion of situation, self doubt didn't have time to get hold of her, and Bea had gently guided her until her confidence grew.

But today, thoughts and worries had started to creep into her head. Bea had two lovers before in her life, two lovers who were probably experienced in making love to a woman, and she worried that she would look like an idiot compared to them, after a while.

Tonight there would be no interruptions, just Bea waiting for her to make love to her. She felt the pressure building.

Bea reached up for a kiss and whispered, "Give me a minute to change into something I hope you'll like. I promised you earlier that you would have all of my attention, and you're going to get it."

George gulped hard as she watched Bea walk away with a gentle sway to her hips, and she prayed she could be all that Bea needed and wanted.

George didn't know what to do with herself while she waited for Bea. She'd gone from sitting on the bed to standing and back again. The passing of time was doing nothing for her nerves.

She got up, took off her jacket, and started undoing her bow tie as she walked over to the mirror on the bedroom wall. She left the bow tie hanging loose around her neck and ran her hand through her hair. As she looked at herself in the mirror, she heard a little voice in her head say, *She's going to find out how boring you are, George.*

She shook her head, trying to get rid of the voice making her more nervous, and as she looked up she saw, reflected in the mirror, Bea walking out of the bathroom.

George gulped hard and for some reason couldn't get her legs to move to turn around. Bea was wearing a fine black see-through kimono, and matching bra and panties. George had never seen a sexier or more erotic sight in her life, and her arousal was instantaneous.

Bea walked up behind her slowly and ran her fingers down the back of her shirt. The simple touch was enough to help her gather her courage to turn around.

"Do you like this, Your Majesty?" Bea asked innocently.

George nearly laughed at the ridiculousness of the question. Like was not a word she would use to describe what she felt about what Bea was wearing. The bra especially was doing insane things to her mind. She had the overwhelming desire to suck on the nipples peeping through the material.

"No, I don't like, I love it, and I want you so much right now, it's scary," George said with almost a growl.

Bea laughed softly and batted away George's hand when she reached out to touch her. "Wait, no touching yet. I want to talk to you first."

"You want to talk, now?" George thought she'd never heard a more ludicrous statement in her life.

Bea started to undo George's shirt buttons slowly, agonizingly slowly. "Just for a few minutes, please?"

Even a few minutes sounded like hours to George, when all she could think of was having Bea under her, but she would do anything for her lover. She felt like a beast in a cage, snarling through the bars, held back and getting more riled up by the second, and Bea was the only one who had the key to her freedom.

When Bea finished unbuttoning her shirt, she kept hold of the bow tie and shrugged the shirt off George's shoulders.

Making short work of the compression T-shirt she wore beneath, George was now bare-chested, and Bea slipped the bow tie loosely back around her neck.

"You wanted to talk?" George croaked, eager to move the pace faster.

Bea ran a manicured fingernail down the front of George's chest and swirled over her hard abs.

The steady beat of arousal was now an incessant throb. George's body demanded she take her lover, and it was so hard to stay in control. "Please, darling, or I may explode."

"I know that you've been tense, perhaps a little nervous about making love, and I want you to tell me why." Bea started to place small kisses on her chest as she waited on an answer.

God, am I that transparent? George was convinced this was part of Bea's plot. Under normal circumstances she would never admit what she was about to say, but she was so turned on that she was convinced her brain had short-circuited. "I've always been scared of being intimate with anyone, until you. I'm nervous with you, but not scared."

Bea caressed her neck and looked deeply into her eyes. "Why?"

"Because they would see my weaknesses and I would look foolish." She felt exposed as soon as she said it, but Bea reassured her by pulling her down by the loose bow tie around her neck and gave her a kiss on the lips.

"Georgie, you're safe with me. I will never betray what is between us. When we're alone, together like this, you're safe. There are no judgements, no expectations, just two people who accept each other for both their strengths and weaknesses."

George rested her forehead on Bea's, closed her eyes, and took a moment to absorb her lover's words.

She wondered how on earth she could have been lucky enough to not only find this woman, but have her love. She couldn't speak but simply nodded her acceptance. "You are everything I've ever dreamed of. Your strong body, to take care of me"—Bea placed kisses on both her biceps and in the middle her chest—"and the biggest heart, to love me the way I've always wanted. I want you to express yourself without fear."

George felt so much emotion at that moment, she had to gulp hard to keep in control. She reached out a shaky hand and caressed Bea's soft skin.

Bea turned her face into George's hand and kissed it. "There's only you and only me, and"—Bea stepped back and loosened the tie to her kimono, opening it and letting it fall at her feet—"I am yours."

George felt her emotional shackles fall away forever. She stepped forward and lifted Bea into her arms and kissed her more passionately than she ever had. Her passion ran deep, and long and felt like a rush of fever that threatened to devour them. The energy that she had held at bay when she was talking to Bea came out like a torrent.

She walked them back to the bed and quickly pulled off her trousers and underwear, before lying on top of her lover. Her mouth went immediately to one of Bea's hard nipples that taunted her through the see-through bra, while her hand pushed under the lace cup and squeezed Bea's other breast. Sucking on her breast felt even better than she'd imagined, the lace creating a little teasing barrier that was driving her wild.

Bea moaned loudly and entwined her fingers through George's hair, pulling at it in desperate need.

George was hungry. She wanted Bea and wanted her everywhere. She repositioned herself on Bea's thigh and started to thrust. When she tried to slip her hand down to touch Bea, Bea grasped her wrist.

"No, just you. It's just for you this time. I want to watch you come on me."

George could've come that second after hearing Bea say those words. She groaned and thrust faster. Her orgasm was seconds away and racing towards her like an unstoppable force.

"Fuck...I'm..."

Bea held her gently and whispered in her ear, "Come on me, Georgie, I'm yours, all for you."

That was it for George. She thrust into Bea a few more times before her orgasm exploded and drained all the tension, the doubts, and worries that she'd felt since she had woken up alone after their first night together. She collapsed onto Bea, gasping. "I love you, I love you."

Bea stroked her back tenderly, until George calmed. She raised up on her elbows and looked down at Bea, smiling. "You are a bad woman, Miss Elliot. You wound me up so tight I thought my head was going to explode."

Bea giggled and pulled her down into a kiss. "I hope I always can, Your Majesty."

When Bea talked to her that way, it made her want to make her moan and scream her name.

Bea reached up to touch her, but George grasped her wrists and held them above her head.

Bea wriggled for a few seconds, and then her cheeky smile was back. "You have me then. What would you do with me, oh mighty Queen?"

George grinned, full of confidence and liberation. She was finally able to be who she was and trust that her lover would always support and never betray her. She lowered her head until her lips were inches from Bea's lips and said, "Everything."

❖

Bea lay on her back, tantalizingly close to an orgasm that was just out of reach. Her plan to get George to talk and get rid of those last insecurities had worked well. George had been an energetic lover before, but since their talk, it was as if she had thrown off the last of her chains and was revelling in her newfound freedom of expression. The focus of that expression was thankfully…Bea.

George thrust two fingers inside her, while her tongue lapped at her clit, building up her orgasm. But having come a few times already, Bea wasn't sure if she could again.

"I'm so close."

George crawled back up her body and slowed her thrusts to a gentle swirl. "Bea, do you remember when we had dinner in France?"

Oh God, yes. Bea held on to George's head and looked into her eyes. "Yes, tell me."

"I said, *Ti amo, la mia regina Beatrice.* I love you my Queen Beatrice." That was it, she needed to hear George's voice. She remembered how aroused she'd felt that night, as George spoke to her in Italian.

Bea dug her nails into George's shoulders. "Again…"

"*La mia regina Beatrice. Ti amo, ti amo.*"

This time the wave of pleasure didn't stop. George gave her a deep kiss, as her orgasm crashed over her. "Oh God, I love you," Bea said breathlessly.

George rolled off and pulled Bea into her arms.

"For someone who is new to this, Georgie, you're certainly good at it and have a lot of stamina. I think I might die if I have one more orgasm." She heard and felt George's laughter rumble in her chest below her.

"I like to please you, my darling."

"You certainly do that, but I like to please you just as much, Your Majesty." Bea saw George close her eyes and felt her stomach clench beneath her fingers. "Oh, I think you have one more left in you."

George nodded and, feeling emotional, said, "I was so lonely without you. I can't believe you chose to come back to me."

Her heart ached. The time they spent apart had been awful, but now they were together, and Bea vowed to herself that she would never let George feel that way again.

"Let me kiss away the loneliness, so you never feel it again." Bea kissed her way down her chest and stomach, until she disappeared under the covers.

CHAPTER TWENTY-NINE

Bea became aware of a loud droning noise, rudely waking her from sleep. "Argh." Her eyes popped open to find she was lying on top of George, who was wide awake and smiling.

"Good morning, my darling."

"Morning, Georgie. What is that dreadful noise?"

George looked a bit confused. "What noise…? Oh, you mean the piper? He plays below my window every morning to signal the start of the day."

"You mean, I've got to put up with that every morning for the rest of my life?" Bea said with a mock frown.

George smiled broadly realizing what that meant. "Yes, for as long as you're willing to share my bed, Miss Elliot."

Bea lowered her lips closer to George's and said, "Oh, I think you can safely say that I will willingly share your bed for the rest of my life. In fact, after last night, I may force you to stay here in bed forever."

George tickled her ribs mercilessly. "Oh, you think a little thing like you can keep me here?"

They laughed, talked, and held each other, as they should have been able to do after their first morning together.

Bea popped her head up from George's chest suddenly and said, "Am I keeping you from your work?"

"One morning won't hurt—besides I'm on holiday. I'll do my boxes later, while you get dressed."

They lay in silence, just holding each other and enjoying the quiet. "Balmoral looks magical from what I've seen so far."

George kissed her head. "You haven't seen half of it yet. I can't wait to show you around."

"It seems more like a castle than a palace, and the tartan curtains, carpet, it's everywhere, and gives it an ancient atmosphere."

"Hmm. Nothing has really changed since Queen Victoria and Prince Albert's time. We try to keep it the same, traditional. We like it that way."

Bea remembered she'd brought Georgie a gift and jumped up to rummage through her bags.

George grinned broadly. "I think this is the best view of the day."

A very naked Bea walked back to the bed, clutching a gift box. "Behave, Your Majesty, or you won't get your gift."

"I'm sorry. Can I have my gift? Pretty please?"

"All right, since you've been so good. Here." She handed over the box, and George opened it quickly.

"I thought we could build it together, while we're here at Balmoral. I hope you don't have this boat…ship…thing, whatever it is. I asked Cammy, but—"

Bea was tackled down to the bed and found herself underneath George.

"You are just a dream, my darling. I don't know how I was lucky enough to find you, but I promise I'm never going to let you go. You are just perfect, and I love you more than life."

"I love you too."

❖

Later that morning, while George attended to her morning paperwork, Bea took her time having a leisurely bath and getting ready for the day. George had told her the family planned a lunchtime picnic. She looked down at Rexie, who had decided to stay on with her, rather than follow the Queen and other dogs, and said, "Will I do, Rexie?"

Before Rex had a chance to pass his opinion, there was a knock at the door. She opened it to find Cammy waiting there.

"Ma'am?"

"Morning, Cammy. Oh, my, that's a unique outfit."

Cammy appeared to be wearing full Highland dress, although Bea wasn't quite sure. It was a colourful sight. The kilt was red, bottle green, and yellow, and on top she wore a brown tweed jacket and a brown cap with a small pom-pom.

"Morning. Yes, thank you. It's traditional to wear Highland dress at Balmoral," Cammy said.

Bea had noticed the previous evening that all the pages were in kilts, unlike their counterparts at the English palaces.

"The Queen and the family are waiting for you downstairs. I'll escort you if you're ready, ma'am."

"Since when do you call me *ma'am*, Captain?" she teased.

Cammy gave her a charming smile back. "Since you are the Queen's—"

"What am I, Captain?" Bea asked with amusement.

Without missing a beat Cammy said, "The Queen's lassie."

Bea laughed out loud. "My, my, Captain. Lali is right in thinking you are charming."

Cammy seemed surprised by that comment. "She does?"

"Uh-huh, but don't tell her I told you."

"Oh, I won't. Thank you for telling me."

"So, will I do for the picnic? I wasn't sure what was appropriate to wear." She indicated a figure-hugging wool jumper, jeans, and designer wellington boots that her mother had advised her to buy before going. She'd explained the royals' country style was always practical.

Cammy appraised her and gave a quirky smile. "Aye. You look fine, lassie. The Queen is very lucky. I would put on a warm jacket though. It's a bit cold here if you're not used to it."

Bea walked over to her wardrobe and got out a green country raincoat. "I did notice it looked a bit gloomy outside. They're really going to cook and eat outdoors in this?"

"Aye, it's often been said that the royal family would go out in weather you wouldn't put a dog out in."

Bea chuckled at Cammy's colourful description and thought back to what her mother said about Balmoral being a testing ground for new members. *I hope I pass.* "They seem to love it up here."

"They are outdoors sorts of people, and Her Majesty especially, with her military background, enjoys being out in the fresh air and being active."

Her mind flashed back to last night and the energy George had displayed, tiring her out completely. "Yes, she does have a lot of energy."

Cammy smiled. "If you're ready?"

"Yes, of course. Come, Rexie." Her new best friend bounded after her.

Bea walked down the stairs leading to the entrance hallway. It was busy with staff going back and forth to the Land Rovers with tables, chairs, and picnic baskets. Then she caught sight of George, talking and organizing the outing with her family and staff. As if sensing her coming down the stairs, George turned and smiled up at her, wearing similar Highland dress to Cammy.

George came to meet her at the bottom of the stairs and offered her hand. She took it and curtsied to her Queen, while Rexie wandered off to meet up with the other dogs.

"Hello, my darling. I've missed you."

"I've missed you, Your Majesty, but what on God's green earth are you wearing?"

George looked down at her outfit. "What? You mean my kilt? The family always wears tartan and kilts when we're here—well, not Theo, he thinks it's too old fashioned. It's part of the way we do things here."

Bea looked round and all the male members of the family were similarly dressed to the Queen. The older female members had tartan skirts and country jackets, although Vicki was dressed similar to herself.

"Do you not like it?"

Bea saw the worried look on George's face and immediately wanted to reassure her. "Oh no, I just wasn't expecting it, but you look rather handsome in it, actually."

George kissed her cheek and smiled. "Excellent. Well, let's go and have some fun, shall we?"

George insisted on driving Bea and herself down to the picnic spot, which sat idyllically on the River Dee. As they drove, Bea sneaked her hand over to George's bare leg and softly stroked her hard muscled thigh.

"I can see the benefits of the kilt, Your Majesty," Bea said mischievously.

George grabbed the teasing hand before it could creep any further up her thigh. "My darling, as much as I love you to touch me, I am liable to drive us into a tree if you don't stop."

Bea stuck her tongue out. "Spoilsport."

George smiled indulgently back.

"So tell me about your outfit then. Which tartan is this?"

"This is Royal Stewart. There are different versions for different occasions, but this one is Hunting Stewart. It has muted colours so you don't look too garish while hunting."

"So why do you wear the Stewart tartan when you are Buckinghams?" Bea asked.

"We are related to the House of Stuart through my ancestor, Queen Victoria. The Stuarts were kings of both Scotland and England, so that entitles us to use that as our family tartan. We also have a Balmoral tartan, but you need the express permission of the sovereign to wear it."

Bea smiled cheekily. "Oh, and what would happen if I wore it without your permission? Would you punish me, Your Majesty?"

George's eyes widened and she gulped audibly. "We're in danger of crashing into that tree again with that sort of talk."

"Oops. I'll be on my best behaviour, I promise. What is Cammy's then? And what is that funny hat she's wearing with the bobble on top?"

"The captain's family tartan is Cameron, of course, and the funny hat, as you call it, is a glengarry—it's traditional to wear one if you have a military background. I wear them with some of my Scottish regiment uniforms with a feather added, because I am a chieftain."

"I wonder what my tartan would be."

"Do you have any Scottish blood in you, my darling?"

"Yes," Bea said excitedly, "my grandma was Scottish."

George smiled broadly. "Granny will be pleased. She is very proud of our family's Scottish blood. What was your grandma's name? We can check what your tartan would be, and then you could wear it on your dress for the Ghillies Ball."

"Really? Oh, that would be great. I would feel like one of the natives then. Her name was Buchanan."

"Excellent, we can ask Granny about Buchanan. She's a mine of information."

When they arrived at the picnic area, by the edge of the freshwater loch, George jumped out quickly and moved round to help Bea out of the Land Rover. Seeing that everyone else was otherwise occupied with preparations, George gave her a tender kiss. "I love you, Bea, and I can't tell you how wonderful it is to have you here to share this. It's so important to me that you feel like one of the family."

Bea kissed George's chin. "I love you too, and your family are lovely people. They've made me very welcome."

George laughed and took her hand, leading her down to the picnic area. "You're so sweet, my darling."

"Why?"

"Why? Oh, too many reasons to mention, but one of them is, you're so short, that you always kiss me on the chin."

Bea play-hit George on the arm. "I'm not small, you're just a giant, Your Majesty."

"Ouch! Don't hit me, Miss Elliot, you're so strong." George play-acted, making them both laugh.

"I'm not that small, am I?"

George put her arm round her shoulders and kissed her head. "Yes, you're my little cute smout."

"Wait, what's a smout?"

She grinned cheekily at Bea and said, "A good Scottish word for a small, shrimp-like person."

Bea looked at George as if unsure if she should be annoyed or pleased. "Hmm. Smout? It's cute, I like it. Now kiss me again before your family see us."

❖

Bea had never been to a picnic like this before. The staff had set up everything—tables, chairs, plates, cutlery, even a drinks table with every spirit and beverage that could be needed—and left the family to do everything else themselves. George seemed to be in charge of the old-fashioned charcoal barbecue, with Max assisting, while Queen Sofia and Princess Grace saw to the salad and other side dishes.

Further down the bank, George's Uncle Bran, Vicki, and Theo were fishing with the help of an estate worker. It was slightly surreal to see these lofty, untouchable people taking part in very ordinary everyday tasks.

Bea was sitting on a folding camp chair beside the Dowager Queen Adrianna.

"It's a beautiful day, isn't it, Beatrice?"

It was in fact chilly by Bea's standards, but the royals seemed to be made of tougher stuff. "Yes, it's so picturesque here. I've never been in Scotland, although my grandma was Scottish."

Queen Adrianna beamed. "Really? Oh, that's wonderful. You are an even better match for our dear George then. My mother was Scottish, and there is a great affinity for all things Scottish in our family."

"The Queen said to ask you about what my tartan would be. She thought I could wear the colour to the Ghillies Ball. My grandma's name was Buchanan."

The Dowager Queen tapped her walking stick against the earth below them, appearing to think very hard. "Hmm. I seem to recall it's quite a bold tartan with greens and yellow colours, but I will find out from my private secretary. She's an expert in these sorts of matters."

"Bea, darling?" George shouted and beckoned her with a big smile.

"Would you excuse me, Ma'am?"

Queen Adrianna patted Bea on the knee. "Of course. It seems Her Majesty can't do without you, my dear."

Bea literally skipped over to George. She'd never felt as relaxed as this in a long time, and spending time with George's family was really fun. "What can I do for you, Your Majesty?"

George put her arm round Bea and pulled her in for a kiss. "Nothing. I just missed you, and perhaps I wanted to show off my cooking skills."

She rested her head against George's shoulder, watching the fire burn down and the charcoals burn white. "I didn't know you had any cooking skills. When does a Queen have to cook?"

"Well, I've only ever cooked field rations before during my officer training, and helped my Papa with this, but the head of the family always does the cooking. This is my first year."

Bea saw a distant, faraway look come over George's face, and she realized this was yet another thing that reminded her of her loss and of her responsibility.

She bumped George's hip. "You'll do very well, Georgie, and if you get stuck, then I'm here to lend a hand. That's what I'm here for."

"Thank you. I'm just getting used to that. Having someone to support me, I mean," George explained.

"I know. It's a learning process for us both, but I'll be at your side as long as you want me."

"Thank you, darling."

Bea lifted up one of the plates with the finest Aberdeen Angus steaks and said, "Now enough lovey-doveyness, make my food, oh mighty Queen."

❖

George sat with her mother, enjoying a drink after their large meal, watching Bea being taught the rudiments of fly fishing by the head keeper and Queen Adrianna.

"Do you think Granny will ever give up fishing?" George asked her mother with a smile.

"I doubt it. Not as long as she can get a seat by the riverbank. She has always loved it as long as I've known her. Your papa said she was even better than your Grandpa Freddie, and now she has inveigled Bea into it, you may never see your young lady again."

She watched Bea with pride. "She has fit in exceptionally well, don't you think, Mama?"

Queen Sofia smiled fondly at her doting daughter. "Oh yes, indeed. She's not a young lady who's afraid to get stuck in. I think you've made a perfect choice. This holiday could have been so melancholy, the first trip to Balmoral without dear Eddie, but seeing you so happy and so much in love has lifted everyone's spirits."

George looked seriously at her mother. "You approve then, Mama?"

"I do indeed. When do you intend to make it official?"

"I'm taking her to Loch Muick, to spend the day and night there. I've had Cammy make some preparations for me, and I hope to ask her then."

Her mother stroked her head. "It's a stunningly romantic spot. You're a good girl, George, and a dutiful monarch. Eddie would have been so proud."

George looked over to see her lover casting out the fishing line, only to get it caught in the nearby tree. Theo, Vicki, Max, Granny, and Bea all laughed together, while Uncle Bran was sent to retrieve it.

"I surely hope so, Mama."

CHAPTER THIRTY

George and Bea set off early the next morning to start their day out at Loch Muick. George wanted as much privacy as possible, and so didn't want any security with her for the day, but Inspector Lang had insisted on two of his men sitting on surveillance outside the royal lodge by the loch.

George pulled the Land Rover up in front of the house and helped Bea out of the truck. "Here we are, darling. This is Glas Allt Shiel house. It was built by Queen Victoria for the views over the loch. It wasn't used a great deal after her death, but Papa had it refurbished. It's not some grand royal residence, more like a comfortable country squire's home."

"It looks perfect. Are we still on Balmoral estate?"

George walked to the back of the Rover and started getting their bags out. "Yes. We have 49,000 acres on the estate, but this isn't our personal playground, it's a working estate. We have grouse moors, forestry, and farmland, as well as managed herds of deer, Highland cattle, and ponies. When the family head back down to London, the estate keeps working, making money for its upkeep and providing jobs."

Bea held her hands up. "You don't have to justify yourself to me, Georgie."

George dropped the bags and walked over to her. "I'm sorry. I just don't want you to think we're extravagant. This is a private estate, and we finance it ourselves. I just wanted you to know that."

Bea reached up and kissed her on the chin. "I understand. I'm learning and taking on board everything you say. Now just relax."

"Okay, before we take our things in, I want you to get a taste of what lies ahead." George pulled her by the hand excitedly, down past a line of trees, and suddenly the view of the loch opened out in front of them.

"Oh, my God, Georgie. This is…it's stunning."

George was delighted by Bea's reaction and very proud that she could share this with her. Bea had told her how she and her sister had been city girls, never venturing out of London, so it was wonderful to see she appreciated the dramatic, glacier-scarred land. "I'm so glad you like it. Come on, I'll put our things inside and get our day started."

As she walked off Bea shouted, "Are you sure you won't be cold?"

George looked down at her army issue cargo shorts and T-shirt and smiled. "Don't you worry. I'm well used to the Aberdeenshire climate. I'll just be a few minutes."

She put their belongings into the house and set off to start their walk. They walked hand in hand along the loch trail, George carrying a backpack with all the things they needed for the day. It was a bright day, and after a couple of miles, Bea dispensed with her jumper, leaving her in a tight-fitting dark blue camisole, to match three-quarter-length jeans. George took every opportunity to place an arm round her bare shoulders or cast her eyes down for a nice view of her breasts.

The snow-peaked tips of the surrounding mountains slipped steadily into slate greys and then muted browns and greens of the grasses and heather further down, ending in the calm glassy blackness of the loch.

"I can't believe how quiet and peaceful it is, Georgie. I've never experienced a place like this. It has such an ancient atmosphere."

"This is why I love it here, Bea." George stopped and turned Bea towards the loch. She placed her hands on Bea's shoulders and whispered, "Close your eyes, clear your mind, and tell me what can you hear."

"Birds singing, water splashing, the breeze whistling through the trees."

"Peace. That's what I hear, peace."

George hugged her from behind and said, "You can see why Balmoral is so special to me. After living in London and touring about the world most of the year, to come here in the summer is something special. I can feel my cares leaving as soon as I arrive, and to have you here makes it all the more special." George then whispered in her ear, "There's a way to experience this, that's even more special though. Well, I think so. Do you want to see?"

"Yes," Bea said excitedly.

George took her hand and they both walked on, following the trail to a small brick building, halfway round the loch. "This is the boathouse. I thought we could go out on the loch and eat our lunch out there."

Bea looked a little worried. "A boat? Out there? I've never been on a boat."

"Don't look so worried, darling, it's just a dinghy, nothing too big, and I am an excellent sailor." George gave her a wink and then opened up the big double doors of the building.

There were boats of different sizes in there, from a few bigger ones down to simple rowing boats, but George headed for the big one with a sail, which was down at the moment.

"That's a dinghy?" Bea asked with surprise.

George looked up and said, "Yes, a simple two-man dinghy with a sail. You can't really have anything much bigger in a loch like this."

She saw the tense look on Bea's face and walked up to her, taking her hands. "You will be absolutely fine. Remember, I can sail huge battleships, so I think we'll be safe enough in this. If you don't like it, we can come back in."

Bea nodded. "I trust you."

George gave her a quick kiss on the cheek and went off to bring out the dinghy. She wheeled it out on a boat trailer, down to the water.

❖

Bea watched the play of the strong muscles in George's shoulders, arms, and legs as she set up the boat. *Now I feel much better about sailing.*

Once they got out onto the water, it wasn't so intimidating. They sailed into the middle of the loch and got out the sandwiches Cook had packed them. "This is wonderful, Georgie. I've never done anything like this. You're filling my life with experiences I'd never thought I'd have."

George smiled brightly. "I hope I can always give you a rich and loving life, my darling, but I have one more thing I think you might like."

She put away the rubbish and left over sandwiches and brought a rectangular plastic food box out of the backpack. "Would you like dessert?"

"Oh, you know I would." Bea smiled.

George moved to sit on the floor of the boat, her head resting against the boat seat. "Come and lie with me." She patted the space between her legs.

Bea was unsure. "Will the boat not tip over if I move?"

"No, it'll take more than your little smout body to turn over this boat. Come on, trust me." George beckoned her with a crooked finger.

Bea moved gingerly over to her, and lay back onto George's chest.

"Remember I said there was one thing better than the peace you heard?"

Bea nodded.

"That thing is peace on the water. Close your eyes, darling, and let yourself float in the peace."

She did as asked and listened to the sounds of nature around them, while being held lovingly in George's arms. Every so often George would place soft kisses on her head and cheeks, whispering *I love you* in her ear.

They floated like that for a few minutes before Bea opened her eyes and looked up to her love above her. "Georgie, no one has ever done something so simple and yet so romantic for me. I love you."

"You deserve more romantic days than I could come up with, but I'll always try to show you how much I love you. Now, how about that dessert?"

Bea nodded enthusiastically. "Oh yes, what have you got for us?"

George opened up her plastic container and pulled out the reddest and plumpest strawberry Bea had seen, which had been dipped in chocolate.

"You spoil me," Bea said.

"I hope I always will. These were grown on the estate. I hope you like them. Take a bite." George lovingly fed the strawberries to her, taking occasional bites at Bea's insistence.

Bea had her eyes closed, enjoying being held in George's arms and waiting on the next bite of plump fruit. When it didn't materialize, she opened her eyes slowly to be faced with a ring box. Her mind was unsure of what was happening, but her heart raced instinctively knowing this was going to be a special moment.

"Beatrice Elliot, the day you gave me that annoyed look across the boardroom at Timmy's, I knew you were special. You brought colour and laughter back to my world, when my heart was broken and aching with grief. You supported me as a friend and looked after me, despite our differences, and you came to be with me, even though you knew your life would change forever."

George opened the ring box, and Bea held her hand to her mouth as she gasped.

"This was my great-great-grandmother Queen Mary's engagement ring. She was the last sovereign Queen of this country and sat on the throne for fifty years. I thought it fitting that as the next Queen to follow her, I give it to my wife, if you'll have me. I love you with all my heart, my darling. Would you do me the great honour of becoming my wife and consort?"

Even though Bea knew when she came to Scotland that she was committing to George, and marriage would follow in time, it was still a shock to be asked and so soon. The ring had a large solitaire diamond and smaller diamonds set on either side, making the band look as if it were all set in the precious stones. "George, are you absolutely sure you want someone like me to be your consort?"

George lifted her hand and held the ring next to her ring finger as if waiting to see if it would be accepted. "I am certain you are the perfect person to share my throne, and to help govern my people. All you do is care for others and work tirelessly for charity, and my family love you. That makes you the perfect person for the job. I know you're sceptical about some of the ways we do things in the royal family, but you can help me by questioning what we do, and helping me modernize and keep the monarchy relevant to this changing world. Please? Say yes."

Somewhere deep inside, Bea knew she was meant to do this, meant to be the one to love the Queen and help her and carry out whatever duties befell her. She took a deep breath and said, "Yes, Georgie, I love you, and I will marry you."

George slid the ring onto her fiancée's finger and turned on her side so she could kiss her. Bea gasped as the boat rocked from side to side but was soon engulfed in a deep, passionate kiss, which left them both breathless.

George leaned up on her elbow. "When I look at you all I can hear are the words of the immortal bard Robert Burns. *But to see her was to love her, love but her, and love for ever.* Thank you for coming into my life. I love you," George said, before lavishing Bea's lips with some gentler, loving kisses, as they floated along Loch Muick.

They burst through the front door dripping wet, but in good spirits and laughing. "You weren't wrong about rain, Georgie. That was unbelievable."

"It was fun though, wasn't it? The locals call it rude rain. It can be sunny one moment, and the next, you're drenched." George smiled.

"Oh yes, lots of fun." Bea realized they were both dripping all over the floor. "Have you got some towels?"

"Yes, I'll get them. You go on through and get warmed by the fire."

"But it wasn't lit before we came out. I don't know if I could—"

George took hold of her shoulders and pushed her towards the drawing room door. "Just go. I'll be back in a minute." George ran off up the stairs, and Bea walked into the room.

"Georgie, you are just too perfect." She found the huge open fire burning warm and bright, and a bottle of champagne sitting in a chiller. It made for a very cosy scene with the large, thick sheepskin rug set in front of the fire. George must have had Cammy set this up.

Bea pulled off her soaking wet jumper and jeans and tried to warm herself in front of the fire.

"I've got towels darling…"

She turned and caught George's gaze hungrily raking over her body, and her hands were holding the towels so hard, her knuckles were turning white.

"Can I have a towel, please?" Bea asked.

"What? Oh…yes. Sorry." George handed over the towel and took off her shoes and began to towel off.

"This was so nice to come back to, Georgie. You're so romantic."

"I wanted to make it nice for you."

Bea bent over and wrapped her long wet hair in the towel, hoping she wouldn't look like a drowned cat.

George moaned.

Bea looked up and saw George looking like she wanted to devour her. She felt her stomach clench and a steady throb begin. The moisture dripping off George's wet dark hair and running slowly down the pronounced muscles in her shoulders and arms made her ache to be touched. Her fingertips started stroking gently over her own hard nipples.

"Georgie," she whispered.

Their eyes never left each other as George pulled off her T-shirt and walked towards her. She stood in front of Bea, bare chested and waiting.

Bea trailed a fingernail from George's neck, down the centre of her chest, over her stomach, and swirling round her navel, which drew a moan from George. She opened the button at the top of George's shorts and let them fall, and they were soon kicked away.

"I want you, Bea," George said huskily.

Bea smiled and turned her back to her, lifting her hair onto her shoulder, allowing George access to her bra clasp. "Then take me, Your Majesty."

George groaned deep in her throat. Bea had noticed that this term of address got George hugely turned on.

She felt her bra being loosened and pulled off, and as soon as her breasts were free, they were taken into George's hands. She gasped at the sensation, as George's hands were still wet and cold from the rain, making her nipples go painfully hard. Bea placed her hands on top of George's, encouraging her to squeeze harder.

"You like this, my darling?"

"Yes, Your Majesty," she moaned.

George lowered her lips to Bea's ear and turned the heat up even more. "I thought you weren't anyone's subject, Miss Elliot?"

Bea moaned as George placed kisses and soft bites down the side of her neck. She looked up at the mirror above the fireplace to meet George's eyes. "I was wrong. I am your subject, Your Majesty, and I am yours to command." She lowered her eyes submissively.

George's nostrils flared. "Lie down on your front on the rug."

Bea did as asked, and once George had gotten rid of both their underwear, she lay on her side next to Bea.

George began by stroking her fingers from Bea's neck down her spine and lingering over her buttocks, which made Bea squirm and moan. "You liked to be touched here?"

"Yes, Your majesty," Bea groaned.

Bea opened her legs, knowing where she wanted George's fingers. George dipped her fingers quickly into her slit and then up to her arse, spreading the wetness around and teasing the hole.

Bea gasped. "Oh, please, Georgie." Bea had never experienced this sort of overwhelming passion before in any of her relationships, and she'd certainly never begged, but she felt anything was possible with George.

"What?" George continued teasing both holes with her fingers. "Tell me what you want."

"Fuck me, Your Majesty."

Those words made George shiver with pleasure. Only in her deepest, darkest, private fantasies had she ever thought about this kind of play, and she was loving it. "Get up on your hands and knees, my darling."

George knelt behind Bea and groaned when she saw the abundant wetness coming from her sex, painting her inner thighs. She thrust two fingers inside her without warning.

"Oh yes." Bea cried out at the sudden fullness.

George groaned in pleasure as she always did at the warm, velvety feeling of being inside Bea. "You feel so good, Bea, I love you so much." George kept up a steady rhythm with her fingers.

Bea turned her head and said breathlessly, "Love you. Harder, please?"

George smiled and grasped her shoulder while thrusting with her hips into her hand, to make it harder, rougher. Every time she thrust, her own sex hit her hand, and her orgasm built. Then, as Bea got nearer and nearer the edge, she thrust back on George's fingers. "That's it my darling, come in my hand."

"I'm so close...can't. I need more." Bea's groans turned to higher-pitched cries when George curled her fingers and rubbed deep inside. "*Georgie.* Too much..."

Bea sounded as if she was almost in tears, so great was her arousal. "That's it my darling, come for me. I'm here, you can take it for me."

Bea screamed in a low, guttural, primal tone as she went over the edge and collapsed to the rug, bringing George with her.

George was very close, and she ground her clit against Bea's buttocks below. It was more passionate than any fantasy she'd ever had, and it was all because of Bea. "Oh God, I'm going to come on you." Bea helped by pushing her behind up into George's sex.

"Love you, love you, love you," George moaned, like a mantra, her hips thrusting faster and faster, until she gave a hoarse cry and her hips started to jerk erratically as her orgasm hit.

They both lay there panting, George kissing Bea on the shoulder and the side of her neck. "Thank you so much, my darling. I haven't felt anything like that before." She rolled to the side and took Bea into her arms.

"You don't have to thank me. No one has ever made love to me like you. It feels so raw, so passionate with you, like nothing else matters."

"When I look at you, nothing else does matter to me. All I want to do is show you how much I love you, and bring you pleasure. You are my greatest treasure." George leaned in and gave Bea one of the softest kisses they had ever shared.

Sometime later, they lay together on the rug with a blanket over them. They had shared some of the champagne and were now just enjoying holding each other, Bea with her head on George's chest, and George holding her tight.

Bea lifted her hand above them and admired her engagement ring. "It's so beautiful, Georgie. I just can't believe it's happening."

"I'm so glad you like it. I feel so lucky to have found you, Bea. You are the only woman I will ever love." George brought her hand to her lips and kissed it.

"I think everyone in the country would say I'm the lucky one, Georgie. It's not every day that an ordinary girl gets to marry a Queen."

George shook her head. "No, they'd be wrong. Bea, I've looked at the love my parents shared, and I prayed that I would be as lucky, but I didn't think I would be. I thought I'd be forced to live out my life with someone I didn't truly love, but when this little smout came along, determined to dislike me, I lost my heart and found my Queen Consort."

Bea giggled and tickled George's well-defined stomach. "I just wonder, why me though? Why choose me as your Queen Consort? I have no experience and I'll have to learn everything from scratch. Someone like Princess Eleanor would do the job better. When I saw she was with you at Ascot, I thought I'd given her exactly what she wanted, and it broke my heart."

George turned to face her. "I chose you because you understand that being royal isn't about showing off, it's about doing your duties without any fuss. It's not enough just to be a Queen Consort, you have to get out there and do it. Eleanor might have a royal background, but she would never understand that concept, whereas you do. You are my perfect Queen Consort. I told her exactly that, in no uncertain terms, when she tried to ingratiate herself to me at the races. She left the country soon after."

"You are sweet."

"Not sweet, my darling, just honest." George watched as Bea played with her hand nervously.

"I've got a lot to learn, and I want to do the job properly, working hard for lots of charities. Will you help me?"

"Of course I will. So will my family. But you'll have lots of other help. A private secretary, ladies-in-waiting, and other staff. Plus, you'll always have me, my darling. I will always protect you and try to guide you."

Bea nodded. "It feels so intimate, so private here at Balmoral, but I suppose the world is waiting for us out there."

"Yes, Bastian informs me that speculation is at fever pitch, wondering why you're here at Balmoral with us, but don't worry about what comes next. It will all be planned out. The prime minister arrives tomorrow, and we can discuss plans with her then."

"Does she always come when you're here? You don't even get a break from the government when you're on holiday?"

"No, the prime minister must come to see me at Balmoral to keep me informed on world events and government business."

Bea hugged her tighter. "Wait till Mum and Dad hear about this. They'll be so excited. I do hope they get on all right with your family."

"Of course they will. Mama and Granny are very good at putting people at their ease. I must also speak to your father privately and ask for permission to marry you."

Bea sat up and gave George a strange look. "Ask his permission? Georgie, do you know what century it is?"

George reached up and stroked her hair tenderly. "Yes, I do, but I'm also a very traditional person, as you know. I'm not asking permission because your dad owns you or something. It's just about showing him respect, and showing him that his little girl will be well loved and looked after."

"You are the sweetest and most loving person I have ever met."

"It's just how I feel. I wouldn't want someone marrying our daughter without asking me."

"Our daughter?" Bea husked. They hadn't talked about it yet, but she knew children were essential for the succession. It was no hardship for her, because the thought of having George's children made her heart fill with joy.

"Of course. If you will share that gift with me, your children will sit on the throne of Great Britain for generations to come."

In that moment she wanted to let George know how special she was. "Georgie, you truly are the handsome prince from a fairy tale. I didn't think people like you existed anymore, but you've proved me wrong. I love you with all my heart, and I want to show you." She took George's hand and placed it between her legs. "Do you feel what you do to me? How wet I am for you?"

George groaned and nodded her head. "Yes, let me…"

Bea felt her about to roll her over. "Oh no, you don't. I know you like to take charge, but let me give you pleasure and show you how much I love you, Your Majesty."

"Yes…"

Bea got up and rummaged in the overnight bag she'd brought with her and pulled out an Intelliflesh strap-on.

A grin appeared on George's face when she saw what Bea was carrying.

"I brought one from London—I thought you might like to use one again, since you enjoyed it so much the first time."

"Oh yes. I would love that."

She smacked George's hands away, when she tried to take it from her. "Uh-uh. No touching, you don't have to do a thing. Just lie back and enjoy, Your Majesty."

Once she attached it properly, Bea kissed and nibbled at George's lips and jaw, all the time stroking and pumping George's cock in a soft massage.

"Bea…I can feel it."

Bea smiled down at her. "I know, and I can feel you in my hand. Are you enjoying this?" She kissed her way down her chest, her stomach, and then nuzzled and sucked at the cock.

"Oh yes. It's so good…"

Bea took her full in her mouth, and George arched her back.

"Oh God."

After a few minutes, she slid her mouth off with an audible pop and crawled up George's body to kiss her lips. George's arms circled Bea's back.

George hummed in pleasure into the kiss, and pulled back to say, "Let me? Inside, please?"

Bea smiled at the great restraint George was showing and said, "Yes, but I'm in charge, okay?"

George nodded. "Anything. Just want to feel inside you."

Bea gave her exactly what she wanted. She lifted her hips and guided George inside her. They both groaned as they came together.

George took hold of Bea's hips, while rocking her hips in a gentle thrust. Bea matched her gentle rhythm and grasped her own breasts, moaning at the touch. Then, as the full feeling was propelling Bea too quickly, she slowed the rhythm right down and allowed George to slip out.

"Darling, what…?"

George sounded confused. But her eyes went wide when Bea gave her a smile and a wink and said, "Shh. You're going to enjoy this."

She spun round, so she was facing away from George, took hold of her cock, and slipped it back inside, then lifted George's hands and placed them back on her hips.

"Bloody hell, woman!" was the last coherent thing the Queen said before all she could manage were grunts and groans.

Chapter Thirty-one

The Queen stood alone in one of the smaller sitting rooms in the castle, waiting for the prime minister to be shown in. Since this was her holiday, she didn't wear anything formal. Just some jeans and her trusty old cricket jumper.

There was a knock and Bodicia Dixon was shown in. She curtsied, and George invited her to sit on a tartan-covered armchair.

"Thank you, Your Majesty. I hope you're having a pleasant holiday."

"Very much so, Prime Minister, and I hope you will enjoy your few days here with us."

"I'm looking forward to it."

George laughed inside. She knew Bo was not a country woman in the slightest, and she could just imagine her trying to walk the Balmoral estate, and attend their many picnics, in her short skirt and the highest of high heels.

George listened to everything the prime minister said with great interest and asked pertinent questions when she felt the need to. When they had finished with all the political business, George took the opportunity to speak to Bo about her own situation. "Prime Minister, I am sure you are aware that Miss Elliot is staying here with my family," George said very seriously.

"Yes, Ma'am. It's all the media can talk about, and I understand it's the main topic of conversation with the public up and down the land."

"Well, I'm pleased to inform you that I have asked Miss Elliot to marry me, and she has graciously accepted."

"Congratulations, Your Majesty. Your cabinet and your government will be delighted for you, Ma'am."

"And the rest of the House of Commons, and the House of Lords?" George smiled as she asked.

Bo gave a soft laugh. "I'm quite sure the vast majority will share your joy, Ma'am. After all, it puts both the government and country at ease to see the succession secure, and your marriage is the first step towards that."

George chuckled. "Indeed, Prime Minister, although I hope no one points that out to my fiancée. She has a tendency to see these matters—of, shall we say, dynastic concerns—unromantic."

"I can certainly understand that, Ma'am. The realities of our system of government can seem very dry to some ladies."

George found the prime minister a very hard one to read. At times she was convinced she was gay, and at other times she saw her use her sexuality to influence the men she met. She supposed that was the prime minister's great skill; she was all things to all people.

"Quite, and my people, Prime Minister? Do you believe that public opinion has sufficiently changed? Will they accept her?"

"Oh yes, Ma'am. The work that both Sebastian and my man Felix have done to counteract the adverse publicity has changed the public's mind. I understand the latest polls are ninety percent for, ten percent against. A politician would give their right arm for those numbers, and I can assure you, when you announce your engagement, the country, if not the world, will go royal-wedding crazy."

"Excellent. There is just one thing though. Is there time to organize a wedding before the coronation? I think it's very important that my consort is crowned with me at the ceremony, in order that she be legitimized in her role as royal consort, and as mother of the future monarch. Particularly because we will be the first gay couple to sit on the throne of Great Britain, there must be no question that any offspring from our union come from two royal parents."

The prime minister nodded in understanding. "I agree with you, and I have no doubt that we can put together a magnificent royal occasion before the coronation. After all, ceremonies and pageantry are what we do best. Leave it with me, Ma'am, and I'll have my team put together a plan in conjunction with the Lord Chamberlain, the Duke of Norfolk, and your man Bastian."

The Queen stood and extended her hand in thanks. "Many thanks, Prime Minister. Now I believe we are expected for a hike followed by a picnic. I hope you'll enjoy the fresh air of Aberdeenshire."

"I can't wait, Your Majesty," Bo said with little enthusiasm.

❖

Bea had been a nervous wreck before her parents arrived at Balmoral. She supposed all couples would be nervous at their two families meeting, but this was even more nerve-racking. Her very ordinary mum and dad from East London were meeting the in-laws, who just happened to be the royal family.

After letting them rest and settle in after their long journey, Bea led them down to the drawing room to have afternoon tea with the family. They decided to keep the meeting to just George's mother and granny at first, so as to not overwhelm Sarah and Reg. The dogs, of course, were allowed to be there, as they always were.

As Bea watched her mother and father chatting with Queen Sofia and Queen Adrianna, she knew she shouldn't have worried. Both women possessed the great skill of putting people at their ease very quickly. Bea looked at George and smiled. George had assured her that the meeting would go well, and it had.

George, again very smartly dressed in her kilt, stood and indicated for everyone to stay seated. She gave Bea a wink, and then turned to Reg. "Mr. Elliot, would you like to see our gardens here? I think they would perhaps interest you."

Reg put down his teacup and said nervously, "Yes, Your Majesty. That would be nice, thank you."

Bea rolled her eyes; she knew exactly what George was up to. A part of her felt she should be annoyed that her fiancée was asking her father's permission, but she just couldn't be annoyed with George. It was who she was, old-fashioned and terribly traditional, but that was one of the many parts of George's character that made her unique and so loveable.

At least when the Queen returned, she could tell her mother the good news and they could all start talking weddings. She'd purposely not worn her engagement ring so she could surprise her mother with the news, after George had spoken to her father.

"The gardens are beautiful, Dad. You'll love them," Bea told her nervous-looking father, who nodded and followed George out of the drawing room, followed be Baxter and Shadow. Rexie, as he usually did these days, stayed at Bea's feet.

George led Reg across the large lawn and into one of her favourite parts of the formal garden. A large square of flowers and plants was set out to follow a pathway leading to a central fountain. The dogs ran ahead, playing together and roughhousing.

Reg hadn't said a word since they left the castle, and George was keen to put him at his ease. "Bea has told me a great deal about your landscaping work, Mr. Elliot. I'm very much an outdoors person myself, so I greatly admire anyone who works with the land for their living. I hope you approve of our gardens here."

"Oh yes, Your Majesty. It truly is a beautiful garden. Sarah and I have always enjoyed walking round your gardens at Windsor Castle, so it's a privilege to see your gardens here."

George stopped beside the fountain and said, "Mr. Elliot, if we are in private, please call me George."

Reg's eyes went wide. "Are you sure, Ma'am?"

"Of course. I hope we can become friends," George said with a reassuring smile.

"I would like that, Ma'am…George, and you must call me Reg."

"Thank you, Reg. Shall we?" George indicated for him to walk on. "We have a wonderful greenhouse further down, with some beautiful exotic flowers I'm sure you'll appreciate."

"Oh, I'd love to see that."

They walked onward and George decided to take this opportunity to broach the subject of Bea. "Reg, I wanted to have a bit of a chinwag with you about Beatrice and myself. I expect you know that we have very strong feelings for each other."

"Yes. Apparently my wife suspected that Bea had feelings for you for some time, but Bea wouldn't talk about it, and I didn't know for definite until that day it went all over the news. She was very upset."

George sighed, remembering the pain and trauma of that day. "It was extremely unfortunate the way it came out, and I'm deeply sorry for the effect it had on your family, but I do hope you know I took steps to help, and to find out why it happened."

Reg nodded. "Bea told us, yes. I was worried that your family shared the same opinion of my daughter as Viscount Anglesey, but then I met the Queen Mother and Queen Adrianna today and saw that couldn't be true."

George stopped stone dead and said, "I want you to know, Reg, that no one else in my family shares that opinion. They all greatly respect and like Bea, and because of Viscount Anglesey's actions he has been relegated to the outer reaches of our family circle."

"Thank you. I wouldn't want Bea to be hurt like that. She's had a lot to deal with in her young life. Has she told you about Abby?"

"Yes, she did, and I'm very sorry for your loss, Reg." George saw the pain on the older man's face and said, "Let's have a seat here." She indicated the garden bench by the path.

When they sat, she said, "I went with Bea to Abigail's grave a few months ago. I was honoured that she would share that with me."

Reg nodded sadly. "Sarah won't go. She still hurts too much to face seeing the grave. She wants to remember her as the lively, playful little girl she was before. But I make myself go. As her father, I think it's my duty to take care of her, even though she's no longer here. Does that make sense?"

George nodded. "Yes. Duty is something I understand well, Reg."

"It isn't much, but I plant and tend the flowers around her grave, keep it tidy and clean. It's all I can do for her now. Things were so different when the girls were young. A lot of dads secretly hope for a boy, but not me. I couldn't have been prouder of my two daughters, and I used to refer to Sarah, Abby, and Bea as my three girls. I couldn't have been happier. I'm telling you this, George, because I want you to know how much I love my family, and how much more protective I am of Bea, now that Abby is gone. You might be the Queen, but Bea will always be my princess. Do you understand?"

That was a very polite warning you got there, George. "I totally understand what you're saying Reg, and I respect you for saying it to me, face to face."

Reg shrugged. "When you have children George, you'll understand you would stand up to the devil himself for them, no matter the cost. Bea is a very modern woman and she may appear tough, but she has a soft, romantic heart and doesn't deserve someone who isn't prepared to give their all to her."

George turned slightly so she could look Reg in the eye. "I want you to know that I adore your daughter. I adore, love, and respect her and would never give her anything but my all. So to that end, I would like to ask for permission to marry Beatrice."

"I'm not quite sure what to say, Your Majesty."

"Just tell me the truth, Reg. I want there to be no awkwardness between our families. Please tell me how you really feel."

He took a breath and said, "I would never stand in the way of my daughter's happiness, and it's obvious she loves you."

"I feel a but coming," George said with a smile.

Reg looked very uncomfortable. "You're from very different worlds. I was a great admirer of your father the King—he had good principles and worked hard for his people. I know you will be the same because he always showed how proud he was of you. But in the past, outsiders who came into the royal family didn't fare too well, and they weren't even ordinary girls from a working-class background."

"I understand your fears, but I can promise you, I and all my family will protect and guide Bea as she learns the ropes. I am very loyal to those I love, and I promise you that I would never do anything to disrespect your daughter, our marriage, or her position as Queen Consort."

Reg smiled at her. "Not many people, man or woman, would ask a father's permission in this day and age. I can see that you really are your father's daughter."

"Tradition is very important to me, Reg."

The older man extended his hand to the Queen and said, "Then I would be delighted to give my daughter away to you in church, Your Majesty."

George mentally punched the air with delight. She took Reg's hand. "Thank you. I won't let you down."

"You do realize what a feisty young woman she is? Bea doesn't have a high tolerance for the establishment."

George laughed and patted her future father-in-law on the back. "That's exactly what I love about her. She challenges me to think about things in a different way. She will be a wonderful consort."

Reg shook his head in disbelief. "My little girl, the Queen Consort. It's unbelievable."

George stood and said, "Let's go and have a look at the greenhouse and get back to the house. I know Bea is anxious to tell her mother."

❖

"Oh, sweetheart, I'm so happy for you." Sarah threw her arms round her daughter.

"Thanks, Mum. I couldn't wait to tell you," Bea looked up adoringly at George. "We're really happy."

Sarah went to embrace George but pulled back, suddenly realizing who she was about to hug. "I'm sorry, Your Majesty."

George immediately leaned in, kissed Sarah on the cheek, and said, "Please, Mrs. Elliot, we are going to be family now. I told your husband the same thing, in private please call me George."

"Beatrice? Are you going to show your mother your engagement ring?" Queen Sofia said.

"Oh, of course. Can I have it, Georgie?" Bea said.

Everyone sniggered as George pulled the ring box out of the sporran in front of her kilt. "What? The sporran is the closest I get to a handbag."

She took the ring out, insisted on placing it on her fiancée's finger, and gave her hand a kiss before Bea held her hand for her mother's inspection.

Sarah clasped her hand to her mouth. "Oh, my, that is beautiful."

"It belonged to George's great-great-grandmother, Queen Mary. I absolutely adore it, Mum."

Two pages came in with silver trays with champagne for the guests. Queen Adrianna took one and said, "Thank the Lord. My mouth was as dry as my old bones."

Once everyone took a glass, the Dowager Queen knocked her stick on the floor, bringing everyone to attention. "I would like to say a few words that I'm sure my son Eddie would have done if he were here today."

George put her arm around Bea and smiled over at her mother.

"George, ever since you were little, we all knew you would be a remarkable monarch. You've been dutiful, hardworking, and as your father did before you, put your country first, but your mother and I know that the role of sovereign can be a lonely one. We all prayed that you would find that special someone who would ease that heavy burden of your destiny, and seeing the way you look at each other, we know you have found her. Beatrice, I know my son would have welcomed you into our family with open arms, and so will the rest of our family. You two will be the first couple of your kind and will be remembered for generations. I have a feeling that, together, you will lead this family and the country with distinction. To Her Majesty the Queen, and her future consort."

As the family toasted them, George pulled Bea into a kiss and said, "I love you, my darling."

"I love you, Georgie."

"Put her down, Georgie." Theo came sauntering into the room with a huge smile on his face.

Reg and Sarah bowed and curtsied to the prince.

"Mr. and Mrs. Elliot, delighted to see you again. Wonderful news, isn't it?"

"Oh, it is indeed, sir. Reg and I are delighted."

Theo leaned in and said in a stage whisper, "Theo, please. I'm not as stuffy as the rest of them."

Bea's parents laughed and were immediately put at their ease.

He snagged a glass of champagne and greeted his sister and Bea, giving them each a kiss. "So you managed to catch a girl at last, eh, Georgie?"

George simply pulled Bea closer to her and said, "I was waiting for perfection, and I found her."

"Well, well, very smooth, Georgie. Welcome to the family, Bea, we're a loony bunch, but very loving."

"So what's next? When are you announcing the engagement, George?" her mother asked.

George indicated for everyone to sit down, and she did herself, taking Bea's hand in hers. "Well, we realize we have to do a press call and interview, but Bea is quite keen we do that in London, not here."

Bea gazed at George with a dreamy look on her face. "Yes, this has been such a special, private time for us here at Balmoral, and I really don't want to invite the press into this sanctuary."

"I'm glad you think of it that way, my dear. It's an important place for the family," the Dowager Queen said.

"The Ghillies Ball will be our first semipublic engagement. We want to go to that as a couple, so I'll have Sebastian liaise with Number Ten and announce it the morning of the ball. Then I'm afraid we'll have to head to London to meet the press. I hope you all don't mind cutting the holiday short."

Bea looked confused. "What do you mean cut it short? I thought the ball marked the end of your holiday here?"

"No, we normally take a week's cruise around the Scottish Islands on the royal yacht."

"Oh, well don't—"

"Of course we don't mind," Queen Sofia interrupted. "This is much more important, my dear one."

"Thank you, Mama. Theo? Could you find Aunt Grace and our cousins? I'd like them to meet the Elliots and share in this."

Prince Theo winked at his sister. "Of course. I'll be right back."

Chapter Thirty-two

B o Dixon closed the top-secret file she'd been reading on her tablet and held her head in her hands. Felix walked into her office and said, "You've read it then?"

Bo nodded and remained silent. The projected screen on the wall showed pictures of the Queen and her fiancée dancing at the Ghillies Ball in Scotland. The newly engaged couple's interview was due to go live at any moment, and the news channels were filling up time with all the footage they had of the pair.

"There's no doubt that Anglesey is involved?" Bo asked Felix.

"No doubt."

Bo growled in frustration. "Just when I thought I had given the people their fairy tale. The world's media have descended on London to see the poor girl plucked from obscurity to be made a Queen, and this has to come along and threaten it."

Felix smiled and said sarcastically, "You're such a romantic, Bo."

"Hardly."

"I suppose every fairy tale needs a wicked villain. The story will be even more exciting as long as the Queen and her village girl win through. What's their next public engagement as a couple?"

"I believe they're attending Prince Theo's graduation from Goldsmiths Art College. The Queen Mother, the Dowager Queen, Her Majesty, and Miss Elliot will be there," Felix told her.

"All three generations in the same hall? I don't like it, Felix."

"Neither do Sir Walter or his MI5 agents, but apparently the Queen Mother and Queen Adrianna insist. You can't really say no to them. Well, I wouldn't like to try. All the other guests at the ceremony have been rigorously checked, and the royal family will be surrounded by MI5 agents and their own protection officers."

Bo sat back in her leather chair and said, "I suppose I don't have much choice then. Just make sure you tell Sir Walter, that if anything happens to the Queen or her fiancée, I'll chop off his bollocks and make them into a handbag."

Felix gulped audibly. "Yes, Bo." He looked up to the screen. "Look, it's starting."

❖

Bea smoothed down her petrol-green jersey dress nervously. "Do I look all right?" she whispered to George.

They were waiting to start their first official interview as a couple. This one interview was to be carried by all the media and TV channels live, and waiting for it to start was nerve-racking for Bea.

"Of course, you look beautiful, my darling," George told her. "I especially love your hair."

Bea had asked her friend Holly to do her hair and make-up for the interview, and she'd styled her locks in a soft wave, giving a slight bounce every time she moved.

"Thank you. I'm glad you like it."

"I do, very much so."

Bea ran her hand over the lapel of George's blue three-piece suit. "And you look as dashing as always."

George laughed softly. "I try. Now don't be so nervous, you'll be wonderful. If you get tongue-tied or don't want to answer a certain question, just give my hand a squeeze and I'll take over. Okay?"

Bea nodded, but it was hard to be anything but nervous, standing in the ornate white drawing room of Buckingham Palace. The gold cornicing, gold-embroidered furniture, and the large paintings of queens and kings of the past made her realize what an enormous task she was undertaking. Up at Balmoral, everything seemed so simple. They were just two people who loved each other, in the privacy of that large estate.

As soon as they left that sanctuary, they were thrust into a storm of public attention and press interest from every corner of the globe. It had been quite frightening at first, knowing that she could never just pop out on a whim or down to the corner shop again, but George helped her every step of the way, and kept her as protected as possible.

Bea knew, no matter how hard it got, George's love was worth any discomfort or intrusion on her private life.

The interviewer, Carl Mason, walked over to them and bowed to George. "Your Majesty, we are ready for you both now."

Abby, I know you're watching over me. Help me not make a fool of myself.

❖

Julian's hand shook as he watched his cousin's engagement interview. He'd lost control of everything. Princess Eleanor had given up and headed home, and the British public had sickeningly bought into all this fairy tale stuff about the couple. Even his parents and siblings loved Beatrice.

"Only I can see what a sick pervert you are, George."

It had been bad enough bowing at his cousin's feet all his life, but come the wedding, he would have to bow down to Beatrice Elliot, from Bethnal Green.

Never. He didn't realize he was holding his glass of wine so tightly until it broke in his hand. Julian looked at the dripping blood with fascination.

"I think it's high time you felt some pain of your own, George."

Julian called a number on his secure line. "The warning wasn't enough. I want this brought to an end. You will be greatly rewarded."

❖

Today was to be a graduation like no other at Goldsmiths College. The college had been honoured when the young Prince Theodore had chosen them to study fine art, but today would be even more exciting, as the Queen would attend with her new fiancée.

Security was extremely tight. Each student was permitted only two guests, and everyone had full security checks done on them. MI5 agents were posted around the hall and the college, with Cammy, Inspector Lang, and the other protection officers surrounding the Queen and her fiancée.

The couple had arrived early but were being held in a secure office until the rest of the audience were scanned, searched, and seated.

George had only been informed that a specific threat had been made against her person. The delay wasn't helping Bea's nerves any, and she paced up and down the office, watched by George and Cammy. The Queen Mother and Dowager Queen were being held in a separate location for security reasons.

George sat in a relaxed posture at the principal's desk. "Darling, please sit down. You're making me dizzy."

"I can't. I'm too nervous." Bea fiddled with her engagement ring.

"You've been lots of places with me before."

Bea sighed and continued pacing. "Not like this, not going in with you as your fiancée. Everyone's going to be looking at me as well as you this time. They used to just look at you."

George signalled for Cammy to step outside for a moment, then took her into her arms. "Listen, you'll be absolutely splendid. You handled the Ghillies Ball well. You attended as my fiancée then."

Bea rested her head on George's chest. "Those were the Balmoral staff and the villagers. They were very supportive. This is Theo's special day, your family's special day. I don't want to do something stupid and ruin it."

George lightly grasped her chin. "Now listen here, my little smout. You always behave with faultless decorum in whatever you do in life, and today will be no different. You could never let me down. I will be the proudest person in the world, walking in with you on my arm. I love you. Understand?"

George always had a way of making her feel better. She was like a solid rock of reassurance that Bea could always lean on. "I understand," she said with a smile and leaned up to kiss her love on the chin.

❖

George and Bea sat in the front row alongside Queen Sofia, Queen Adrianna, and Cammy. MI5 agents and police protection officers were dotted around the room. Although the other students' families might not be aware of all of them, George was acutely aware of the beefed-up security, and she was sorry it had to be this way on Theo's special day.

She looked up to him on the stage, in his cap and gown, and her heart burst with pride. Theo had come so far since their father's death, and she knew with certainty the King was looking down on the day, equally as proud.

The speeches finished up and it was now time for the students to receive their scrolls. She could tell from here, Theo was a little nervous, but not as nervous as the young man who sat next to him. He'd caught her attention because he looked the odd one out in the company of the other students. His hands trembled, and unlike the other students who were listening to the speeches and smiling, he looked straight ahead throughout the whole ceremony.

The young man's name was called, and at first he didn't react, until someone behind nudged him. He walked across the stage and shook hands with the professor with no visible emotion, collecting his scroll as he went.

Then it was Theo's turn. "BA Fine Arts. Prince Theodore, Duke of York." The crowd clapped and cheered, none more so than the Queen and Beatrice. He looked towards her and she gave him a wink in return.

Just as Theo reached the professor, the student who had gone before him, who hadn't reached the other end of the stage, turned and ran back towards Theo. He pulled out a shining silver hunting knife and stabbed Theo in the side. Everything then seemed to happen in slow motion, as Theo fell. "No, Theo!" George jumped up shouting.

The concealed agents moved towards the stage, and the student pulled out a weapon and aimed for George. In seconds she felt her shoulder being hit so hard it nearly knocked her down, and then a burning pain radiated out from the impact.

She heard Bea scream her name, but the room became a blur as officers tackled her to the floor, covering her from further attack.

From her position on the floor she saw Cammy pull out her weapon and shoot the student in the head, as agents piled onto the stage.

She could hear deafening shouts and screams from the audience, and Inspector Lang order the room cleared.

Bea, Theo. I have to get to them. "Get off me," George shouted from underneath the pile of agents."

"Georgie? Georgie? Are you all right?" Bea cried.

Standing up, George pulled off her suit jacket to reveal a bloody gunshot wound in her shoulder.

"Oh my God!" Bea clasped her hands to her mouth in shock.

"It's fine. Are you hurt?" George pulled Bea to her, checking her for injuries.

"No, no. I'm okay. Theo?"

"Cammy? Secure the Queen Mother and the Dowager Queen. Don't let anyone you haven't seen before near them."

"Yes, Ma'am."

The Queen made her way to the stage, where Inspector Lang stood guard. "Ma'am, please stay back where you can be secured."

"I want to see my brother. Go, take care of my fiancée, Lang."

He bowed and let her climb up on stage. She sank to her knees when she saw her brother's state. The whole right-hand side of his shirt was bloody, and an MI5 agent was pushing a compress down on the wound trying to stem the flow of blood.

"Theo?" George took his hand when he raised it.

"Georgie…is that you?" Theo asked, his breathing very laboured.

She tried to soothe him by stroking his brow. "Shh, don't talk. The paramedics will be here soon."

"I don't know if I can hold on, Georgie. Need to close…my eyes. I don't want to die, Georgie."

George looked him right in the eye and said, "Don't you dare, Theodore. Do you hear me? I'm commanding you to keep those eyes open. If you die, I'll kick your bloody arse up and down Horse Guards Parade. Do you understand me, Theo?"

She saw a slight smile come to her brother's face. "I'll try."

"Don't try, Theo. Just do as you're told. Keep squeezing my hand and talking to me. Stay awake, little brother."

"Were you…?"

Theo's voice receded to a whisper. "Was I what, Theo? Talk to me."

"Were you proud of me? Wanted to make you proud."

George leaned over and kissed his forehead. "I am always proud of you, Theo. I love you, little brother."

"Love you too, Georgie."

Bea came up to the stage and stood very close to George. "Theo? Stay with us. Your sister needs you."

"She needs you…Bea. Look after her."

The paramedics appeared at their side and immediately set to work. Bea pulled George into her arms, until a second crew came and started to tend to the Queen. "Leave me. Just help my brother," George shouted at them.

"He has all the help he needs at the moment, Ma'am. We have a chopper waiting to take him to the hospital immediately."

"Georgie? Let them look at you," Bea told her.

She nodded and watched her brother wheeled away to the waiting helicopter. It was at that moment the adrenaline that had kept her going suddenly left her and all the energy was sucked out of her body. The last thing she heard as she fell was Bea's scream.

Chapter Thirty-three

The whole of London was put on lockdown, as the counter-terrorism measures came into effect. Airspace closed over the whole of Great Britain, and all public transportation in and around the major cities was suspended.

The Queen Mother and Queen Adrianna were not allowed to follow Bea to the hospital, and for security were taken to a secret location.

Bea sat with Cammy in the deserted accident and emergency waiting room. When it became clear the casualties en route were the Queen and the first-in-line to the throne, all those who were waiting to be seen and who could be safely moved were transported to the hospital in the next town, so as to clear the department and ensure all necessary security measures could be taken.

"Ma'am? I got you a cup of tea. I can't attest to its quality, it's just from a machine."

Bea looked at Cammy through her tears. "Thank you, and I'm not *ma'am*, Cammy. I might never be."

Cammy sat down beside her. "Don't you say that, lassie. George will be walking you down the aisle. Mark my words."

"Why did she have to stand up and make herself a target, Cammy? The agents were about to take him down."

"It's who she is. Even though she's the Queen, George doesn't think herself more important than anyone else."

Bea nodded sadly. "I'm so glad you shot that man, Cammy. It could have gotten so much worse. You're a hero."

Cammy shook her head. "Not me—just doing what I'm trained to do. I'm only sorry I couldn't take the bullet for her, and then she'd be sitting here with you."

"Don't say that. You killed him before he could do any more damage. That's enough. Who would want to hurt Theo? He's such a harmless boy."

"He's also heir to the throne, until the Queen has any offspring. He may be a harmless boy, but he's a very important player."

Bea looked at her quizzically. "What do you mean? You think…?"

"I don't know what I mean, really. It just strikes me as something different than a terrorist attack."

As Bea was contemplating that, a doctor came out of the A&E double doors. "Miss Elliot, I'm Jeremy Frobisher, senior consultant here at Central Hospital."

Bea shook his hand. "How are the Queen and Prince Theo?"

"The Queen is going to be fine. The bullet didn't shatter any bone, and the entry wound was fairly clean. We were able to remove the bullet and wash out the wound here in A&E, without going to surgery."

Bea let out a long breath, and her tears started anew. "And Theo?"

"The prince is on his way to surgery as we speak. I won't mince words, Miss Elliot, his condition is very serious. He's lost a lot of blood, but we're doing all we can. The royal physician is on his way, so he's going to have the best possible care."

Bea couldn't speak. The emotions just overwhelmed her.

Cammy put her arm around Bea and tried to calm her. "Has someone informed the rest of the family, Doctor?" Cammy asked.

"Yes, I contacted the prime minister to keep her informed about the Queen and Prince Theo's conditions, and she is going to keep both Their Majesties up to date."

"Can I see her, Doctor?" Bea managed to say.

"Of course, Miss Elliot. She's asking for you. Follow me."

The prime minister sat at the head of a large table in a secret meeting room in Whitehall. As soon as the news of the attack hit, the Prime Minster immediately called for a Cobra meeting. The meeting brought together government ministers, the police, secret services, and emergency services in times of national crisis.

"Ladies and gentlemen, today an attack was launched at the heart of the British constitution. Luckily, Her Majesty looks to be on the mend, but Prince Theodore is in very serious condition. I want to know what we know, and how and why it happened. Sir Walter? Why don't you start us off?"

The head of MI5 gulped and looked decidedly nervous. "We believe the individual is simply a hired gun—it's who hired him that is the more worrying piece of news. My agents that have been monitoring Viscount Anglesey have reported that he left his flat in town just after it was announced that the Queen had survived. They let him leave in order to see if he would attempt to contact anyone. They stopped him at Heathrow, trying to flee the country."

Bo sat back in shock. "Good God. I knew that weasel was involved somehow. The Buckingham family is starting to look like a Greek tragedy. Right, well let's wait and see what he can tell us. Let's reconvene in three hours. I have to make an address to the nation. Let's make sure we work hard on this. If that man had taken out the Queen and her heir…Well, it doesn't bear thinking about. Get to work."

❖

The Queen had been placed in a private room, in the most secure area of the hospital. There were agents and police officers at every entrance and exit of the hospital, and only a select group of doctors and nurses were being permitted to care for her and her brother.

Bea sat at the side of the bed and watched the royal physician, Mark Battlefield, check over her wound.

"It's been well taken care of, Your Majesty. The wound will heal very well, I believe."

George nodded her head and said, "And Prince Theo?"

"I'm just on my way to check on him now, Ma'am. He's being brought from theatre. I'll come back and check on you soon, Your Majesty."

George felt her barely contained anger bubbling towards the surface. "Don't bother about me, Battlefield. Just concentrate on my brother," George snapped.

Bea smiled and said, "Thank you, Doctor. If you would pop back later on, I'm sure Her Majesty would appreciate that."

"Of course, Miss Elliott. I'll report on Prince Theodore's condition as soon as I know more."

Once he left, George looked at Bea angrily. "Countermanding my orders now?" She wasn't used to feeling the helplessness of injury. Her brother was in some other part of the hospital teetering between life and death, and she could do nothing about it. This out of control feeling was making her feel panicked and sick.

"Well, someone has to, when you're behaving like a spoilt brat and incapable of making sensible judgements."

"Who do you think you are? You are talking to the Queen, or have you forgotten that?" George shouted.

Bea looked shocked at her outburst. "I thought I was your fiancée, soon to be your wife. It looks like you think I am yours to be commanded like the rest of your lapdogs."

George watched in horror as Bea's face crumbled into tears, and she ran from the room. "Bea, no, come back. I didn't mean—" George tried to sit up and felt the hot searing pain lance through her shoulder. "Argh!"

Cammy ran in. "Are you all right, Ma'am?"

"No, I'm a bloody arsehole who deserves a swift kick in the proverbial bollocks."

"Why?" Cammy asked.

George held on to her wound, as if the pressure would ease her pain. "I think I really hurt Bea."

George replayed the conversation with Bea, and Cammy said, "Bloody hell. If you'll forgive me, Ma'am, you *are* a bloody arsehole. That lassie has been out of her mind with worry in that waiting room. She was crying on my shoulder, and then you talk to her like that?"

Cammy was the only one who could give George a dressing down like that. She smacked her head back against the pillow. "I know, I know. Can you help me up? I need to speak to her."

"I don't think there's any way you can walk, George. You've lost a lot of blood. Let me go and find her."

"No, please. I need to do it myself. Can you get me a wheelchair?" Cammy nodded.

"Oh, and one more thing, Cammy…"

When Bea rushed from George's room, she'd no idea where to go and found herself making her way towards Theo's room. She wasn't allowed in, since she wasn't family yet, but felt better just being able to sit outside. The protection officers who all knew her well had no problem with her presence.

I was stupid to ever think I could be the same as them. Is she always going to think I'm lesser?

She looked up when she heard her name called and saw the unusual sight of Captain Cameron pushing Queen Georgina down the corridor with a bunch of flowers in her lap.

"Bea—can I talk to you, please?" George asked.

"You shouldn't be out of bed."

"I know. I just had to talk to you. I'll go back as soon as I'm finished," George promised.

Bea sighed and nodded. She got up and followed Cammy as she wheeled the Queen down the corridor a bit, to give them some privacy, and then left them.

"These are for you. They're just from the hospital shop, but I promise that when we all get home safely, I'll have the royal florist make you up the most magnificent bunch you've ever seen."

Bea took the flowers and said sarcastically, "You have a royal florist? Really?"

"Yes, and if you forgive me for being an insensitive, bloody plonker, then there'll be a fresh bunch placed in our bedroom and your office, every morning of our life together."

Bea couldn't help but smile at this but still wanted to make her point. "You really hurt me."

"I know. I felt helpless, impotent, and powerless. I'm the head of my family, I'm supposed to be the one who takes care of everything, and now my brother is lying near death in there, and I can't do anything about it."

Bea cupped George's cheek. "Listen, you can't be this control-freak superhero all the time. Sometimes you've got to trust others are the best people for the job. We just have to wait and pray that Theo will pull through. Now, don't be a bad Queen. Behave."

George smiled softly and kissed her hand. "Thank you."

The consultant came out of Theo's room and made his way over to them. "Your Majesty, you shouldn't be out of bed."

"I know, I'll go back, but can you tell me how Theo is first?"

"Yes, Ma'am. We took him straight to theatre and repaired the internal damage caused by the knife wound. All went well in theatre, but he lost a great deal of blood. He's resting now, but he's not conscious."

Bea held George's hand, squeezing it in support. "Will he regain consciousness, Doctor? What are his chances?"

The doctor looked down at the floor, unwilling to answer.

"It's all right, Doctor. You won't be hung, drawn, and quartered if you get it wrong."

"I'd say fifty-fifty."

The Queen took a deep breath, trying to control her emotions. "Thank you for your honesty. Can I see him before I go back?"

"Yes. Just five minutes though, and get back to your room."

Cammy walked over and took the wheelchair from Bea. "Let me, Ma'am."

Bea walked at the side holding George's hand. "Let's go and see that baby brother of yours."

❖

Viscount Anglesey was taken to MI5 headquarters for questioning. The agents guarding the room wouldn't even look at him. His well-ordered and privileged life was falling around his ears, and he was scared—scared of what he'd done and scared of what it would mean.

The interview room door finally opened, and in walked Sir Walter and another agent, carrying a battered-looking computer unit.

"Well, well, Julian. We have been a busy boy, haven't we?"

The overfamiliar language infuriated him. No matter what he'd done, he still merited the respect of his position. "Do you know who you're talking to?" he spat.

"Indeed I do, Julian. A dirty little traitor who deserves to be horsewhipped," Sir Walter said with disgust.

"I don't know what you're talking about."

"Really? Well, what if I tell you we've had your London flat bugged and your conversations recorded?"

Julian stared ahead silently.

"And what if told you that this computer, taken from the dead man who tried to kill the Queen and Prince Theodore, could be traced to yours?"

Again, Julian responded only with silence.

"Julian, conspiring to kill your sovereign and the next in line to the throne? It's positively Shakespearean."

His hands began to shake.

"I think you'll be the first person charged with treason in eighty-two years. I think it's safe to say you'll be staying at Her Majesty's pleasure for a long time to come."

The rage and panic in Julian boiled over. "No! It should be mine. That crown is mine!" He jumped up, grabbed a chair, and went to smash it over Sir Walter's head, but he was tackled to the ground by the three agents in the room. He struggled and screamed, "It's mine, mine. No one can stop me." And then he started smashing his forehead off the floor.

Chapter Thirty-four

In the small TV studio, built to look high over Buckingham Palace, TV presenter Crispin Jacobson waited on his cue to go live on the most important broadcast of his career.

Good morning, ladies and gentlemen. My name is Crispin Jacobson and I would like to welcome you to the day the country and the world have been waiting for. The wedding of Queen Georgina and Miss Beatrice Elliot. It's a day to heal the wounds inflicted on the House of Buckingham over the past year and a bit, and to bring joy back to Britain's favourite family.

The event has been christened The Day Fairy Tales Come True, *and we will bring you every second of this special day, live in your own living room. We have reporters down lining the route with the well-wishers, some that have camped out for a whole week, to get the best places. We have reporters in the royal parks, where this program is being shown on large screens.*

The TV images changed to footage in the parks, where thousands had turned up to watch and be part of the occasion. The people had Union Flags and hats, and were decked out in other patriotic outfits. They had picnic baskets, champagne, and were generally in a jolly mood already.

We also have a reporter at Beatrice's house. The once very ordinary Albion Road, a row of little houses now made famous around the world because our very own Queen Georgina fell in love with a very normal working-class girl. We can cross there now to speak to our reporter, Tricia Godfrey. Tricia, can you tell us what's happening?

A cheer from crowds surrounding the location went up, as the reporter smiled and prepared herself to speak.

Thank you, Crispin. I hope you can hear me, the crowds of well-wishers are in great spirits here as they wait for the first glimpse of the royal bride. As we all know, this wedding has a lot of firsts, and one first is the fact the bride is leaving from her own humble home.

The royal couple took pains to make this wedding the way they want it, and I understand Beatrice was very insistent on leaving from her family home. The police have cordoned off Albion Road for two days, because of the growing crowds, only allowing the other residents access.

This morning, a lot of people have been coming and going from the property, including Beatrice's hair and make-up team led by her friend Holly Murphy, the dress designer, royal florist, and her chief bridesmaid, Lali Ramesh. In keeping with her determination to make this her day, two of the flower girls are the daughters of her university friends Greta and Riley Garrison, in addition to three flower girls and one pageboy from Queen Georgina's extended family. They have been getting ready at a separate location and will meet up with the chief bridesmaid later in the day.

I have with me a well-wisher who has been camping out for six days, just to get to see the royal bride leave with her father. Gina, can you tell us why it was so important for you to be here today?

The woman was dressed in a hat resembling a wedding cake with figures representing Queen Georgina and Beatrice.

I just had to be here to see this. It's a historic day—one day I can tell my grandchildren that I was there.

And why do you think it's so historic, Gina? Tricia asked.

Well, it's a fairy tale, isn't it? I think people thought fairy tales and happy ever after didn't happen anymore, but that young woman is going to leave her house, just like millions of other houses up and down the country, and by the end of the day, she's going home as a Queen Consort to her new home at Buckingham Palace. Bea is one of us, and she made it, she bagged a Queen. It doesn't get any more romantic than that.

I couldn't have put it better myself. Back to you Crispin, the reporter said.

❖

Queen Georgina stood by her father's tomb in St George's Chapel, Windsor, dressed in her ceremonial Royal Navy uniform. She put her hand against the stone, wanting to feel closer to him.

"Papa? I wish you could be here with me today, but I know you will be there in the Abbey with me in spirit. I've found my Queen Consort, and I love her so much. The way you loved Mama. I know you would have adored her as a daughter-in-law. She challenges me and makes me a better person. I know she'll do a fantastic job for my people."

Cammy came in the door of the church and cleared her throat. "Your Majesty? It's time."

She nodded and leaned over to kiss the stone. "I love you, Papa. Watch over us."

❖

Crispin very nearly squealed with excitement during his voice-over, as he narrated the scene to the viewing public.

And the Queen's car has just arrived at the Abbey, to much cheering by those lucky enough to have a spot outside. After much speculation, we can see the Queen has chosen to wear her Royal Navy uniform. We understand this is in tribute to her father, the late King Edward. The gold tassels and braiding look resplendent against the black of the uniform. On her chest, blue Order of the Garter sash and diamond Order of the Garter. On her hip, she carries her father's gold and silver admiral's sword.

And of course, the whole country is delighted to see her brother, Prince Theodore, by her side, after several months' recuperation at Sandringham, where we are told the Queen's fiancée took an important role in helping care for her brother-in-law to be. He stands proudly today as his sister's best man.

❖

"Princess?"

Bea opened her bedroom door at her father's knock. "Dad?"

Her father gasped at the sight of her.

"Princess, you are…I can't find the words. Beautiful doesn't seem a good enough word, but you are. Beautiful, just beautiful."

Bea watched as the tears ran down her father's cheeks. "Don't cry, Dad."

Reg took her hand and kissed it. "I can't help it—you're my little girl, and you always will be."

"Do you think Abby would be proud? I've been thinking a lot about her today. She should have been my bridesmaid, enjoying the day with me."

"She will be with you. Just think of her, and know she'll be watching over you."

Bea smiled and said, "Well, this is it. I just can't believe this is happening to me. Have you seen all the people outside?"

"Yes, you should see the crowds lining the route. They can't wait to see you."

The nerves bubbled and churned around in Bea's stomach. "I'm doing the right thing, aren't I?"

"You know you are, princess. George is the kind of partner a father dreams of for his daughter. Not because she is a Queen, but because she loves you, respects you, will protect you from harm, and understands the importance of family."

Bea agreed with her father wholeheartedly and was certain that George's character would have been the same, whether she had been a farmer, a manual labourer, or a Queen. "You're right, Dad. I suppose we should get going."

Reg reached out and took both his daughter's hands. "When you leave the house, your life will change forever. I just want you to know that no matter how busy you are, jet-setting around the world, Mum and I will always be thinking of you and are so proud of you."

The tears started to well up in Bea's eyes.

"Don't you cry and waste that lovely make-up, princess. Come on."

❖

"Georgie, would you sit down, you're making me nervous." They were waiting in the Abbey vestry for the bride to arrive, but while Theo was calmly sitting, the Queen was nervously pacing.

"I was fine when we came in and met all the clergy—it's just this waiting. I want to get married now."

"I've never met anyone more desperate to get married than you, Georgie." Theo chortled.

George finally came and sat down. "Can you blame me? Bea is just…I don't have the words, but she is matchless. There is no one more perfect than her. I love her."

"Wow, I hope I meet someone that makes me say things like that."

George looked round at her brother. "You do think she's right for me, don't you? I mean my people think so too, don't they?"

"Of course. Did you see the crowds outside? The banners, the placards, all for Queen Bea. They love her."

George nodded and said, "Are you all right? Feeling strong enough?"

"Of course I'm all right. Stop worrying. I'm back to full health. I might not be as strong as I was, but I'll get there."

"Of course you will, but it's my job to worry. You're my brother." George patted him on the shoulder.

Theo looked thoughtful for a minute and said, "I wonder how they're dealing with Julian today."

Very soon after the assassination attempt, Julian had a complete mental breakdown and was committed to Broadmoor criminal psychiatric hospital. He would be treated there until such time as he was capable of standing trial.

"I'm sure they'll keep all forms of media away from him, since the doctor said he seems to be focused on and obsessed with me."

George was aware Theo still had nightmares about that day. When he was recuperating at Sandringham, both Bea and herself had seen the way it affected him. It was such a support having her fiancée at her side through that time. Bea had shown such care to her brother, that George grew ever more in love with her, even though that didn't seem possible.

"You've handled everything perfectly, Georgie, as you always will."

"Oh, I don't know about that, Theo."

Theo shook his head. "Even after all he's done, and how angry we are at him, you still got the best psychiatrist on Harley Street to visit him every week."

"Being head of the family means you help the lost sheep as well as the rest of the family. It's for Aunt Grace as much as anyone. His betrayal of the family has nearly destroyed her, and it's what Papa would have done. I don't think I could have been as generous if you had died, Theo. The pain would have blinded me."

"I don't believe so. It's who you are, Georgie. It was a lovely touch to include little Charles and Mary in the wedding party."

In a show of family unity, Julian's son Charles was asked to be a pageboy for Bea, and Mary a flower girl.

"They bear no blame for the sins of their father. As much as their mother doesn't particularly like Bea, she had nothing to do with what Julian did, and as long as she behaves correctly, she and the children will always be welcome."

One of the ceremonial guards popped his head round the door, and said, "Your Majesty? They're ready for you. The bride's car is five minutes away."

George jumped up quickly. "We're under starter's orders, Theo."

"Calm down, Georgie, take a breath, or you'll fall arse over tit in front of the whole Abbey."

"Okay, okay. I'm calm. Let's go and get my consort," George said with glee.

❖

The Elliots' glass-topped car made its way along the route to the Abbey. Bea was humbled by the crowds that had turned out to see her and wish her well, and she made sure she acknowledged them with a wave at every opportunity.

"Can you believe this, Dad? All these people, just to see us married."

Reg laughed gently. "And you thought the British people would like a republic."

"Well, I was wrong. It's obviously the will of the people. That's what George is always preaching to me."

She pointed out flags being waved by some of the well-wishers. "Look—Canadian, French, American flags, they've come a long way just to be part of this." Then a sudden realization hit her. "Oh God, the whole world's watching this as we speak, aren't they? I'm going to be sick."

Reg took hold of her hand. "Breathe, princess, breathe, you were doing fine. Just don't think about the people watching on TV. Just think about the Queen."

She did as her dad told her and felt the panic subside. The car pulled up in front of the Abbey. The steps and front entrance had been covered in red carpet. Very regal indeed. The car door was opened by one of the high-ranking soldiers standing guard, and she saw Lali descend the Abbey steps to help her with the dress.

"You look wonderful, Bea. Are you ready to change your life?" Lali said, helping her out and holding the train for her.

Bea made sure to wave to those countless people behind the barriers around the entrance. A huge cheer went up, and at last everyone got a chance to see the dress that the world had been speculating about.

"I'm ready."

The fanfare sounded, the choir began to sing, and her father led her by the hand down the aisle of the ancient Westminster Abbey, followed by Lali and the rest of the wedding party. As they passed each row, the guests smiled warmly and whispered about the beauty of her dress or the cuteness of her pageboys and flower girls. She passed the row where Greta and her partner Riley and Holly were sitting and saw Greta with tears running down her face, watching her children. She was so glad she could share this with her friends.

Lastly, she passed the prime minister, who had organized the most central seat for herself, in order to ensure the greatest camera time of all the foreign and domestic dignitaries. Bea saw her wide sparkling smile and thought, with an internal chuckle, *Are you happier for me or for you, Prime Minister?*

They walked through the arch into the area where the families were seated, and she spotted her mother and smiled. She looked overwhelmed with happiness and joy. The Queen Mother and the rest of the family smiled warmly as she passed, and then she saw George, waiting for her, waiting to change her life.

❖

George itched to turn around and look at her bride, especially when she saw her brother's face light up when he looked round, but she kept her eyes forward, disciplined as always.

Then she was there, by her side. When George looked at her bride, she stopped breathing. Bea's dress was sleeveless, ivory and lace with a long veil resting on a long, lace-covered train. It was simple and traditional. "You are beautiful," George mouthed to her bride.

Bea smiled shyly back at her.

George turned her eyes back to the Archbishop, in his rich golden robe and tall mitre. He began the ceremony, and it seemed like a blur to the couple, who could only keep giving each other loving glances and smiles.

George was soon brought to earth when she heard the Archbishop say, "Georgina Mary Edwina Louise. Will thou have this woman to thy wedded wife? To live together in God's law, in the holiest state of matrimony? Wilt thou love her, comfort her, honour and keep her, in sickness and in health, and forsaking all others, keep thee only unto her, as long as ye both shall live?"

"I will," George said confidently.

The Archbishop repeated the same to Bea.

"I will."

"Who giveth this woman to be married to Her Majesty?"

Reg stood confidently, took his daughter's hand and gave it to the Archbishop, who handed her to the Queen.

George smiled at him, knowing how nervous he'd been, and he stepped back.

George turned to Bea, and looked deeply into her eyes, and at that moment there were no nerves. It was as if there was only the two of them, repeating the vows that the Archbishop read out to them.

"I, Georgina Mary Edwina Louise, take thee, Beatrice Anne, to my wedded wife. To have and to hold from this day forward. For better or for worse. For richer or for poorer. In sickness and in health. To love and to cherish. Till death us do part. According to God's holy law, and thereto I pledge thee my troth."

Once Bea had repeated those vows, Theo was called upon to hand over the rings. George gave him a panicked look when he pretended, for a second, he couldn't find them. Ever the joker, Theo handed the Archbishop the rings and George a shook her head at him.

You are *feeling better, little brother.*

They exchanged rings, and it all suddenly began to feel very real. When George had imagined and rehearsed the ceremony, it seemed as if it took forever, but now in the moment it felt like it was racing by, and she wanted to savour every part of it for her memories.

The Archbishop bade the couple to kneel and bound their hands "Those whom God has put together, may no one put asunder." The gold cloth was taken from their hands and he continued. "For as much as Georgina and Beatrice have consented together in holy wedlock, and have witnessed the same before God and this company, and thereto have given their troth, either to each other, and the same of giving and receiving of a ring, and joining of hands, I pronounce that they be married together, in the name of the father, the son and the Holy Ghost."

With that simple statement, their lives as well as their hearts were joined forever, and all that was left was to share the joy with their people.

After a rendition of the national anthem, George escorted her new consort down the aisle to the sound of trumpets. At the Abbey door an open-topped carriage waited to take them back to the palace.

❖

The carriage ride back to Buckingham Palace was magical. The crowds screamed and cheered as they went by, and George smiled watching Bea learning one of her most important royal duties: waving to the crowds, and engaging with the people.

"They're wonderful, Georgie."

"They are happy that I have you. I'm so lucky, my darling."

Bea laughed. "I think they would see me as the lucky one. Have you seen how stunning you look in that uniform?"

"I'm nothing compared to you. You are very good at waving, by the way. I think I'll keep you as my consort."

"It's a bit late to change your mind now."

The carriage pulled into Buckingham Palace and through the archway so they were out of sight. Waiting for them as they got out of the carriage were their three dogs, Shadow, Baxter, and Rexie.

They barked excitedly as George helped her wife down from the carriage. "No jumping, you three. Stay down or you'll ruin your mama's dress."

Bea was caught by surprise by that comment and smiled.

"Well, you are," George said defensively.

"And you are too sweet."

George felt a blush come to her cheeks, and the staff waiting to assist them smiled. "Come on. Let's give the people their happy ending."

❖

Bea and George walked into the centre room, which led out to the famous balcony. All the guests were catching their breath after the ceremony and carriage ride. The staff were waiting with trays of drinks of every kind.

Bea felt very strange. Every member of the family that approached her bowed or curtsied before greeting her. In a matter of hours, she'd changed from an ordinary girl to second in the royal order of precedence.

The etiquette coach that George had organized for her in the run-up to the wedding had schooled her in every aspect of her new role, but it was still strange when it actually happened. It was even weirder when her mum and dad bowed and curtsied.

Bea protested, but Sarah said to her in a whisper, "Don't make us different, sweetheart. It's just who you are now."

Bea nodded and accepted her mother's wish not to be different. It would always be strange, but it would cause her parents more embarrassment to make a fuss about it.

She was happy to see all their friends and family there. Greta, Riley, and Holly looked slightly overwhelmed to be in a room full of royals, but the children less so, running about with their new friends, the royal children. Lali was off in another corner being entertained by the persistent Captain Cameron.

Sarah gave her new daughter-in-law a kiss on the cheek. "It was a beautiful ceremony, Ma'am."

"I'm glad you liked it, Sarah. I hope you will like the last part of the ceremony, going out on the balcony. Bea told me that you and Reg brought your daughters to see my family go out on the balcony for Granny's birthday, one year. Now you'll get to see it from the other side."

"I'm not sure whether to be scared or excited, Ma'am, the crowds are so large," Sarah said.

"How do you think I feel, Mum? I've got to go out first. I'm worried I might faint," Bea said.

George laughed softly. "You'll both be fine. I can see it would be overwhelming if you're not used to it. Just remember, everyone is there to wish you well, and besides you'll be hanging on to my arm. I'll keep you up."

Sarah wandered over to Reg, who was deep in conversation with George's uncle Bran, leaving them alone.

"How long till we go out, Georgie?" Bea asked.

"Around five or ten minutes. The police are just opening up the area in front of the palace gates and removing security barriers, allowing the people to fill up the Royal Mall and outside the palace gates."

Bea gulped and remained quiet. She was starting to feel queasy with nerves.

"Don't be nervous. It'll be wonderful. I'll be there and I love you, my darling wife."

They were interrupted when the Princess Royal walked over to them, with Vicki and Max. "Congratulations, George. It's been a wonderful day," she said with a hint of sadness.

Bea knew that Julian's actions weighed heavily on George's aunt's mind. She felt guilty, even though she had no bearing on what her son had done.

George pulled her aunt into a hug. "Aunt Grace, please. There is no one more loyal to the family than you. Stop taking the blame for what happened, I can see it pulling you down. I love you, Aunt Grace, and nothing will change that."

Grace held on to her niece tightly. "Thank you. I'm sorry."

Behind their mother's back, Vicki and Max smiled at George and mouthed, "Thank you," to her, as they had been so worried about their mother.

The Master of the Household came over to the Queen and said, "The crowds are waiting, Ma'am, and the RAF fly-past has an ETA of ten minutes."

"Thank you. Announce it, please, and could you look after Mr. and Mrs. Elliot? They will be unsure of what to do."

"Of course, Ma'am."

Bea hugged George's arm tightly, feeling like the luckiest woman on the planet. It was such a kind thought to have someone look after her parents, but then, that was George. She never did or said anything without thinking of its effect on those around her.

The Master of the Household chimed the side of a glass to get the room's attention. "Your Majesties, Your Royal Highnesses, Lords, Ladies, and gentlemen. The Queen and Queen Consort are about to step onto the balcony. If the wedding party could get themselves prepared, I will signal you to follow them after a few minutes."

The Queen Mother and Queen Adrianna joined them, as they would be next out on the balcony, by order of precedence.

Queen Adrianna whispered to Bea, "It doesn't hurt a bit. You'll do very well."

Theo threw an arm around his sister's shoulders and winked at Bea. "Well, Your Majesties, you better get busy making little baby Georges. I want to be bumped down the order of succession as soon as possible."

"Theodore. You'll feel my stick on your backside if I hear any more out of you," his grandmother threatened.

Bea laughed. They could always rely on Theo to make things more light-hearted.

George offered her wife an arm. "Shall we, my darling? Our people await."

Bea finished the last of her drink, hoping it would give her courage, and followed George.

Two pages opened the balcony doors and the new couple stepped out, to be hit with a wall of noise. Bea gasped. "Oh, my goodness."

The people were so great in number and so tightly packed, that they looked like ants from up on the balcony. They covered the whole area around the Victoria Memorial fountain in front of the palace gates, and right up the length of the Royal Mall, further than the eye could see.

"There must be hundreds of thousands of them." Bea smiled and waved along with George.

"And they're all here for you, my darling. You are the consort of the people—they love you, and so do I."

Gradually the rest of the family and the flower girls and pageboys joined them on the balcony to wave.

A chant started to come from the crowds. "Kiss, kiss, kiss, kiss!"

George pulled Bea into a kiss, and the crowds went wild.

When they pulled away, George asked her wife, "Well, you've done it now. You're one of us, Your Majesty. Are you happy?"

"Yes. Everyone says this is the day fairy tales came true. Thank you, Georgie, for giving me my fairy tale. I love you."

The crowds went wild as the royal couple kissed again, this time with much more passion.

EPILOGUE

Two months later

Queen Georgina and the Queen Consort proceeded along the route they had taken on their wedding day, in the golden state coach. They didn't have long to enjoy their honeymoon aboard the royal yacht, but Bea had adored it. It was peaceful and idyllic, much like their time at Balmoral, cut off from the outside world with only their most trusted staff. It didn't last long though, until duty brought them back to London to begin preparations for their coronation.

Bea ran her hands over her ivory satin dress, and marvelled at its beauty. They were both to be dressed in medieval style, and when she was shown the designs for her dress, embroidered with emblems representing the countries of the United Kingdom and the Commonwealth, she knew it was going to be special.

George looked stunning to Bea, dressed in ivory satin breeches and hose, and a satin shirt. The simple outfit was merely a background to the rich robes that would be placed on her during the ceremony.

Bea took her hand. "Are you nervous?"

George thought about it for a moment and said, "My whole life's been leading to this moment, and the vows I will make, just like my wedding vows, I'll keep until my last breath. So I should be nervous, but I'm not. I feel calm, and that's because I have you by my side. My wife, my consort, you allow me to feel I can take on anything. I love you, Queen Beatrice, you are my anchor and my strength."

In a breach of royal protocol, Queen Georgina leaned in and kissed her consort. And Bea knew that while they might be the first couple of their kind to reign over that ancient kingdom, no royal couple before them had ever had a greater love.

About the Author

Jenny Frame is from the small town of Motherwell in Scotland, where she lives with her partner, Lou, and their well loved and very spoiled dog.

She has a diverse range of qualifications, including a BA in public management and a diploma in acting and performance. Nowadays, she likes to put her creative energies into writing rather than treading the boards.

When not writing or reading, Jenny loves cheering on her local football team, which is not always an easy task!

Jenny can be contacted at jennyframe91@yahoo.com
Website: http://www.jennyframe.com/

Books Available from Bold Strokes Books

The 45th Parallel by Lisa Girolami. Burying her mother isn't the worst thing that can happen to Val Montague when she returns to the woodsy but peculiar town of Hemlock, Oregon. (978-1-62639-342-4)

A Royal Romance by Jenny Frame. In a country where class still divides, can love topple the last social taboo and allow Queen Georgina and Beatrice Elliot, a working class girl, their happy ever after? (978-1-62639-360-8)

Bouncing by Jaime Maddox. Basketball Coach Alex Dalton has been bouncing from woman to woman, because no one ever held her interest, until she meets her new assistant, Britain Dodge. (978-1-62639-344-8)

Same Time Next Week by Emily Smith. A chance encounter between Alex Harris and the beautiful Michelle Masters leads to a whirlwind friendship, and causes Alex to question everything she's ever known—including her own marriage. (978-1-62639-345-5)

All Things Rise by Missouri Vaun. Cole rescues a striking pilot who crash-lands near her family's farm, setting in motion a chain of events that will forever alter the course of her life. (978-1-62639-346-2)

Riding Passion by D. Jackson Leigh. Mount up for the ride through a sizzling anthology of chance encounters, buried desires, romantic surprises, and blazing passion. (978-1-62639-349-3)

Love's Bounty by Yolanda Wallace. Lobster boat captain Jake Myers stopped living the day she cheated death, but meeting greenhorn Shy Silva stirs her back to life. (978-1-62639334-9)

Just Three Words by Melissa Brayden. Sometimes the one you want is the one you least suspect. Accountant Samantha Ennis has her ordered life disrupted when heartbreaker Hunter Blair moves into her trendy Soho loft. (978-1-62639-335-6)

Lay Down the Law by Carsen Taite. Attorney Peyton Davis returns to her Texas roots to take on big oil and the Mexican Mafia, but will her investigation thwart her chance at true love? (978-1-62639-336-3)

Playing in Shadow by Lesley Davis. Survivor's guilt threatens to keep Bryce trapped in her nightmare world unless Scarlet's love can pull her out of the darkness back into the light. (978-1-62639-337-0)

Soul Selecta by Gill McKnight. Soul mates are hell to work with. (978-1-62639-338-7)

The Revelation of Beatrice Darby by Jean Copeland. Adolescence is complicated, but Beatrice Darby is about to discover how impossible it can seem to a lesbian coming of age in conservative 1950s New England. (978-1-62639-339-4)

Twice Lucky by Mardi Alexander. For firefighter Mackenzie James and Dr. Sarah Macarthur, there's suddenly a whole lot more in life to understand, to consider, to risk…someone will need to fight for her life. (978-1-62639-325-7)

Shadow Hunt by L.L. Raand. With young to raise and her Pack under attack, Sylvan, Alpha of the wolf Weres, takes on her greatest challenge when she determines to uncover the faceless enemies known as the Shadow Lords. A Midnight Hunters novel. (978-1-62639-326-4)

Heart of the Game by Rachel Spangler. A baseball writer falls for a single mom, but can she ever love anything as much as she loves the game? (978-1-62639-327-1)

Getting Lost by Michelle Grubb. Twenty-eight days, thirteen European countries, a tour manager fighting attraction, and an accused murderer: Stella and Phoebe's journey of a lifetime begins here. (978-1-62639-328-8)

Prayer of the Handmaiden by Merry Shannon. Celibate priestess Kadrian must defend the kingdom of Ithyria from a dangerous enemy and ultimately choose between her duty to the Goddess and the love of her childhood sweetheart, Erinda. (978-1-62639-329-5)

The Witch of Stalingrad by Justine Saracen. A Soviet "night witch" pilot and American journalist meet on the Eastern Front in WW II and struggle through carnage, conflicting politics, and the deadly Russian winter. (978-1-62639-330-1)

Pedal to the Metal by Jesse J. Thoma. When unreformed thief Dubs Williams is released from prison to help Max Winters bust a car theft ring, Max learns that to catch a thief, get in bed with one. (978-1-62639-239-7)

Dragon Horse War by D. Jackson Leigh. A priestess of peace and a fiery warrior must defeat a vicious uprising that entwines their destinies and ultimately their hearts. (978-1-62639-240-3)

For the Love of Cake by Erin Dutton. When everything is on the line, and one taste can break a heart, will pastry chefs Maya and Shannon take a chance on reality? (978-1-62639-241-0)

Betting on Love by Alyssa Linn Palmer. A quiet country-girl-at-heart and a live-life-to-the-fullest biker take a risk at offering each other their hearts. (978-1-62639-242-7)

The Deadening by Yvonne Heidt. The lines between good and evil, right and wrong, have always been blurry for Shade. When Raven's actions force her to choose, which side will she come out on? (978-1-62639-243-4)

Ordinary Mayhem by Victoria A. Brownworth. Faye Blakemore has been taking photographs since she was ten, but those same photographs threaten to destroy everything she knows and everything she loves. (978-1-62639-315-8)

One Last Thing by Kim Baldwin & Xenia Alexiou. Blood is thicker than pride. The final book in the Elite Operative Series brings together foes, family, and friends to start a new order. (978-1-62639-230-4)

Songs Unfinished by Holly Stratimore. Two aspiring rock stars learn that falling in love while pursuing their dreams can be harmonious—if they can only keep their pasts from throwing them out of tune. (978-1-62639-231-1)

Beyond the Ridge by L.T. Marie. Will a contractor and a horse rancher overcome their family differences and find common ground to build a life together? (978-1-62639-232-8)

Swordfish by Andrea Bramhall. Four women battle the demons from their pasts. Will they learn to let go, or will happiness be forever beyond their grasp? (978-1-62639-233-5)

The Fiend Queen by Barbara Ann Wright. Princess Katya and her consort Starbride must turn evil against evil in order to banish Fiendish power from their kingdom, and only love will pull them back from the brink. (978-1-62639-234-2)

Up the Ante by PJ Trebelhorn. When Jordan Stryker and Ashley Noble meet again fifteen years after a short-lived affair, are either of them prepared to gamble on a chance at love? (978-1-62639-237-3)

Speakeasy by MJ Williamz. When mob leader Helen Byrne sets her sights on the girlfriend of Al Capone's right-hand man, passion and tempers flare on the streets of Chicago. (978-1-62639-238-0)

Venus in Love by Tina Michele. Morgan Blake can't afford any distractions and Ainsley Dencourt can't afford to lose control—but the beauty of life and art usually lies in the unpredictable strokes of the artist's brush. (978-1-62639-220-5)

Rules of Revenge by AJ Quinn. When a lethal operative on a collision course with her past agrees to help a CIA analyst on a critical assignment, the encounter proves explosive in ways neither woman anticipated. (978-1-62639-221-2)

The Romance Vote by Ali Vali. Chili Alexander is a sought-after campaign consultant who isn't prepared when her boss's daughter, Samantha Pellegrin, comes to work at the firm and shakes up Chili's life from the first day. (978-1-62639-222-9)

Advance: Exodus Book One by Gun Brooke. Admiral Dael Caydoc's mission to find a new homeworld for the Oconodian people is hazardous, but working with the infuriating Commander Aniwyn "Spinner" Seclan endangers her heart and soul. (978-1-62639-224-3)

UnCatholic Conduct by Stevie Mikayne. Jil Kidd goes undercover to investigate fraud at St. Marguerite's Catholic School, but life gets complicated when her student is killed—and she begins to fall for her prime target. (978-1-62639-304-2)

Season's Meetings by Amy Dunne. Catherine Birch reluctantly ventures on the festive road trip from hell with beautiful stranger Holly Daniels only to discover the road to true love has its own obstacles to maneuver. (978-1-62639-227-4)

Myth and Magic: Queer Fairy Tales edited by Radclyffe and Stacia Seaman. Myth, magic, and monsters—the stuff of childhood dreams (or nightmares) and adult fantasies. (978-1-62639-225-0)

Nine Nights on the Windy Tree by Martha Miller. Recovering drug addict, Bertha Brannon, is an attorney who is trying to stay clean when a murder sends her back to the bad end of town. (978-1-62639-179-6)

Driving Lessons by Annameekee Hesik. Dive into Abbey Brooks's sophomore year as she attempts to figure out the amazing, but sometimes complicated, life of a you-know-who girl at Gila High School. (978-1-62639-228-1)

Asher's Shot by Elizabeth Wheeler. Asher Price's candid photographs capture the truth, but when his success requires exposing an enemy, Asher discovers his only shot at happiness involves revealing secrets of his own. (978-1-62639-229-8)

Courtship by Carsen Taite. Love and justice—a lethal mix or a perfect match? (978-1-62639-210-6)

Against Doctor's Orders by Radclyffe. Corporate financier Presley Worth wants to shut down Argyle Community Hospital, but Dr. Harper Rivers will fight her every step of the way, if she can also fight their growing attraction. (978-1-62639-211-3)

A Spark of Heavenly Fire by Kathleen Knowles. Kerry and Beth are building their life together, but unexpected circumstances could destroy their happiness. (978-1-62639-212-0)

Never Too Late by Julie Blair. When Dr. Jamie Hammond is forced to hire a new office manager, she's shocked to come face to face with Carla Grant and memories from her past. (978-1-62639-213-7)

Widow by Martha Miller. Judge Bertha Brannon must solve the murder of her lover, a policewoman she thought she'd grow old with. As more bodies pile up, the murderer starts coming for her. (978-1-62639-214-4)

Twisted Echoes by Sheri Lewis Wohl. What's a woman to do when she realizes the voices in her head are real? (978-1-62639-215-1)

boldstrokesbooks.com

Bold Strokes Books

Quality and Diversity in LGBTQ Literature

 victory EDITIONS

Drama

 MATINEE BOOKS

E-BOOKS

SCI-FI

MYSTERY

 erotica

 SOLILOQUY

EROTICA

YOUNG ADULT

 BOLD STROKES BOOKS

 LIBERTY EDITION

Romance

W·E·B·S·T·O·R·E

PRINT AND EBOOKS